The View From Rampart Street

by Mary Lou Widmer

Strategic Book Publishing and Rights Co.

Strategic Book Publishing and Rights Co.
12620 FM 1960, Suite A4-507
Houston, TX 77065
www.sbpra.com

Hardcover version published in 2009.
Softcover version published in 2011.

ISBN 978-1-61204-909-0

Book Design: Linda W. Rigsbee

DEDICATION

To Al, as always,
for love and support.

New Orleans, 1840

CHAPTER 1

With each step up the curving mahogany staircase, Mariette Delon caught fuller glimpses of pastel evening gowns swirling around the dance floor. Reaching the top step, she kicked back the bottom flounce of her blue silk dress, tightened her lips, cracked open her fan, and glanced back to see if her mother had caught the gesture. Desiree Delon's frown told her she had. Following her up the stairs, her head turbaned in a crisp white tignon, her earlobes hung with golden loops, Desiree puffed from the exertion of climbing the stairs and the constraints of her stays.

Mariette looked about her. She had never been in the Quadroon Ballroom before, had vowed never to be here, but although she had fought relentlessly against coming tonight, being put up on the auction block, as she saw it, she had apparently lost the first round. She would never have admitted it to her mother, but she was curious about the place where so many connections were made, so many contracts arranged, so many lives changed forever.

The musicians, seated near the floor-length windows at the street end of the ballroom, were playing a quadrille. Dancers in four squares of eight whirled gracefully across the polished parquet floor, and viewers kept time with gloved hands, as Mariette moved toward a lineup of brocaded chairs against the wall.

Finding two vacant chairs, she sat, and her mother sat beside her. She needed the rest. She was exhausted, exhausted from the day, from the week, from the whole preceding year, when she had daily told her mother she would *not* become a *placée*. And yet here she was, elaborately dressed and coiffed as though she planned to attract a rich Creole gentleman who would offer to be her *patron*.

Today had been the worst day ever. Maman had been appalled to find her reading in her boudoir at four o'clock, no rag curlers in her hair, no nap taken, no stays or chemise laid out. And for her part, Mariette had literally been shocked to see her mother carrying in the blue tissue silk dress she was wearing tonight, a dress made by Madame Delacroix without her knowledge, *behind her back,* so there would be no last minute excuse about not having a dress to wear. *But she has your measurements, Mariette,* her mother had said, as if that was the point of the argument. Mariette had narrowed her eyes in anger, and their voices had risen again.

It was a one-sided discussion, for Mariette had repeated her own views often enough for her mother to know them; yet, her mother would have her way. Desiree got the preparations moving, ordering Celine to bring in water for Mariette's bath, to heat the curling irons on the wood stove, to lay out her limerick gloves. And while she was being bathed and powdered, dressed and coiffed, while Celine rolled the stovepipe curls and Desiree fanned her with a huge palmetto fan, Mariette sat like a statue, her angry gaze riveted on the flagged patio outside her window, where the banana trees had wilted in the oppressive Indian summer.

On her dressing table, where brushes, buttonhooks, and hair

receivers were scattered about in abandon, two night candles, their threadlike flames unwavering in the airless room, illuminated Mariette's changing image in the looking glass. First came her hosiery, then her drawers, her stays and her chemise. Then, while still in her underclothes, she had watched the long and tedious hairdo take shape. It was parted in the middle, ornamented with ringlets and loops at the sides, and finished off with long curls that lay beside her throat. As the elaborate hairdo progressed, it was secured with hidden combs and hairpins. But when Desiree and Celine were trying to decide whether the whole affair should be topped with a tiara or a coronet, Mariette stood up abruptly, faced her mother defiantly, and declared that it was *enough!* Then Desiree, fearing that heat and anger would mar her daughter's already flushed complexion, had nodded that yes, all right, it was enough.

"You look beautiful!" she'd said, knowing it would both anger and please her daughter. The dress had come last, the tissue silk, so cloudlike Mariette could hardly feel the weight of it on her body. She would never have admitted it, but it was a gossamer thing, like a butterfly's wing: the most beautiful dress she'd ever seen.

So here she was at the ball, just as her mother had said she would be. *Plaçage* was what she had been trained for all her life, and it was going to happen. At least, that's what Desiree said. So Mariette knew that tonight, at least, there was nothing she could do about it. The afternoon debacle had progressed from arguments to tears and finally to a compromise. If Mariette went to the ball with an open mind, to dance and try to enjoy herself, Desiree would not force her to become a *placée* against her will. That was the best promise her mother had made all year; that is, if she planned to keep it.

Mariette knew her mother hoped in her secret heart that she'd meet someone tonight, someone handsome and wealthy who would offer for her, and she'd change her mind about having a protector. But that would never happen, Mariette knew. She had better plans for her future than waiting on a Creole hand and foot and warming his bed.

She looked around. The room was oval, high-ceilinged, and magnificent. The windows were dressed in gold damask that pooled on the shining floor. Veined marble columns at the four corners of the dance floor supported the medallioned ceiling, from which hung two enormous gasoliers. Potted palms stood in shadowed corners.

To her far right, in the curve in the oval, two young men in formal attire sat on chairs like her own, sipping whiskey from shot glasses. From the time she sat down, she was aware that the taller of the two was looking her way. Now, without a word to his companion, he put his glass on a small table, stood up, and started walking in her direction. Mariette saw others in his circle doing the same, and the young man quickened his pace. Reaching her first, he bowed. "*Mademoiselle,*" he said, "may I have the next dance?"

"*Oui, M'sieur,*" she said. She closed her fan and opened the dance card dangling from her wrist.

"Will you sign my card?"

Without taking his gaze from her eyes, he fumbled for her card and scribbled his name. Almost at once, the quadrille ended, the dance floor cleared, and a slower dance began.

The tall Creole turned to the other admirers coming to ask the beautiful young woman for dances. "Sorry, gentlemen," he said. "This is my dance. You'll have to see *Mademoiselle* later." The men backed away resentfully. "*Mam'selle,*" he said, extending his gloved hand.

CHAPTER 2

Although she tried to ignore it, Mariette felt a little jolt of excitement at being the center of attention and the partner selected by this extraordinary-looking man. She placed her gloved hand in his and rose from the billows of her skirts to walk with him to the dance floor. Facing him, she marveled at the width of his shoulders and the clearly defined musculature beneath. He stood out among Creoles, she mused, who scorned a muscled figure as that of a menial laborer. Their idea of masculine elegance took the shape of a slender gentleman, who spent his days seated on his gallery, sipping black coffee and reading the latest business news.

The young man took her to the opposite side of the dance floor, which suited her well, for there she could escape her mother's constant scrutiny. At last he stopped and led her most adeptly into the steps of the dance. She looked up into his eyes. At first she had thought them brown, but now, in the amber light of the gasoliers, she could see they were a deep green. His nose was well made, his lips wide and sensual, his hair growing long into his collar and curling at the sideboards.

When his hand touched the back of her gown, just above her waist, a ripple of shivers ran to her shoulders. It was a thrill to be in the luxurious ballroom, dancing to the heart-tugging sweep of violin music. Even if it were only for this one night, it would give her something to remember.

"*Mam'selle*," he said, "I am Philippe Grillet, and I'm honored to have the first dance with you."

My first dance ever, she thought, *at my very first ball, which will also be my last. Till now, I've been a prisoner in my mother's house, not knowing how lovely it was in this ballroom, just blocks away. And to think, I didn't want to come!*

"*Merci, M'sieur*," she said. "My name is Mariette Delon."

"Are you from New Orleans, *Mam'selle*?"

"Of course."

"Then why have I never seen you before?"

"Because this is my coming-out ball, *M'sieur*. I'm being introduced tonight." She pinched her lips and lowered her eyes.

"You say that as if it doesn't please you."

"It doesn't please me at all," she said, tilting her head and lowering her lids. "I have no intention of becoming a *placée*."

"Then why are you here?"

"Because it is my mother's wish that I take a *patron*."

She looked up into his eyes, and wondered what his thoughts were on the subject of *plaçage*. He favored it, of course. Why else would he be here? Only Creoles in search of quadroon mistresses came to the Orleans Ballroom. It was a system selective and elite, well respected by colored and white alike.

"I see," he said, his brows knitted. "Well..." He laughed softly. "I don't really see."

Mariette frowned. "You think I'm out of place here?"

"Oh, no. It isn't that. It's just that...well...please forgive me, Mam'selle. I had no right..."

"You have every right," she said coolly. "If you're here to look over the coterie and make a selection, you'd certainly want to know all the facts."

"Well, no. That's not my intention. My cousin Gabriel comes to town once or twice a year from his father's plantation and he expects me to entertain him."

"So you brought him here to see the latest offering of quadroons," she said.

"Well...yes."

"Hmmm...well, that should entertain him." She laughed coquettishly. "Young women, delicately raised, offered by their mothers for contracts. You can't find that down on the farm, I'm sure."

"My choice of words was poor," he said. "Please let me explain."

"No need. I'll make it easy for you." Her anger was returning. "Do you see that lady in the chair against the wall?" she asked, nodding in her mother's direction. "The one in lavender with a white tignon? The one whose eyes have never left you?"

Philippe followed her gaze and saw a pretty mulattress the color of milk chocolate, frowning in his direction. "Yes."

"She is my mother." She'd said it bluntly, with neither pride nor shame. He looked astonished, but he seemed not to care who or what she was. He might not have come to select a *placée*, but he certainly seemed to admire her, just the same.

"Please, *Mam'selle*," he said. "Don't let them talk you into *plaçage*."

"Oh??"

"Oh, I know this must sound presumptuous, coming from a total stranger, but somehow I know that the life of a *placée* is not for you."

Mariette's cheeks grew warm. She felt affronted by the remark, yet strangely hopeful. "I can't help feeling you *are* presumptuous, *M'sieur*, since you know nothing at all about me," she said, not unkindly. "If the life of a *placée* is not for me, then what life would suit me better?" She was prodding him now, hoping to hear some suggestion she had not yet considered. He was a total stranger. She would never see him again. Why not play this little game of *what is to become of my life?*

"I think you should be the *wife* of a Creole," he said. "The lady on his arm at the opera, the chatelaine of his estate."

Mariette laughed softly. "Yes, and I think the moon is made of cream cheese."

"But I'm serious, *Mam'selle*.

"But there are laws, *M'sieur*, laws of the state, laws followed by the Church. Or do you think I should ignore them?" She searched his eyes, feeling the impact of their sea-green intensity. She could not allow herself to take him seriously, for when she awakened from the dream, she'd still be at the mercy of her father, whose plans for her were set in stone. It was her father's plan that had made her mother so adamant about the Qadroon Ball. And now, Philippe Grillet had put into words her own hidden desires, but she dared not hope for the impossible. "And how could I ignore the laws," she asked, "in a city where Maman and I are known as mother and daughter?"

"I don't know," he said, "but I'm sure it could be done."

He whirled her around the floor, her bell skirt describing tilted circles on the parquet, but neither the music nor the steps intruded upon her concentration. She could not believe what she'd heard. She'd been raised in the home of a *placée*, sheltered and hidden from the world, brought up to be accomplished, articulate, and desirable to a wealthy aristocrat, and on her first night in the company of gentlemen, a Creole had expressed her own deepest wish for herself. Her heart leapt. Hadn't she always believed that anything was possible if one wanted it badly enough?

"Was your mother a *placée?*" he asked.

"*Oui, M'sieur.* She still is."

"And knowing what that life is like, she wants the same for you?"

Again, he was mouthing her resentment. Soberly, she answered, "My mother is a very happy woman."

"That is not the point, Mam'selle. She knows the limitations of *plaçage.* She should want more for you."

Mariette did not answer. She probably should be arguing on her mother's behalf, or not arguing at all. How could she totally reverse her position of a half hour earlier on the subject of *plaçage?* Her posture on that subject had already hurt her mother, would hurt her again when her father made his demands. She regretted that, but she had to be true to her own sentiments and her own determination. "You know, *M'sieur,* a young quadroon woman cannot live on fantasies." Her mother's words. "In truth, we have few choices." She waited to hear his retort.

"You have all the choices in the world. You can do anything you want. You're beautiful, you're charming, and you're...so very fair. If you become a *placée,* it's because that's what you *want* to be."

"No, *M'sieur,* that isn't so." A lump formed in her throat, but she smothered her anger under a facetious light-heartedness. "It will go something like this. My mother will say to me, 'Come, Mariette, *ma cherie.* Three suitors have offered for you. A tall one, a short one, and an old one. But all are very rich. And you may have your pick. Each has promised you a house, a rig, two servants, and the finest silver service."

"Only three?" Philippe laughed, falling into her jocular mood.

In a swift mood swing, Mariette frowned and pressed her lips together. She had been making light of it, but now, she was plunged back into the depressing reality of her situation.

"I'm sorry," Philippe said. "I thought you were jesting."

"I was, but it isn't a jest, *M'sieur.* It's a lifetime plan," she said sadly.

Philippe looked down into her eyes and became serious. "Do me a favor, will you?"

"And what would that be, *M'sieur?*"

"Try to defy your mother in this. Say 'no' to the suitors who come to offer for you."

"Why should I do that?" It was exactly what she planned to do.

"Because I think you deserve a better life than you'll have with a protector."

Mariette's heart melted inside her; but, although he appeared to be her champion, he clearly had no intention of making her a part of his future.

Again they danced in silence. Mariette wondered if she was only imagining it, or if he had drawn her closer and if his hand was holding hers more firmly. Her eyes grew moist. She lowered her head so he would not see her face. Bad days were ahead for her, for the suitors would surely come. It was no joke. But her mother had promised...well, she had promised so*mething.*

In the privacy he had created for them inside the circle of dancers, she felt the brush of his cheek against hers and the warmth of his breath on her hair. She closed her eyes and let the strange and unexpected pleasure of his nearness wash over her.

The music stopped. Mariette felt him release her and stand away from her, still meeting her gaze. Her reluctance to leave him surprised her. She would probably never see this man again. As if in a dream, she placed her hand on his arm and let him walk her back to her mother. The hope he had planted in her heart had nurtured her own determination to defy her parents, the world, the way things were. She resolved once again not to give in.

"*Mam'selle*," he said. They were back at the row of chairs against the wall, and her mother was watching. He sketched a bow over her gloved hand. "Thank you for the dance."

"Thank you, *M'sieur*," she said, dropping a curtsey.

She felt her fingers slip away from his, and she sat down beside her mother. Men standing around her were all talking at once, asking for dances, but for Mariette, the excitement had gone out of the evening. In a space between two dark-coated shoulders, she saw Philippe Grillet walk toward the men's bar and out of her life. She glanced up at the young men bending over her, forced a trembling smile, and let them sign her dance card.

CHAPTER 3

"Mariette! Mariette! Wake up!" Celine whispered urgently, shaking her awake. Mariette frowned and turned away from the maid, pulling the covers over her head. "Dey're comin' awready," Celine insisted, shaking her more briskly.

Mariette turned the covers back down again. "Who's coming, Celine?" she asked, still hoarse from sleep.

"De suitors, *chere.*"

Instantly, Mariette sat bolt upright, a long strand of black hair hanging over her eye. "The suitors?"

"*Oui.* To ask fo' a contrack...to be your *patron*. De fust young man, he be here now, talkin' to your Maman in de pah-lor."

Mariette came awake. Her eyes narrowed and her nostrils thinned. "I knew this would happen if I went to that ball." She got out of bed and walked to her wash basin, while Celine poured water for her morning ablutions. "What time is it, Celine?"

"Six o'clock."

"*Mon Dieu!*" she said irritably. Then, in a sudden change of mood,

"What does he look like, Celine?" she asked, wondering if it could be Philippe Grillet.

"Handsome. Young. He look nice to me." She handed Mariette a wash cloth, a bar of lemon soap, and her tooth brush. Mariette lathered the cloth and began washing her face.

"Is he tall? Does he have dark hair?"

"No. He short, wit light hair."

Mariette made a mouth. Celine began to lay out her clothes. "Yo' Maman was still sleepin' when he knock at de door."

"Well, I guess so, at this hour," Mariette said, while brushing her teeth.

"She put on her robe and let him in de pah-lor. Den she s'cuse herse'f to dress and comb her hair. She tole me t'come git you ready. You gotta dress quick now and go take a look at him. She said she'd let you make de choice."

"And I told her I would not be a *placée*," Mariette said as she dried her face. She hurried to get herself dressed so she could make sure her mother did not accept the caller's offer. After he left, she'd have it well understood with her mother that she'd take none of them, no matter how rich or handsome they were. She'd run away first.

She recalled Philippe Grillet's admonition. *Don't let them do this to you.* Her heart warmed at the memory of his words. They had shored up her courage. She recalled his tall, handsome figure, his clean-cut, boyish face with the crisp brown curls falling over his forehead. And what glorious eyes he had!

Celine stood waiting with her stays and her dress. When the stays had been laced and the calico dress buttoned down the back, Mariette sat at the dressing table for Celine to brush her long hair and tie it at the nape of her neck with a ribbon.

Mariette smiled, recalling the slight, warm pressure of Philippe's hand at her waistline. He had danced divinely, with surprising grace for a tall, muscular man.

"Mariette," Celine whispered from the hallway, "*vite, vite, cherie.*"

In minutes, Mariette appeared in the parlor, freshly scrubbed, her hair falling in little corkscrews over her forehead. She curtsied to the young gentleman, who bowed and waved his hat almost to the floor. Desiree looked at her daughter, then at the Creole, who proceeded to blush furiously.

"Andrew Le Vasseur, at your service, Mademoiselle," the young man said. "If you remember, I had the privilege of dancing with you Saturday night."

"But of course, M'sieur," Mariette said. Mariette did not remember the man at all. After that first dance, all the faces above the dark coats and white collars began to run together. The man standing before her was short, indeed, and blond. He was quite young, not much older than Mariette herself. He was immaculately attired for such an early hour. It occurred to Mariette that he must have gotten up at four o'clock to be here at the crack of dawn, so well put together in doeskin riding breeches, frock coat, and leather boots. His hair was well barbered and his manners were impeccable, but Mariette wondered, without really caring, how one so young could afford such an expensive lifestyle.

Apparently her mother had questioned him along these lines, for now she said, "Monsieur Le Vasseur's father is a sugar planter in Lafayette City, and M'sieur himself supervises the plantation. He and I have had a nice talk, and if you'll thank him for his visit, Mariette, then you and I can discuss his proposal."

"Thank you, M'sieur," Mariette said.

The young man handed Desiree his *carte de visite.*

"If you will come back later today?" Desiree asked.

M'sieur Le Vasseur departed reluctantly, mounted a roan mare, and rode away. Mariette walked to the window of the parlor, drew back the lace curtain and followed his departure with her eyes. She saw another young man crossing Rampart Street, coming in the direction of her house. Leaving the parlor, she retreated to her bedroom. Desiree followed.

Mariette began unbuttoning the loops she could reach at the back of her bodice.

"What are you doing?" Desiree asked peevishly. "You can't undress, Mariette. Others will be coming. Stop that," she said, taking hold of her daughter's hand. She looked harshly into Mariette's eyes. "Tell me what you think of the young man who just left. He made a very generous offer. He said he'd buy you a house as fine as this one, with furnishings of the same quality, and..."

"Maman!" Mariette shouted. "I will not be a *placee*! I told you that Saturday night. I said it a year ago, on my sixteenth birthday, and I've said it a hundred times since. You hear only what you want to hear. When he returns, tell him I'm not going to accept any offer at all."

"But you were at the ball. It's understood. I can't..." She stopped, her lips trembling. She was upset and angry.

"You can. You must. You've broken your promise to me. I'm going to stay in my room until they're all gone."

"And what am I to tell them?" Desiree asked.

"Tell them I'm sick. Tell them I died. I don't care what you tell them."

Desiree did not move. Her mouth was a tight, hard line. Finally, she departed for the parlor. From her room, Mariette heard a knock at the parlor door. She heard a muted voice asking questions and her mother's voice answering. She heard the front door open and close as one caller after another came to offer for her.

When the crystal clock on her dressing table showed twelve noon, she heard Desiree walking back from the parlor down the hall in the direction of her bedroom. Her heavy footsteps signaled her anger, but Mariette was not going to be intimidated. She had kept her part of the bargain. Now her mother must keep hers. Desiree's footsteps did not stop at her room but continued on to the dining room. Minutes later, Celine knocked.

"Come in," said Mariette.

"Your Maman wants to see you in the dinin' room."

"I'll bet she does," Mariette said. Celine started to leave. "Wait, Celine," she said. "Is she angry?"

"She ain't happy."

"Please button me up again," Mariette asked. Celine came into the bedroom and re-did the few loops Mariette had undone. Mariette smoothed her hair, shook out her skirt, and left her room. Slowly she approached the dining room table. Her mother was seated there, saying nothing but breathing hard, and that was a bad sign.

Celine had set the table in their absence. Now she brought in cold sliced chicken and red, ripe tomatoes from the food safe, new potatoes she'd boiled while Desiree interviewed the men, and rolls she'd purchased from a vendor. She poured water into their glasses and left, so as not to get caught in the crossfire.

CHAPTER 4

Mariette sat at the table. Her mother crossed herself and said Grace, as if she were ordering someone's execution. Mariette ate hungrily, for she'd had no breakfast, but she was fully aware of her mother's icy stare. After they'd eaten in silence for a few minutes, Desiree put her fork across the plate. It was time for the confrontation.

"You had the prettiest dress at the ball," Desiree said. "Celine and I spent an hour in the heat, dressing you and doing your hair. Men swarmed around you like bees all night, and you danced till your slippers were all but worn through. And now that they're coming to the door, promising houses and rigs and anything else you want, you don't even have the courtesy to come to the parlor and meet them."

"Why does that surprise you, Maman?" Mariette asked. "Wasn't that our agreement? I'd go to the ball, and you would not force me to become a *plaçee*? You promised. I know you hoped I'd meet someone there that struck my fancy, but that didn't happen."

"And so for this great favor you did me, I had Madame Delacroix make you the most gorgeous dress in the city."

"I didn't ask for the dress." She got up from the table and walked to the window, hands behind her back, looking out. "I told you a year ago that I wouldn't take a *patron*."

"Once more. Tell me why. I'm getting old. I forget."

Mariette turned around and faced her mother. "Because…well, because it's degrading." Mariette's voice broke on the words. She lowered her eyes.

"Degrading. I see. For me, it was good enough, but for Princess Mariette, it's degrading."

Mariette came back to the table and placed her hands over her mother's. "Why do you force me to hurt you, Maman? What I'm saying is not meant to reflect on your life. It's been a good life for you. But it's not for me. You made your decision about *plaçage*. Now I must make mine."

"I had no mother to advise me," Desiree said somberly. She looked at Mariette. "Maybe you think that was lucky for me."

"Oh, no, Maman." Mariette squeezed her mother's hand. "You know how much I love you."

Desiree's face was hard, her shoulders stiff. She gazed at nothing in particular, her mind absorbed with some unseen memory. Mariette knew she was lost in the past. "I came to this city with no mother, no sister, no friends, except for M'sieur Tabary, who'd been like a father to me in the five years our group had been in Havana. Then, when war broke out between France and Spain, we were set adrift in little boats with hardly any food or water. We were lucky to make it to New Orleans." She turned to look into her daughter's eyes. "I had no one to care about me, Mariette. It was only when M'sieur saw me on the stage and offered to be my protector that my life became comfortable, and I knew what it was to be happy."

"I know, Maman," Mariette said, gently fondling her mother's hand. "It was good for you. But don't you see? I've never wanted for anything, so I have no need to be... rescued. Besides, if I took a protector, I'd have to give up my dream of becoming an actress, and you know that's my heart's desire. I'd always have to be at home, waiting for him to arrive, always anxious, always ready, like a..."

Desiree looked up, frowning. "A what?"

"A slave." Mariette looked away from her mother. She had done it again. Words were hard to find, and only hateful words would make her meaning clear.

Desiree gazed into the hall leading to the back of the house, to make sure Celine had not heard. "A slave!" she said in a harsh whisper. Her eyes narrowed with venom. "Do you call me a slave?"

"No, Maman. No."

"Do you know any slaves who own their own houses, with mahogany furniture and lace curtains?" Desiree fairly spat out the words. "You are the third generation of *gens de couleur libre* in this family, not the first."

Mariette's eyes smarted. "I know, Maman, and I know you consider us fortunate. But I have feelings of my own about M'sieur."

"Oh? And what might they be?" There was a new kind of curiosity in her question.

"Well, whenever he comes to the house, we must all be confined like prisoners. We can never go out with him, not to Church or on a picnic, or even for a stroll."

"We both know why, Mariette. Must we punish each other by speaking of it?"

Desiree watched the familiar signs of distress transform her daughter's features. How often had she or Mariette read about Raoul Delissard's wife, the aristocratic Honorée LeCourt Delissard, in the society notes of *Le Moniteur*? Once, Desiree recalled, the article said she was pouring coffee during the intermission at the opera. On another occasion, her daughter Celeste was being entertained at a lawn party for her seventeenth birthday. Celeste and Mariette were the same age.

In her training for *plaçage*, Mariette had been taught to be articulate, accomplished, and most of all, interesting, for an interesting *placée* was visited more often and given expensive gifts. Mariette had learned how to converse pleasurably with a man, about his health and his interests, but never, ever, about his other family and his real home. All this she knew.

More than anything else, she dreaded the physical intimacy which would be her most important duty as a *placée*. An image of her mother and father together in bed, which she'd accidentally seen from her treetop hideaway when she was seven, could not be erased from her mind. It had sickened her. But somehow, she'd matured and accepted the fact that a *placée* was the gentleman's lover, his mistress. A *placée's* expertise in the bedroom was what kept him coming back and made the elaborate lifestyle worthwhile.

"I want to speak about my future, Maman," Mariette said

"What else have we been discussing?"

"The future I plan is not *plaçage*."

"Then what, Mariette? Will you be a seamstress? A beautician? We hoped you'd have more security than a job of menial labor could provide."

"You left out marriage, Maman."

"And who would you marry? A man of color?"

"Why not?"

"Because your skin is white. Your children must be white. It is your obligation to them."

Mariette sighed audibly. She was hearing it again, the dream and the duty of every free woman of color to lighten the skin of her children, and in so doing, lighten their burdens.

"And you cannot marry a white man," Desiree continued. "Not in this city."

"So I have no choice. Is that what you're telling me?"

"Yes. More's the pity, *ma cherie.*" She looked into Mariette's eyes and patted her hand. "I'd make things different for you if I could, Mariette. But this is the way it is for us. And we should not fight it. Not when you consider how happy I've been with M'sieur." Desiree sighed. "Besides, what has it all been for—the singing lessons, the dancing lessons, the English lessons—if not to make you a charming companion to a wealthy Creole gentleman?"

"Let me talk, Maman. Please."

Desiree frowned, knowing the matter was far from settled. But she nodded.

"I don't want to argue with you or be disrespectful. But this is my life we're planning here. And you must let me speak my mind, and promise to listen."

"Speak, then."

Mariette drew in a deep breath. "When I was a child, I did anything you wanted." She took her mother's hand and rubbed the back of it gently. "I went to the schools you selected. Why wouldn't I? I didn't know what would be expected in return." The image flashed again, but Mariette willed it away.

"But Mariette, you've been a grown girl for a long time now. Surely you knew what kind of life you'd soon be entering."

"Yes, I knew. I saw how men looked at me and my friends when we passed them in the market. But they were content to wait and put in a bid for us with our mothers' blessing. It's so much more civilized that way." She knew she was being impertinent now, but the time had come to stand up for her rights, if indeed she had any rights, or she would be lost forever in a life she despised.

"Mariette!" A touch of impatience? Of pity? "Why didn't you talk to me?"

"We can't talk, Maman, you and I. We always wind up arguing. I hate that! But I can't live the life of a *placée*. I just can't."

"You would be treated like royalty," Desiree persisted. Mariette wanted to walk out of the room, but instead, she shook her head impatiently. "Look at your friend Denise," Desiree continued. "Look how happy she is. She has everything a young woman could want."

"Everything but marriage…and respect…and dignity."

"Dignity?" Desiree's eyes widened. "You think I have no dignity? You think M'sieur does not respect me?"

The image came again. Mariette refused to let it linger.

Desiree continued. "You have been spoiled and pampered all your life, *ma fille*. Raised on a satin cushion. These hands," she said, taking Mariette's hands in her own, "have never known the dishpan or the dust rag."

"I didn't ask to be spoiled and pampered," Mariette said. "There are some things I simply will not do out of gratitude for being raised 'on a satin cushion.'"

Desiree's dark eyes flashed. "Your father and I want to know you have a secure future with a man who will care for you."

"…and who is free to leave me at will."

"And if he did, you would be fixed for life, with a house and furnishings and a nice income."

"I care nothing for these things, Maman. I lived my life in obedience to you, hoping that when this time came and we had this talk, you would understand."

"And what am I to understand?"

"That I want to be an actress, like you were when you first came to New Orleans. I want to sing and dance on the stage. That will make me financially independent. I won't need a *patron*."

"Mariette…"

"No. Let me finish. When I was a little girl, the actresses came here to visit, even though you were no longer on the stage. They sat in the parlor, sipping little glasses of anisette."

"And eating sponge cake," Desiree added, smiling wanly, as if suddenly enjoying the recollection..

Mariette gazed into space. "They taught me how to walk on stage, how to laugh, how to cry." Her eyes filled. She brought her hands together, gathering in the cherished memories. "I adored them, Maman. I wanted to be like them."

"They brought you gifts. I remember that. They were generous with you."

"Oh, yes." Mariette got up from the table and looked outside again. Then, turning back to face her mother, she laced her fingers together. "They were so extravagant. So flamboyant. I longed to be a part of their world. Even now, when I go to the Camp Street Theater, I hang on every word the actors say. This is what I must do, Maman," she said, sitting down and taking her mother's hands. "Surely you, of all people, can understand that."

Desiree shook her head sadly. "It can't be done today, *ma cherie*, not by a quadroon. When I arrived here in 1805, things were different. The people of New Orleans were starved for entertainment. And we were experienced actors. We'd been together five years in Havana. We could do anything from comedy to Shakespeare. We packed the theater every night. People didn't care that we were mulattos and quadroons.

"But the theater has come a long way in thirty years, especially since M'sieur Caldwell came here. They don't need colored actresses any more, Mariette." She met her daughter's gaze, begging her to accept reality.

"Then I won't tell them," Mariette said, smiling brightly, "and they'll never know."

Desiree knew this was true. Mariette could "pass," at least in Caldwell's theater. It was in the American Sector of town, where all the Kaintocks and Irishmen and Northerners had settled since Louisiana became a state. Few French people from the Vieux Carre went there. Yes, Desiree thought, she's right. There, she could get by.

"But it's an English-speaking theater," Desiree pressed on with objections.

"And don't I know English? Why did M'sieur spend all that money on my education if I don't use English when I have a need to?"

Desiree pinched her lips. "Suppose we say we'll talk to M'sieur about it when he comes to visit." She got up from the chair, put her hands to the small of her back, and stretched. Suddenly she frowned and met Mariette's eyes, as if something had just occurred to her. "What about that young man who rushed to have the first dance with you at the ball?"

Philippe Grillet. Mariette flushed. She went suddenly weak. "What about him?"

"Why wasn't he here this morning?" Desiree brightened. "Was he the one you were waiting for?"

"No, Maman, at least not the way you think."

"Explain that, Mariette." She remained standing, gripping the back of her chair.

"He said I should not be a *placée*."

"I see. And just what did he say you should be?"

Mariette lifted her chin, in a small gesture of defiance. "He said I should be the chatelaine of an estate." She gazed past her mother, a smile trembling on her lips. "He said I should have a Creole for a husband."

Desiree barked a short laugh. "Of course. He'll fill your head with dreams, and you'll be so grateful you'll let him take you to bed while you wait for the fantasy to happen. He's duping you, Mariette. He wants to be your lover without the expense or the obligation of *plaçage*. Can't you see that, you foolish child?"

The thought had, of course, occurred to her. He might only be toying with her, hinting of marriage to take advantage of her. She had pushed it aside, not wanting to believe it.

"I knew you'd say that, Maman, but he is not a liar. I know it. He has a very honest face."

"And he's handsome, too, so you believe anything he says. You're a child, Mariette. You know nothing at all about men."

"That may be true, but he says I can do anything I want with my life, and I believe that." She paused. "Will you deny me even hope?" Tears found release now, and Mariette gave into them. She lowered her face to her hands and wept in deep, anguished sobs.

Desiree listened, suffering as much as Mariette, but offering no words of sympathy, for there were none to offer. "Did he ask you to marry him?"

"Of course not."

"Or even be his *placée?*"

"No. I told you. He said I shouldn't be a *placée.*"

"He has no right to express such opinions, when he offers you no other options." Desiree was angry now. "Did you tell him you wanted to be an actress?"

"No." She looked at her mother quizzically. "Why should I tell him that?"

"No reason." She waved her hand to dismiss the question. "It's good you didn't. Society people think actors are low, common people, very little better than…"

"Whores?" Mariette asked. She gave her mother an oblique glance. "*Placées?*"

"That will be quite enough, Mariette," Desiree said, pushing her chair beneath the table in anger. "I wash my hands of it. We cannot talk, you and I. I'll leave it all to M'sieur. You'll talk to him about everything and let him decide. I'm going to have my nap now. I need it. You've exhausted me."

M'sieur, Mariette mused. Always *M'sieur.* Never Papa. No. He couldn't risk telling the world that Raoul Delissard had a second family and had fathered a quadroon daughter.

CHAPTER 5

Raoul Delissard's visit was not long in coming. A week after Mariette's argument with her mother, a letter was delivered, saying he'd arrive in a few days. Praise the Lord! Her mother's mood changed miraculously to bright smiles and high spirits.

His visits were always anticipated with brisk housecleaning and arduous food preparation. That would take her mother's mind off their disagreements of the past week. She and her mother would shop together at the French Market for her father's favorite foods and liqueurs and cigars.

He always brought a bit of excitement into their quiet, humdrum lives. He was a handsome man, a treat to behold in his planter's hat, frock coat, and leather boots. When he visited, he sat with her mother on the parlor settee. The house was still in "summer dress," with oyster white linen slipcovers pulled tightly over the horsehair settee and chairs. The wool carpets were stored in the attic, rolled with tobacco leaves to ward off moths, and the gleaming hardwood floors were covered here and there with area rush mats. The brass fireplace fan was open, and standing in a row before it were pots of red geraniums and striped Schefflera Mariette had brought indoors for a spot of color. The room was like a summer garden, with its scents of lemon oil furniture polish and potpourri in cutglass jars.

When Mariette was a little girl, she sat on a footstool at her father's feet and rested her head against his knee, while he lazily fingered the strands of her hair. She told him about her studies and her dancing lessons and her friends.

But ever since that day long ago when she'd seen him from her treetop aerie, undressed in her mother's bed, holding her mother in his arms, she'd never felt the same about him again. At first she'd been repulsed by him, though her mother had shown up soon after, holding his hand, beaming as he smiled down at her. With maturity, Mariette had come to understand what she'd seen, even if she'd never been pleased by it. She'd never felt the same reverence toward her mother, either. The pedestal was gone. Her heroine had feet of clay.

This time, when her father came, she'd have to talk with him about her opposition to *plaçage*. She was frightened, knowing his sentiments on the subject and knowing, too, that he had spent a fortune training her for that life. Naturally, he supported the system itself. He had personally benefited from it for the past twenty-three years. But for his daughter? Maybe he would want something better, as Philippe had suggested. She could hope for that.

When he arrived, Desiree greeted him at the door, kissing and embracing him so eagerly that his packages were crushed between them. Laughing, he handed them over toCeline. "*Bon après-midi, mon amour,*" he said to Desiree. Then looking at Mariette, "*Et ma 'tite 'fant.*" He reached over to kiss her cheek.

"*Bon après-midi, M'sieur,*" Mariette said warmly, taking his scarf and his coat. Desiree's eyes were shining with tears. How she loves that man, Mariette mused. At least that's one person who makes her happy.

"Come. Let's sit down in the parlor," Desiree said. "Open the windows, Celine, and get my fan, please."

"*Bonjour,* Celine," M'sieur called out to the maid, as she walked away to follow orders.

Celine returned with Desiree's fan and disappeared to finish preparing the mid-afternoon meal.

With Desiree beside him on the settee, he presented his gifts. He handed Desiree a hatbox and her mouth formed an O as she took it carefully and untied the bow. Gingerly, she lifted a bonnet out of its bed of silk paper, and as she turned the wide-brimmed straw, trimmed with silk ruching and pink ribbons, she exclaimed that it was without a doubt the loveliest bonnet in New Orleans. "But M'sieur," she protested, "it is far too fine, too extravagant for me. I have no dresses that would be equal to it."

"Then we must get you some," he said, smiling magnanimously. He pulled out a roll of bills and dropped them on the cherrywood *escritoire* close by. "Get that seamstress, that Madame Delacroix, to make you something beautiful to match the bonnet."

Desiree leaned over and kissed his cheek. "And where will I go with such an outfit?" she asked. Mariette knew her mother was not hinting that he take her anywhere, for she was not devious. She knew what was impossible and never complained about her lot.

"To the theater, of course, *BéBé,*" he said, calling her by his pet name. "You still love the theater if your name is Desiree." He put his arms around her and hugged her close, and Desiree smiled with pride. This was all she wanted of life, Mariette thought, these few caresses, these few days of sharing her bed with him. And then he would go again, and she'd never ask when he would return. All the rules had been laid down long ago. *But how can she live that way?*

"Now for *mon 'tit chou*," her father said, handing her a tiny package.

Mariette opened the box to find an exquisite pair of drop earrings, fashioned like tiny roses carved out of ivory. She drew in a breath before speaking. "Oh, M'sieur, they're so beautiful." She got up and kissed his cheek. "If only I'd had them the night of the ball!"

"Oh, by the way, how did things go at the ball?" he asked.

Desiree was silent. Mariette answered. "Oh, M'sieur, the Orleans Ballroom is so beautiful! And the music was wonderful!"

"Well!" Delissard said expansively. "Were you the belle of the ball?"

"She was," Desiree said stiffly.

At that moment, Celine called them in to dinner and they spoke no more about the ball. The meal was superb. Even Desiree loosened up and laughed after her second glass of Madiera. After dinner, the evening passed in conversation.

"You can look for some wonderful plays this season," M'sieur told Desiree. "Caldwell has even engaged Edwin Forrest to star in one of his productions."

Desiree smiled and nodded. Mariette's eyes widened at the news of impresario James Caldwell and the coming theatrical season. Then she and her mother exchanged knowing glances, and the merriment over the news diminished.

"But if you go to the Camp Street Theater, hire a carriage," he added, raising an admonishing finger. "I'll leave you enough money. Don't go in the rig. I've heard there are thugs in the American Sector at night, and there's very little street lighting beyond the theater."

At ten o'clock, Desiree retired to her bedroom, and Mariette was alone in the parlor with her father. Mariette watched as he poured a small liqueur and took out a cheroot. She brought the tinderbox and lit the cigar for him, as she'd seen her mother do so often. He stretched out his booted legs and rested them on the footstool.

"Sit here beside me, *cherie*," he told Mariette. She joined him on the settee.

"I have to talk to you, M'sieur," she said with a tremor in her voice.

'What is it, Mariette?" he asked. "You look so troubled, *ma fille!*" He took her hand and fondled it gently. Her father's hands were the hands of a gentleman, soft, with slender fingers and well-trimmed nails. "Did any of the young men from the Ball come to offer for you?"

Tears brimmed in Mariette's dark eyes. "Oh, yes, M'sieur, but I have no wish to be a *placée*."

"Is this something new? I haven't heard this before. I thought we all understood about your future. Your mother and I don't want you to have to work in any menial capacity."

"But I *want* to earn my own living. I want to be an actress, like Maman was when you first saw her on the stage."

Delissard smiled, remembering. "*Ma belle Desiree*," he said, gazing into space, reminiscing. Mariette waited. Then, he gave her his attention. "But you must understand, *ma petite*, that a quadroon would have a hard time getting into an acting company today."

"Maman said that. But if I don't tell them, they won't know."

He, too, was silenced by the irrefutable fact. But he had more to say. "Now suppose you did get into an acting company and then met a wealthy Creole who wanted to take care of you."

"No, M'sieur. I won't be a *placée*, ever." She met his gaze. "I deplore the idea of *plaçage*."

Silence fell between them for a moment. Raoul Delissard put his arm around his daughter's shoulder and drew her to him, trying to find the words he'd come to say.

CHAPTER 6

"You may be surprised to hear this but I'm glad you didn't take any of the suitors who offered for you," he said.

"Oh, M'sieur, I'm so relieved," she said. The words came easily now. "I know how happy Maman has been with you, but this life is not for me. I want to be an actress, at least for a little while, and then I must marry, even if I marry a quadroon."

"Oh, no, Mariette, you must not do that," he said. "Your skin is like cream, *ma petite*, and your children must also be white. Don't lower yourself."

"The only way I could do that is by becoming a *placée*," she said boldly, avoiding his eyes. "If I married another quadroon, at least our children would be legitimate."

She felt as if she had struck her father. She'd never meant to give him pain. True, she resented the role in which he'd placed her mother, for Desiree's life was one of secrecy and confinement, in spite of the material things she enjoyed. In light of that, who was he to say she'd be lowering herself to marry a quadroon? At least, she'd be able to tell the world who her husband was.

"I came here to propose something to you, Mariette," he said soberly, "but I don't want you to give me your answer tonight. I can see now that it will not sit well with you at first."

Mariette's heart thudded.

"I have a good friend, a planter, whose property is adjacent to mine in Jefferson City. His name is Louis Soniat. He is a man my own age. I've been trying for years to acquire a large portion of his land along the River Road. This would double my holdings and allow me more docking space on the riverfront."

"Yes, M'sieur." Mariette wondered why her father was telling her these things.

"Louis is a bachelor," Delissard said.

Instantly, she understood.

"He knows about my life here, and he has seen you often and admired you. He asked me if I would talk with you about becoming his *placée.*" He waited while she turned a pair of dark, disbelieving eyes in his direction. "He would be good to you, Mariette. You would be treated like a queen. Louis is enormously wealthy."

Mariette felt as if all the blood had drained from her body. "I have no desire for great wealth, M'sieur," she said weakly. She knew that her father's friend had promised him the land he wanted if she agreed to his proposal. She felt sick, disillusioned. She could not believe her father would use her this way, in exchange for convenient docking space.

Delissard once again drew her close, and she felt herself stiffen against his embrace. "You'll soon change your mind when you get used to an opulent home, expensive jewels, and a household of servants at your command."

"No, M'sieur, I will not change."

"Please don't give me an answer now. Think about it. The only life for you in this time and place is as a *placée, ma fille*. And no finer man could be your *patron* than Louis Soniat. He is kind and gentle, and since he is a bachelor, he would be almost entirely at your disposal. Will you promise me to think about it?"

Mariette shrugged, not looking at her father. Would she do him this favor? Give up her life for his docking space? Is this what he had raised her for, *spoiled* her for? To trade her for land, as he would a slave? She'd always thought he'd done it out of love.

She backed away and looked at her father. She saw a stranger. She did not know the man at all. Something hot and painful roiled inside her chest. Never again would she feel a quickening of affection in his presence. She was not his daughter any more. She was his merchandise.

She spoke now, boldly, no longer afraid to express her innermost feelings. Her father had not hesitated to express his, although they involved the sacrifice of her entire future.

"Your friend is much too old for me, M'sieur," she said.

"Nonsense," said Delissard. "Don't you know that the best protector a young woman can have is a man with maturity and experience? Not only has he had time to acquire wealth, but he treats his young *placée* tenderly, as a precious possession."

Possession! I am no man's possession! Not the wealthiest, gentlest man in all Louisiana. How can my dear, tender father think of me as his friend's possession or his own merchandise? I will hold back my feelings no longer.

"I met a young Creole at the ball," she said, looking away from her father. "I was very much attracted to him. He said I should be the wife of a Creole, not a *placée.*"

"Don't live in hope of that," Delissard said quickly. "That man did you no favor, planting such a fantasy in your head."

"It was already there."

"What was his name?"

"Philippe Grillet."

"I know the Grillets well. They are commission merchants. The father also has a sugar plantation on Bayou St. John." He sighed heavily, irritated that his own proposal had been sidetracked. "They are high society, Mariette. They will arrange for their son to marry a wealthy socialite, and he won't even remember a quadroon girl he once met and flattered."

Tears filled Mariette's eyes and spilled down her cheeks, but she squared her shoulders and said what was in her heart. "Suppose he would say he was going to marry me."

Delissard smiled indulgently. "He cannot do that, Mariette," he said. "It's against the law."

"Suppose he tried to pass me off as white," she argued. Suddenly, Mariette was aware that Philippe Grillet had promised her nothing, had probably already forgotten her; but the fantasies he'd awakened still burned hot inside her, and she had to speak. She was trying to salvage her life.

Delissard shook his head. "It won't happen, Mariette. Take my word for it. A family like the Grillets would expect a well-known family tree and a very generous dowry." He sighed heavily. "How can I give you that, *ma fille?* It would mean I would have to acknowledge you as my daughter. And surely you can see the consequences."

"Of course. You'd have to tell your wife you've had a mulatto mistress for twenty-three years and you have a quadroon daughter." It was the first time she'd ever mentioned his wife, and she knew that stepping into his other life was unforgivable. She knew her words were like arrows shot into his heart, and she was glad.

Delissard threw his cigar into the fireplace and his gaze followed it to the glowing coals. Without looking up, he said. "We'll speak of this another time, Mariette. I am very tired."

Mariette felt strong now in her resolve. She must see to her own happiness, for there was no one else who would. "Very soon, I'll be going to the theater to try out my talents," she said. She was telling him now, not asking him.

He locked eyes with her and sighed. "Go, if you must. See James Caldwell at the Camp Street Theater. He is the best. You will use the name Delon, of course."

"Of course," she said, bitterly. "I always have."

CHAPTER 7

Mariette sat on a cotton bale on the riverfront, sorting out her heartaches. She was soothed by the soporific pflum-pflum-pflum of a paddle-wheeler coming into port. She had walked the six blocks through the French Quarter from Rampart Street to the docks to distract herself by watching the rafts, keelboats, canoes and scows sailing in on the wide, fast-moving, mud-colored river.

Pyramids of cotton bales lined the docks, and draymen sat holding the reins of their horses, smoking cigars, awaiting the arrival of ships. Muscled stevedores, black men and white, unloaded vessels, their bare arms glistening in the sun. The wharf was alive with pitchmen, peddlers, vendors, and beggars. Vessels, lined up double and triple file, waited to be relieved of their cargoes of indigo, sugar, molasses, animal skins, and cotton.

She watched the sturdy flatboatsmen jockeying for docking space, bending their muscle-corded arms to the oars. These "Kaintocks" were a dirty, uncouth lot, who usually hung around the bawdy houses of Gallatin Street. The presence of such men on the riverfront made the place "off limits" for Mariette. She had slipped out of the house while her mother and Celine were napping.

She had much to think about. Two weeks had passed since her father had asked her to be Louis Soniat's *placée*. The next time he came, he'd want an answer. Her answer would be no, but it would not stop there. Too much hung in the balance for her father to give in to her whims.

She knew now that he'd educated her and groomed her so that one day, he'd be able to cash in on his investment. But he was soon to discover he was wrong if he'd counted on her willing submission, for that he would never get.

She loosened the strings of her reticule and counted her money. From the bills he'd left on the *escritoire* for silks and baubles to keep his *placée* and his daughter content, she'd squirreled away three dollars this time. Added to what she'd picked up on previous occasions, she had the better part of her steamship ticket to St. Louis, if she should be forced to make the trip. She'd do it in the blink of an eye if he forced her into *plaçage* with Louis Soniat. In St. Louis, no one knew her, and she could pass for white. She wasn't afraid to go away alone. In fact, she looked forward to it.

She'd have other expenses besides her ticket money, though. She'd need money for room and board. Then she'd have to find work. She knew nothing about the theaters in St. Louis. Perhaps there were none. If so, she'd have to look for work as a seamstress. She'd learned dressmaking from Madame Delacroix in the past two years, ever since the day she'd gone for a fitting and noticed a young Negro girl sitting on the floor, pulling out basting threads. She'd asked Madame if she, too, could come help her in the afternoons after school. Madame had been glad for the extra help, and Mariette had explained that she was working just to learn how to sew. It never hurt to know a trade.

She'd made up her mind to be able to support herself, if ever she had to run away. As time went by, Madame taught her to cut out a pattern and later, to alter a dress. Madame never asked her why she was there. And now Madame had started paying her for piece work. These wages also went into her savings.

Mariette's fondest hope was that she'd be able to audition for James Caldwell and be taken into his acting troupe at the Camp Street Theater. This would make her financially independent. But even if that happened, she'd still be here in New Orleans, where her father could put pressure on her to become Louis Soniat's *placée*.

She gazed out at the water and thought how nice it would be to be married to a handsome young man, living in a townhouse somewhere in the Quarter or maybe in the American Sector, raising children who could proudly tell the world who their parents were. But quickly, she took control of herself. Things were as they were, and the best one could do was live with her problems or try to solve them. She was young and strong and able to take care of herself. With enough money, she could go to St. Louis, pass for white, get a position, and make a new life. She would hate leaving her mother, but as far as she could see, there was no help for it.

"Wanta buy a purty *chapeau*, little lady?" a toothless, bearded vendor asked.

Mariette jumped. She had not seen the man coming. Suddenly, he bent over her, holding out a dirty taffeta bonnet he'd probably retrieved from someone's trash can. She grimaced and moved away. She walked briskly toward the *banquette* of New Levee Street. He followed her for a while. Then, cursing under his breath, he gave up and returned to the dock. This was why her mother forbade her to come here alone. Good reason, she mused.

Dodging vendors and beggars, Mariette entered the French

Market, where the chaos was more organized. Here, under a Spanish-tiled roof stretched a line of stalls on both sides of a narrow aisle two city blocks long, where vendors sold everything from fresh produce to raw oysters to cooked food.

Mariette smelled the intoxicating aroma of okra gumbo. She reached into her reticule for a few coins. She had eaten little at lunch. The crisp air and the enticing aroma had whetted her appetite. She walked to the booth and ordered a cup.

The thick, rich soup was delicious. Mariette stood at the counter, eating it ravenously, dipping crusts of French bread into the brown broth. People passed her by, brushing her skirt in the crowded aisle, but she didn't care. It was good to be on her own for once, just another stranger in the crowd.

"You're not dipping that French bread properly, you know," a genteel voice said. Mariette was stunned motionless. "The way you're doing it, you've got the gumbo dripping down your chin."

Before she turned around, Mariette knew who it was. Philippe Grillet. He was standing at the counter, enjoying his own gumbo. Smiling, he took his napkin and pressed it to her chin.

Mariette giggled. "Philippe Grillet, I do believe," she said, using the napkin and then returning it.

He bowed and nodded. "You remembered my name."

"I did. And when did you become an expert on dunking bread into gumbo?" she asked, still laughing.

"When I was about six, I think. One day, I remember it well, I said to myself, I said, 'These people are doing it all wrong. You must dip the curl of the slice under the broth, like a spoon, and lift out as much of it as possible. Without spilling it on your chin.'"

Mariette smiled and dimpled. He was even more handsome than she remembered. When he took off his top hat, his dark curly hair danced in the river breezes and his eyes held as many colors as a bayou swamp at dawn.

"And so, Mam'selle Mariette," he said, "what are you doing alone in the French Market on a weekday afternoon?"

"You remembered my name, too."

"But of course. A man does not forget such a radiant beauty."

"Oh, I don't know," she said. "You managed to do so for the past two weeks."

He threw his head back and laughed. "You're very frank."

She shrugged. "Why not?"

"Why not indeed?" His generous mouth curved upwards in a smile. "I've thought of you often. But I didn't know where you lived."

Mariette's heart did a crazy little dance inside her chest. Was it possible? Would he have looked for her if he'd known her address?

"Mariette...may I call you Mariette?"

"Of course. And I shall call you Philippe."

"Are you out without a chaperone?" he asked, looking around.

"Yes. My mother and my maid Celine are taking their naps. They think I'm napping, too. But the weather was so beautiful; I just had to get a change of scenery. The riverfront is just a few blocks from our house."

"Suppose they wake up."

"They won't. Napping is a sacrament to them."

Philippe's eyes crinkled with amusement. "It is to most Creoles, too," he said.

"Maman and Celine nap two full hours every afternoon, and they sleep so hard, they wake up with sheet creases that don't go away till bedtime."

Philippe laughed again.

"And what about you?" she asked. "What are you doing here?"

"Having lunch. I come here almost every day. Our commission house is just a few blocks away on the *Rue Royale.*"

We've been only blocks apart all this time, she mused. "And what do you do there?" she asked.

"We buy and sell goods, usually shiploads of them, cotton, sugar, whatever our clients produce."

"I see. That must be very interesting."

"Oh, yes. Fascinating." He smiled at her broadly. "And where were you planning to go this lovely afternoon, after you'd had your gumbo?"

"No place in particular," she answered pleasantly. "Just for a walk."

He sensed a trace of sadness in her voice. "May I walk with you, then?" he asked.

"Of course. I came to the riverfront to think through some of my problems. Then I was hungry, so I stopped for a cup of gumbo. Now I think I'll walk to a place I dearly love in the *Rue Royale.*" She touched her napkin to her lips and dropped it on the counter. Philippe did the same.

"And what is it in the *Rue Royale* that so intrigues you, Mariette?"

She smiled. "Instead of telling you, I'll show you," she said. She laughed light-heartedly, delighted at the unexpected encounter. She'd thought of him so often in the past two weeks and fantasized about meeting him casually on the street. And here it was happening, just as she'd imagined.

She took his right hand to lead him down the *Rue Chartres.* Feeling a raised area on the back of his hand, she stopped suddenly and lifted it to look at it well. A bad burn scar ran up his hand and appeared to continue past his shirt cuff. He saw her looking at the scar but he offered no explanation, and she asked for none.

She tucked her hand in the crook of his arm and continued her stroll. By a circuitous route, they wound up on the *banquette* in front of a residence in the *Rue Royale*, where she stopped. Close upon the sidewalk was an extraordinary cast-iron cornstalk fence that marked off the front yard. Now, clasping her hands before her, she smiled and sighed.

"This fence is one of my favorite things," she said. "Isn't it beautiful?"

"It is," he agreed.

"It's new," she explained, "and terribly expensive. The molten iron is poured into a cast, giving the cornstalks depth. Then a second cast is made and fitted to the first, and the stalk becomes three-dimensional. My father told me about it."

She lowered her eyes and gave in to her sadness. She was thinking of her father and what she must do to get his land for him. Facing Philippe, her head down, she knew he could see the flush in her cheeks and the movement of her shoulders as silent sobs took control of her. She looked up now, directly into his eyes, and picked up her explanation. "The most beautiful thing about it is that the corn is painted yellow"... her long, slender finger traced the corn... "the stalks are green..." her forefinger moved down the length of the stalk... "and the morning glories growing up the stalks are blue." She cupped a morning glory in her palms. Philippe watched her, seemingly mesmerized by her movements.

She looked up at him again. "Don't you think it's a lovely sight?" she asked with a catch in her throat.

"Lovely," he said. He took her hand. "And now it's my turn to choose a place. Let's go to Vincent's for coffee."

"Won't you be missed at work?" she asked

"I make my own hours," he said. "I wrapped up two big contracts this morning, so I owe myself a half holiday."

"Then let's have coffee," Mariette said.

He pulled her hand through the crook of his arm. Together they walked a few blocks down *Royale*, Philippe chatting congenially, discussing the weather, Mariette giving in to a light laugh from time to time, and at last finding herself outside the confectioner's parlor.

Inside the shop, Philippe ordered their *café au lait,* and they each selected a meringue. Then, settled at a tiny marble-top table, Mariette put sugar in her coffee and began eating her meringue greedily. She could feel a sugary crumb at the corner of her mouth but before she could lick it off, Philippe lifted it with his fingertips and put it in his mouth. It was such an intimate gesture—almost like a kiss—and Mariette felt her face flushing almost to her hairline.

"Did the suitors call on your mother after the ball?" he asked.

She sighed heavily. "Yes. They came," she said, thrust back into sadness once again.

"Well? Did your mother choose a protector?" he asked, having to know.

"No. I told her even before the ball I would not be a *placée.*"

Philippe smiled. *With relief?* "I'm happy to hear you say that, Mariette." Gently, he placed his hand over hers.

CHAPTER 8

Mariette smiled. The warmth of his hand on hers sent little rivulets of fire through her veins. She closed her eyes for the briefest moment, composing herself, but she did not withdraw her hand, and he did not move his. He lifted her hand and held it in both his own.

"Something is making you sad today," he said. "Can you tell me what it is?"

She put her fork down and looked into his eyes. She felt his concern. He had the self confidence of maturity; yet there lingered in him the gentleness of a boy. She decided to tell him about her father's proposal.

"….And so you see," she said, when she'd told him everything, "although I'm determined not to become a *placée*, I don't know how I can defy my father. I may be able to put him off for a while, but in the end..." She shook her head, lowered her gaze to her cup.

Philippe lifted her chin with his thumb and forefinger. "You must refuse him, Mariette," he said peremptorily. "He has no right to dictate the course of your life. You are his daughter, not his slave."

Mariette shook her head and laughed softly, pleased by his sentiments but aware how little weight that argument would carry. "This afternoon, I sat at the docks and thought about taking a steamboat upriver to St. Louis, where I could pass for white." She looked into Philippe's eyes. "I have most of the money for my passage saved already. And I am a good seamstress. Not a modiste, but I will be soon. And I do have other options. I could marry, perhaps."

Men would line up from New Orleans to St. Louis, Philippe thought. But he had no intention of encouraging her to go. "Don't run away, Mariette," Philippe begged. "Just refuse your father. He cannot force you to live with the man. He cannot use you as a bargaining chip.

"Oh, I think he can," she said. "We are all manipulated, Philippe. Even you, though you may not know it."

A short laugh. "Me? How am I manipulated?"

She finished the last drop of her coffee and pressed her serviette to her lips. "Someday, your parents will find a wealthy young debutante, and they'll arrange a marriage for you." She locked eyes with Philippe. "They'll put such pressure on you, you'll be forced to give in. Perhaps the young lady's father will have political influence to bring big contracts to your commission house."

"I'd never let them force me into a marriage of convenience."

She leaned back in her bent-wire chair and sighed. "You think not, but you will. And that makes you just as much a slave to their wishes as I am to my father's."

Neither spoke for a moment, and the coffee was forgotten.

"Then perhaps it's time we broke out of bondage," he said, smiling a teasing smile.

Mariette did not understand his meaning, but her heart quickened. They sought each other's eyes and an undeniable vibration passed between them. He took her hand and pressed it to his lips. Mariette felt as if she'd been torn from the universe and spirited away to another place, where the wonderful feeling that was passing between them could blossom into something deeper. Whatever happened later in her life, she'd always have this moment.

"Don't give in to your father," he said, his lips so close to hers that she could feel his breath on her face. "Give me time to think about your problem. There has to be another way."

She frowned and tilted her head. "Why would you do that, Philippe?"

"Because I hate to see a life sacrificed for no other reason than monetary gain."

She nodded. She loved his words. She loved the fact that he cared what happened to her. He was the only one who did. She pressed her fingertips to the edge of the table. "Truth to tell," she said, "it's my mother who signs the contract. In theory, my father has no control over her, because they are not legally married. So she makes the decision. But she's always done whatever he said, so how can I persuade her to do otherwise? Especially since she thinks it's best for me."

Philippe took a calling card from his waistcoat and placed it on the table. He found a pencil in his coat pocket. "Here," he said, "write your address on the back of this card. I need to know where you live. I can't count on running into you when you take a walk to the riverfront."

She smiled. She wrote the address and pushed the card back to him. He slipped it into his pocket. "But, you mustn't come to my house," she said. "My father might be visiting." She thought for a moment. "And if my mother sees you, she'll think you've come to offer for me. I don't want you to feel trapped or embarrassed."

"I won't come to your house. But we could plan to meet at the

French Market. I usually have my lunch there at about one o'clock. At the gumbo counter or somewhere close by."

"So if I should decide to take a walk at nap time," she said smiling.

"You'll know where to find me."

Mariette smiled a satisfied smile. "My father did grant me one concession," she said.

"Oh?"

She looked squarely into his eyes. "He said I could audition for M'sieur James Caldwell at the Camp Street Theater."

"Caldwell?"

"Yes. The British actor, the great impresario." She smiled.

"Oh, I know who he is," Philippe said brusquely.

"I want to be an actress with his company. Then I could be financially independent."

"Mariette, do you know what you'd be getting into, becoming a part of that company?" His tone showed blatant disapproval.

"I only hope I'll have a chance to find out," she retorted, her own voice becoming crisper.

"Mariette, *ma cherie*, theater people are low and common, certainly not fit company for a well-raised young woman like yourself. Please don't do this, I beg you."

Mariette sat back in her chair and folded her arms. "It's been my lifelong dream," she said. "I have no intention of giving it up now, unless, of course, Caldwell doesn't take me."

"Oh, he'll take you, all right, in more ways than one."

"What do you mean?"

"The man's a womanizer. Everyone knows that. He'll promise you a leading role, but he'll ask you little favors in return."

Mariette's mouth dropped open. She could feel the heat rising in her neck and her cheeks. "And you think I'd do such things? How dare you suggest..."

"I'm not saying you'll do them." He lowered his voice so as not to attract attention. "I'm saying he'll embarrass you by asking."

Mariette frowned. "Why must everyone tell me what to do?" she asked. "My mother, my father, and now you."

Philippe dropped some coins on the table, took Mariette's hand, and led her from the shop. He walked her down the street to an abandoned store and pulled her into the arcade. "Mariette, if you become an actress, you will regret it," he said. "You will be looked down upon. You will see coarseness and intimacies you can not even imagine. You've been sheltered all your life. You're not prepared for such things."

"And what is that to you, Philippe Grillet?" she asked, her eyes narrowing. "First, I'm not allowed to refuse *plaçage*," she said, her cheeks growing hot with anger. "Then I'm not allowed to refuse my father's selfish and cruel request. Well, I may just have to endure those things, because my parents say so, but you, Monsieur Grillet, I do not have to obey. I have my parents' permission to audition for Caldwell, and I'm going to audition."

Her voice had risen in volume as she spoke, and she could see that it was all Philippe could do to repress a smile of amusement at her fiery explosion. Instead, he pulled her into his arms and kissed her hard on the mouth. The kiss became more tender as it lengthened, and the embrace more passionate. Her bonnet fell back with the impact of his grasp and hung dangling down her back by its ribbons. Shocked at first, she was soon aware that his lips were warm and soft beyond her imagining. She closed her eyes, placed her hands lightly against his hard chest, and felt ashamed when a sound very much like a purr escaped her lips.

In his arms, she felt the embrace gentling. He was holding her as if she were something precious, as if he knew she would not withdraw. Her knees were so weak from the kiss that, had he not been holding her, she would most surely have collapsed.

Slowly he released her and looked into her eyes. She stood, gazing stupidly, reeling from the kiss. Awkwardly, she tried to right her bonnet and tie the bow, but her hands seemed unable to function. Philippe found the bonnet ribbons and tied them in a saucy bow beneath her chin.

With his index finger, he gently brushed a loosened strand of hair from her brow. "I'm going to walk you home," he said. "Or nearly home. It's late, and it isn't safe to be out alone. Besides, they'll be missing you at home."

Mariette didn't answer, but she took the arm he offered and walked along beside him, feeling an incredible sense of well-being. She felt as if she were weaving drunkenly. She feared she might lose her balance or trip on the uneven planks of the *banquette*.

Her heart was still pounding, her cheeks heated. She shot a sideward glance at Philippe. What a man he was! And what a kiss he'd given her! She'd forgotten whatever it was she'd been so angry about. She'd have to go over it again in her head when she got her good sense back. For now, she could remember only that unguarded moment when he'd pulled her into his arms and lowered his mouth to hers. Her willing response had surprised her. Now she could barely draw a breath as she walked briskly beside him, trying to keep up with his long strides. She knew she should have objected to the kiss, but she had reveled in it and did not know how to pretend otherwise. She could think only of his strong commanding grasp, the sweetness of his mouth on hers, and the faint delicious taste of coffee on his lips.

CHAPTER 9

Mariette couldn't believe she was actually walking down the aisle of the darkened Camp Street Theater while a rehearsal was in progress. This was what she'd always yearned to see, the inner workings of a theater. She slipped quietly into one of the back rows. Her mother, shawled and tignoned, moved into the row behind her, like a proper maid.

They had agreed between them that Mariette could not go into the American Sector unchaperoned, and if they went into the theater as mother and daughter, Mariette would not be taken. Desiree had therefore come in the guise of Mariette's maid. They had even agreed that Mariette would always call her Desiree, even at home, so that she would become accustomed to it, and she would avoid a mistake that might cost her her career. Desiree was not put off by this.

In fact, Mariette sensed in her mother an excitement to be in the theater again. Mariette knew that in her secret heart, Desiree was not totally opposed to her theatrical ambitions.

The play in rehearsal was one Mariette had seen before—*The*

Boarding House. Smiling, she rested her forearms on the back of the seat in front of her and sat forward, a smile on her face. The stage was set with a long dining table in the center. A middle-aged actress was speaking.

"Take a seat at the end of the table, Mr. Smith," the actress said. "When your bill is paid, you'll move back into the roast beef section."

Mariette laughed softly. Her heart was lighter than it had been in a long time. To her delight, she understood the English words perfectly. She knew her mother did not, but she seemed to be enjoying herself just the same.

Despite's Philippe's disapproval of her acting ambitions, Mariette had taken the first step to make them a reality.

"But, Mrs. Malone," the actor replied, "I have been promised employment by Monday."

Suddenly a tall imposing figure rose from a seat in the middle of the theater, startling Mariette. "No! No!" the man called out to the actor. "Face the audience, Ernest, and project! I can't hear you out here." Ernest nodded and tried again. "That's better," the dark figure called out, and the rehearsal continued. A quarter of an hour later, the director rose again. "Take ten minutes," he called out to the actors.

"This is your chance," Desiree whispered over Mariette's shoulder. "That's Caldwell."

Mariette gasped. "Are you sure?" she asked.

"Yes. Go. Introduce yourself."

Mariette felt her heart beat against her ribs. She didn't know when she'd been so nervous, but this was the most important moment of her life, and she had no intention of ruining her chances. She pulled down the peplum of her new green walking suit, adjusted the ribbons of her bonnet, and walked down the aisle toward her destiny.

"M'sieur Caldwell," she called out to him.

Standing, he turned and, in the darkness, with the stage lights behind him, his face was not clearly visible, but his tall, broad-shouldered frame appeared formidable. "Yes?"

Mariette approached him, her hands at her sides.

"I want to introduce myself," she said in English. "I am Mariette Delon. I'm seventeen years old and I'd like to be an actress with your company."

Caldwell seemed to be restraining an urge to smile. He looked her over, and since she now knew he was a womanizer, she couldn't help feeling like merchandise on display. Her cheeks warmed.

"And why do you think you can act, Miss Delon?" he asked.

"Well, my mother was a great actress, and she and her friends taught me, even as a child. My mother worked with the great Fontaine, Madame Marsan, and the Champignys."

Caldwell smiled. He seemed to be studying her every movement, her figure, even the way she used her hands. "Very notable theater personalities," he said.

She drew in a deep breath and laced her fingers at her waistline. "As for me," she said, "I took voice lessons from M'sieur Pelagie..."

"Good teacher."

"...and I studied dancing under M'sieur Francisquy."

"I'm impressed with your resumé."

Now's the time, Mariette thought. "I hoped you would give me a chance to work with you."

Caldwell, standing in the aisle, waved her to pass him by. "Could we have a sample of your talents?" he asked smiling.

"Now?"

"Please. Why don't you sing something for us?"

"I know 'Girl at the Garden Gate," she said, "and I brought the music." She made a move to go back to her seat for it.

"We have no accompanist today," he said, "but perhaps you'd be willing to try it '*a capella*'?"

"Very well, M'sieur."

Desiree's heart went out to her daughter, knowing the fear and hope that must be warring against each other inside her. But oh, how proudly she walked down the aisle toward the stage, her head held high, her small shoulders back. Lifting her skirt daintily, she climbed the steps to the stage and stopped center front.

She stood where the light would be most flattering, clasped her hands at her waist, and sang one chorus of the song in her clear soprano voice. At the very first note, the actors in the wings came quietly to the back of the stage and stood listening.

How beautifully she sings, Desiree thought. Her notes are true, even without accompaniment, and she has such quality and control.

When the chorus ended, Mariette stepped easily into a soft-shoe dance to the rhythm of the song she had just finished. Oh, yes, she's graceful, Desiree thought, and look how she smiles at the audience. She has a natural instinct for the stage. He'll take her, of course. Maybe not today, but soon. He'd be a fool not to. This is where she belongs. Let her enjoy it for a while. She's young.

When the dance ended, the actors who had formed a half-circle behind her applauded. Mariette turned around, surprised and delighted. Caldwell approached the stage.

"Miss Delon," he said, taking the steps two at a time, "You sing and dance beautifully. You are a pretty young woman, and I'm impressed with your talents, but I have no openings in my company at this time." A small frown of disappointment played between

Mariette's eyebrows. "We have a complete repertory company for the season, which has already begun. But if you'd like to come sit in the theater during rehearsals, you are welcome," he said.

Mariette's eyes widened. "Oh, M'sieur," she said. "I would be most grateful. I'll bring my notebook. I'll study the blocking and listen to your directions. Then, if you ever do have a place for me, I'll be better prepared."

"Good idea! Young actresses come and go. They get married. They have babies. Parts become available. In time, I'm sure you'll be an actress."

He held out his hand to shake hers, American-style. Mariette placed her hand in his.

"Thank you, M'sieur," she said.

"Wait," he said. "Let me give you something." He walked to a desk at the back of the stage and returned, holding a thick paper package. "Here is a copy of the script for the next play, *The Day after the Wedding*. Perhaps you'd like to study the ingenue role of Letitia, just for practice?"

She took the package in both hands and clasped it to her bosom. "Oh, thank you, M'sieur."

Caldwell peered out into the darkness of the empty theater. "You didn't come alone, I hope," he said.

"No, M'sieur. My maid Desiree is with me. Our rig is just outside."

"Good. Now may I make one more suggestion?"

Mariette nodded, smiling.

"Your English is good. You know the words, I mean. But if you were ever to act here, in the American theater, you'd have to do something about your accent. If it is too French, no one will understand you."

"Oh, dear," Mariette said. "What do you suggest, M'sieur?"

"Well," Caldwell said, "I could give you elocution lessons." He smiled, tilting his head. One actress nudged another. "Can you come here at eleven each morning?"

"Oh, yes, M'sieur," she replied. Knowing now that the impresario was a womanizer, she was aware that his intentions might be suspect, but she was willing to take a chance. It was a foot in the door. Wouldn't her mother be with her, wherever the lessons took place, as her maid and chaperone?

"Then I will see you tomorrow, Miss Mariette, at eleven? Here in the theater? This means, of course, I'll no longer be able to sleep till noon, but," he waved his hand dramatically, "I think it will be worth it. Something tells me that someday you'll be a fine actress."

Mariette smiled. She was thrilled. She loved being called Miss Mariette. She extended her hand to Caldwell. This time, he bowed over it, European-style.

In the bright gas footlights, she could now see Caldwell clearly. He was an extremely good-looking man with thick, wavy hair and dark penetrating eyes. He had heavy eyebrows and an oversized jaw, but the overall effect was one of virility.

Mariette walked down the aisle of the theater. Before she reached her mother, the rehearsal had resumed. Out in the glare of mid-afternoon, Mariette climbed into the rig, and Desiree took the seat beside her. Mariette smiled gleefully. After leaving the rig at the livery stable on Rampart Street, Mariette took her mother's arm and walked toward the house, stopping every few seconds to laugh and hug her. Perhaps she'd have a future in the theater after all.

CHAPTER 10

By nine o'clock, Celine and Desiree had retired. Mariette, now in her gown and wrapper, sat in the parlor, reading the script by the light of the girandole. She was lost in the fantasy world of *The Day after the Wedding*. When she came to the lines marked *Letitia*, she read them aloud.

Suddenly, the silence was broken by a tapping on the glass half of the front door. Mariette jumped. Who could it be to come at such an hour? Perhaps someone had been watching her through the window. Her heart was in her throat.

She walked to the door and lifted the pongee curtain. She gasped, for she was face to face with a man, but she saw him only in silhouette with the whale-oil street lamp behind him. She returned to pick up the girandole. She carried it slowly back to the door, her heart racing. Then, fearfully lifting the curtain once again, she discerned the handsome face of Philippe Grillet. Relieved and thrilled at the sight of him, she dropped the curtain and hurried to unlock the door.

She replaced the candle-holder and walked out onto the gallery, pulling the door closed softly behind her. "It's very late, Philippe," she whispered. "My mother has retired for the night."

"I was hoping she had," he said smiling.

Shyly, she walked to the top step and sat down. Then looking up at him, she patted the place beside her, and Philippe sat too. He took her hand, warming it between his own.

"How are you, Philippe?" she asked, trying to ignore the fact that his warm hands holding hers were awakening every nerve ending in her body.

"I'm fine. And you, *mon ange?*" he asked, smiling his devastating smile.

"Fine, too," she said. "Oh, Philippe, I'm so glad you came to see me. I have news, although I doubt you'll be as pleased with it as I am."

"Well, tell me."

"I went to see Caldwell today at the Camp Street Theater." She watched for his reaction. Except for a tightness about his lips, he registered no expression.

"Go on," he said.

"I sang and danced for him, and he said I was talented but he had no place for me in his company."

"You're luckier than you know."

"But he did invite me to come to rehearsals and he offered to give me lessons in speaking English, you know, without an accent."

"Elocution lessons."

"Yes. He gave me a copy of the script for his next play, so I can practice."

"And you don't see that the man is a womanizer?"

"No," Mariette lied. "Why would I think that?"

"Mariette," he said in an exasperated tone, "the man gave you a script, although he didn't give you a part in the play. Doesn't that tell you something? And although he has no place for you in his company, he invited you to come to rehearsals and offered to give you private speech lessons. Do you think he does that for everyone that walks in off the street?"

A smile tugged at the corners of her mouth.

"Why, you little vixen," he said. "You knew what he was up to all the time." Now, suddenly, he was serious. "And yet you encouraged him with your wide-eyed innocence? What do you plan to do when he pounces in the privacy of his dressing room?"

Mariette allowed herself a hearty laugh. "Why, Philippe, I think you're jealous," she said.

"I'm not jealous, Mariette," he said, breathing audibly. "It just infuriates me to see a sensible girl walk into a spider's web with her eyes wide open, just for a part in a play."

"I'll be in no danger, Philippe." She placed her hand on his arm. His expression did not soften, but he did not move his arm away. "My mother will be with me as my maid and chaperone. Wherever I go, she'll go. What can he do with a middle-aged woman in the room?"

"More than you think."

"Besides, if he gets disrespectful, I'll just leave the room."

"Disrespectful!" Philippe slapped his forehead and laughed a sardonic laugh. "Oh, my poor little innocent! What a lot you have to learn! And doesn't he know it! I really don't want you to go back there any more. The place is bulging at the seams with lascivious people, the worst of whom is Caldwell himself."

"*You* don't want? And what have you to say about it, M'sieur? I've told you before, you're not my father, though you seem to think you are. I'm going to be an actress in Caldwell's Company, and I'm willing to take a chance."

"Take a chance!" He laughed again."Oh, *pauv"tit 'fant!* The man is a boa constrictor. He won't pounce on you. Forget that. He'll bedazzle you. He'll oil his way around you. He'll promise you stardom and wealth and fame, then he'll make himself so charming, so irresistible, you won't be able to help yourself. You'll give in to him."

"Give in to him! I think I'm intelligent enough to know when a man's making himself charming and irresistible."

"Don't be too sure about that. You have no experience with men, Mariette. It has nothing to do with intelligence. And as for your mother, *cherie*, he'll dispose of her easily enough. He'll send her on a little errand or ask her to do him a favor. It's so simple." He laughed sardonically.

"I may not have experience but I have common sense." She slanted a frown in his direction and saw his jaw was still clenched in disapproval. "I'm not going to give up my dream of being on the stage, Philippe," she said with determination. "I'll just have to be on my guard against boa constrictors and close my eyes to immoral behavior."

He huffed angrily, but she suddenly lifted her head and looked into his eyes.

"*Mon Dieu*, you are so beautiful," he said. He reached out to touch her cheek with his fingertips, and she closed her eyes to receive his touch. "You skin is so smooth, *cherie*. It glows, even in this meager light. I've thought of you every day since we walked down the *Rue Royale* to see the cornstalk fence."

"Have you, Philippe?" She longed to touch the curls that swept around his ears and the collar of his shirt, but she was not that bold. Not yet.

"I keep remembering your fingers on the cornstalks," he said. He took both her hands in his and lifted them to his lips, pressing a kiss into each palm. A thrill danced up her arms. She found it difficult to breathe. "I wanted my face to be in your palms, like those morning glories. I wanted to feel the softness of your fingers. I think of that at night when I'm lying in my bed."

She turned to meet his eyes, and then slowly, shyly, lifted her trembling hands and cupped his face. His eyes fell shut, and his breath caught. Mariette blushed, but she did not move her hands. She loved the roughness of the day's growth of beard against her palms. Philippe's eyes opened. He took her hands in his and placed them against his chest. Then, taking her in his arms, he kissed her softly on the mouth. Mariette's lips opened to his. She felt herself drowning in the sweetness of his kiss. He kissed her deeply and passionately, and when he drew away, his eyes still filled with longing, he kissed her twice again, in short, staccato kisses.

Philippe took her head in his hand and drew it to rest in the curve of his shoulder. She listened to the beat of his heart and rubbed her face against the fabric of his coat.

"So, if I keep on going to rehearsals and to elocution lessons...?"

Philippe tensed. He let out a harsh breath. Then he drew away and stood up. She was sorry she had so abruptly ended their very special moment, but didn't she have to know?

"When you act on the stage," he said, "you leave all refinement behind you."

"And do I leave you behind, Philippe?"

The hopelessness of their situation descended upon her like a great weight. She could so easily fall in love with this man. Acting was her life-long ambition, but he could see only that it made her cheap and common. She had no hold on him. He was probably just infatuated, and if the going got too rough, he'd forget all about her.

"I had hoped we could mean more to each other, Mariette."

"And you're saying we can't, if I don't give up acting?"

"I didn't mean it to be an ultimatum."

"You hoped you wouldn't need an ultimatum," she said.

"Yes, I suppose that's true."

Then, after the warm and wondrous kisses, after the memories he'd recalled, after the fire he'd ignited in her just by holding her hand, he stood up, brushed off the seat of his pants, and gave her one last look. "I have to go now. And you'd better get to bed. It's late. Goodnight, Mariette."

CHAPTER 11

"Miss Mariette," Caldwell said pleasantly, stopping her halfway through a line, "there are three ways to pronounce that word. You say it with a French accent. *Bee-ter*." He raised his hands, touching thumbs to forefingers in a typical French gesture. "New Orleanians say it with a soft Southern drawl. *Bid-der*." He shook his head with disdain. "And *I* say it the correct way. *Bit-tah*. Please say it my way."

"Oui, M'sieur," Mariette said. "Bit-tah."

He smiled a one-sided smile and lowered his gaze flirtatiously. "That's fine. Do you think you can call me 'Mister Caldwell'?"

"Yes, Meester Caldwell."

"*Mister*. Oh, hell, call me Jemmy. All my friends do."

"Oh, no, Mees...Mis-ter Caldwell."

Caldwell laughed. "All right, Miss Mariette. Now read your next line."

As the elocution lesson in Caldwell's dressing room proceeded, Desiree sat quietly in the corner with her knitting. No one questioned her presence there. Mariette was young, and chaperones, even in the theater, were part of the scenery.

For the past two weeks, Mariette had been coming to the theater daily to watch rehearsals. She'd studied the role of the ingenue Letitia in the upcoming production of *The Day after the Wedding* till she knew it by heart. She'd arrived each day at eleven for lessons in the correct pronunciation of the words of the English play. Who better for such instruction than Caldwell, an Englishman by birth? She had only to keep him at arm's length, and all would be well.

Four weeks had passed since her father had asked her to become Soniat's *placée*. He had not yet returned for her answer. As far as Mariette was concerned, he could not stay away long enough. She had counted the days since she'd last seen Philippe. It had hurt her deeply when he'd walked away so brusquely from her gallery that night. She had cried herself to sleep, but she'd done her best since then to forget him. She had enough people running her life without taking on another, especially when he was demanding that she give up the one thing she wanted more than anything else in the world. And promising her nothing in return.

She had not lied to him. She'd made it clear how important the theater was to her. Maybe he'd decided a relationship with a quadroon, one he had neither the right nor the desire to marry, was complicated enough, without the added factor of her acting with the womanizing Caldwell. Perhaps he'd also decided that if she was willing to put up with Caldwell's undisguised flirtation, she was too low and common to be of any interest to him.

At least the elocution lessons were going well. Caldwell had told her she was a quick study and an amazing mimic. And as he read with her, pronouncing the words, she felt herself becoming more British in her articulation every day.

As for Caldwell, he seemed to glory in her love of the theater and her willingness to watch and learn and prepare herself for a future career.

The Boarding House finished its run, and rehearsals for *The Day after the Wedding* began. Mariette had of course seen the current ingenue, Madeline Duval, when they'd passed in the wings. She shot Mariette a look that could have frozen molten lava.

Madeline and Caldwell had had an affair a few months back, according to theater gossip. While Mariette was not an understudy in the play, the only role she could conceivably fill was Madeline's. This would happen only if Madeline became ill and had to miss a performance. So it must appear to the ingenue that Mariette was waiting for her to break an arm or come down with influenza. She was undoubtedly furious with Caldwell for allowing Mariette to watch rehearsals and for helping her along. It was as if he too hoped for the worst for Madeline, so that he could put his new girl in the role.

One day Mariette saw Madeline in an ardent embrace with a handsome young bit player, who had taken the liberty of squeezing her *derriere* in the public corridor, where all the world could see. Perhaps she had allowed him this privilege just to make Caldwell jealous. At any rate, Mariette had seen it, and the grapevine had it that Caldwell knew about it too. The whole affair was becoming explosive.

Mariette knew that Caldwell was fond of her. So, it seemed, did everyone else. Desiree heard him talk to another actor about her "adorable" French accent, and from her corner of Caldwell's dressing room, Desiree had seen through the open door, two girls raise their eyebrows when Caldwell and Mariette laughed at something during the "private" elocution lessons. Like most theater people, they thrived on gossip and resented the little French girl who'd turned the director's head.

Mariette soon discovered that Philippe's assessment of Caldwell was not groundless. One day in the third week of their lessons, Caldwell turned to Desiree. "Desiree," he said, "would you mind going to the restaurant across the street for me?" He reached in his pocket for change. "Ask them to make me a pot of coffee and buy some *croissants*. A half dozen should do. I, for one, have had no breakfast, and I'm sure you'd both enjoy a little something."

Mariette translated for her mother, and a bell went off in her head.

"*Bien sur, M'sieur*," Desiree answered, obviously not suspicious of his intentions. But Desiree was no sooner out the door than Caldwell made his move. He came to the tiny settee where Mariette sat, put one arm around her waist, and slid his other hand beneath her skirt and petticoats up to her thigh, which he proceeded to fondle. Mariette let out a little cry of surprise.

This was not a man "oiling his way around her," as Philippe had described it. This man was pouncing. In spite of all she'd heard about Caldwell, she had never believed he'd make advances during their lessons. He'd seemed so protective of her innocence.

She got to her feet in one sudden move, pushing him aside angrily. "I'm sorry, Mister Caldwell, but I am not accustomed to being handled that way, and I think it might be best if the lessons ended for good."

Caldwell rested against the sofa, a roguish grin on his face. "I thought we were good friends," he said.

"Too good, I had hoped, for this kind of intimacy."

"*Touché*!" Caldwell said. He straightened his clothes and left the room. She did not come in the next day at eleven, and Caldwell went back to his habit of sleeping till noon.

The theater itself, she discovered, was one big den of iniquity. Philippe had been right about that, too. Once, through an open door, Mariette saw an actor and actress making wild, passionate love, with only a tangled sheet to hide their nakedness. Mariette had been shocked.

Caldwell, a married man, seemed attracted to every woman in his company, and she was sure he'd had affairs with most of them. For this reason, Mariette took it as neither a compliment nor an insult that he'd tried the same with her.

On opening night of *The Day after the Wedding*, Mariette sat in the box seat Caldwell had reserved for her. Though she didn't have a part in the production, she'd watched every rehearsal. She felt "involved" in the play and nervous for the actors. The theater was packed and for good reason. The cast included Caldwell, of course; the well-known Lydia Kelly; and Mariette's nemesis, Madeline Duval, as the ingenue.

As she took her seat, the musicians were tuning up, and there was the wondrous sound of subdued excitement in the audience. She saw things now in the brightly-lit theater she hadn't seen at rehearsals, when the theater was dark: the dome of the ceiling, with a blue background and a canopied center painted with clouds and studded with silver stars; the cut-glass chandelier; and the three tiers of boxes, each decorated with wreaths of roses. She wondered if her mother and Celine, who were sitting in the top tier, would see and hear well enough.

The house lights dimmed. Mariette pictured all the actors backstage, taking a last-minute look at their makeup, then rushing to their places in the wings. Her heart was suddenly heavy. She yearned to be part of this company. How could she have thought it would be so easy? Caldwell's troupe had been complete and doing quite well before she'd auditioned for him. It would continue to do so, whether or not he took her in.

She faced the fact that he might never take her at all. Maybe the closest she'd ever get was where she was tonight, in the stage box. Maybe he'd allowed her to come to rehearsals just to have someone new and different to flirt with. But now that the elocution lessons were over, even the flirtation had ended. Mariette sighed heavily and gazed toward the stage as the heavy curtains parted.

Applause greeted Lydia Kelly as she walked onstage and spoke her first line, projecting it musically into the silence of the theater. When the performance ended and the applause began, Lydia Kelly walked onstage alone to a thunderous ovation. Then Caldwell came out alone for his usual tumultuous applause. Again and again, they were called back until they'd taken five curtain calls.

In the midst of the noise and confusion, Mariette felt a soft tap on her shoulder. She looked around to see an usher trying to get her attention. He gave her a note and left. Frowning in wonder, she opened it and read it.

"I'll come to your house tonight. P."

Philippe! He had been out there, somewhere in the darkness. He'd seen her in the box and sent her the note. Her sadness vanished. She would see Philippe tonight. Her heart was filled to overflowing.

Mariette met her mother and Celine in the lobby of the theater. As her father had advised, they took a hired carriage home. In the darkness of the cab, Mariette fingered the note she had tucked away in her reticule.

She realized she'd never told her mother about the day she'd met Philippe in the French Market at the gumbo counter. Nor had she mentioned his nocturnal visit after she'd auditioned for Caldwell. She planned to tell her everything in time, but she'd never been certain how Philippe felt about her or what plans he had for their future, if indeed he had any at all.

CHAPTER 12

At midnight, when Desiree and Celine were asleep, Mariette sat in the parlor waiting. When Philippe tapped at the glass half of the door, she rushed to open it and join him in the shadows of the gallery. Without words, he took her face between his hands and gently kissed her lips, and then embraced her possessively.

"I got your note," she said, when she caught her breath. She looked up into his shadowed countenance. "I was so happy you were in the audience tonight. I was feeling depressed, sitting there in the box, when I wanted so badly to be on stage." Suddenly, she asked, "Why *were* you there, Philippe? I thought you hated the theater."

"Oh, no! I love good plays. I just don't like the idea of your being mixed up with low-life people every day."

Mariette shrugged. They'd never see eye to eye on this. Her chin trembled. "I was sitting there, thinking I'd probably never realize my ambition in the theater, and then the usher brought your note. It gave me something to look forward to tonight."

Without words, he took her in his arms and held her close, rocking her gently, as if she were a child. "Then I'm glad I came."

"So am I," she said, her head still pressed to his chest. She could hear his heart beat. She drew in a deep unhappy sigh. "Nothing is turning out right in my life."

Releasing her from his embrace, he took her hand and led her to sit on the top step, as they'd done on his first visit. He put his arm around her shoulder. "Tell me about it, *mon ange.*

"My father will come back any time now, and he'll want my answer. He'll push me into *plaçage* with that old man."

"Tell him no, Mariette. You must."

"Oh, that's easy to say, but without a career in the theater to give me an income, I'm at his mercy, don't you see?"

Before he answered, he lifted her chin to look into her eyes in the light of the street lamp. "Don't despair, *ma belle fille.* Things can turn around in a minute."

"How?" She sniffed.

He offered her his handkerchief. "Tell your mother she must refuse to sign the contract. You said it was all in her hands."

Mariette shook her head. "She's used to giving in to him."

"But she'll do it for you, Mariette. She loves you."

"She's afraid of him."

"Well, if you can't get into Caldwell's troupe, what about working for that modiste you spoke of?"

Mariette shrugged her shoulders. That was not the career she had looked forward to at all.

"My parents will not accept that. They want me set up with a rich man, someone who can do my father some good."

"Oh, *ma belle Mariette*," Philippe said. "I've been so miserable since we last argued and parted angry." He took her in his arms and nuzzled her ear as he spoke. "I can't eat." He pressed a soft kiss to her cheek. "I can't sleep" Another kiss to her brow. "I can't work."

Another to the pulse beneath her chin. "I think I may be losing my heart to you."

"Oh, Philippe." She wrapped her arms around his neck and rested her cheek against his, rubbing it gently.

Philippe took her in his arms possessively. She felt his lips brush across hers, teasing her, testing her response. Then holding his hand to her nape, he took her lips with his own and kissed her deeply. She went weak in his arms. At last he pulled away, breathing hard. She knew he did not trust himself to restrain his impulses. She rested her head against his shoulder.

As they sat together on the step, Mariette held his right hand in hers. She fingered the back of his hand lovingly, and felt the scarred area again. "What is this on your hand, Philippe?" she asked, turning the cuff back at his wrist. She saw a long, angry red scar.

He withdrew his hand from hers. "It's a burn scar from my childhood."

"How did you get it? Do you mind saying?"

"No." He drew in a deep breath. "I was spending a few days with a friend, Charles Deslattes, at his father's plantation in Golden Meadow, downriver."

Mariette nodded.

"It was the middle of the night. We were all asleep, when suddenly I heard screams and I smelled smoke. I opened my eyes to see flames reflected in the mirror in Charles's bedroom. I was terrified. I shook Charles awake and ran from the room. I thought he was behind me."

"But he wasn't," Mariette injected.

"No. When I got outside, his mother was there, with a blanket wrapped around her shoulders. She was counting heads. It was a big family. She looked at me frantically and asked, 'Where is

Charles?' I told her I thought he was right behind me. But he wasn't there." He shook his head. "The house was an inferno at this point. So I ..." He hesitated. He grimaced, and Mariette knew he was seeing a conflagration that had haunted him all his life. "I took the blanket from Madame Deslattes' shoulders and soaked it in a horse trough nearby. I wrapped it around me and ran back up the steps and into the house."

"Oh, Philippe, you could have been killed."

"I wasn't able to get to him. The staircase had collapsed in the flames. I called out to him, and I think I heard him call back. But when I saw that the ceiling was about to give way, I ran back outside. I didn't save him."

"But you tried," she said compassionately. "It wasn't your fault."

"I've always thought it was."

"And the burn?"

"It was very bad for a while. But like everything else," he shrugged his shoulders, "you get better or you die." His voice was almost a whisper when he added. "Charles died."

"It wasn't your fault." She rubbed the scar gently and pressed his hand to her lips.

He gazed out into the street, and she knew he was re-living the pain of guilt. "I should have turned around to see if he was there. He may have been trapped in some way, and I could've helped."

"Have you thought of it often, Philippe?" she asked.

"All my life. And I'm deathly afraid of fires."

"I don't wonder." She held his hand to her cheek and then kissed it again.

"I must go now," he whispered, "but I'm not angry." He smiled his handsome smile. "I'll try to think of a way to help you. To help us both. And I'll be back."

He stood. Then taking her hand in his, helped her to her feet and took her in his arms. Lowering his head, he covered her mouth with his and moaned with repressed yearning. With his hand spread wide against her back, he pressed her body to his, increasing the heat that was building between them.

She slipped her hands inside his frock coat to circle his warm, hard body, and bring it closer still to hers. She was aflame with desire for him. Then he broke away and placed his finger against her lips. She smiled beneath his finger, but in her secret heart she answered, *Yes, Philippe, my darling Philippe. Please come back to me.*

CHAPTER 13

Before she'd even had her morning coffee, Mariette opened *Le Moniteur* to the theater page to read the review of *The Day after the Wedding*. Critics praised the play and the actors with equal enthusiasm. Folding the paper, she handed it to Desiree, who was coming into the dining room in her nightrobe. "Take a look at this, Desiree," she said, pointing to the coumn. She walked over to the dresser and poured two cups of coffee. She had remembered to call her mother by her first name, as they'd agreed, but the term sounded foreign to her ears. "Does it offend you when I call you Desiree?" she asked.

Desiree smiled. "No, *ma fille*, not at all." Then, returning her attention to the newspaper, she said, "Just wait till the critics see *you* in an ingenue role. Then they'll have something to write about."

"That's something they may never see," Mariette said sadly.

"Of course they will. Give yourself time. No one was ever taken into a well-known company overnight."

"But when *M'sieur* comes back, he'll want my answer about becoming a *placée* to his friend."

"So? What has one thing to do with the other?"

"If I have no acting job as a means of earning a living, he can force me into *plaçage*."

"No, no, Mariette. That he cannot do. I am the one who must sign the contract." She put sugar in her coffee and stirred it. "Only the *patron* and I. Don't forget that. Your father has no control over it."

"But he has control over *you*. Will you say no to him if he asks you? Will you do that for me?" Mariette held her breath, waiting for her mother's answer.

"I don't know, Mariette. Perhaps it would be a good thing for you to take this M'sieur Soniat. Your father says he is a very rich man."

"I don't care about that. I despise *plaçage*, especially with a man as old as my father."

"And Philippe?" Desiree asked, with a hooded glance over her coffee cup. "What does he say?"

Mariette shot a side glance at her mother. Desiree knew Philippe had come last night. There was little she could hide from her mother. "Philippe says I must refuse to become a *placée* to my father's friend."

"Well, I expected that. But has he offered you any alternative?"

"No, but I'm hoping he will."

Desiree shook her head. There was nothing more to say. Although in theory, she and only she could sign the contract, Raoul Delissard could make life hell for her if she didn't. "I'll try to say no, Mariette. I promise you that." She sighed wearily. "I don't know how much good it will do."

Mariette got up from her chair and gave her mother a hug. "Desiree," she said, enjoying addressing her mother like a girlfriend, "your promise means more to me than you will ever know."

CHAPTER 14

In his office on the *Rue Royale*, Philippe sprawled lazily in his swivel chair, one booted leg resting on an open drawer, as he absentmindedly drew lines enclosing the corners of a scratch pad. He could think of nothing but Mariette's angelic face, her sweet smile, her creamy white breasts partially bared in her wrapper. She was such a temptation to him, it was all he could do to keep his hands off her. And yet she was not a girl he wanted to take into *plaçage*. He genuinely cared about her. Had it not been for all the obstacles in their path, he would have courted her with the intention of marrying her. Yet he knew how impossible that was in the time and place they were living in.

He would not set her up in a prostitute's cottage on Rampart Street. He respected her too much for that. He knew she'd probably give in to the inevitability of it, and do so more readily if *he* asked her than if she had to accept her father's friend. He smiled absently, thinking of the dimple beside her delicious mouth. Oh, God, how he wanted that girl!

Through the half-glassed wall surrounding his office, he had an unobstructed view of the front door. He was waiting for Armand to come in. Armand was already two hours late for work and had missed an appointment with the *Henry Clay*, a ship he'd been scheduled to meet earlier this morning. Philippe had gone in his place, but there was still the paper work to be done in the transaction, and it needed immediate attention.

Armand was so madly in love with his *placée* that his morning love-making could not find a stopping place. He came to the office later and later each day and did nothing at his desk but smile and write little love notes to Monique. Philippe would have to talk to him about that. But more than anything, he wanted to confide in him about his own problem.

In Philippe's more rational moments, he knew he had gotten in over his head in an impossible romance. As recently as the night at the Orleans Ballroom, he'd been determined to remain a bachelor. He didn't even want to take a *placée*. He'd wanted no one and nothing to tie him down. When he'd remarked to his cousin Gabriel about Mariette's beauty, Gabriel had feigned surprise that he, Philippe, the Don Juan of New Orleans, would be so moved by a pretty face. The eldest of nine male cousins and still a bachelor at twenty-nine, Philippe was considered by the others a roué with a harem of women stashed all over New Orleans. He'd never dispelled the myth. He'd only wished it were so.

In actual fact, before that night, only two women had occasionally relieved his semi-celibate existence. The widow Duclos, his mother's friend, had stopped by his townhouse one afternoon a year ago to get "fresh young ideas" for decorating her new apartment. She'd stayed for tea, and one thing had led to another. The ideas she had come for were fresh and young but hardly on the subject of decorating.

Philippe grinned, remembering. Mme. Duclos was a master of bedroom delights. He'd fixed her breakfast the next morning and looked forward to her monthly visits ever since.

His sister's friend Elise was the other side of the coin. A pale, convent-bred girl, she came to town to shop, but always made time for a friendly visit to Philippe's apartment. She left him feeling as if he'd ravaged a virgin. They both knew better, but what fun it was to play the game!

But no more! In the past two months, he'd forgotten them completely and would never entertain them again. For the first time in his life, he was in love. Incredible though it seemed, he was sitting here, ruminating on the fairness of the state laws regarding mixed marriages. And how could the Church follow those laws? He was in search of answers to questions he'd never considered before. The Sacrament of marriage should be available to all people, no matter their color. It was ludicrous. What it came down to was: He could not legally have Mariette as his wife. Not in New Orleans.

Needless to say, his parents would consider him a pariah if he tried to legalize a relationship with a woman of color. His inheritance, which was considerable, would be lost. His partnership in a thriving commission house would end. Friends and family would shun him, once the truth about Mariette's heritage was known. His business contacts would be severed. His father's clients would never have dealings with a Creole married to a colored woman, even if such a marriage could take place. But why should he care? He was twenty-nine years old. He had twelve years experience as a merchant. He could set up his own business and trade with the Americans, who did not know him. Was he or was he not a man?

Excited at the prospect, he stood up, hands on his hips, and smiled at the ceiling. He wanted to laugh aloud. It was so simple. To start with, he could rent an office in the American Sector and, now that the New Basin Canal was finished, make a fortune on his own, along with all the Kaintocks and Americans who'd come south after the Louisiana Purchase. Through the canal, New Orleans merchants were now in touch with Gulf Coast planters who were eager to trade, and soon, the streets of the American Sector would be paved with gold. Everyone said so.

He began pacing around his desk. He took a cheroot from a teakwood box, clipped the end, lit it and puffed until the aromatic smoke hung in a blue haze above his head. Just knowing he might not have to give her up set his pulses racing. There had to be a way he could marry her. Maybe they could go to a priest who didn't know that Mariette was a quadroon. No, that wouldn't work. Birth certificates were needed. He could alter the birth certificates, but...

Think, man, think. He sat down at his desk, put his cheroot in an onyx ash tray, and ran his fingers through his hair. Suppose they were to marry in New York. There was no *Code Noir* in New York. Mixed marriages were legal there. And in the big port city, there would be more clients than he could handle.

But would Mariette go? Leave her mother? Leave New Orleans? Her horizons, though limited, were dear to her. Could she leave the theater? The damned theater! Well, why not? She hadn't been a success here. Not yet, anyway. Caldwell hadn't even taken her into his troupe. Maybe she could act on the stage in New York. At least until she was *enciente*. Then, hopefully, she'd be willing to forget about the theater.

Why should he give her up? Now that he'd found Mariette, held her in his arms, kissed her delicious lips, nothing would ever be the same again.

But perhaps before making such a drastic break from home and family, he just might try passing her off as white to his parents. She certainly looked white, far whiter than he, who like most Creoles was olive-complexioned. He could make up a whole new identity for her. No, it would never work. But then, he'd never know unless he tried.

The brass bell over the front door clanged as Armand burst in, flushed, clean-shaven. Philippe stood up and made an overt gesture of taking out his pocket watch. Twelve noon? What kind of hours were these? Armand's honeymoon would have to end, if he wanted to keep his position. He was taking advantage of their leniency. Knowing his righteousness grew out of jealousy, Philippe felt hypocritical. He signaled his friend to come to his office. Armand took a seat across the desk from Philippe.

"Armand, this is the third time this week you've come in hours late. This morning I had to go in your place to meet the *Henry Clay*. That was bad enough, but there's paper work to do, and I'll be damned if I'm going to do that for you."

Armand's mouth fell open, and he consulted his own pocket watch. "*Mon Dieu*, I'm sorry, Philippe. I was ..." a small grin turned up the corners of his mouth.

"I know what you were doing, Armand. It's no secret. You're mad for Monique. Look at you. You didn't even comb your hair. You've got to get hold of yourself, *mon vieux*."

Philippe looked at Armand's crestfallen face. He felt like a bastard scolding him, when he would have given anything to be in his place, if he could have Armand's peace of mind about *plaçage*, and if Mariette could have Monique's.

"I'm truly sorry, Philippe. It won't happen again."

"Very well. I have your word, and that's good enough for me." Philippe took another pull on his cheroot and his expression sobered. He put out the cigar. "There's something else I want to talk to you about," he said. "You are quite obviously the expert on the subject of *plaçage*."

Armand smiled. "How can I help you, *mon ami*? Is it about Mariette? Are you going to approach her mother with a contract?"

Philippe shook his head. "No. If that were the case, I could manage on my own."

"Well, then..."

Leaning forward conspiratorially, Philippe said, "I want to marry her, Armand."

Armand chuckled. "You're jesting, *mon ami, n'est-ce pas?*"

"No," Philippe answered quickly. "I've never been more serious in my life."

"It cannot be done," Armand said. "*Voyons*, Philippe. Face up to life. Your parents would laugh at your proposal and put an end to it."

"But suppose they didn't know. Suppose they believed she was white. What then?"

"But they will want background, Philippe. You know Creoles. If she were a woman of property, I mean great property, or if she came with an enormous *dot*, that might be another story. But things being what they are..." He shrugged. "Why make things so hard on yourself? Why don't you take her for your *placée*? With no wife in the picture, you could spend all your free time with her, as I do with Monique." Armand smiled wickedly. "You would not regret it, *mon vieux*."

Philippe did not return the smile. He rubbed his lower lip with his forefinger. "She hates *plaçage*, Armand." Looking into his friend's eyes, he became animated. "You have never seen Mariette, *mon ami*. You cannot imagine such beauty. And she's not only beautiful, she's talented, educated, accomplished."

"They all are, Philippe. If not, why would we love them so? Monique, too, could pass for white, but the idea of marriage is futile, my friend. My father would track her down like a bloodhound until every slave in her family history was dug up. And so," he lifted his palms, "I am willing to compromise. I live with her, and if Papa discovers my little love nest, he will understand, *n'est-ce pas?*"

Philippe sighed audibly. "I want to spend my life with Mariette," he said.

"And so you can. With your father's blessing in the bargain, even if a suitable marriage is later arranged for you."

"But I'd never marry anyone else. That's what I'm trying to tell you. How could I," Philippe asked, "when I've lost my heart to her?" Philippe sat down on the front of the desk.

Armand placed his hand on his friend's arm. "You say that now, Philippe, because you're besotted with her. But after a time, when your passions cool, there may come a day when your father will suggest an heiress as a suitable bride. And then, in a more pragmatic state of mind, you'll realize that with two words, you could double or triple your wealth. And the beauty of it is, you could go on visiting Mariette, just as you always have. Are you sure you could turn down such an arrangement?"

"Yes. Very sure. What kind of hypocrisy would that be?"

"The kind many men in New Orleans live with quite comfortably." Armand got up from his chair. Several of his co-workers had come into the office, returning from meetings with ships' captains and planters. All were hard at work on receipts and follow-up arrangements.

"So you'll try to pass her as white to your parents," Armand said. Philippe nodded.

"Well," just for a moment, consider the humiliation your beloved

Mariette will suffer when your parents discover her true heritage. It is inevitable, you know. Some simple thing will happen. They might see her embracing her mother on the street one day."

Philippe nodded. "I've thought of all that."

"Have you thought of taking her away from New Orleans?"

"Yes. And that might be the answer, if Mariette is willing to go. If my parents reject her, I'll do it. But there's something else." Armand waited. "Her father wants her to take his friend as a *patron*," Philippe said. "He lives in Jefferson City. He's an older man, a bachelor. Louis Soniat. Do you know him?"

"No."

Philippe pressed his hands to the desk and hardened his jaw. "The thought of her going to bed with that middle-aged lecher is like a fist turning in my stomach. He's a millionaire planter, but that means nothing to Mariette."

"Are you quite sure, Philippe?"

Philippe gazed into his friend's eyes. "Quite sure. Mariette has very simple tastes. She hates *plaçage*. But unless she marries or runs away, she'll have to give in sooner or later. Her scheming father is planning to use her in exchange for a great parcel of riverfront land."

"Well," Armand said, brightening. "If she must inevitably become a *placée*, she would certainly prefer to become your *placée, n'est-ce pas?*"

"I suppose."

"Then beat the old man to it. Ask her mother to accept your offer."

"But her father won't let that happen. You see, I don't come with valuable riverfront property." He shook his head sorrowfully.

"I see." Armand paused, weighing the facts. "Then perhaps you'd better let her go, Philippe. There's too much working against you."

"I know you're right, but I can't. I'm determined to marry her, one way or another."

"So!" Armand grinned a one-sided grin. "What has happened to our intrepid leader? The last of the confirmed bachelors?"

Philippe smirked. "We always think we know exactly what we want. That's because we haven't found it yet."

"You're right, *mon ami*. I hope you can work it out. But I wouldn't want to have your problems. *Jamais!*"

"I'll be leaving soon for Northern Louisiana," Philippe said. "I'll be gone five or six weeks. That will give me time to think and plan."

"Ah! Your Christmas trip. I envy you the dances and parties."

"I wish I didn't have to go at all this year, but my father thinks it's good business, to party with our clients at harvest time, when they have dollar signs before their eyes."

"Try to relax. Have a good time."

Philippe frowned and shook his head. "No. I won't have a good time at all. I'm going because I must. You know how my father is. I can't win with him."

"Will you tell Mariette you're going?"

"Of course. She must know I haven't abandoned her."

"I wish you luck, Philippe," Armand said, with the tone of one who knew his friend would need it.

CHAPTER 15

At one o'clock, Mariette walked over to the French Market and approached the gumbo counter. She prayed Philippe would come today. She sat on a bent-wire chair at a small table between the gumbo counter and the oyster bar. She'd hold the table for their lunch. Seeing the waiter approach, she waved him away and kept her eyes on the busy aisle in the market.

The weather had turned cold overnight and even in her warm hooded pelisse, she shivered in the brisk river winds. At last, she saw him and stood in greeting. He took her hand and lifted it to his lips. She yearned to have him embrace her, that she might draw strength from him. In the babble and confusion of the market, they would probably never be noticed, but her rigid upbringing made her keep her distance.

"I kept a table for us," she said.

He sat across from her at the table, and she had a chance to look him over well. He was wearing a greatcoat with a capelet and a slouch hat. She loved the wintry smell of him, of wool and bay rum and tobacco.

"I'm so glad you're here," he said before she could speak. "I wanted to tell you I'll be going on a trip in another day or two. It's business. I'll be away several weeks."

Mariette's eyebrows tented. She moved closer to him. "Where are you going, Philippe?"

"Every year, about this time, my father sends me to visit the sugar planters in northern Louisiana whose crops we handle."

"I see." She felt sick at heart. "But why now?" she asked. Her voice broke on the words. She must steel herself against tears.

"Because this is sugar-making time." He spoke softly and took her hand again to hold it as he spoke. "The harvest is in, and once the sugar has been ground and prepared for shipping, the planters give the darkies a few days off to celebrate. The planters invite their friends from all along the River Road. Then during Christmas week, the partying begins. There's food and music and dancing. It's good business for our clients to see us then, on a social basis."

"I'm sure it is." Her voice trembled again. She must not burden him by crying. Her problems were not his problems, and she must not assume they were. He had never made her a commitment.

"Since I was a boy of fourteen or fifteen," he said, "I've been going with my father on this trip. I used to play for the couples to dance."

"Play?"

"The piano. I studied piano for several years. I was no virtuoso," he said smiling, "but at least it was music. At one of the plantations, a slave played the fiddle and I accompanied him."

Mariette forced a smile. "So they've seen you growing up, the planters."

"Yes, they have. In the last few years, I've been making the trip alone, without my father."

"And are there pretty young ladies on those plantations?" She tried for a light tone but her voice broke on the words.

He sensed her distress and frowned with compassion. "None that interest me," he said.

Now, she simply had to get his attention and his advice. "So you won't be in New Orleans for Christmas."

"No, *mon ange.*"

Not even on my gallery at midnight. She had not expected to see him on Christmas Day. Surely he'd have to spend Christmas with his family, if he were here. But she'd hoped he'd find a few minutes for a visit on Christmas night.

What good would it do to repeat that her father would probably be returning while he was gone and would want an answer to his proposal? They'd covered that ground already. What could he do about it anyway? Only her mother could help her now.

"But I wanted you to know that I hadn't abandoned you."

Aren't you abandoning me, Philippe, in my moment of need?

"And while I'm away, I'll try to work out a plan for us," he said.

She looked up, a small frown playing between her eyebrows. "A plan to do what?"

"For us to be married, *mon amour.* Do you want to marry me?"

Mariette's breath caught. She plumbed the depth of his eyes. He'd never spoken of marriage before. He'd said she should marry a Creole, but he'd never said that *he* should be that Creole. Truly, his feelings for her were genuine. She smiled. She wanted to take his face between her hands and press her lips to his. Marry him? It was the dream of her life, but didn't he know how impossible it was? Especially if he were leaving her now, now at this crucial moment.

She felt tears burning her eyes. "Of course I want to marry you, Philippe, more than anything in this world. But it will be too late.

My father will be back before then. He'll want an answer. And my father is a very determined man."

The waiter approached again. Philippe signaled him to come to the table. Mariette quickly lowered her head and brushed the tears from her lashes.

"What would you like, Mariette?" he asked.

"I can't eat, Philippe. I have no appetite," she said.

"Later," he told the waiter, and the man left the table. Then turning to Mariette, he said, "Listen to me, Mariette. What I have to tell you is very important." He looked around to be sure no one was listening. "When I come home, the first thing I'm going to do is tell my parents I've found a young woman I'd like to marry. That should please them in one way. They've been urging me to settle down."

She nodded, although she knew the plan was futile.

"I'll arrange to take you to my father's plantation on Bayou St. John. While I'm away, I'll make up a whole new identity for you. I'll make it convincing, wait and see. Then, if they give us their blessing, we'll say we want a quiet, private wedding, and we'll be married in the new parish of St. Patrick in the American Sector, where none of the priests know us."

"But, Philippe, your parents will want..."

"...a big wedding, I know. But we'll marry secretly and tell them afterwards."

"But the birth certificates."

"I know about the certificates. Leave that to me. I can change them. My friends in school used to say I could have been the world's greatest forger."

Mariette continued frowning and shook her head. "It will never work."

"It will. Have confidence."

"And if it doesn't?"

"I'll marry you anyway, and we'll live in the American Sector or even in another city."

"You'll lose everything," she said.

"As long as I have you, *mon ange*, I'll have the world."

"Oh, Philippe, I love you so. But there are so many pitfalls, and of course, the worst of them is..."

"...is what, *mon amour?*"

"…that while you're away, my father will come to town with his friend Louis Soniat. How am I to hold him off?"

"Tell him no." Seeing that she was shaking her head, he said, "Tell him you want to think about it." He hesitated. "Or better yet, tell him yes, but you need a few weeks to get ready."

Mariette nodded, not trusting herself to speak.

"I know you're worried," Philippe said. With his forefinger, he traced the furrow in her brow. "I'd cancel the trip if I could, but my father would want to know why, and I don't want to tell him anything about my plan until I have the details worked out. He'd start checking into it. He'd talk to my friend Armand, who knows all my secrets, and the whole thing would blow sky high."

She held his hand between her own. "Get back as soon as you can," she begged.

"I will. And ask your mother not to sign the contract."

"I already have," she said in a small voice. "She promised she'd try."

"Then that's all we can do for now."

Mariette nodded. She tried to envision Philippe's father's plantation, his mansion, and the unreality of her fitting in there. What if his parents rejected her? They would, of course, if they found out about her heritage. She would be humiliated, and Philippe would be shunned, ruined.

They stood up. Philippe took her arm and walked her to the *Rue Royale*, where they exchanged one last look of anguish before parting. As she crossed the street, she knew he was standing behind her, watching her. So, with a sinking feeling in her heart, she squared her shoulders and walked briskly to her mother's house on Rampart Street.

CHAPTER 16

"It's so damp and cold! It goes right to the bone!" Desiree said, walking into the parlor, rubbing her hands together.

Mariette did not answer. Sitting on a high velvet-tufted stool before her needlepoint screen, she was a picture of desolation. She pushed the needle through the screen absently. The overcast atmosphere suited her mood.

"Typical Christmas weather," Desiree added, casting a sidelong glance at her daughter.

Mariette sighed audibly. Her mother was trying to make her talk, to get her mind off her problems, but she had no more concern with the weather than she did with the Christmas season. She hadn't been out of the house in more than a week, and then only to run an errand. The Belgian block streets of the Quarter were slick with moisture, and the winds off the river were so cutting she'd had to pull the hood of her pelisse tight around her head.

Desiree shook her head and walked back to the kitchen.

Mariette thought of Philippe and sank her teeth in her full lower lip. She jabbed her needle into the screen in temper, pricking a finger of her left hand. She jumped and brought the finger to her lips.

Three weeks and no word from Philippe. She felt upset and angry about his "good will" tour to the plantations. It had taken him away just when she was going to need him. True, he couldn't help her in any direct way. He couldn't confront her father unless he himself wanted her for a *placée*.

Mariette knew Philippe loved her. He'd asked her to marry him. He'd held her tenderly and kissed her passionately. He'd spoken of plans for their future. But what good were plans, if her father arrived now?

She had only to close her eyes to conjure up the image of Philippe's fresh, clean-shaven face, the feel of his warm lips pressed against her eyelids, her cheeks. Each time, she lost her breath, remembering. She loved him, and she wanted him.

Where was he now? Dancing with some beautiful plantation belle? *He could have a good future without me*, Mariette thought. *He doesn't need all the trouble I will bring into his life.*

She wove her needle into the screen and got up, putting her hands on her hips. For now, she didn't even have the theater to distract her. The play, *The Day after the Wedding*, had closed, and rehearsals had not yet begun for the next production, *Lock and Key*. It made little difference to her, in any case. There was no part for her in the play.

She gazed through the glass top of the front door. Any time now, her father could be arriving. She sighed heavily and clasped her hands together until her knuckles were white. His sickening proposal haunted her. "Say no," Philippe had said. "You must refuse him." Easy to say, if you were hundreds of miles away at a Christmas party.

And Mariette knew her father. He was stubborn and determined to have his way. She would not be able to refuse him indefinitely, not without a reason. She walked back across the parlor.

Christmas was coming. Neighbors were baking gingerbread men and taking out the fruitcakes and the blackberry cordial they'd made months ago in preparation for the season. Packages tied with red bows were appearing in windows all along Rampart Street. Mariette wished she could sleep through it all until New Year's Day.

Desiree came back to the room and shook her head. "Come shopping with me, Mariette," she begged. "We'll look in the stores along *Rue Chartres*. Everything is decorated for Christmas. Don't you want to go?"

Mariette sighed. "No, not today. I'm very tired. Anyway, I have only two presents to buy, for you and Celine, and I have plenty of time for that."

"What about your father?" Desiree asked.

Mariette gave Desiree a black look. How could her mother think she'd give a gift to a man who would barter her for land? How could she still care for him after his blatant display of greed and indifference toward his daughter? Mariette got up to leave the parlor, but a sudden sharp rap at the door startled her and stopped her. Her mother opened the door to a messenger.

"I am to wait for an answer," the messenger said.

Desiree nodded. "Mariette, it's for you." She raised her eyebrows and handed her the note.

Mariette broke the seal and unfolded the letter. "It's from Caldwell," she said. "He wants me to take a bit part in his new production, *Lock and Key*. He says it's not a big role but a good one. A French maid. It's perfect for me, he says. He thinks I should take it. He wants an answer. Rehearsals begin at three o'clock today." She looked up at her mother, a smile forming on her lips. "What do you think, Desiree?"

"Yes. I think you should take it," Desiree said, smiling.

Mariette's heart was instantly lightened. She smiled a full smile. "Then I will. Can you come with me?"

"Of course. Send him your answer."

Mariette walked over to the *escritoire*, wrote a note, and gave it to the messenger. Then she gave her mother a hug. At least one thing in her life was going in the right direction.

***

Everyone was in high spirits at the Camp Street Theater. After saying hello to the regulars in Caldwell's troupe, except for Madeline, who managed to keep her back turned, Mariette shook the impresario's hand and thanked him for the role. "I don't care if it's a small role, Mister Caldwell," she said, smiling, remembering her English pronunciation. "I'm finally getting into your company. That's what matters."

"Good girl, Mariette," the impresario said. "Bigger roles will come. You'll see."

Mariette was more than a little surprised when, the week before the new play opened, his prophecy came true. One day, Mariette arrived at the theater to discover that Madeline Duval, the ingenue, had run away with the bit player she'd been kissing in the wings during the run of the last play. They'd signed on for leading roles in a play soon to start in Atlanta.

Caldwell called Mariette to his office. As usual, the room looked as if a hurricane had swept through. But he had his legs up on his desk and he was smiling, apparently not at all perturbed by the shipwrecked appearance of his office or by having lost one of his leading ladies.

"How would you like to play the part of Odette in *Lock and Key*?" he asked. He raised his eyebrows to his hairline. He looked like the cat that had swallowed the canary.

Mariette was, of course, hoping for that plum of a role. "Oh, Mister Caldwell!" she exclaimed, wanting to run up and hug him, but holding back. "I'd be thrilled to play it."

"Then it's yours," he said, as delighted at the prospect as she. "You know, Mariette, you're a very lucky young lady."

"Oh, I know that, Sir."

"No, I mean it's such a wonderful time for a beautiful young actress to be starting her career in New Orleans. I'm building a theater at this very moment that will be the biggest and most luxurious in the South. The St. Charles Theater. What a showcase for a young talent!"

"How soon will it be finished?" Mariette asked, picturing herself on such a stage.

"By May first. No later."

"Then I'll be waiting anxiously."

"So will I." He laughed his exuberant laugh.

Rehearsals continued. Mariette knew her lines in a matter of days, which were all that remained before opening night. To her delight, the theater was packed. It was Standing Room Only for the run of the play. *If only Philippe could be here*!

Opening night, the musicians were tuning up. "Five minutes!" the stagehand called out. Mariette gave a start. She ran quickly to the ingenue's dressing room, which was now hers. She took one last look in the mirror, just as she'd imagined the actors doing when she'd been sitting in the stage box watching the last production. She hugged her mother. Her heart was beating so hard, she thought it would fly from her body.

"I'm terrified," she said.

"You'll be just fine," Desiree said. "As soon as you've said your first line, you'll relax and it will go beautifully."

Mariette nodded. She didn't trust herself to speak. From the wings, she watched as the leading lady walked onstage, and the audience broke into applause. The performance had begun. There was no turning back now. Halfway through the first act, she listened for her cue. Hearing it, she amazed herself by walking onstage and saying her first line.

The words resounded clearly. No rasping. No cracking. She began to feel comfortable, just as her mother had said. She felt the warmth of encouragement of hundreds of people in the audience radiating toward her. She felt their eyes on her, imagined them smiling into the darkness, smiling their good wishes for her to succeed.

After Act One, she returned to the dressing room to the arms of her mother who was waiting, misty-eyed, to tell her how well she'd performed. Mariette had only two lines in the Second Act, but Act Three was almost all hers. She felt that she was delivering her lines with clarity and control, so that even Celine, sitting up in the highest balcony, could surely understand every word.

When the play ended, a deafening round of applause filled the theater, and Mariette knew the first real thrill of her career. The leading lady walked out for her ovation. Then came Caldwell, who accepted his applause with dramatic humility. Finally, Caldwell stepped in front of the curtain, holding Mariette's hand. The volume of applause doubled. Now Caldwell waved her to take a bow alone.

Again and again, Mariette was called back until she had taken five curtain calls. She could feel her face flushing, and her tears could no longer be held back. Flowers were brought onstage for the leading lady and for Mariette. Caldwell saw how Mariette charmed the audience by her genuine surprise that the flowers were for her. What innocence, he thought, to go along with her talent and beauty!

After the curtain calls, Mariette's dressing room was crowded with actors. Everyone in the play came by to kiss her or shake her hand and add their congratulations. She was glad when the excitement ended and she was alone with her mother, taking off her makeup and changing into her street clothes. She felt emotionally drained. Just as she was ready to leave her dressing room, Caldwell appeared.

"You were wonderful, Miss Mariette," he said. "The unexpected star of the show."

"Thank you, Mr. Caldwell," she said.

"I'm sure this is the first of many triumphs for you in the theater. Now go home and get a good night's sleep." He took her hand and bowed over it.

Caldwell's words proved true. Over breakfast the next morning, Mariette read the critic's review aloud for her mother to hear. "Mariette Delon," [the critic said], "'a bright new star in the Caldwell constellation, was an unexpected delight in the ingenue role in the first performance of *Lock and Key* at the Camp Street Theater last night.'"

Her hands trembled, holding the newspaper.

"Go on," Desiree urged.

"'In the role of Odette, she was every inch the professional. Her acting was superb, rivaling that of the light-comedy star, Lily Wells. Where has Caldwell been keeping this jewel of an actress? We hope to see lots more of her this season.'"

"Oh, *ma fille!*" Desiree beamed. "I knew the critics would rave when they got a look at you!" Then she opened her arms wide and Mariette came to her mother for a heartfelt embrace.

CHAPTER 17

Two days after the play opened, Mariette was in her room, taking the pins from her hair in preparation for her nap. She heard the front door open, then the voices of her mother and her father. Her heart gave a violent jump, and her knees turned to jelly. Her father would want an answer today, and she knew what the answer must be. Her door opened, and Celine took her in at a glance, in her camisole and pantalets, her hair loose from its pins.

"You can't take no nap, Mariette. M'sieur Delissard is here, with another gen'mun, an' he wonts t'see you."

"Who's the other man, Celine?"

"Ah don' know." She paused. "You look pale as a ghost, chile. Want me to he'p you dress?"

Mariette nodded, and Celine stepped into the room and closed the door behind her.

"Where's Desiree?" Mariette asked.

"She be entertainin' the mens till you gets dere."

It was Soniat, of course. She was heartsick. A middle-aged man, a man old enough to be her father! And she was to take him as her lover! How could she let him invade her body, take her virginity? How could she let herself be bound to him in vows as strong as marriage, so long as he chose to keep them?

Mariette quickly pulled her chemise back over her head, circled her waist with her stays and turned to let Celine pull the strings and tie them. She stepped into a petticoat which Celine buttoned at the waist. From her armoire, she took out a daytime calico dress, a print of mauve and brown flowers, with a line of tiny buttons down the back. Then, putting on the dress, she pulled her long hair over one shoulder to let Celine fasten her down the back. At last, she sat at the dressing table, exhausted with fear, apprehension, and heartache.

"Ah better not take time to do yo' hair, Mariette," Celine said. "Just leave it hangin' down. I'll brush it for you."

Mariette didn't care. After a few strokes of the brush, she raised her hand to put an end to the brushing and drew her hair like two ebony ropes over her shoulders. It was good enough. If he didn't like how she looked, maybe he'd withdraw his request.

In the parlor, her father sat stiffly on the edge of the settee, with a man his own age sitting down facing him. They put down their cordial glasses and rose as she entered.

"Ah, Mariette," her father said. "There you are at last."

Mariette walked to her father and dropped a curtsey, but she backed away when he moved toward her to kiss her. "I'm sorry I kept you waiting," she said. "I didn't know you were coming."

"Of course, my dear," he said kindly, taking no apparent heed of her stiffness. "I'm anxious to have you meet M'sieur Louis Soniat, my long-time friend and neighbor in Jefferson City. Louis, may I present my daughter Mariette."

It was the first time Mariette had ever heard her father acknowledge their kinship in the presence of another human being. She looked at him, her eyes narrowed, telling him this. Now she turned her gaze to Soniat. He was a fine figure of a man for someone in his middle forties, which she supposed him to be. He wore a small, neatly-trimmed beard and mustache of jet-black threaded with silver. He smiled, bowed over her hand.

"Mademoiselle Mariette," he said, "I have looked forward to meeting you for a very long time."

"Have you, M'sieur?"

Everything about him spoke of wealth, from his well-tailored clothes to the diamond rings on his fingers. He had obviously gotten himself up especially well for this meeting.

"I've told Mariette all about you," Delissard told Soniat.

Liar! You've told me almost nothing about the man, except for his wealth and his land.

"She's been waiting to meet you," Delissard went on.

More lies! She wanted to cry out the word, but her face remained expressionless. Anger brought heat to her cheeks. She prayed Soniat would not mistake it for a virginal blush.

Her father's face was wreathed in smiles. "M'sieur Soniat has something beautiful to show you, *mon petit chou,*" he said. "A magnificent home in Faubourg Marigny. He's already furnished it, but he wanted..."

Soniat put his hand on Delissard's arm. He shook his head almost imperceptibly. He wanted to speak for himself. "I'm anxious to see if you like the house, Mam'selle. If not, I'll sell it, and we'll look for another. But I'd be most pleased if you'd let me take you and your mother there this afternoon. Would that be convenient?"

Mariette glanced at her father, who was nodding so strenuously he looked like a doll with a spring in its neck. His pretense of fatherly love and devotion sickened her, but of course he was trying to impress Soniat with his daughter's docility. She wanted to slap him. Instead she found his gaze and held it, sending him an unmistakable message of loathing.

So the house is ready and I haven't even agreed to the contract yet.

"Would you get our wraps and our bonnets, Celine?" Desiree asked. Decisions were being taken out of Mariette's hands. Her mother and father were shaping her life. But Soniat kept his eyes fixed on Mariette, waiting for her answer.

"*Tres bien, M'sieur,*" Mariette said, smiling wanly. "I'd love to see the house." *Have I made a commitment with that answer? I hope not.*

Desiree got up from the settee. "Come, *ma cherie,*" she said to Mariette. Celine approached them with their things.

They rode in Soniat's huge black-lacquered carriage, the most beautiful carriage Mariette had ever seen. It was upholstered in maroon velvet, with shirred pockets in the interior and deeply-cushioned vis-a-vis seats. His liveried driver slapped the reins and a handsome pair of chestnut mares took off at a brisk trot down Rampart Street. They crossed Esplanade Avenue to enter Faubourg Marigny.

"Mam'selle Mariette," Soniat said, "I saw you in Caldwell's new production at the Camp. What is it called? *Lock and Key?*" Mariette nodded. "You were wonderful! Your acting is so professional. Ladies around me were moved to tears in the last act."

"Thank you, M'sieur," she said. She knew she must converse with the man. Her father was expecting it. "I had begun to think he'd never have a part for me," she forced herself to add, "but two weeks ago, he sent for me." She could have said more. She could have explained how she accidentally got the part, but the constriction in her throat was painful, and she could speak no more. Nor did she wish to entertain this man, who would shape her future and ruin her life.

"The role was ideal for you." Soniat smiled benignly.

"Thank you." She cleared her throat. "Do you like the theater, M'sieur?" she asked in a thin, unnatural voice.

"It is one of my favorite *divertissements*," he said, enthusiastically.

Mariette smiled. She looked into the man's brown eyes, alive with admiration. He was really quite smitten. He looked like the young boys who waited outside the stage door, looking up at the actresses with calf-eyes.

Seated facing Soniat, her knees just inches from his, she felt self-conscious with her hair hanging down to her waist in streamers, like a schoolgirl who didn't know how to coif herself, but his adoring look told her he was pleased with her just as she was. She felt sorry for the man. None of this was his fault. He was a bachelor, and he'd fallen in love. He wanted to take a *placée*. In that he was no different from dozens of men in New Orleans.

The carriage stopped before a huge, magnificent house in New Levee Road on the riverfront. It was a breath-taking mansion, two-storied and multi-gabled, situated in the center of an acre of land, surrounded by trees and gardens.

The coachman hopped down from his seat, opened the carriage door, and helped the ladies down to the carriage block. They walked toward an arched wrought-iron gate, over which purple bougainvillea had been trained. The gate opened onto a brick walk leading to the wide steps of a two-storied mansion, with balconies lending shade to the galleries. Mariette was overwhelmed.

CHAPTER 18

S urely there was some mistake, Mariette thought. Louis Soniat couldn't have bought this home for her to live in as his *placée*. Gentlemen bought small unobtrusive houses for their mistresses, not mansions to call attention to their secret lives. But he was leading her toward the house, his fingers at her elbow almost proprietarily, giving every indication that he *had* bought it for her. She was both frightened and angry, since this opulent home had undoubtedly cost a fortune, and she had no intention of living in it.

The interior of the house was like nothing Mariette had ever seen. They walked through the huge front door, crowned with a stained-glass fanlight which threw multi-colored rays into the corridor. As they strolled down the corridor, which was graced with crystal gasoliers, Mariette looked through the open doorways leading off the corridor into the double parlors on her right and the drawing room and dining room on her left. All the rooms were elaborately furnished and lavishly decorated, with cupids of bronze d'or gracing the corners of white marble mantels. Friezes and medallions with open pierced designs on the high ceilings were truly the handwork of masters.

Realizing her every reaction was being measured, she restrained her compliments. If she appeared too elated, both men would assume the arrangement was a *fait accompli*. Desiree, however, felt no such restraint. She clasped her hands before her breast as if in prayer and walked through the rooms, exclaiming over everything, studying her daughter's face, and trying to evoke a similar reaction from her. But Mariette said nothing.

At last they all sat down in the first of two identical parlors, mirrored at both ends, creating a sense of infinity. Soniat sat beside Mariette on one settee, facing her parents on another.

"Well, Mariette," Delissard began, "what do you think of this house?" He was smiling the radiant smile of a victor. It was he who had prodded Soniat to create this palace for her, so she would not be able to resist its opulence. He was waiting for her answer now, confident it was all over but the signing. Mariette turned a look of cool aversion toward her father and watched the smile melt slowly from his face.

Now she turned to Soniat, who was awaiting her reaction. "It is the most beautiful house I've ever seen, M'sieur," she said. "Please do not mistake my silence for lack of appreciation, but the arrangement between us has never been finalized, and I think we need to talk, you and I." She lowered her eyes, refusing to speak in the presence of the father she despised.

"But, Mariette, I told you," her father began, but she stopped him mid-sentence with another scathing look.

"You *asked* me," she said, "and I have never yet given you my answer."

Delissard lips tightened. He drew in a deep breath. Mariette knew he could see his lands slipping away from him.

"Mam'selle," Soniat began, "I beg your forgiveness. I misunderstood. You're right. We must talk alone."

Turning to her father, Mariette said, "If you will excuse us?"

With almost comic alacrity, Delissard took Desiree's arm and ushered her across the polished floor, through the corridor, and down the outside stairway to the grounds below. When they were out of earshot, Mariette turned back to Soniat.

"M'sieur Soniat," she began, looking into his eyes, "please forgive me for appearing indifferent. When my father wants something, he takes it for granted that everyone will comply. He spoke of you only once, and asked if I would consider becoming your *placée*. That is your desire, I presume?"

"Oui, Mam'selle," Soniat answered. It was as if he were the teenager now, and she the woman taking charge of proceedings.

"I am flattered that you admire me, M'sieur."

"Anyone who sees you admires you, M'amselle. *I* am in love with you. I have been for years, watching you grow up into a lovely woman. And now," he said, his eyes devouring her, "there isn't another in the city whose beauty can compare to yours."

Mariette bit her lower lip. How was she to tell him? He seemed a kind man, and he'd declared his love for her. Yet she must make it clear that she was in love with Philippe, and she hoped for some possible future with him. Her concern here and now was to avoid becoming Soniat's *placée*. *Refuse him*. Philippe's words haunted her. *Tell your father no!*

"M'sieur, may I confide in you?"

He took both her hands in his. "Of course, Mam'selle."

She drew in a deep breath and tried to compose her thoughts. Withdrawing her hands from his, she clasped them in her lap. "A few months ago," she began, "I met a young man, a Creole, who begged me not to become a *placée*. He said I deserved to be the wife of a Creole, the chatelaine of his estate."

Color rose in Soniat's face. "Who was this young man?"

"I'm sorry, M'sieur, I can not tell you that. He is away now for several weeks on business. Before he left, he kissed me and told me he wanted to marry me. He told me not to become your *placée*." She lowered her gaze to her hands. "I thought you had a right to know that."

Soniat nodded. He lifted her chin and looked into her eyes, saddened by what he had heard. "Mam'selle, this young man will never marry you. I think you know that."

She nodded. "Perhaps that's true."

Encouraged, he continued. "He made you empty promises and gave you false hopes." He got up and walked before her, pacing with his hands behind his back. "I know we've just met. You know nothing about me. I don't expect you to love me. I'm forty-five years old, old enough to be your father. But I, too, would marry you if I could." Now he returned to the settee and took her hands again. "There is, however, one way in which I differ from your unrealistic young swain. I know it cannot be done. Others have tried without success. The secret of the quadroon's heritage is always discovered, and the marriage is always annulled. It is an exercise in futility." He sighed audibly. "And so, unlike your young man, I accept things as they are and make the best of them. Actually, I am in a far better position to marry you than he is. I have no family to hold me back, and I am one of the wealthiest planters in the South. I can live to suit myself, and society be hanged, but I would not put you in a position where, in time, you would be ridiculed."

He took out his handkerchief and pressed it to his forehead and his temples. He went on. "If I take you as my *placée*, people may disapprove of the riches I will lavish upon you, but they will accept you as part of an old New Orleans tradition. If I marry you, those who know you and those who later find out about you will despise you. They can't hurt me. My fortune is made, and their approval is of no concern to me, but they could make your life unbearable. Believe what I tell you. Your young man has filled your head with fantasies."

He was right. Philippe could never marry her. That did not mean, however, that she had to accept *plaçage*. Now that she'd been taken into Caldwell's company and received rave reviews, she felt confident her career would be made. If she didn't earn enough to support herself by acting, she could work with Madame Delacroix as a seamstress to supplement her wages. And, all else failing, she would take a steamship to St. Louis. She would not be a concubine!

Stiffening her spine, she spoke the words she knew could bring her world crashing down on her head. "I know what you say is true, M'sieur, but I think it only fair for you to know that I still have feelings for this young man."

"I'm glad you told me, Mariette." It was the first time he'd spoken her name.

He thinks I'm coming around.

"I know love doesn't come and go in the wink of an eye," he said. "I'll be patient, and I'll try to make you forget him, if you give me the chance."

"I'm sorry, M'sieur. I can not. It has nothing to do with you. It's simply that I cannot enter a life of *plaçage*. To me, it's demeaning. I hope this does not give you too much heartache. And I truly hope you can sell this beautiful house."

Louis Soniat was incensed. His color rose until his face was beet-red. Trembling inside, Mariette stood staunchly before him, trying to read his thoughts. He had been promised a *placée* whom he'd loved and patiently waited for. To him, that justified entitlement. He had offered her father some of the best land in Jefferson City. He had bought her a mansion, and she had rejected him. He couldn't believe it. Clearly, he was a man who was rarely refused, especially when making such a generous offer.

No doubt he would pressure her father to get Desiree to sign the contract. He would certainly not walk away from his dream so easily.

CHAPTER 19

On the carriage ride back to Rampart Street, no one spoke, but vibrations of anger were heavy in the air. Soniat's face was a mask of outrage. He said nothing to Mariette's father; yet Delissard surely knew she'd refused the offer of *plaçage*. He looked as if he would have a seizure of apoplexy. His gaze did not leave Mariette, and the veins in his neck were rigid. Her mother was so confused and upset by the seething unspoken accusations that Mariette expected her to break down and cry at any moment.

Mariette wanted only to get away from her father and Louis Soniat. She wanted to go to her bedroom and think through everything she'd said to Soniat and try to figure out what would happen next. It would undoubtedly be bad for her mother, who supposedly wielded the most power in this little drama of contract signing. Her father would be irate that Desiree had not talked Mariette into agreeing to his self-serving plan. But whether Mariette agreed or not, he could force Desiree to sign. Why hadn't she anticipated that? God only knew what her father would do to get that land.

At the house on Rampart Street, the driver helped the ladies down. Soniat sat as silent as stone. Her father, unprepared for this turn of events, didn't know whether to get out with the ladies or ride on with Soniat and try to explain his daughter's unexpected behavior, perhaps promise that he could talk her into the arrangement.

Mariette walked slowly up the bricked walk toward the door, purposely hanging back to hear her father's words as he stood outside the carriage talking to Soniat. Her heart was beating wildly with fear of his vengeance.

"My dear Soniat," she heard him say, "please forgive my daughter. She's young and foolish, and I'm afraid we've spoiled her. I'll talk to her, and my wife will sign for you. I promise you that."

Mariette, almost at the house, glimpsed beneath her lashes to see Soniat's reaction. He was looking straight ahead, not even acknowledging her father's words. Her father moved back away from the carriage. "I'll be in touch with you soon," he added.

Inside his carriage, Soniat rapped the ceiling with his walking cane, and the vehicle rolled away. Mariette's father approached the house, his heavy footfalls signaling his anger. Mariette hastened her own steps.

In her room, she pressed her ear to the door and listened. At first she heard only restrained accusations from her father and mewling apologies from her mother. Words were not audible, but the meaning was clear. She opened her door a crack.

"...and she refused him! I can't believe it. What have you been doing all this time, Desiree, if you weren't preparing her for Soniat?"

"She doesn't want *plaçage*, Raoul," her mother said, sheepishly.

"She doesn't want! And what does she have to say about it? We are her parents. We decide what's best for her. I thought that was understood. I thought all these weeks..." Mariette could hear only bits and pieces. "...showers and parties... make her look forward... fallen down on your job, Desiree."

Mariette was frightened for her mother. Her father's voice was trembling with rage. "I told you what this meant to me, the land, the riverfront land." At this point his voice was so loud she was certain everyone in the neighborhood could hear him.

Mariette heard a crack, like a whip snapping. She staggered back as if she herself had been hit. Recovering from her shock, she opened her bedroom door and ran down the hall to the parlor. In the bright, airy room, she saw her father holding her mother by the arm, his right hand raised, ready to strike her again.

"He's an old man to her, Raoul," Desiree cried out, tears falling down her face, "and she's in love with somebody else." As Mariette watched, unseen, he slapped her mother again, even harder than before, and as his right hand came back in the same arc, it was rolled into a fist that struck her mouth.

Mariette gasped. As Desiree fell from his grasp, she grabbed at the lace scarf on the small table beside the settee, pulling the scarf and the candle-holder with it. A resounding crash followed.

"Don't hit her again!" Mariette shouted. "Hit me if you must hit someone. It's my fault. I'm the one who asked her not to sign." Mariette was seized with terror at the rage in her father's eyes, but she held her shoulders straight and pinned him with her own dark gaze.

"Well, here she is, my grateful little daughter," her father said facetiously. "Come here, *mon petit chou*," he said, curling his fingers back toward himself, signaling her to come.

She stood her ground behind the settee, which separated her from him. "I will not be an old man's whore!" She flung the words at her father, outraged that he had hurt her mother, seething with indignation, yet trembling inside for fear of what he would do to her.

She had surprised him with her declaration. He stood stock still in the middle of the room, looking at her, trying to decide what tack to use. Taking advantage of his temporary calm, Mariette went to her mother and helped her up to the settee. A trickle of blood fell from the corner of her mouth. Mariette took her handkerchief from her sleeve and wiped it. Her mother's face was turning a deep shade of red. By tomorrow, it would be purple. How could he do this to her? She sat beside her mother and put her arms around her. Tears welled in her eyes.

Her father sat on the settee facing theirs. "Mariette, we must talk, you and I," he said.

Desiree patted Mariette's arm, telling her to do as her father said. Mariette remained where she was, waiting, never losing eye contact with the man she loathed.

"The home he offered you was a mansion, *ma fille*," her father said, in what she took as a conciliatory attempt.

"So?" Inside she was shaking, but she did not let him see it. His dark brown eyes were filled with venom. "It's only a house. Do you want me to trade my virginity for it?"

"Yes!" The sibilance of the word resounded in the little room. "It's what you were trained for. It's all you are good for. And you will never get a better offer."

"I don't want any offer at all. I despise *plaçage*."

His outrage flared once again. He got up from the settee and grabbed her arm. He pulled her to her feet, so that her face would be a target for his hand.

"I reject *pla*..." The blow landed on her face before she could finish the word. A blow from his fist, so hard that she saw flashing colors before the pain began to register. With the force of the blow, she fell to the floor. Slowly, she put her hand to her face, a reflex action to comfort the wounded area. Her head was beginning to pound. She'd expected him to be furious with her, but she'd never really expected him to hit her. It was the first time in her life that he had. A thought flashed across her brain. She would not be acting on Caldwell's stage tonight.

"Are you going to hit me again?" she asked, every tooth in her mouth aching, "or can we talk civilly?"

He walked away, as if to remove the danger from her immediate vicinity. He stood with his back to the glass partition in the front door. Mariette got up. She sat beside her mother once again.

"I'll have to send word to Caldwell that I won't be acting tonight," she said. "I'll tell him my father struck me, and I'm disfigured from the blow. I swear that's what I'll tell him if you hit me or my mother again."

He stood before the door, breathing heavily, his fine nostrils thinning in his rage. He knew Caldwell. She felt sure he wouldn't want the gossipmonger to know about his private life.

"As you heard earlier, I'm an actress now in Caldwell's company," Mariette said, her jaw throbbing. "I can earn my own living and move into my own quarters. You need not support me any longer. I'm leaving this house today. I will not be Soniat's *placée.*"

Her father came charging back like a madman. "You will do what I tell you to do," he said, raising his hand once again.

"Or?" she asked. Now her trembling was visible. One look into her father's eyes told her his threat to hit her again would not work. He refused to be the loser in this all-important fight.

"...or your mother will be beaten until you realize that I know what's best for you. And Caldwell be damned!" With brute force, he took Desiree's arm and lifted her to a standing position. Desiree sobbed aloud in fear. Raising his right arm again, he slapped her face, first with his palm, then with the back of his hand, his diamond ring cracking viciously against her face, bringing blood. Mariette feared he might dislocate her jaw or break her nose.

Mariette tried to take hold of his arm and stop his blows, but he had the strength of ten men in his rage. She was pushed back to the settee by a blow to her breast with his open palm. Then, looking up, she saw her father's hand raised once more to hit her mother.

"Don't!" Mariette cried out. "She can sign."

Delissard's hand stopped in mid air, and he let Desiree go. She slumped back down to the settee beside her daughter. Slowly, Delissard recovered. He raked his hair with his fingers, pulled his waistcoat back down in place, and righted the rest of his clothes. The women watched, motionless.

He pulled a contract from his inside coat pocket. He walked over to the *escritoire*, found a pen, and opened the inkwell. He dipped the pen point. "Come," he said to Desiree. "Sign it."

Desiree looked at her daughter. Mariette wanted to cry at the sight of her mother. One eye was almost closed. Her cheeks were both swollen and already discolored. God only knew what bones were broken inside the delicate face. And she knew from the pain in her own face that she, too, was swollen and discolored. The brassy taste of blood was in her mouth.

"Go, Maman. Sign it," she said.

It was difficult to talk. Her mouth hurt. Her head throbbed. This was the one eventuality she had not even considered. What would she do now, with all her determination? She supposed she would become a *placée*, with the finest house in Faubourg Marigny.

As Desiree signed her name with a shaking hand, Raoul Delissard turned to Mariette. "Don't even think of running away," he warned. "I'll find you wherever you go, and I'll make you sorry."

He took the signed contract and left the house, slamming the door behind him.

CHAPTER 20

"As I told you in the note I wrote yesterday, Desiree and I were in a terrible accident," Mariette said, when Caldwell saw their faces. "The horse car we were in stopped suddenly, and we were thrown against the front wall."

"My God!" Caldwell said. "Let's hope the makeup will cover it. One night's receipts are all I can afford to lose. As it is, we had to tell last night's ticket-holders we'd put on one more performance at the end of the run for them. They were outraged, nonetheless, at the inconvenience." He paced his office, smoking a cheroot, stopping from time to time to look at Mariette. "That beautiful face! That's your fortune, you know. You must be more careful."

"Yes, Mister Caldwell. Next time, I'll pick a softer place to fall." She tried to smile, but every facial movement was torture.

"I only hope you fully recover from those bruises and the swelling."

"I will," she said firmly. "I'm young and strong. Wait and see."

"I hope we don't have to wait too long."

Mariette got the distinct impression that if her appearance didn't improve, she might no longer have a place in Caldwell's company.

He paid little attention to Desiree's injuries. Her presence in Mariette's dressing room was a matter of indifference to him. *Her bruises do help substantiate my story, however,* Mariette thought. The idea of a man beating up two women was not something that leapt easily to mind. So Caldwell believed her. All she had to do now was lose her swelling and bruises and get back to being an attractive young ingenue. *Bon Dieu,* please let it happen.

Every night before the performance, Caldwell's own makeup man came to her room and helped disguise her discoloration. The swelling would have to take care of itself. Fortunately, she had lost no teeth. Nothing in her face felt as if it were broken, and her headaches went away within a few days.

After performances and during the day, Celine put cold compresses on her face and Mariette lay very still, praying for her face to resume its normal contours. She thanked God Philippe would never have to see her this way. By the time he returned, she should have recovered, if she were ever going to recover. And if she were ever going to see him again.

Philippe! If only he'd been here to protect her! she mused, as she lay with a compress on her face. But he couldn't have struck her father! Perhaps it wouldn't have come to that if he'd been here. Philippe wouldn't have allowed her to go to Soniat's house in the first place. And how would he have prevented it, she wondered. Would he have married her? On the spot? With her father's knowledge? And Soniat's? No, to all questions.

She was back again, on that interminable merry-go-round. But the story had an ending now. The carousel ride was over. She was contracted to Soniat, and she would be his *placée* by the time

Philippe returned. She was beyond heartsick. She was distraught, heartbroken, and inconsolable. A headache of mammoth proportions descended upon her.

In the next two weeks, she awoke each day with a headache, had her breakfast, lay down with her cold compresses, had dinner at noon, "notes" and rehearsals in the early afternoon, more compresses, a late-afternoon rest, a *petit dejeuner* at five, and then she bathed and dressed for the theater. Within that framework of daily activity, she moved like an automaton. Nothing to look forward to but an ugly life as a whore to a man she detested. And no escape from the father she despised. She endured the passing days, and her face somehow restored itself to its original contours.

The happiest part of her day was when the curtain went up at the Camp. Sometimes she believed she was happy only in a make-believe world. Perhaps that was why she'd been so willing to believe Philippe's fairy tales. As the play became the hit of the season, her performance in the part of Odette became the talk of theater-goers. Her own heartache was poured out each night in the words of her character, and when the performance ended, she felt emptied of sorrow, only to face it again the following day.

CHAPTER 21

The day of her move to Soniat's house had been arranged by her father for a Tuesday, five days before the end of the play. It was clear to Mariette that the run of the play was of little concern to her father. Acting was not to be her main occupation in life from this time on. It would be up to Soniat, after she was established under his roof, to decide whether or not she continued acting. But Soniat had already told her how much he admired her talent. *Oh, Dear Lord, what did it matter? What did any of it matter?*

Mariette got up at the crack of dawn to have plenty of time to dress, have Celine do her hair, and decide on a few things to pack in her *valise* before Soniat arrived. He had said to bring nothing; he would buy her a complete wardrobe. They would go shopping together. But everything could not be bought in a day. And wouldn't she need her comb and hairbrush, her wrapper and carpet slippers, and a few chemises, camisoles, pantalets, and stays? Underthings could not be bought in a shop with a man. She might have to be a *placée*, but she didn't have to be a trollop.

On that terrible day, it was not hard to rise early, for she had not slept all night. Too much was happening at once, and all of it bad. With her move into her new life, she was losing Philippe forever. That was the hardest blow of all. Besides that, she was entering a life she deplored, and her emotions were in turmoil. She feared physical intimacy with Louis Soniat. She shuddered when she thought of it. Exhausted with fear and anxiety, she sat down fully dressed on the side of her bed and pressed her head to the bedpost.

Where was Philippe at this moment? Was he sleeping late after a party last night? Had he been playing the piano, while the guests sang Christmas carols? His face was always before her, chatting, laughing in his personable way. She loved him and wanted him, but her life with him was over. He would not be back, and she would grieve for him and yearn for his hard body and his arms holding her close. Philippe had been the one bright spot in her life, her hope for a lasting love and possibly for marriage. But she would never see him again. She threw herself across the bed and sobbed.

Then, suddenly realizing her face would be splotched and her eyes red and swollen when Soniat came, she quickly checked her tears. The bed ropes squeaked as she let herself down. She dabbed at her eyes with her handkerchief and blew her nose. She would cry no more. This was life. No one had said it would be easy. Her father had beaten that knowledge into her. She was a woman now, and she could do whatever she had to do.

Last night after the performance, she'd returned home late, keyed up, knowing today was the beginning of a terrible new life. She'd tossed and turned in bed, resorting to tears, then to prayers, and finally to walking the floors. In the clear light of day, she was trying to convince herself that she was going to be a *placée,* and the life she'd envisioned with Philippe could never be.

Soniat had said one thing that kept coming back to her. Mixed marriages were always discovered and annulled. It was better for Philippe's sake that they never attempt such a fraud. Perhaps Philippe had recognized that. Maybe that was why he'd made no definite plans on the eve of his departure.

Even if he'd really wanted to marry her, it was too late now. When he returned, she'd already be locked into a contracted alliance. She already was, *n'est-ce pas?* Mariette drew in a ragged breath. She would have to resign herself. At least, Soniat loved her and he'd be good to her. He seemed to be pleased with her acting career, even proud of it. All things considered, it was probably the best life she could salvage for herself.

She dried her face once more and squared her shoulders. She took a look in the pier glass at the outfit she'd chosen for her first day as a *placée*, and tried to see herself as Louis would see her. It would be hard to call him Louis, a man of his age, but he would want her to.

She smoothed the peplum of her brown velvet jacket and straightened her skirt. Then with her fingertips, she opened the cream-colored lace ruffles of the *fichu* at her throat. She checked the hairdo Celine had created, with its figure-eight twist at the nape and the small corkscrew curls on the forehead. Opening the armoire door, she found her brown velvet bonnet. All her accessories had been made to match, her parasol, her reticule, and her fringed shawl, and she'd bought herself an expensive pair of English walking boots.

She was well-dressed for a *placée's* daughter. She sighed once again. Her inner battle was not yet over. From her bedroom, she could hear Celine and her mother hustling about, tidying the parlor, making coffee for M'sieur Soniat when he arrived. Her mother was not laughing or singing, as was her way when she went about her household tasks. No, Desiree would probably never laugh again.

The shocking episode with her father had removed all joy and laughter from her life.

With a final touch to her chignon, Mariette picked up her things and opened the door to the corridor. Finding her mother fussing over the coffee tray in the parlor, she sat on one of the settees to keep her company.

Desiree sat beside her and took her hand. "You look beautiful, *ma cherie,*" she said. Mariette shrugged. "Mariette, I know this is not the way you hoped things would turn out. But try to find some contentment in your life, *ma fille.* At least, you will want for nothing."

Except Philippe, Mariette thought. She said nothing, but she frowned and shook her head, and Desiree understood. Possessions had never been important to Mariette.

"It's just that..."

"I know, *ma fille.*" Desiree patted her daughter's hand. "I know." Now looking into her daughter's eyes, she said, "Mariette, nothing is ever perfect in this world." Desiree gazed into a middle distance, deep in thought. "When your father and I first settled here in this little house, we loved each other, and so our alliance seemed perfect to me. And then, one day, when I hadn't seen him in several months, I read in the paper that he had married. An aristocrat, like himself. Honorée LeCourt. Even the name was aristocratic."

"He hadn't told you he was going to marry her?"

"No. He owed me no explanation, I knew that, and yet, I thought it was different with us. I thought if he had to make a marriage of convenience, he'd tell me, so I'd know whether or not I could ever hope to see him again. But, no." She waved her hand. "I was told nothing. It hurt, because I understood then that to him, I was just a *placée.* Nothing more."

A great deal less, Mariette thought, remembering the blows her mother had taken. Her pretty face had healed, too. No one would ever know how cruelly her father had beaten them.

"Pauv' Maman!"

Abstractedly, Desiree rubbed the back of her daughter's hand. "Some months after his wedding," she went on, "I heard a knock at the door. It was Raoul, back to see me again, as if nothing had ever happened. We resumed our life together. That was when I became *enciente*." Her mother smiled, and then suddenly, a small frown appeared over her eyebrows. "His wife Honorée was also *enciente* at the time. She had a little girl, too. Celeste, they called her."

Mariette's eyes narrowed. "You should never have taken him back," she said with venom. "He is evil, Maman."

"No, Mariette. Just determined to have his way. We should never have refused to do as he said, you and I." Desiree dabbed at her eyes with her handkerchief. "I know you think *plaçage* was easier for me because I loved your father. But even with love, as you've seen, things are never perfect, *cherie*. Love may bring happiness, but it also brings much pain, especially to us."

Us, Mariette thought. Quadroon women, forbidden to marry white men, unwilling to marry black, never knowing who or what we are.

"I know you don't love M'sieur Soniat. But believe me, you can make your life comfortable, *ma cherie*. You'll be fabulously wealthy. He will want you to buy every kind of luxury. Take advantage of that. You're entitled to it. He's a bachelor with no family to account to. He'll take you wherever he likes and care nothing if people are shocked by it. You won't have to be a hothouse plant like me."

Mariette looked at her mother with pity. Her life had been sad, and yet, for some reason Mariette couldn't fathom, she'd loved Raoul Delissard. Mariette would never speak of him again.

"No matter what you tell me, Desiree, I still love Philippe."

"You didn't tell M'sieur Soniat about Philippe, did you?"

"Yes, I told him," Mariette said. Desiree gasped. "Not his name, of course." Mariette shrugged. "He said he understood. I really don't care if he did or not. He said if a mixed marriage were possible, he would have asked to marry me." Mariette laughed a short, bitter laugh. "I think I'd let my father kill me first."

The front door knocker clacked, and suddenly the house came to life. Celine ran to answer the door, Mariette pasted a thin smile on her face, and Desiree quickly dried her eyes. Within minutes, Soniat had been admitted, had had his coffee, had said his goodbyes, and Mariette was taking her last walk down the brick path as a virgin. The tightness in her throat grew painful.

Alone in the carriage with Soniat, she was aware that his eyes never left her.

"*Ma reine,*" he said. "You are truly beautiful today. As always. And your performance last night was outstanding."

"Thank you, M'sieur," she said woodenly.

"Louis, please."

"Louis." She felt the need to say something. She looked him over well. "You look quite handsome today yourself."

He smiled, acknowledging the compliment. He was even more elaborately attired today than the day he'd taken them to see the house. He was wearing a greatcoat, a black beaver hat, and polished black leather boots. A diamond winked in his cravat. He was immaculately barbered, his mustache neatly trimmed, his fingernails buffed to a shine. He was dressed as if for his wedding, and she considered that this was as close as he'd ever come to a wedding, since she was the woman he loved, and he could not marry her. He took her hand in his, and she wanted to recoil at his touch. Physical contact with him was almost unbearable. She supposed she'd have to get used to it. Soniat seemed satisfied to attribute her skittishness to innocence.

"Now what would you like to do today, *mon ange?*" he asked. "Shall we shop for fabrics or shoes or pretty bonnets? The choice is yours. I am totally at your disposal."

Mariette looked into his light brown eyes. It was as if the world had just opened for him. A wealthy man, an aristocrat, a planter, and yet she, Mariette Delon, was all he wanted. He was easy to please.

He was waiting for her answer. If she said she wanted nothing, which was truly the case, he would be disappointed. "I would like to shop for fabrics in a silk shop," she said, feeling like an actress in a play. "Then tomorrow, we must send for Madame Delacroix to come and sew at the house until the dresses are made. A few daytime dresses, and a few dinner dresses, that is, if you'd like me to dress for dinner."

"I'd like you to do whatever your heart desires, *mon amour.*" He brought her hand to his lips and pressed a kiss to it. At the touch of his lips and his mustache, a little shudder ran down her spine, not the kind she'd known when Philippe had kissed her hand, but a frisson of disgust. She turned her head toward the carriage window.

She was suddenly aware that from every house on Rampart Street, neighbors were watching. Eyes appeared at windows, taking in the carriage, the horses, the liveried driver, and Mariette Delon, who seemed to have struck it rich on her very first alliance! Mariette pulled the little velvet curtain along the rod and sank back against the seat. Her cheeks flamed.

Louis Soniat lifted his hand to his mustache as if to groom it but Mariette could see that behind it he was hiding a smile. It seemed that she could do nothing wrong in his eyes. She detested his adoration.

CHAPTER 22

The doors of the Chartres Street stores opened wide to Soniat, for those who did not know him personally knew what kind of wealth he represented. His driver followed in their wake, carrying back to the carriage paper parcels containing lengths of watered silks and satins, velvets, bombazines, and trimmings suitable to the fabrics.

In a millinery shop, they purchased two bonnets to match the fabrics. From a cobbler, they ordered a dozen pairs of the most expensive English shoes—soft as butter with exquisite stitching. Then they were off to Tyler's Jewelry Store in the *Rue Royale*, where every bracelet and necklace in the establishment was laid out before them on black velvet cloths. At first, Mariette refused to try on such expensive baubles, saying she had a few nice pieces that would do quite well. But when she saw how eager he was to spend his money, she selected a delicate gold bracelet with an opal stone in the center.

"Don't wrap it," he told the fawning clerk. And then to Mariette, he said, "I want you to wear it, *mon amour.*" And he put the band around her wrist.

"Thank you, Louis," she said, simply. She could not make herself say more.

She did not miss the raised eyebrows of the clerk and the cashier. A man of Soniat's age and a girl young enough to be his daughter! For the first time, Mariette felt her feathers ruffled. What business was it of theirs if he chose to buy her the whole jewelry shop? She wished now she had let him buy her a diamond bracelet. She gave them a small self-satisfied smile that equated with a swift kick in the breeches.

After an exhausting afternoon, Mariette arrived at the mansion on New Levee Road. She wished her mother and Celine were there, that she might show them her purchases. Well, those days were gone forever. She was a woman now and head of the house. She might not be a Creole's *wife*, but she was in every respect his chatelaine. She was discovering how much she hated that role.

The driver stopped at the front steps, helped her out, then drove the carriage to the rear. Soniat took her elbow and they walked up the front stairway to the wide gallery. He unlocked the door and they entered.

"You must be tired, *mon amour*," he said. "I'll take you to your bedchamber. I'll send up the woman I hired as your personal maid. She'll help you get comfortable for your nap."

Your bedroom? Your personal maid? Your nap? Mariette couldn't believe her ears. Was she to have her own bedroom apart from his? And a maid of her own? She'd expected a maid who would clean and cook, but if she was to have a personal maid, then there would be other servants, as well.

And now he expected her to take a nap. He had no intention, then, of coming to her room. At least not yet. All day long, fear had been building inside her when she thought of going home. She couldn't help wondering how soon he'd expect to claim his rights. After all, he had a big investment in her, and he was in love. Her mother had signed a contract, giving him access to her bed and her body. But now, praise God, he had put her mind at rest about everything. At least for the day.

"Thank you, Louis," she said, this time with genuine gratitude. She touched the lapel of his frock coat and saw the color rise in his face. "I'm very tired, and I must leave for the theater at seven."

Soniat beamed. "I'm looking forward to it, *ma belle*," he said. "I'll see that you have a tray in your room at five. Will that be convenient?"

"That will be fine," she said. "Just toast and tea. My stomach is jumpy before a performance."

"Of course." He pressed his lips to her hand, caught her eyes with a look of restrained longing, and left her in the doorway to her bedroom.

Mariette closed the door behind her. As she pulled off her gloves, she looked around in amazement at the size and richness of the boudoir. Exhausted though she was from a day of endless purchases and fawning clerks, she was still astonished.

The room had been decorated in the palest shades of blue and cream and green. The focal point of the room was a four-poster bed of gleaming burnished mahogany, and against the walls were matching pieces: a huge mirrored armoire, a dressing table, an *escritoire*, and two loveseats flanking a fireplace with a white marble mantel. The walls were of green damask, the fringed draperies a shade darker. A thick carpet in pastel tones marked off the area where the settees faced each other.

A soft knock at the door startled her. "*Oui?*" she said.

"*Pardonnez-moi, Mam'selle*," said a small feminine voice. "*C'est Adelle, votre bonne de chambre.*"

"*Entrez*," Mariette said.

The young woman could not have been more than twenty. She was a mulattress, as small and slender as a child, with skin like milk chocolate. "*Parles-tu Anglais?*" Mariette asked.

"*Oui, Mam'selle*," Adelle said, and Mariette wondered how much English she really understood.

"I speak English as much as possible," Mariette said, "to learn the language well. I'm an actress in the American theater."

Adelle smiled and nodded. She was strong and quick for her size. In minutes, she'd taken the watered silk counterpane from the bed and folded it over the frame, turned back the blanket and sheets, and was standing before Mariette, unbuttoning her jacket and helping her out of her clothes. Soon, the maid had undressed her, slipped her nightgown over her head, and brushed her hair. Mariette fell into bed and sighed as her head sank into the goose-down pillows. Adelle pulled up her covers.

Struggling with her English, Adelle said, "I come with you for tea *à cinq heures*, Mam'selle."

"Thank you," Mariette answered, and before Adelle had left the room, Mariette felt herself falling into a deep, exhausted slumber.

CHAPTER 23

The role of Odette in the play *Lock and Key* was such a perfect vehicle for Mariette, it might have been written with her in mind. Odette was a young girl whose parents refused to let her wed the man of her choice, a handsome young clerk whose state in life was beneath her own. Though the social status of the lovers was reversed in Mariette's own life, Odette's heartache was very real to her. In the third act, when Odette cried for her lost love, Mariette played the scene so convincingly there was never a dry eye in the house. The newspapers called her "extraordinary, the best new talent to come along since Jane Placide."

Mariette was glad she'd studied the part so well and the words came to her so naturally, because the first time Soniat escorted her to the Camp, she had a great deal on her mind besides her lines. Mariette had never dreamed that he would insist on going with her to the theater and bringing Adelle along to help her. Not only that, he wanted to be backstage, in on the goings-on. Mariette knew what the other actresses would make of that, and it upset her terribly.

His carriage alone attracted much attention, for the likes of it were rarely seen in New Orleans. Then as they walked from the stage door to her dressing room, she was aware of a little cluster of actresses gathering to look at the gentleman who'd brought her to the theater in such style and to whisper behind their hands about Mariette's "arrangement."

Let them talk, she decided. *Why should I care? They have something juicy to gossip about. It changes nothing for me.*

She introduced Soniat to no one, but led him directly to her dressing room. He doffed his top hat along the way to the ladies of the cast, thrilled as a star-struck schoolboy to be backstage. Mariette knew, of course, that she'd find Desiree inside, and that presented another problem. After closing the door, she embraced her mother. Quickly she informed both Soniat and Adelle in French about their secret with Caldwell. "Be careful not to mention that Desiree is my mother while we're in the theater," she said. "Caldwell knows. He's known for a long time, but he's passing me as white. He and I have agreed to say that Desiree is my maid."

"*Mais non, mon amour,*" Soniat said.

"It's all right, Louis," Mariette said, forcing herself to talk to him, to use his first name, although it was like gall on her tongue. "Maman understands. Caldwell isn't a bigot. Far to the contrary. He wouldn't be able to keep me in his company if my heritage were known. My mother is happy about my acting. She knows this is how it has to be." She shrugged.

Soniat nodded but his frown remained.

Now Desiree spoke up. "I wasn't sure you'd still need me," she said sadly. Her eyes shifted to Adelle, and Mariette knew her mother felt as if she were being replaced.

Mariette put her arms around her mother. "I thought you might be relieved not to have to come every night, Maman," she said softly.

"Perhaps," said Desiree, but she seemed depressed. Mariette suddenly realized that this would be the only way she and her mother would get to see each other now.

"I think it might be nice to have some time to myself," Desiree said woodenly.

Mariette smiled and took her mother's hand. "Please keep on coming if it pleases you," she said. "I love having you with me."

Desiree brightened.

"Just show Adelle where things are," Mariette added, "and if ever you aren't well, you can feel free to stay home, knowing she'll be here to dress me."

Desiree smiled and nodded. With this hurdle leaped, Mariette was ready to change into her costume. She glanced at Soniat, who sat on a cane-back chair, his hands on his walking stick, watching the proceedings with undisguised delight.

"Louis," Mariette said. "Come with me. I want you to meet Caldwell. When the play starts, you can stand in the wings to watch the performance. Would you like that?"

"Oh, *ma belle*, I would consider it a privilege."

Desiree smiled as they left the dressing room, relieved that Mariette seemed to be accepting her role in Soniat's life. She'd been forced into it, but she did it so well, catering to him, just as she, Desiree, had always catered to Raoul. And she was so beautiful! The girl had only to notice him to have him eating out of her hand! *Mon Dieu*, she mused, the world could be hers!

Caldwell answered to a knock and after Mariette had introduced Soniat as her "friend," Caldwell treated him royally. Romantic intrigue was Caldwell's specialty. He promised Mariette he would see Louis comfortably situated before the first act began. Playfully, he shooed her from his room.

On the way back to her dressing room, she slowed her steps in the corridor as two other young actresses approached her. They smiled wickedly. She met their stares.

"So you've found yourself a lover, Mariette," said Agnes Bayard. Mariette did not answer.

"And a rich one, at that," said Louise D'Aquin. "Good for you, my girl. But you are full of surprises. First Caldwell, then that young Creole you were so cozy with at the French Market, and now.." She nodded her head in the direction of Caldwell's dressing room.

"That young Creole was good-looking," Agnes said. Mariette felt her cheeks grow hot. "But money is everything, *cherie.*"

Mariette did not grace their remarks with a reply, but her heart hammered against her ribs. She could hardly believe that she and Philippe had been seen together at the market. New Orleans was indeed a small city, where everyone knew everyone and saw everything.

The performance went well as always. Soniat watched from the wings and applauded till his hands were swollen, but to his credit, he did not enter her dressing room throughout the play and did not speak to her. Afterwards, however, he waited outside her door, clearly supervising her departure. Mariette lowered her lids and her cheeks flamed, for he could not have made it clearer that he was her proprietor, her *patron*. She told her mother goodnight, and, ignoring the stares of the other cast members, left through the stage door, Soniat holding her elbow and Adelle following in her wake, like a faithful minion. On the way home, Mariette had such a terrible headache that she could not respond to Soniat's incessant compliments and his chatter. And by the time the carriage arrived at the house on New Levee Road, she was trembling so badly she could hardly walk up the front steps. She could not conceal her tremors from Soniat.

"What is it, *ma cherie?*" he asked, as they entered the corridor. "Are you ill?"

"No, Louis," she answered. "Just exhausted and nervous."

"Well, of course you must be, *ma poupée*," he said, taking her in his arms and petting her like a child. "You've had so much to contend with in such a short time. The new house, the servants, the play...and me," he said, smiling apologetically. "Come. We'll go upstairs. Adelle, fix Mam'selle a cup of chocolate and bring it to her room."

Mariette felt the tears stinging her eyes. She was repulsed by Soniat's arm at her waist, helping her up the stairs and into her bedroom, into the setting for the greatest crisis in her life.

CHAPTER 24

"Louis," she said, starting to sob, "I think if I don't cry, I'll be terribly sick."

"Of course, *BéBé*," he said, taking her in his arms like a father. Mariette wept freely. He stroked her back and made comforting sounds. "Now, *viens 'ci, cherie*, sit down."

He led her to one of the settees flanking the fireplace, where a small fire, laid in anticipation of her return, crackled cheerfully. They sat together, with his arm around her shoulder, she crying as she had rarely cried before in her life. When her crying had subsided to an occasional ragged sob, Adelle returned with her chocolate.

"Here, *BéBé*, drink this," Louis said, lifting the cup to her lips. She sipped it, but when she started crying again, he motioned Adelle to take it away. The maid left the room. Louis gave Mariette his handkerchief, and she wiped her eyes and blew her nose. Finally, when she had cried herself dry, Louis spoke.

"Listen to me, Mariette," he said. "And answer me truthfully. Are you a virgin?"

"Yes, Louis."

"Are you afraid of going to bed with me?"

She looked up into his eyes, and she knew she detested him. The thought of being touched intimately by his well-manicured hands made her feel sick to the stomach. "Yes, Louis," she answered. Her sobbing began again.

"You're having a crying jag, Mariette," he said impatiently. "Now stop it. You're acting like a child. Grow up. You're a woman now, and you're my *placée*. You know I love you and I'll never hurt you."

He's going to do it now, Mariette thought.

He pulled off one boot and Mariette wailed as though he'd struck her. Taking her by the shoulders, he turned her to face him. Firelight reflected in his eyes as he held her.

"I'm going to take you to bed, Mariette. It's going to happen, so you might as well make up your mind to it. You must stop this childish sobbing. This can be easy and pleasant for you, or it can be difficult; but either way, it's going to happen."

He pulled off his other boot and looked at Mariette. She stifled her urge to cry and released her misery in little anguished hiccoughs. He walked over and locked the door to the corridor with a loud clack. Mariette whimpered. He began to undress himself before her eyes. She couldn't believe it. Piece by piece his clothes fell to the floor in a pile until he was standing before her in the shifting firelight in nothing but his long underwear. She lowered her gaze to her lap.

"Look at me!" he said peremptorily.

Lifting her head, she looked. She saw his thick shoulders and his hair-matted chest. She hated his body. He was strong. He could beat her into submission as her father had. His waistline was thick, his drawers giving an indication of a paunchy stomach and a well-defined male area that terrified her.

She bit her bottom lip and looked up into his face, her breathing punctuated by occasional sobs.

"Stand up, Mariette," he ordered.

Mariette stood. She closed her eyes. She would not see what he did to her. She would transport herself out of her body and let it happen as she watched from afar. He could not hurt her that way. There was no escape. All the preparations, the beatings, the waiting, the gifts he'd given her had led up to this one moment. Louis Soniat would no longer be denied.

He unbuttoned her dress. She heard it slither to the floor. Like a rag doll she stepped out of it and moved when he turned her body until, at last, the warmth of the fire on her back and her calves told her she had been stripped of every stitch of clothing.

From her spirit's vantage point high up above them both, she saw him pick her up in his powerful arms and place her on the bed that had been turned down for her. Then he removed his long underwear and climbed in beside her, pulling the featherbed over them both.

What followed was too ugly for even her spirit to watch. She was back in the treetop, watching her father on top of her mother, hearing her mother purr. Then, suddenly, her tender thighs were pried apart and she was impaled in her most private part by his tumescent manhood.

All her life her parents had told her she was being prepared for this. But they had lied. Nothing had prepared her for this ravishment, this humiliation, this rape of the soul. Hot, silent tears fell from beneath her closed eyelids and trickled into her hair.

He drove himself harshly into her virginal body until something tore and bled. It hurt, but she did not cry aloud. She would not respond to him in any way. But it was not over yet. Again and again, he pummeled into her rawness, until once again, she sought refuge outside herself, where there was no pain and no humiliation. And there, from her lofty perch, she let it happen.

It would be over soon. She could tell. He was panting like an animal and sweating. And then, without warning or prior knowledge, she felt a pulsation as a fiery liquid entered her body. His seed. His detested seed. It was done.

He stayed with her a minute or two, his heavy weight pinioning her body. She didn't move or speak. At last, he kissed her cheek. Perhaps he felt the wetness of her tears, because he said, "The first time is always bad for the woman, Mariette. It will get better. I'll buy you something beautiful tomorrow."

CHAPTER 25

Mariette slept late the following morning. After her humiliating experience with Louis, she'd wept for a long time and been unable to sleep. At last, fatigue had overcome her and she'd fallen into a restless slumber. Awakening, she felt sore where he had hurt her. She called for hot water and washed well. She brushed her teeth and rang for Adelle to comb her hair. Then, in a daytime calico dress, her hair pulled back to her nape, she joined Louis at the long rosewood table in the dining room. The dresser was lined with covered silver salvers of hotcakes, coddled eggs, bacon, biscuits, and steaming *café au lait*. But Mariette took only half a biscuit with her coffee.

Two household servants had been added to the staff, both Negresses as dark as Celine. Soniat presented them to her before breakfast. Octavie was the cleaning woman, Pauline the cook. Mariette nodded and the women curtsied politely, served them, and left the dining room.

Louis had brought them both from Oak Manor, his plantation in Jefferson City, which augured a kind of permanence to his residence at the New Levee home. This Mariette had not anticipated. Her father's absences were usually of long duration. But then, her father had another family.

Mariette had grown up thinking that *placées* spent a good deal of time alone. She'd been looking forward to that, even more so since last night. How often would he want to do it to her? Every night? Twice a night? She would not be able to endure it. And yet, she knew she must.

Surely Louis would be called away for long periods of time. He had a huge plantation in Jefferson City, which had kept him totally occupied till now. Problems would come up, demanding his attention. She hoped for that.

Each morning for the remaining days of the play, Mariette arrived at eleven at the Camp for notes. Louis took her there and sat in the theater, enjoying the feeling of being an insider. After notes, she and Louis were free to do as they wished until time for her rest, her *petit dejeuner*, and her trip to the theater. Louis made the most of their hours together.

One day, to distract her from her new bedroom experiences and her whole new status in life, he took her to the race track, where members of the exclusive Jockey Club exchanged tips. The men scrutinized Mariette with such brazen curiosity, her face felt scorched. Soniat gave her a handful of bills to place her bets. When a drum sounded, all betting stopped, and the slave jockeys wearing the colors of their owners approached the starting gate. Soniat's horses won three of the five heats, and Mariette left the track with a bagful of money. She smiled, but the smile never reached her eyes. She knew she didn't appear as elated as Soniat would have liked.

When they got home, he visited her bedroom before she took her nap, dismissing Adelle, telling the maid he'd see to Mam'selle's comfort. What he saw to was her further pain and humiliation. She clenched her teeth while he was inside her, thrusting, thrusting until she felt as if she would scream at any moment, but the wait was not long. In a short time, she knew her punishment was over. She released a sigh of relief that he could not misunderstand.

Each day, to reward her for the pleasure of the last, he took her to a shop and bought her something. She bitterly resented the gift, wanted to throw it in his face. Yet she knew she must not anger him by refusing. Like her father, Soniat was a man whose anger seemed close to the surface. She was afraid that her attitude of cool contempt might offend him at any moment.

He took her on other outings, like the ride on the Pontchartrain Railway to Milneburg, a colorful little fishing village of camps built on stilts out over the lake. There they had a picnic lunch, which he'd had Pauline prepare. They ate it in the shade of a summer house on a long pier extending out over the water. He'd probably expected her to enjoy herself, and her unresponsive attitude seemed not to satisfy him. Neither of them spoke on the return trip.

Nothing had ever been so welcome as the arrival of her monthly period. For one thing, she knew she was not pregnant with Soniat's child. For another, it would give her a few days' respite from the constant anxiety over his nightly visits. This he agreed to respect, but she didn't know for how long.

During this blessed hiatus, Christmas came. A few days before the holiday, Mariette had asked if she might go shopping alone, and Louis had magnanimously agreed, lending her the carriage and his driver Remy. He thought, no doubt, that she needed time alone to buy him a gift.

At Tyler's, she'd bought him a gold pocket watch with a deer in flight embossed on its cover, and inside, she'd had the jeweler inscribe the words, *Merry Christmas to Louis from Mariette, 12/25/1840*. She knew he'd expected a more affectionate message, but that was where she drew the line. If she hadn't been afraid of reprisals, she'd have gotten him nothing at all.

Mariette bought her mother a sterling silver heart on a chain. For Celine, she bought a new fringed shawl, and for each of the servants, wool stockings and flannel nightgowns. She wrapped her gifts in tissue paper and hid them on the floor of her armoire.

On Christmas morning, Louis took her hand and led her to the first parlor, where he arranged a stack of packages at her feet. When she saw how many there were, all wrapped with huge red bows, she knew he expected her to gasp with delight. But she gave him only a small smile as she suffered his kiss on her cheek.

"Sit down, *ma reine*," he said, leading her to a wingback chair, "and I'll hand you your presents one by one."

Mariette sat and Louis handed her the largest of the gifts. She opened the box to find an exquisite house robe of dubonnet velvet lined with cream-colored quilted satin. "It's lovely, Louis," she said with forced enthusiasm. She got up and put it on over her wrapper. It tied at the waist with a sash and clung to her body, making her feel warm and elegant. She tried to concentrate on the gift, to distract herself from painful memories, but they nonetheless intruded. *It's Christmas Day, and where is Philippe?*

She shook her head to dispel the question and turned her attention to Louis. "Thank you, Louis. You're very kind. I know I'll enjoy it." For something so expensive, she should have been exclaiming and embracing him. But she couldn't do it.

In a smaller box, she found a diamond pendant surrounded by sapphires, hanging from a silver chain. "It's beautiful," she said. "But the robe would have been enough."

"*Ma cherie*," he said, touching her face with his fingers. She almost recoiled but stayed herself. "I've been waiting all my life to have someone I loved to spend my money on. Don't deny me that pleasure." She put on a false smile and nodded. "Let me put it around your neck." Turning her back to him, she lifted her hair, and he hooked the delicate chain. He kissed her nape, and she wanted to shiver with revulsion, but she held herself stiff as a rod.

The other boxes held bottles of perfume from France, cashmere nightgowns, silk stockings, leather-bound books, and a box of chocolate-covered nougat *dragées*.

Mariette's expression of thanks was lukewarm for each.

At noon, he sent his driver Remy to pick up Desiree, and at one o'clock, they sat down to a dinner fit for royalty. Covered dishes in an endless procession were carried to the dresser, and Pauline served each plate with slices of turkey, oyster dressing, pork roast, yams, cranberry jam, cauliflower, peas, and stuffed mirlitons, each prepared in her own delectable culinary style. Octavie lit the candles, and Remy, doubling as butler, poured the wine.

There was one thing for which Mariette was grateful. Her mother, for the first time in her life, could sit at the table and be waited on like a lady. If Soniat chose to entertain a mulattress at his table, he offered no apologies. Mariette knew no one else who could have done this for her mother.

She thought about her life. Her worst loss, of course, was Philippe, for he would never want her now. She was damaged goods. Also, she was just as much a prisoner as her mother ever was, albeit in a mansion. In spite of all this, if she didn't have to be intimate with Louis, she could have tried to live with it.

Fool! she chided herself. Why do you think he brought you here? Bought this mansion? Dressed you in silks? Gave you diamonds and sapphires? There's always a price to pay. He wants to drown himself in carnal pleasure. He's paid dearly for this set-up and he plans to get his money's worth.

Late Christmas afternoon, a runner came with a message that Soniat was needed at Oak Manor. He seemed terribly disgruntled that he'd have to leave Mariette today. It was Christmas, and the play had ended. He had perhaps planned a special evening of sipping cordials before the fire in Mariette's room. Now that her menses was ending, he would be back in her bed again. Perhaps he had planned to take a longer time than usual with their lovemaking, perhaps even stay the night in her bed. She shuddered inwardly.

The emergency had changed his plans. Three runaway slaves, he explained, had been caught and returned. Two men and a woman.

"What will you do to them, Louis?" Mariette asked. This was a side of Soniat's life she knew nothing about.

"I'm not sure. It might be best to sell them. They've run away before. I don't need headaches like that. It's upsetting to the other field hands. But of course they'll need to be punished first or the others will do the same."

"How will you punish them?" she asked in a whisper.

"A few stripes, I suppose. A beating won't kill them, and it will restore order to Oak Manor."

"Even the woman?"

"Especially the woman. She's the instigator." He was frowning distractedly, and she knew he'd forgotten all about her. His thoughts were on Oak Manor, the runaways, and the manner in which he would have them whipped and disposed of, perhaps sold away from their children.

Mariette felt nauseated. In her sheltered life, she'd known little about runaway slaves and beatings. Celine was a slave, but Celine was like a member of the family. She was free to leave the house at will. Their trust in her was implicit. City life for house servants was nothing at all like that of field hands on a plantation, the type of slavery Soniat saw every day. She looked up into his eyes, and her loathing for him took on a new dimension. She could not measure her hatred for him.

A short time later, she and her mother watched from the gallery as he rode away on his black stallion. He would make better time on horseback, he said, and he wanted to leave Remy and the carriage for Mariette's use in his absence. Mariette looked sorrowfully at her mother.

"God knows what will happen to those poor slaves," she said.

Desiree nodded. "Do you want to come home for a few days, *cherie?*"

"No, Maman. I have all my things here now. And he'll expect me to be here when he comes back."

The two women exchanged knowing glances. This was what it was to be a *placée*. You were "placed," situated, where you could be found when you were wanted. That was the sum of it. Desiree stayed till five o'clock. Octavie prepared a dish for her to take back for herself and Celine. Then Remy took her home.

CHAPTER 26

Alone at last, Mariette went to her room and changed into her new woolen nightgown and velvet robe. Then, remembering they were gifts from Louis, she took them off, folded them in the armoire, and put on her old brushed cotton gown and wrapper. She lay on her bed.

Hatred for Soniat welled up in her like a fountain. She was distraught with it, limp with it. Yet, she must never let him know of her revulsion. She wondered how she could ever extricate herself from the trap in which she was so hopelessly caught. After his brutal treatment of the past week, she had only contempt for him. Every time he came to her bed, she knew she was in for pain and revulsion. His visits were not long, for he came only to satisfy himself, and that was quickly done. But they were so painful to her soul that they seemed to last forever.

What on God's earth did she have to look forward to? If she complained, he might beat her. He sometimes looked tempted to do so, when he was displeased with her lack of gratitude or enthusiasm. And if she ran away, her father would seek her out and take his own revenge. Her life was ended. Her heart was as cold as a grave. She thanked God the play was over. She didn't know how she would have found the strength to perform tonight.

She got up and walked to the fireplace and added a log to the fire. She touched a taper to the fire, cupped her hand around the flame, and lit the night candle on her bedside table. Then she turned down the featherbed and the silk sheets on her mattress. After taking off her robe, she slipped beneath the covers.

For a long time, she lay very still and listened to the sounds in the house. The servants were working downstairs. She heard the delicate clink of china dishes being put back in the dresser. Then the thinner chink of silver as the utensils were returned to their felt-lined drawers. Each quarter hour, she heard the tinny chime of the mantel clock. Then nothing.

Twilight invaded her bedroom. Adelle came to check on her, and Mariette sent her away for the night, saying she was tired and would certainly not eat again after the heavy midday meal. "Take the rest of the evening for yourself."

So now she was alone, facing the medallion on the ceiling. Her four-poster bed had no canopy, and in winter time, no mosquito net, so her view of the ceiling was unobstructed. She studied the intricate pattern of the medallion and thought of Philippe. Christmas Day, and where was her love? She was heartsore, for no matter how busy she kept herself, how many outings she endured, how many gifts she received, she never lost the image of his sea-green eyes, his smooth skin, his curly hair. Philippe, Philippe. She loved him, God help her. And now she would never have him.

The door knocker clacked. Her heart raced. Frightened at what or whom she would find, she got up, put on her wrapper and slippers and let herself out of the room. Flattening herself against the wall so she would not be visible to the caller through the sidelights, she inched her way down the stairs. She glanced down the first floor corridor, hoping to see one of the servants coming, but no one was there. By now, Adelle would be back in the servants' quarters, a separate building behind the main house. Mariette was alone in the mansion.

Fear gripped her. Should she pull the bell cord for Remy? A stranger could be on the gallery. She might be in danger. In the dusky corridor, she tried to look through the sidelights to see who was there, but the caller was not in her line of vision. Cautiously she opened the heavy wooden door, keeping the chain secured.

"Yes?" she said.

"Mariette?"

Her knees went weak. She tried hard to breathe, but found it almost impossible. She knew who it was, calling her name at twilight on Christmas night. She wanted to throw the door open and run into his arms. Yet she could not help the anger that roiled inside her, that he'd abandoned her in her need, nor the fear that he might leave her now, after he knew she'd been sullied. Why was he coming back to her now? Now, when it was too late.

"Let me in, Mariette," he said. "We have to talk."

CHAPTER 27

Mariette lifted the chain and opened the door. Philippe entered the vestibule. Mariette stood facing him, tears welling in her eyes. Unable to restrain her relief and her happiness, she rushed to him and threw her arms around his neck, but he stood stiffly, his hands at his sides.

"Philippe?" She backed away quickly, as if she'd been burned. She was hurt and confused. Her gaze probed the depths of his eyes, where a myriad of emotions played. What was he thinking? So much had happened since he'd left, so much that he didn't know. All their plans remained unresolved, and would always remain so now.

Philippe gazed down the wide corridor, now shrouded in shadows, as if expecting at any moment to see Soniat coming toward them. But Mariette's eyes never left Philippe.

Oh, Philippe, Mariette cried out inside herself, *why didn't you embrace me?* She choked on a sob but to him she said nothing. She wasn't sure if she hated him for deserting her and condemning her to this life, and now apparently blaming her for it, or if she adored him and wanted to lose herself in his arms and forget everything that had happened since he left.

She ached to hold him again, but he must make the next move. And before that, there were things she must explain and things she had to know. And in the end, what good would all the knowing do? What was left for them to share, but aborted dreams and the memory of a few sweet kisses?

"Where is he?" Philippe asked.

"Jefferson City. Some trouble at his plantation."

Philippe took two steps from the vestibule into the corridor and peered into the darkening parlor. It wasn't that he doubted her, she knew that. It was human instinct to want to be forewarned in the enemy camp.

As he passed her, she glimpsed his profile, his fine nose and strong chin, outlined against the waning daylight framed by the sidelight window. Her heart lurched, and she knew that she'd always love him, no matter what. When he was near her, his overwhelming presence and the sensations he aroused in her infused her aching heart with the only happiness she'd ever known. With him she felt secure, protected, complete. She wanted to wrap herself in him and let the rest of the world fall away. But nothing was ever that simple.

Who had told him where she was? Only her mother knew, and she'd been sworn to secrecy. Had he come to rescue her from Soniat? If he'd come back to say his plan was all worked out to present her to his family, he was too late. She was committed. Contracted for. She was not supposed to have emotions to love one man and despise another. She was a quadroon.

Her breast heaved with anger. She wished she had never let him in. She had no apologies to make to him. She faced him in the dusky corridor, her chin high, her shoulders back. "What do you want, Philippe?" she asked.

"How long have you been here with him?"

"Three weeks," she said. She felt dirty and used, but she did not rush to explain. Why should she? A single tear fell down her face, and quickly she brushed it aside.

Feet wide apart, Philippe stood with his fists clenched and cast his gaze to the ceiling. His heavy dark eyebrows came together and his hard jaw told her he was exercising great restraint over his fury. He removed his planter's hat and hung it on the newel post.

Gray twilight settled in the corridor, broken only by the strips of illumination from the sidelights and the fanlight above the door. Mariette walked to the foot of the stairs, and he followed her.

"You cannot stay here, Philippe. You must go."

"How many times have you made love to him, Mariette?" he asked, his voice harsh and mean. "Every day? Twice a day? More than twice?" His voice rose in volume with each question.

"I don't have to answer your questions," Mariette paried. "I have a new life now, Philippe, one you abandoned me to." She closed her eyelids. "You must leave now."

A nerve in his cheek quivered. "Answer me before I go," he said. "Is he a good lover? Is he gentle because of your youth and innocence?" He was speaking cruelly now, and Mariette felt the hot tears falling down her face. "Or does he come at you like a tiger to get his money's worth, after setting you up like this?" He waved his hand to take in their majestic surroundings.

Mariette was trembling, not from fear but from anger. He was making her feel ashamed for something he knew nothing about, something she'd had no control over. Pride had sealed her lips, since she wanted

Philippe to suffer, but now pride in her own integrity opened them.

"Many times," she said, shamed by his look of loathing. "But don't call it 'making love.' There was no love. He took me forcefully, brutally. Why not? He had every right. I am his property now."

Their eyes locked and held, and she could see the revulsion in his gaze. Was it revulsion with her or with what had happened to her? She couldn't tell. He lifted her under her arms and stood her on the bottom step of the stairway, so that their eyes were on the same level. Then, taking her in his arms, he crushed his lips to hers so harshly she could feel his teeth hard against her mouth. He held her body to his so forcefully that she could not catch her breath.

Even as the kiss continued, she began to weep heart-rending sobs. He held her close, his embrace becoming gentler, more caring. He kissed her face, now wet with tears, her lips, her throat. But where his first kiss had been hard and punishing, those that followed were warm and sweet and loving. He, too, was emotionally torn apart, suddenly realizing he was to blame for it all. He wanted her, but he could not have her. He was aware that he had left her to the will of another man. Two other men. And even now, holding her in his arms, he did not know how to remedy the terrible wrong.

She continued to sob, eyes closed, too frightened to move, too heartbroken to resist. She was shaking and crying from the depths of her soul, but she clung to him for support. Weakly, she lowered herself to sit on the second step. Philippe sat beside her. She dried her tears on the sleeve of her wrapper.

"Why did you do it?" he asked in a hoarse whisper. "Didn't I tell you to wait for me, that I would work things out?"

"You made me wait too long, Philippe. I had no choice."

"You always have a choice, Mariette. You could have said no. What would he have done? Carried you here..." he looked about him..."to this mausoleum, kicking and screaming? I don't think he's young enough for that."

"My father managed it all for him." Her voice broke on the words. "He struck my mother viciously because she would not sign the contract." She sobbed. Philippe's face registered disbelief. "He beat me, too, on the face with his fist. I was disfigured. Caldwell had to cancel the performance of the play for a time, and then use heavy makeup after that to hide the bruises." She shrugged, as if her performances were of little consequence at this juncture.

Philippe looked as if he had been struck. A frown line appeared between his brows.

Mariette went on. "I didn't care about the theater. It meant nothing to me, compared to what was happening in real life. What mattered was, I couldn't let my mother be beaten again."

Philippe took her in his arms and held her close, but gently now, rocking her body, stroking her back. "Oh, Mariette, *mon amour*, please forgive me. I didn't know. It was my fault. All my fault. I should never have left New Orleans. He wouldn't have struck you if I'd been here."

"Oh, I think he would. And if not that, he would have tried another way. He has many devious methods, my father. He might have threatened to tell *your* father about me. Did you ever think about that?"

"I wouldn't have cared. He could have done whatever he liked. I would have taken you away, left town, gone anywhere with you."

Mariette shook her head and smiled an indulgent smile. "You didn't even stay *home* to be with me, Philippe," she said gently, and he knew it was the truth. She saw a frown forming on his brow, a frown of self-accusation for the torment she'd been through. Now, as she watched, she could almost see the wheels turning in his head, as one thought led to another. Soniat had taken her virginity. This too was his fault and a source of anguish to him.

They sat together, staring toward the sidelights, Philippe's face a mask of pain. Mariette waited. She knew that he was tortured with guilt. "I want you to know I wasn't running away from our problems," he said. "If I had known the extent of your father's cruelty…if I had known how soon Soniat would come to claim you," he said, turning to face her and brushing her cheeks with his thumbs, "I would never have gone. Believe me. As it is, I cut my trip short to come home because I was anxious to take you to *Belle Fleur* to meet my parents."

"It's too late, Philippe. I belong to Soniat now."

He frowned. "You belong to no one but yourself. No one owns your soul, Mariette."

It was what she'd been telling herself every time Soniat came to her bed, that her soul was still her own. *Oh, Philippe, I love you so.*

They were lost in shadows, sitting in the dusky twilight at the foot of the stairs. Mariette reached out and touched Philippe's hair, then tunneled her fingers through the thick crisp curls at his temple. He took her hand and drew it to his lips, kissing the palm, then pressing it to his cold face.

He moved back to look at her, and she saw only his eyes, his marvelous eyes, wide and sorrowful and sensitive. She put her arms around his neck and pressed her cheek to his. She could feel his warm breath in her hair.

The mantel clock chimed in the dining room, that faraway tinny chime she'd heard earlier that evening from her bedroom. It was a sound she would forever associate with this moment of shame and hopeless burning love.

CHAPTER 28

"I'd put a lamp on but I don't know how to light gas fixtures," she said. "I'm afraid to start a fire."

"Are you alone?"

"Yes."

"Just stay here beside me. I don't know how to light them either. I have candles in my townhouse. I'm not a millionaire."

Her heart was thrumming, her blood singing at his nearness. She couldn't believe he was here, and for tonight at least, he was hers. The choice between *plaçage* and marriage seemed to diminish in importance. If Philippe still wanted her, she'd surrender willingly to him, although she was another man's *placée*. She loved him so. And for the first time in her life, she knew what it was to be stunned by a scorching desire.

"Mariette," he said gently, "if you had to be someone's *placée*, why wouldn't you be mine?" His voice was despondent, spiritless.

She reached up in the dark and felt that his cheeks were wet with tears. "You didn't ask me," she said, pressing her head to his shoulder, weeping too. "You could not commit yourself, even to that."

He took her by her shoulders and found her eyes in the shadows. "Would you have?"

"Yes."

"But what about your father? And the land he was to get?"

"I suppose he still could have forced my mother to sign the contract for Soniat, but if you had been here, then maybe…oh, Philippe, I don't know."

"I do. I would have killed the bastard. And then, we could have run away together."

He took her in his arms and held her close against him, but this time, it was a tender embrace. Finding his greatcoat a hindrance, he struggled out of it and left it where it fell. He reached out for her now in the darkness and took her in his arms. She felt his warm, soft lips on hers, biting them, drawing them inside his own, and she melted in his embrace. After the kiss, she rested her head in the curve of his shoulder.

"Was it very terrible for you, Mariette?" he asked softly. "Soniat, I mean."

She closed her eyes and shook her head, not wanting to talk about it. "Yes," she said, "it was horrible."

Philippe moaned with anger. His grasp on her upper arm was like a band of steel. He was suffering as much as she.

"I didn't expect to enjoy it," she said. "I didn't *want* to enjoy it. But I didn't think I'd be left shamed and aching, without a shred of dignity. Like his chattel."

"Oh, my God, Mariette," Philippe said. Slowly, penitently, he planted soft little kisses along her throat and the curve of her shoulder. "I would do anything to undo the cruelties you've suffered, but it's too late for that now. So we must go on from here. But first I must know if you still love me, in spite of everything."

"I do," she said without hesitation. "I've thought of nothing but you since I was taken to this house."

"It's more than I deserve, but I'll take it just the same. When I discovered you were here with him, I walked along the levee trying to decide whether to kill him or just kill myself. I decided to see first how things were."

"How did you know I was with him?"

"Your mother told me, but she didn't tell me where."

"So how did you find me?"

"I went to Caldwell."

"But the theater is closed. The play is over."

"I went to his house."

"His house? Even *I* don't know where he lives."

"I found his address. It wasn't hard. He told me about Soniat's mansion on New Levee Road. Apparently the bastard bragged to Caldwell about the place where he'd set you up."

"Caldwell told you all that?"

"Yes. Caldwell's a coward, you know. I think he feared for his life. I guess I looked like a maniac when I went there. He wanted to make sure I knew it wasn't *he* who had signed a contract for you." He fell silent as they gazed into each other's eyes. He took her face between his hands. Her eyelids fell shut. She felt his lips slant over hers, his arms draw her into his embrace.

Mariette gasped at his touch. It was like a firebrand, marking her forever his, legally or illegally. She didn't care. She knew only that she'd never let him go again. Her hand fell against his chest, and she went limp in his arms and motionless. *Oh, God, I want him so!* She was floating in a sea of delicious lethargy. With great difficulty, she revived herself. She stood up and held out her hand. "Come to my room with me, Philippe."

He breathed deeply, mired in his own arousal, but he shook his head. "I won't make love to you, Mariette. I won't make a whore out of you."

She choked on a sob. "I'm afraid that's already been done."

He leaned his head against her knee and breathed a ragged sigh. "Forgive me."

"Come with me. I don't want to be found here with you if my maid should come back to the main house."

He took her hand and followed her up the stairs and through the door to her bedroom. Closing the door behind her, she turned the key in the lock.

The night candle flickered in its brass holder, casting their shadows against the damask wall. She took his hand and drew him to sit beside her on the small settee facing the fire.

Flames still burned low, blue in the fireplace, giving off a meager light. The logs whooshed and dropped between the andirons. Philippe got up and added a log, and in seconds the flames leapt around the pile, giving off a brighter light. Now they could see each other's faces aglow with passion, eyes bright with love, lips wet with kisses.

Resting in the corner of the settee, he took her hand and pulled her to lie in the curve of his arm. She laid her hand on his chest, her palm feeling the drumming of his heart. She felt intoxicated, euphoric. She grew aware of an undulation, low down in her body. It was the first time she'd ever known this wondrous rhythm she had no desire to quell. It was a pulsation that begged for some release she did not know.

"Philippe," she whispered. "Won't you take me to bed and just hold me? It would be so warm and cozy there."

"Much too cozy, my love," he said hoarsely. "No, I won't do that."

He shook his head. "Not until we're married." Taking her by the shoulders gently, he moved her away from him. He got up from the settee, straightened his clothes and rested both hands against the marble mantel, breathing unevenly, trying to regain his self-control.

"I love you, Philippe. If you want me, I'll gladly have you in my bed. To me, it will be my bridal night, and all the bad memories of Soniat will be forgotten."

"Don't say his name to me. I feel such rage against the man, I could kill him without a second thought." He turned and went back to where she was sitting, her long dark hair spilling over her shoulders. He sat on the floor and rested his head in her lap. "I want to talk to you about my plan for marrying you." He looked up into her eyes.

She was shaking her head. It was too late for wedding plans.

"Everything can be carried out as I planned," he said, "in spite of your being here."

"How can that be, Philippe? I'm trapped. The time had passed for us, dear heart."

"Don't say that. I want you to listen to me. Will you do that?"

She nodded, frowning.

He sat on the settee beside her and lifted her chin to make her look into his eyes. "Do you love me?"

"With all my heart."

"And will you marry me?"

She closed her eyes. "Philippe…"

"No, no. You've got to listen. After that, I'll take all your objections." He made her more comfortable in his arms. Even he was anxious to hear the details spoken aloud. It was an impossible plan, but it might work, if she trusted him and did as he said. He took a deep breath and began.

CHAPTER 29

"We're going to try to pass you as white when I take you to meet my mother and father at *Belle Fleur*," he said.

"*Belle Fleur?*"

"My father's sugar plantation on Bayou St. John."

"And what then, Philippe?" She could hear the edge of impatience in her own voice.

"I'll tell them we want to be married and we'd like to have their blessing. If they agree, we'll go to St. Patrick's Church in the American Sector, where all the priests are Irish, just off the boat. They won't know us, and so, with our altered birth certificates, they will marry us. Then we can tell my parents we just couldn't wait for all the preparations for a big wedding." He paused. "What do you think?"

She shook her head. "To start with, they'll never give us their blessing. The priests at St. Patrick's may marry us, but I think your parents will have the marriage annulled when they find out what I really am."

"That's always a possibility, but I don't intend to give you up. What's the worst thing that can happen, even if they do find out?"

"You could lose your inheritance and your partnership in your father's business."

"I don't give a damn about the inheritance. And I can start my own commission house in the American Sector. If the Frenchmen won't do business with me, the Americans will."

Mariette backed away and smiled. "Do you think so, Philippe?"

"I know it. I thought I'd start looking around now for a vacant property in the area of the canal," he said.

She touched his face with her fingers. "Philippe," she said, "do you have any slaves?"

He frowned, confused at the sudden change of subject. "Why do you ask?"

"Well, do you?"

"I have one manservant my father gave me when I moved into my townhouse. I gave him his papers last year. He stayed with me, but he works for wages."

"I'm glad." She gazed past his shoulder. "Does your father have slaves?"

"Well, yes. He has to, for his sugar plantation. If he freed them, they'd all run away."

"I see. Well, does he ever beat them?"

"Beat them? No, never. What brought all this on?"

"That was why Soniat went back to Oak Manor, to see about punishing some runaway slaves that were caught. He said he'd have them beaten. Then he's going to sell them."

"That's slavery, Mariette. I thought you knew that."

"How could I? I've never lived on a plantation or even seen one. Here in the city, slaves run errands. They go to market. Their owners aren't afraid they'll run away. No one I know mistreats them. We love Celine."

"Then you should free her."

"Yes. It's just something we've never thought about. Neither has she, or she would've asked for her papers."

"Now that we have that settled, will you let me go on with my plans?"

"Of course." She pressed a fingertip to his full bottom lip, and he grabbed her hand and kissed it.

"I'll look for a building to rent in the American Sector, preferably one with an office downstairs and living space above. I'll have to sell my town house in the *Rue Royale*, and I may not find a buyer right away. But in the meantime, we can live in my town house till I work things out."

Mariette tried to find his eyes in the meager light of the fire. "I can't do that, Philippe."

"Why not?"

"Because we're not married yet.

"You aren't married to Soniat, and you're living here."

"I know, but I'm his *placée*," she said, rubbing her forearm, gathering her thoughts. "I've had a lifetime of learning about *plaçage*, and this I know. If a protector abandons his *placée* for a wife or another mistress, it's all right. No one loses face because the *placée* keeps the property. That's why contracts are signed. But if the *placée* leaves *him* to become another man's mistress, she's looked upon as a whore. The protector loses face, like a husband who's been cuckolded."

"Well, I know, but..."

"Besides, if you took me to your townhouse, your parents would know I was there, and that would make me such a wanton in their eyes, in addition to having no real certified background, they'd never give you their blessing. No," she said, shaking her head, "my only salvation is to stay here till we're married. And it must be soon, before Soniat gets back, or I'll be lost. Marriage would save my reputation, and Soniat would have no right to challenge you, because you'd be my legal husband."

"Mariette," he began, "let me be sure I have this right. You insist on staying under the roof of a man who has hurt you and who will never marry you, because that keeps you respectable, but you can't come and stay with me, although I love you and plan to marry you, because that would make you a whore. Is that right?"

"That's right."

"Well, what if you're gone when he returns and you refuse to come back? What then?"

"If I'm married, he can't lay a hand on me. But either way, he can take back the land he gave my father."

"Well, I won't lose any sleep over that."

"But my father would come and find me and beat me again."

"Not if I'm alive," Philippe said, his eyes narrowed.

"What would you do, Philippe? Kill him? And hang for it?"

"If it were the only way, yes."

"But it isn't the only way, Philippe. I'm willing to try out your plan. But it must be very soon, before Soniat comes back."

Philippe frowned.

She took his hand and looked into his eyes. "What's the matter? A few minutes ago, you were all excited about those plans. You were sure they would work."

"That's when I thought you'd come away with me to my town-house tonight."

"I can't. Believe me. I wouldn't stay here if I didn't have to. Just get things moving as quickly as you can, and pray he won't come back for a few more weeks."

"All right," Philippe said. "This time, I'll do it your way. I owe you that. Let's talk about our visit to *Belle Fleur*.

CHAPTER 30

She snuggled up to him in the corner of the settee, awash with happiness, waiting to hear his plan.

"I've made up a whole new identity for you," he said. "First your name."

He head snapped around. "Why change my name? They don't know me."

"You're an actress, *n'est-ce pas?* If they read your name in the paper, they can track you down through Caldwell, and find out your mother's a mulattress."

"Oh. But they might just as easily recognize me on the stage."

"With costumes and make-up, you could be anybody. Besides, they don't go to the American theater. They speak only French."

"Oh."

"We'll tell them your father was a planter in Natchez. We'll say your mother died in childbirth and your father was killed in a steamboat accident. I'll go to the library tomorrow and look through some old newspapers, eight or nine years ago for steamboat explosions. There were lots of them. If there was a man in his late thirties in the list of casualties, who was survived by a daughter, he's your father."

Mariette smiled. "Oh, Philippe! Do you think you can get away with it?"

"Of course." He smiled, pleased with his own idea. "So after I see the dead man's name, I'll tell you what your name is. All right?"

"I guess."

"We'll say you were raised by the Ursuline nuns in their orphanage. That should please my mother. She was taught by the Ursulines."

"Suppose she asks them about me."

"She won't. She had a bad falling out with the Mother Abbess when my sister was expelled."

"Oh, that's good!" She sucked in a breath, then laughed. "Not that your sister was expelled, just that your mother won't inquire." She turned to meet his eyes. "Oh, Philippe, do you think there's really a chance?"

He drew her into his arms and held her close. "It has to work. I need you, Mariette. I think we can make my parents believe this story, but we must both concentrate. I'll write you a list of things to memorize—names of your ancestors, birth dates, towns they were born in. You must know them by heart, just as if you were a Creole and these things were vital to you."

"Well, I'm half-Creole. I've heard all my life about these things. Not that my father's ancestry can help me now. But if you write down the facts, or rather the fiction," she said, smiling, "I'll memorize it all. I'm used to studying lines. I'm an actress, remember?"

Turning to lie across his body, she took his face between her hands and touched his lips with hers. She loved him so. He was the man she wanted, and the miracle was that he wanted *her*, enough to give up his inheritance and everything else he held dear. She suddenly believed that it could work. It had to. God couldn't forbid them to spend their lives together...not for an insignificant fraction of difference in their blood.

"Where will you say we met?" she asked, her enthusiasm matching his own. "Who will you say introduced us?"

"I've thought about that. I'll say it was my friend Armand from the commission house. I'll say you're a distant relative of his. He's from an old Creole family. My father will be satisfied with that."

"And what will you tell Armand?"

"Well, he knows about you already. I hope you don't mind that I've told him. I'll just ask his permission to lie a little."

"A little!" She shook her head and grinned.

Mariette got up from the settee and walked to the fireplace and looked down into the blue flames. She spoke quietly. "I keep thinking of what they would do if they knew the truth."

"Don't think about it," Philippe said. "I'll try to set up the dinner for tomorrow night at seven. Do you have something to wear? A dinner dress?"

"Yes. I have some new dresses." She was sorry she'd said that. He'd know who'd given them to her. She didn't want him thinking about that.

Silence fell between them for a moment.

"By the way," he said soberly, "what will your mother say about my proposal?"

Mariette shook her head and bit her bottom lip. Philippe could see that her dark eyes were misty. "I think she would be happy, if it were possible for us to marry."

Philippe held his arms out to her, and she went back to the settee and rested in his embrace. Philippe pressed his lips to her forehead lovingly. "She would have to give you up forever, Mariette. You would not even be able to recognize her on the street. Would she be willing to make that sacrifice? Would you?"

Mariette hesitated. Then suddenly she looked directly into Philippe's eyes. "Yes." She nodded. "She would give me up to see me married, to see me happy."

"And would you be happy, *cherie?*"

"Would I be happy!" she said facetiously. "Don't ask foolish questions." She smiled. Then just as suddenly, she frowned again. "Philippe," she began, "what shall I do if Soniat comes back in the meantime?"

"I don't know. Pray it doesn't happen. He could be gone for weeks. And we could be married in a couple of days."

Mariette shook her head. All her doubts seemed to be returning.

"Suppose we take this one step at a time," he said. "But remember, if he comes back and you want to come to my townhouse, you can. Here's the address." He took out a *carte de visite* and wrote it on the back. "When you find yourself alone, run away. Hire a carriage. We'll worry about what happens after that. My man servant will be there if I'm not. His name is Jean Baptiste. I'll tell him about you."

Mariette nodded. "I'll remember. But I'll pray to the Blessed Mother that doesn't happen."

He decided to try just once more. "Why don't you come with me tonight, Mariette?"

"I told you why. If he finds me there, he'll challenge you."

"Is that what you're worried about, that he'll challenge me?" He laughed a harsh, sardonic laugh. "Do you think I'm afraid to be challenged by Soniat?"

"He's only forty-five, Philippe, and they say he's an expert swordsman."

"I'm an expert swordsman, Mariette," he said, touching his chest with his fingertips, "and a far younger man. Let him challenge me. I'll be glad to do the world a favor and dispose of the bastard."

"Well, I won't come to your townhouse and put you in jeopardy, no matter what you say. So I guess I'll just stay here and hope we can marry before he comes back."

"I'll do my best," Philippe said.

Holding his hand, she walked with him down the stairs. He picked up his greatcoat and his planter's hat where he'd left them. It was pitch dark in the corridor, with only the patches of gray from the side-lights to guide their way.

They kissed in the dark corridor and Mariette slipped the chain lock free and let him go. And after he'd gone, she leaned against the closed door and breathed a sigh of joy, laced heavily with fear.

CHAPTER 31

The chestnut mares clip-clopped down Bayou Road en route to *Belle Fleur.* At 6 p.m., it was already dark at the end of December. Lanterns had been lit outside plantation homes set back from the road, all along the route from the Vieux Carré to Bayou St. John.

Mariette had never been this far from home before. In her sheltered life on Rampart Street, she'd never traveled beyond the French Market on the riverfront. In recent weeks, Soniat had taken her to the Faubourg Marigny, the racetrack and to Milneburg, but never in this direction. Her mother and her neighbors called this area Back-o'-Town, the land outside the walls of the original city.

"The plantations are all so beautiful, Philippe. I always pictured Back-o'-Town as a swamp, with nothing but alligators and snakes."

"Half the land is swamp," he answered, "but there is this one strip of high land that's been inhabited by Frenchmen since the early 1700s… and Indians before that…mostly Choctaws." For a time, they rode in silence, broken only by the clop-clop of the horses' hooves. "My father bought *Belle Fleur* from the descendants of one of the first French settlers," Philippe said. "The house is over a hundred years old."

Mariette felt unnerved hearing this, knowing already that the Grillets were part of the *ancien* population of the city. Knowing she'd be closely scrutinized, she'd spent the day worrying about what to wear to strike the right balance between gentility and humility, so she might win their approval. She wondered if it were possible, no matter what she did.

Another problem they'd had to work out was transportation to *Belle Fleur*. She couldn't have Philippe pick her up at the New Levee house without Adelle and the other servants seeing him and perhaps telling Soniat. She'd had to ask Remy to take her to her mother's house for a party. She'd said she'd have a ride home, he was not to worry. But Remy was taciturn by nature, and therefore inscrutable. Still, he drove her to her mother's house on Rampart Street, and Philippe had picked her up there. Which meant that Desiree, too, was in on the secret. Oh, what a tangled web we weave!

Desiree had done a lot of frowning and head-shaking. A contract had been signed, after all, and the consequences of Mariette's actions could be devastating.

Just before sunset, Jean Baptiste, Philippe's manservant, had pulled up at Desiree's door. He drove the carriage, and Celine, who'd agreed to come along as Mariette's chaperone, climbed up to sit on the perch above the carriage alongside him. Mariette got inside with Philippe.

Mariette smoothed out the fullness of her royal blue taffeta skirt, hoping she'd chosen the right dress. This one had a neckline cut in a modest V and trimmed with a bertha of *ecru* lace, the sleeves a series of puffs that ended below the elbow. She felt pretty in the dress; yet she was certain she had the air of a respectable convent girl.

"Please remember your new name," Philippe cautioned her. "Anne-Marie deBoisblanc. Say it for me."

"Anne-Marie deBoisblanc. I won't forget."

"Your father was Christophe deBoisblanc."

"I know. I know."

After a half-hour ride, the carriage turned off Bayou Road, bringing into view Bayou St. John on one side and the facade of the Grillet mansion on the other. On the bayou side, cool green willows arced gracefully over the shoreline, and cypress trees extended their knobby knees out into the water. Suddenly, thousands of frogs broke out in a raucous chorus, startling Mariette. She tightened her hold on Philippe's arm.

"There's our house," Philippe said. The carriage rolled through an arched wrought-iron gate and followed a semi-circular gravel path to the front of the mansion.

Mariette gazed in amazement at the huge French Colonial home. It was a two-story home, brick on the first floor, cement stucco on the second. Massive white columns ran two stories high, supporting the wide galleries that encircled the upper story. The roof was hipped and very steep, broken by dormer windows.

Awed by the size and majesty of the place, Mariette gave Philippe her hand and stepped from the carriage onto the pebbled walkway. Jean Baptiste helped Celine down, and the servants followed their masters toward the house. Mariette clutched Philippe's arm, alarmed by the aura of power and wealth that surrounded the home. People who lived in such a mansion would never admit her into their family. Why had she ever come here? How could she think they'd have a chance to marry?

The pebbled walk was illuminated by lanterns and flanked by rose trees giving off a delightful perfume in the early evening breeze.

The front door opened to them. A black butler took Philippe's hat and Mariette's shawl, gloves, and bonnet. He smiled at Philippe with a flash of white teeth.

"How do, Michie Philippe."

"Good evening, Andrew."

"Miss Adelaide, she say for you to go on up to the pah-lor."

Philippe nodded. "Andrew, will you see to Celine's comfort?" Philippe asked, nodding in the Negress's direction.

"Ah sho will, suh," Andrew said.

Philippe took Mariette's hand in his. "Your hand is like ice," he whispered.

"I'm scared to death."

"Please don't be. My parents are good people, and I'm here." He kissed her cheek. "It's going to be all right. Trust me."

CHAPTER 32

Mariette's knees felt weak as she climbed the carpeted staircase to the second floor. The circular ascent led to a wide corridor on the second floor with doorways leading into four large rooms. Philippe led her into the first door on the left, where she saw his parents waiting.

His mother, Adelaide Grillet, a French aristocrat, was sitting on one of the two settees flanking a marble fireplace. She made a pretty picture there, a slender beautiful lady in her late forties, in a gown of lavender bombazine, which complimented her black and silver hair. She rose to greet them.

"Welcome to *Belle Fleur*, Mademoiselle deBoisblanc," Adelaide said graciously, taking Mariette's hand. "How lovely you are, my dear. Oh, but your hands are cold. We must get you a sherry to warm you after your carriage ride."

"Thank you, Madame," Mariette said softly.

Philippe introduced Mariette by her new name. After greeting his mother, Mariette turned her eyes to his father, Francois Grillet, who stood beside her. He was a man in his middle fifties, hefty about the waist. He wore a formal dinner jacket and a grey silk embroidered waistcoat. His hair was dark, his sideboards gray, as was his crescent mustache.

"It was good of you both to invite me," Mariette said.

"Our pleasure, Mam'selle," said Francois Grillet. He took her hand and bowed over it.

"Come, sit down," Adelaide said, leading Mariette to the settee. "Andrew," she addressed the butler, "please bring Mam'selle a sherry, and the same for me."

"Bring us each a whiskey, Andrew," the father said. He reached inside his coat pocket for a gold cigar case and offered Philippe a cheroot. Philippe accepted. Both men lit their cigars.

Looking around, Mariette saw that the room was enormous, extending the depth of the house and including both parlor and dining room. French doors in the parlor gave out onto the front gallery which faced the bayou, and those in the dining room led to a rear gallery, overlooking the sugar cane fields in the distance. The doors were closed now against the chill evening breezes, but she could imagine how delightful it must be in summer, with all the doors open and the bayou breezes flowing through unobstructed.

"Philippe tells me you live in the *Vieux Carre*, not far from our commission house," Francois Grillet said.

Philippe tightened his lips. The Inquisition was beginning.

"Yes, M'sieur, I do," she said. She knew she must get control of her nerves and appear confident tonight, just as any society girl would be if invited to dinner. She marshaled her strength and smiled. "I live in a rooming house with a few other single ladies, under the watchful eye of a house mother. The place was recommended to me when I finished my studies with the Ursulines."

"Oh, yes, Philippe told us you'd been educated by the nuns," said Adelaide. "In their orphanage, I believe."

Mariette was brought up short by the way she said *orphanage*, as if it had a bad connotation. "Yes," she said. "My mother died in childbirth, and my father was killed in the explosion of the steamboat *Nellie Belle*, when I was only nine."

"How tragic," Adelaide said, with little feeling. "And your father was a plantation owner, Philippe tells us. In Natchez, I believe?"

"Yes, Madame."

Now it was Francois who continued the interrogation. He said, "deBoisblanc," casting his gaze to the ceiling, as if scanning his memory for the name. "I knew most of the planters in Natchez in the past decade. You say the accident happened in 1831 or thereabouts?"

"Yes, M'sieur, 1831."

Grillet scratched at his mustache. "Strange. I don't recall the name deBoisblanc."

Philippe fidgeted in his wingback chair. "I'm sure you couldn't have known every planter in Natchez, Papa," he said.

"Perhaps not," he agreed, but his tone said otherwise. "Who were your grandparents? Their names might be more familiar."

"Please, Papa," Philippe begged.

"It's all right, Philippe," Mariette said. This was the information Philippe had given her to memorize, and she had rehearsed it carefully. Now she would have her chance to try to convince them. "My father's father was a deBoisblanc, of course, and his mother was a Bienvenu. My mother's father was a Caro, and her mother's maiden name was Denesse."

"Hmm. Denesse is a familiar name," Francois said. "Of course, you have birth records showing all these names."

"Papa, I cannot allow you to harass Mademoiselle deBoisblanc any further."

"Harass?" Grillet asked sharply, offended at his son's choice of words. "I'm certainly not harassing Mademoiselle, Philippe. Wherever do you get such ideas?"

"Philippe," Mariette admonished coolly. "I'm happy to talk to your father about my ancestors." She smiled an artificial smile, an actress's smile, Philippe thought, and turned once more to Francois. "Unfortunately, all our family records were destroyed in a fire in our parish church, the Church of St. Mark in Natchez."

"Unfortunately," Francois said. He could not have said "conveniently" and made his meaning any clearer.

"I would like to change the subject," Philippe said in an authoritative voice.

"And so we shall," said Adelaide. She turned a smiling face to Mariette. "Philippe tells us you speak English quite well."

"Yes, Madame. I learned it at the Convent."

"Remarkable. My daughter never managed that, though she studied with the nuns for years. Sad to say, she parted company with them under bad circumstances. She was unjustly admonished and asked to leave. I've never forgiven them."

Mariette said nothing. She had never met an Ursuline nun in her life, nor Philippe's sister. So she would have been hard put to make a judgment.

"Is your daughter at home this evening?" Mariette asked, smiling.

"Oh, yes." Adelaide sighed heavily. She seemed sorry the girl was at home. "She'll be along. She's still dressing."

Obviously, there was little affection between mother and daughter. Perhaps Adelaide was upset with the girl for her tardiness, but Mariette sensed there was more to it than that.

The butler arrived with a tray bearing small crystal glasses of sherry and cutglass tumblers of whiskey for the men. When all had been served, Francois spoke.

"Tell me, Mademoiselle," he said. "How do you manage your finances, without parents or any visible means of support?"

"Papa, please!" Philippe said, his face reddening. The question was rude and insulting, but he'd known his father would not hold his tongue. To his father, any young woman with no family whatsoever to take her in was hardly worth the trouble to question, but he was straining courtesy for his son's sake.

Philippe cast a glance at Mariette, who was shaking her head at him almost imperceptibly. He was surprised that she appeared calmer, more unruffled as the interview progressed.

She said, "I have a trust fund left me by my paternal grandmother on her death, and another by my father. They are managed for me by an attorney who sends me a stipend each month. I may apply for extra when needed."

She sipped her sherry. She was magnificent, Philippe thought. Calm, in control, and her words had been perfect, just as rehearsed. What an actress! He himself had been tight as a drum, but he felt himself relaxing a bit as she spoke. He hid his proud smile behind his whiskey tumbler. Yes, she would manage this interview admirably. He began to feel more optimistic. It was just possible that they could pull it off, and he would be allowed to marry his beloved girl.

CHAPTER 33

"How are you chaperoned, my dear," Adelaide asked in her most caring voice, "if you are invited out for an evening. To this dinner party, for instance?"

Philippe bristled. He wanted to take Mariette's hand and leave the room, but Mariette parried.

"I have a maid, Madame. Her name is Celine. She goes everywhere with me. She is here tonight, downstairs."

How could they not be impressed with her beauty, Philippe wondered, and her cool, quiet dignity? And yet he knew these were minor considerations, when marriage appeared a possibility. Being an orphan was an extreme disadvantage to begin with, for there were no parents to come forward with lands and dowry and a family Bible tracing their lineage. But it was the role Mariette must play, since the truth was so much worse.

And that aside, Philippe knew that a young woman could have the face of a horse and still be a satisfactory candidate for a Creole marriage, if she could prove she had wealth and background. It amazed him that they wouldn't want their grandchildren to look like Mariette. He ran his fingers through his hair. He wanted desperately to put an end to the interrogation.

Suddenly, his eighteen-year-old sister Jeanine came into the room, her cheeks rouged, her dress revealing more than a modest amount of cleavage.

"Get me a sherry, please, Andrew," she ordered before she'd even been introduced to Mariette.

"Hello, big brother," she said, reaching over to plant a kiss on Philippe's cheek.

"Hello, Sweets," he answered, smiling. Mariette warmed to the way Philippe and his sister seemed genuinely fond of each other. Philippe introduced Mariette to Jeanine. Then Jeanine flopped into a wing chair near the guest of honor. Everyone fell silent at her abrupt and unladylike entry. Jeanine looked at her mother. "Go on talking," she said. "Don't let me interrupt you."

Her mother gave her a look that said she already had. Now Adelaide turned her attention back to Mariette. "Tell me, Mam'selle," she said pleasantly, "what do you do to occupy your time during the day?"

"Oh, I keep busy with reading and sewing," Mariette said, "and I give two days a week as a volunteer at Charity Hospital."

Philippe frowned. They hadn't discussed this "volunteer" business. She was off on her own now, but she seemed totally self-confident. One glance at his mother reassured him she believed every word.

"Oh, my!" Adelaide said, pursing her lips as if she'd tasted something sour. "Don't you find it offensive, handling those poor, unwashed people?"

"No, Madame. They're so very grateful. Especially the children."

"No doubt they are. But that's what we have nuns for."

Where was Mariette pulling these ideas from, Philippe wondered.

She'd never worked in Charity Hospital, much less with unwashed bodies or grateful children.

"Many lay women give volunteer time at Charity," Mariette countered.

"None of my friends do," Adelaide said. "They prefer to make financial contributions and leave the nursing to the nuns."

Mariette smiled. "There are many different ways to help, I'm sure."

My sweet Mariette is backing down, Philippe thought. His mother had a way of intimidating people, even those in her own social circle. How could Mariette win in an exchange with a woman of Adelaide's age and self-righteousness? He came to the rescue and changed the subject.

"Mariette and I had box seats at the Camp Street Theater last week," he said, looking first at his mother, then at his father. "The play was excellent. It was called *Lock and Key*.

At the mention of the Camp Street Theater, Mariette's head turned swiftly toward Philippe, but he did not meet her gaze. *Why is he discussing the theater, when he made such a point that we were not to discuss it?* Then she realized that if she and Philippe were theatergoers, not actors, the whole focus was different.

"We have no box at the Camp," Francois told Philippe.

"Your friend, Maunsel White, invited me to use his," he answered. He hoped his father wouldn't meet Colonel White and mention this slight variance with the truth. "I met him accidentally on the riverfront last week."

Francois drained his glass and placed it on the mantel shelf.

"Was M'sieur Caldwell in the play?" Jeanine asked Mariette, changing the subject back to one she preferred.

"Yes." Mariette smiled. "And he was wonderful."

"Well I think he's the handsomest actor I've ever laid eyes on,"

Jeanine said. "I think I'd absolutely swoon if I met him face to face."

Mariette knew two things. They did sometimes go to the Camp Street Theater. At least Jeanine did. And they hadn't seen this play, so they had no idea she was in it, or had a look-alike in it.

"There's little likelihood of that, Jeanine," her mother stated emphatically.

"I don't know why," Jeanine insisted. "We could invite him to dinner. We've had actors here before."

"Yes, we have," said Adelaide. "And we've always admired their talents and their *joie de vivre.*"

Big of you, Mariette mused.

"But on the whole, such pushy people, don't you find?" Adelaide asked Mariette. "It's hard to explain to one as young as Jeanine the difference between society and theatrical pursuits. She swoons, as she puts it, at the sight of the flashy and the flamboyant."

Mariette found Philippe's gaze fixed on her with an unmistakable message. Say no more about acting. Apparently, to Adelaide Grillet, show people were from one planet and socially acceptable people from another. Philippe needn't worry. She would say nothing about the undignified side of her life. Her "hospital work" had been one mistake. She wouldn't make another.

Andrew announced dinner. Adelaide took Mariette's arm and led her into the dining room, chatting about how lovely her gown was. Obviously, she felt as if she'd made her position clear on the subjects raised, and could now turn to trivia.

Mariette forced a smile, fingering her mother's pearls that lay against her throat. She sat where she was directed at the long table in the dining room, facing the French doors that gave out onto the balcony. Philippe sat beside her. She knew she had not scored well as a serious candidate for the wife of Philippe Grillet. They would not be granted permission to marry. They were different kinds of people, she and Philippe. They lived in different worlds, and Adelaide Grillet meant to keep it that way.

If they knew my grandmother was a slave, they'd throw me in Bayou St. John and never even have to stand trial.

Philippe spread his serviette across his lap. He stole a look at Mariette's face, now devoid of color. Her features were as lifeless as stone. She had understood his parents' questions and his mother's remarks only too well. Any idea of marriage was beyond consideration, from his parents' point of view. Philippe took Mariette's hand in his beneath the tablecloth and squeezed it, as if to say, "Don't despair. I have not yet had my turn."

The meal was beautifully served on Sevres china, with exquisite silverware and delicate crystal. Mariette didn't know what she was eating, though she was sure it was a meal prepared with great care. Somehow they got through dinner and retired to the parlor for coffee.

Mariette watched Philippe move to the edge of the settee. She was frightened. She wondered what he could possibly say to make her look worthy in their eyes.

"As we all know very well," Philippe said, "I did not bring Mademoiselle Anne-Marie here this evening to talk about a play." He put down his coffee cup and took Mariette's hand. He sought his mother's eyes, then his father's. "I brought her here for you to meet her," he said. "I have asked her to marry me, and she has consented. We would like to have your blessing."

Silence fell like a pall in the room. Jeanine sat forward, a smile widening on her face. "Well, you have mine," she said, bouncing out of her chair to kiss both Mariette and Philippe on the cheek. "I think it'll be wonderful having such a beautiful lady as my sister-in-law. I can't wait to tell my friends."

"Jeanine," Adelaide said reprovingly. A frown creased her brow between her jet black eyebrows. "You will tell no one anything, since there is nothing to tell. Now will you please go to your room? We would like to discuss this matter privately."

"I'm staying," Jeanine said. "I want to hear this."

Adelaide sighed. Apparently she hadn't expected Jeanine to obey. Jeanine was the *enfant terrible* of the Grillet family, and Mariette thanked God for her. The girl's presence gave her courage.

"Philippe," Francois began, "you have placed both your mother and me in an embarrassing position. Nevertheless, I'll say what I must. A young man of a Creole family does not enter into marriage hastily or for any imagined romantic motive. Such a marriage must be planned, and who knows better than his parents how to make these plans? It is essential that he marry a young lady with a background like his own, someone who moves in the same social circle, enjoys the same privileges, attends the same gatherings."

Mariette felt her cheeks flush with shame.

"I cannot believe your rudeness," Philippe told his father.

"You force us into an untenable position, Philippe," Grillet said. Then turning to Mariette, "You see, Mam'selle," he said, "there are many things to consider."

"Of course," Philippe said, caustically. "Money and property. If a young woman comes to the marriage with a great deal of either, she is welcomed with open arms, for these arrangements are not marriages, they are mergers." He was speaking loudly now, rudely so. He rose from the settee and stood with his hands clenched at his sides. "'Creoles do not marry for love.' How often have I heard that ridiculous maxim? Well, you won't marry me off to the heiress of your choice, Papa, I can tell you that!" He stood, feet planted apart, breathing hard. "I intend to marry Anne-Marie. She's a fine young woman, decent, intelligent, well-educated, and beautiful, as anyone can see."

"Which is, of course, what has blinded you to all else," Adelaide said.

"No, Maman. I see everything quite clearly. I was attracted to her in the beginning for her beauty. Any man would be. But I've learned to respect her more each time we meet, for her warm, caring ways, and her innocence."

"Innocence!" Adelaide exclaimed scornfully. "In a boarding house? With no older relative to chaperone her?"

"Yes, innocence. We will not discuss this further in Mam'selle's presence. We've embarrassed her enough for one evening. I'll take her home now."

Before Mariette knew what was happening, Philippe took her hand and led her swiftly toward the staircase and down to the first floor. Andrew had heard. He had summoned Celine, who was standing at the door, holding Philippe's hat and Mariette's bonnet and shawl.

In seconds, the door to the Grillet mansion had closed behind them, and Mariette knew that a chapter in her life had ended before it had ever begun.

CHAPTER 34

"What could you have been thinking, Philippe?" Francois Grillet demanded, sitting behind the walnut desk in his office. "Bringing an unknown lower-class woman into our home! Declaring your intention to marry her! And in her very presence! Ahhh," he groaned. "That was too juvenile for a man of your experience." Grillet swiveled the desk chair absently.

"Don't call her low-class, Papa. She is anything but that. And I still intend to marry her," he said adamantly.

"Philippe, my boy, you are our pride and joy. You have known since you reached the age of reason that Creoles marry in their own circle. Love has nothing to do with it. You marry *up*, Philippe. This is not only tradition. It is your obligation as a future leader of the community." He tapped his desk with his thick fingertips, gathering his thoughts. "Even if we rule out wealth, name is still an absolute necessity."

"And love means nothing," Philippe said. He walked to the window and gazed out, hands behind his back.

"That is most often the case, Philippe, although in many an arranged marriage, the husband and wife get along quite well and are even affectionate with each other."

Philippe chuckled sardonically. "That's really funny, Papa!"

"Listen to me, Philippe," Grillet said. "Marriage is not a license for lust. It is a business arrangement. You've always known that, *mon fils.*"

"A business arrangement?" Philippe asked. "Would you say that in front of my mother?"

"There's no need. Your mother's an intelligent woman. She knows how Creole marriages are made."

"Let me ask you something, Papa. Do you love my mother?"

Apparently, no one had ever asked his father that question before. He sat back in his chair and looped his thumbs into his belt before answering. "Well, let's say we have an understanding. We're the same kind of people."

"But you don't love her."

"I love her dignity. I love the order she gives my home. I love her for many things, but if you're referring to carnal appetite, no. She's not the class of woman one would yearn for in such a way."

"Have you had such yearnings for other women?"

Grillet cleared his throat. "Creoles have the same desires as all men, Philippe."

Philippe smirked. "So tell me, Papa, what do they do about them?"

"Ask your friend Armand about his *placée*. He has a young quadroon who takes care of his baser desires."

"Baser desires?" Philippe asked. He laughed at his father's words, but he was still revolted by them.

"Yes. Desires." Grillet got up from his desk and walked around to sit on the front of it. "Later on, he may marry one of his own kind. You will probably do the same." After a moment, he came back to his chair, sat down, and took a cheroot from his cigar box. He bit off the end and lit the cigar. "Too bad your little Anne-Marie isn't a quadroon," he said. "She's a pretty little thing. Articulate, too. You could set her up in a nice little house and get all the lust out of your system."

Philippe knew then that his father had no idea whatsoever that Mariette was of mixed blood. But the picture he'd painted of his life with Mariette was nonetheless degrading. He drew in a deep breath. "Let's suppose I'm not willing to give her up, Papa," Philippe said. "Let's say I'm hard-headed enough to think I can marry her, regardless of her unworthiness. What then?"

Francois's eyebrows come together. "I'll tell you, Philippe," he said. "You know that sign over the door that says 'Grillet & Son'?" He pointed toward the entrance door. "It would thereafter read, 'Francois Grillet, Commission Merchant.'"

"I'd lose my half of the business."

"It isn't *your* half *yet*. No legal document has ever been signed. The commission house is mine, Philippe," he said. "The sign will only remain there if you make a proper marriage."

"I see."

Francois pushed his advantage. "And your inheritance, which is considerable, would also disappear."

Philippe walked to the door of his father's office. He had heard enough. "I'm leaving now, Papa," he said. "I have a boat to meet at the Julia Street wharf."

"Well?" Grillet asked.

"Well what?"

"Are you going to promise me you'll never see her again?" Grillet asked, while Philippe put on his coat and hat.

"No." He frowned at his father. "I won't promise you that."

CHAPTER 35

An errand boy knocked at the door of the New Levee Road mansion with a message for Mariette. He said he'd been ordered to wait for an answer. Standing in the vestibule, her heart racing, she tore open the letter and read:

28 December 1840
Dear Mariette,
   "We've had so many requests for additional performances of Lock and Key that I've decided to call the cast together and run six more shows, beginning tonight. Please come to the Camp at ten this morning. There is much to do."
                                                    Caldwell

Mariette breathed a ragged sigh. It was not from Philippe, as she had hoped, but it was good news and she was grateful for it. She sat at the cherrywood dining table and jotted a note, saying she'd be there on time and handed it to the young man. He tipped his cap, ran down the steps, and hopped from the carriage block onto his horse.

She was glad she'd have to study all day and refresh her memory to perform tonight. Her mind would be occupied. She'd have no time to think about last night's insults and the pain of rejection. The Grillets had made it clear she was unacceptable as a wife to their son and heir. That was no longer the question. Now that Philippe's feet would be put to the fire, she'd find out whether or not he was really willing to give up everything for her. And if he was, could she really let him do that?

Mariette finished her breakfast. She asked Remy to hitch up the carriage to take her to the Camp. Her mind awhirl, she went upstairs to her bedroom and packed a small makeup bag, looked for her copy of the script, and rang the bell cord for Adelle to come to her.

"We'll be leaving for the theater at 9:30," she told the maid. "Would you help me wash and dress, please? And do my hair?"

Before ten, they arrived at the theater. Lines had begun forming at the box office as soon as the sign went up announcing the six additional performances. On arriving, the actors greeted one another cordially, happy at the news that the play had been such a success. Caldwell had run a full-page advertisement in *Le Moniteur* this morning, trusting to luck that all his actors would be well and would agree to come.

Of course they'd come, Mariette reasoned. When an actor didn't work, he didn't get paid. Judging by the long line of patrons waiting for tickets, the extra week would surely be welcomed. The cast would probably be playing to standing-room-only houses. Caldwell was all smiles.

Notes were followed by a rehearsal of the first act. Then Caldwell called a half-hour break, during which lunch orders were taken for the restaurant across the street. Mariette nibbled at a sandwich at the *poudre* table in her dressing room. Adelle had eaten quickly and was now arranging Mariette's costumes on the rack in her dressing room.

A knock at the door startled them both. Adelle took a note from another messenger and handed it to Mariette, while the boy waited. She recognized Philippe's handwriting. She called the boy inside and asked, "How did you know where to find me?"

"The man who wrote it sent me to a house on New Levee Road," he said. "So I went there an' a Nigra man tole me you was at the Camp Street Theater."

A Nigra man. Remy. He'd brought her here in the carriage, and he'd probably returned just as the messenger arrived. Mariette smiled and clasped the note to her breast. "Wait just a minute and I'll have some change for you." She took some coins from her reticule and handed them to the boy.

Swiftly, she broke the seal and pulled out two sheets of paper. The letter was long. It was Philippe's handwriting, and he had written fast. She sat down on the small settee to read.

28 December 1840

My dearest Mariette,

I apologize for the behavior of my parents last night. As I told you on the way home, my mother and father have always expected me to marry someone with name and money, which is the reason why I am still single. I have never found anyone of that description with whom I wished to spend the rest of my life.

I had hoped they'd be as enchanted by your beauty and intelligence as I am and would consider blessing our marriage, although your background is unknown to them. But that was not to be. We must now proceed with our own plans. I took a ride this morning and found a building for lease on Triton Walk. I paid the realtor the first month's rent. It is just what I wanted, an office on the ground floor and an apartment above. Now I need only sell my town house.

Today I will go to St. Patrick's Church to make arrangements for us to be married there tomorrow afternoon. Find your birth certificate and send it to me at my townhouse at 120 Royal Street. My manservant will be expecting it. We'll meet at the church at three p.m. tomorrow. We must arrive separately. Wear a veil. You may be recognized.

I shall be anxiously awaiting the sight of your beautiful face. P.

Mariette pressed the note to her bosom and sighed with euphoria. "Will there be any answer, Mam'selle?" the boy asked.

She realized suddenly that the messenger was still there. "No, thank you, young man," she said. "There is no answer. You are a very wonderful messenger." In a rush of happiness, she kissed the boy on his cheek, and he blushed furiously and ran away.

Mariette sat at her *poudre* table and studied her own eyes in the looking glass. They mirrored her happiness. Philippe still wanted her. He had truly meant what he'd said. He didn't care about the inheritance. The fact was staggering, for his legacy must be enormous, if the opulence of his parents' home was any indication.

How could she let him give up everything for her, even his half of the business? Yet, that was what he wanted to do. Starting his own business seemed a challenge to him. He'd told her repeatedly that she was the only thing he couldn't live without. He'd convinced her of that. It was he who was leading the way, making the arrangements, holding out his arms to her. How could she not run to him?

CHAPTER 36

It had been three weeks since Philippe had sent the note making arrangements for their wedding, but the ceremony had never taken place, and the delay had been no one's fault. First, Desiree had been unable to locate Mariette's birth certificate, and Philippe had gone to the St. Louis Cathedral, Mariette's parish church, and applied for a copy of her baptismal certificate, which he'd been told would suffice. Father Jeansonne, the pastor, had told him that Mariette had to come for it herself. They had returned together, but when the pastor saw the "Q" on her baptismal certificate, he looked first at Mariette, then at Philippe, and then asked Mariette directly, "Are you a Quadroon, M'amselle?" She glanced at Philippe. How could she deny it? It was in the church records.

"Yes, Father," she said.

"Are you two planning to be married?" he asked.

Mariette waited for Philippe to answer. He couldn't lie. It was too obvious. "Yes, Father, we are," he said.

"Well, it can't be done," the pastor said sharply. "It's illegal.

A mixed marriage is against the Code Noir. And of course, and the Church follows the laws of the State."

"But Father, you misunderstand. This is not a mixed marriage," Philippe said. Mariette's head spun around to meet Philippe's gaze, but he would not look at her. "You see, I am a Quadroon, too."

"Oh, no, my son." The priest grinned. "I've never seen a Quadroon with green eyes."

"With all due respect, Father, I have my father's eyes, but my mother is a mulattress."

"It's easy enough to prove, you know. Are you registered in this parish? The record would be here."

"No, Father. My parents were living in Natchez at the time of my birth, and that is where the certificate is recorded." *How smoothly he lies*, Mariette thought.

"I see," the priest said, obviously doubting his words.

"But of course, we have copies of all our vital family records at home," he added.

"Then, you must bring your baptismal certificate to me."

"Yes, Father," Philippe said. He scratched his head and sighed. Then, finding the priest's eyes, he added, "Not that it matters for us, but I've heard there is a priest in Mobile who performs many mixed marriages."

"Yes," the priest agreed, "I've heard that, too. And one in Biloxi, as well."

Philippe's lips were beginning to form a smile.

"But they are breaking the law," Father Jeansonne said sternly, "and the Church does not condone their actions. I'm sure they'll be stopped sooner or later, and the Church will suffer for their legal disobedience." Silence fell for a moment. "Those are renegade priests, who hold that they are saving the immortal souls of the engaged couple, who would otherwise live in sin." He locked eyes with Philippe. "Nevertheless, the priests here at the Cathedral do not perform mixed marriages." The message was clear.

"I understand," Philippe said. "Now if we may have a copy of Miss Delon's certificate, we'll be on our way." The copy was made.

That was the first delay. But Philippe considered it only a delay, for he would not be put off. Next came the search for Philippe's birth certificate. He had never needed it before, and he had no idea where his parents kept it. He dared not ask them for fear they would know he was planning to marry, in spite of their objections. So he decided to do a complete search of the house when they left for their ritual Sunday afternoon visits. He looked through his mother's things first: her scrapbook, her box of souvenirs and mementos, her dresser drawers, all to no avail.

He put the articles back neatly, just as he had found them, and began to go through his father's filing boxes and wardrobe drawers. But no certificate. Suddenly he realized that the family's important papers might be in his father's bank box.

The following day at work, he casually asked his father, "Papa, do you have a bank box where I might put some important papers, so they don't get misplaced? Like the Bill of Sale for my townhouse? Papers I might want to lay my hands on in the future?"

"Well, yes, my boy, I have a bank box at the Louisiana Bank, where I keep some personal records and some insurance policies."

"Would you mind if I put my papers in your box, or would you prefer that I get my own?"

"Oh no, of course you can use mine," Francois Grillet said, trying to make it up to his son for their recent quarrel. "Here. I'll give you the key. Just show it to the clerk, tell him you're my son. He'll have an identical key, and when the two keys are inserted and turned, the bank box will open." And so it was that Philippe located his own birth certificate without his parents knowing it. Now all that remained was the job of changing the "W" to a "Q", a formidable task, but nothing was impossible for a man in love. He felt absolutely charged with power. That night in his room, under a bright light, he dipped his quill pen into the inkwell and carefully changed the bottom of the W to the tail of the Q, deleted the central line with ink remover, and made an oblong connection of the two remaining lines. He examined the results. Perfect. No forger could have done better. He let the paper dry, then folded it neatly and placed it in an envelope beside Mariette's. His second problem had been solved.

Next came his visit to St. Patrick's Church, where, as he'd told Mariette, nobody knew them. He spoke with a young Irish priest, right off the boat, a Father Maher, who looked at the certificates, looked Philippe over, and said, "Sure an' I'd be happy to marry you, Mister Grillet. I cannot perform the ceremony until the weekend, however. We're so shorthanded here, an' I'm scheduled fer confessions an' meetings all the week long."

Philippe regretted the delay, fearing that at any moment Louis Soniat might come riding back into town, but he was so elated to find a priest who was willing to marry them, he decided to take the chance. They made arrangements for Saturday morning at 9 a.m. Philippe left almost on a run, afraid that young Father Maher might change his mind. He'd see Mariette after the performance tonight and give her the good news.

CHAPTER 37

Alone onstage in the third act of *Lock and Key*, Mariette had just begun her lines in the scene where her character Odette cried for her lost love. She wanted, as always, to make the words sound as fresh as if she'd never said them before. She'd taught herself how to start her tears by gazing, unblinking, into the gas footlights that ringed the apron of the stage. The brightness alone was enough to bring on tears, and the gas fumes burned her eyes just enough to get the tears rolling down her face. After that, it was easy. A sob and a sniffle would bring on more tears, and the fact that she was so steeped in Odette's sorrow made each performance a deeply personal experience.

She knew the exact moment to start looking at the gas jets, as though she were lowering her eyes in grief, so that the tears would be ready to accompany the right line. Tonight, however, gazing at the jets, she noticed that they wavered, as if in a draft. Mariette wondered why. No windows or doors were left open in the building in January, the coldest month of the year. Another look confirmed her first observation. The footlight flames were all burning horizontally, almost perpendicular to their jets. Fear seized her. Obviously, someone or *something* had created an opening in the building. Something like...*fire*? Could fire have already burned away part of a wall, allowing a draft of cold air to enter?

Like all theater people, Mariette was mortally afraid of fire. Actors were always at risk, surrounded as they were by flammable paints and scenery. And Caldwell's gas lighting, everyone said, added one more element of danger to the Camp Street Theater. A picture of Philippe as a boy running from the burning plantation house flashed through her mind.

Her heart rushed, but she went on with her lines, her eyes scanning the audience for signs of panic, finding none. Suddenly, she smelled smoke. She stopped in the middle of a line. Eyes wide, she stood in the center of the stage and sniffed. A murmur spread across the first few rows, becoming a rising tide of frenzied shouts as it worked its way down the audience. The standing-room-only patrons began to cry out and were soon climbing over each other in the narrow side aisles to get to the Camp Street exits.

A curl of smoke descended upon the stage from above and screams rang out from the audience.

"Fire!" a patron cried out. Then, everyone was shouting. "Clear the aisles!" "Hurry!" "Oh, sweet Jesus, I see flames."

Mariette saw the flames climbing up the scenery on the side of the stage between her and the dressing rooms. She turned toward the other side, but flames were consuming the scenery there, as well, licking at the gold fringe that edged the red moreen curtains.

Paralyzed with fear, she turned toward the audience, where people were scrambling over theater seats and pushing one another aside, trying frantically to reach the exits. She could not go through the auditorium. She'd be the last person to get out. Surely the roof would fall in before she got to the door.

"Mariette!" a man's voice called out, but all she could see was a jumble of screaming, hysterical people pushing against one another, fighting for every foot of aisle space on their way to the exits.

In desperation, she turned toward the back of the stage. Flames had destroyed the scenery there in those few minutes since she'd first smelled smoke. She saw other actors running in the wings, screaming, making for the stage door at the rear of the building. Lifting her skirts, she rushed toward the back of the stage, climbing over a heavy chair on the set to join the others on their way to the exit. Then she heard a crumbling sound. She looked up to see a beam from the ceiling high above, shifting, starting to fall.

She screamed and raised her arms as a central beam directly overhead came crashing down. One end of the beam hit the stage floor close beside her and then fell toward her, striking her on the head. Everything went black and she felt herself falling.

CHAPTER 38

Sitting in the third row, Philippe heard the word "Fire!" Reacting instinctively, he called out Mariette's name. But at the sight of the first flame, he froze in his seat. His memory of the inferno in his childhood, vivid and terrifying, kept him locked there as effectively as a steel band. In a split second, the heat of that long-ago fire and the pain as it seared his arm came back to him. He sat wide-eyed, stilled by panic.

He saw the beam hit the floor and then strike Mariette, and his panic disappeared. She had turned when he'd called out to her, but it was obvious she could not see him in the vast tangle of moving bodies. He jumped from his seat, climbed across the first two rows, then over the orchestra pit, now alive with screaming musicians, and landed on the stage. He moved the huge beam to release Mariette. Then, with one arm beneath her shoulders and the other under her knees, he lifted her in his arms.

After glancing in all directions, he made a run for it, through the back of the stage, as flying pieces of burning scenery fell around his head and shoulders. He followed the corridor to the stage door exit, now blocked by a sea of humanity. People pushed against one another in their fight to escape from the building, which was now almost totally in flames. In another two minutes, a veritable eternity, he carried her limp body through the exit and down the outside stairs toward his rig in the next door livery stable.

Emerging rigs and men on horseback blocked him again, but at last, he reached the rig and gently laid Mariette against the seat. He took his place beside her. Once out in Camp Street, he could see there was no way he could drive past the front of the theater in the direction of the French Quarter with the traffic now jamming the narrow thoroughfare.

One horse-drawn fire wagon was already on the scene, bells ringing, pumps spewing streams of water against the flaming building. Fire bells of other approaching wagons clanged in the cold, windy night. Hysterical theater patrons lined the sidewalks, crying, hanging on to one another, some stretched out unconscious. Still others continued to issue forth from the double doors.

Rigs that had preceded his were now turning around to go the opposite way, and he found that he was blocking them. Another driver's whip landed on his mare's back, and the animal reared up on her hind legs, threatening to throw Philippe and Mariette from the rig.

A second fire wagon's hose shot another powerful spray into the building, but Philippe could see it was too late. Already, flames were curling out from the third-story windows. The building was gone. Clouds of black smoke rose up into the night as Philippe managed to turn his rig around and escape the mass of vehicles, but he was still besieged by the clanging of bells, and the heart-stopping screams of the sirens.

Philippe raced his mare down Camp Street in the opposite

direction, turned at the next corner and drove to Carondelet, where he turned back toward Canal Street on his way into the French Quarter. When he reached his townhouse, he pulled into the *porte cochere* to find Jean Baptiste waiting for him. The town had been aroused by the sound of fire bells, and people on every street were walking up and down in their night clothes, waiting for news.

"Are you all right, Michie Philippe?" the black man asked.

"Yes, but Mam'selle Delon is unconscious. I don't know how bad off she is. Help me get her upstairs."

Together they lifted Mariette out of the rig, and Philippe carried her up, Jean preceding him with a candle to open doors along the way.

"The guest bedroom," Philippe said, and Jean Baptiste went ahead to turn down the bed. At last, Philippe laid Mariette's head on the pillow and her arms and legs in comfortable repose. He turned to Jean Baptiste. "Go get Dr. Meynard on Chartres Street. Do you know the place?"

"Yassuh. I been dere before."

Jean Baptiste rushed from the room and was halfway down the stairs when Philippe called down to him from the landing. "Don't tell anyone that Mam'selle Delon is here. Do you understand me, Jean?"

"Yassuh."

"Tell the doctor that *I'm* the patient."

Jean Baptiste ran down the stairs, and Philippe returned to the guestroom. He leaned over Mariette's motionless body, and tried to estimate the seriousness of her injuries. A bloody gash marked her forehead, where the beam had struck her, and her face was covered with soot and splinters from the heavy beam. Strands of her long black hair hung over her face, caught in the bleeding wound.

He didn't know what to do first, or if he should touch her at all. If he disturbed a broken bone, more than he may already have by carrying her, he might do her serious harm. He poured water from a pitcher into a bowl on the nightstand. Then, taking a clean face cloth, he soaked it, squeezed it, and gently washed the blood and dirt from her face. She did not move. His heart hammered. He wondered if she was already dead.

He leaned down, placed his cheek above her mouth, and felt the warmth of her breath, but her breathing was shallow. The ringing bells of another fire wagon leaving its station on Chartres Street broke the silence of his townhouse. He continued washing Mariette's face and her neck and arms, gently removing the bloody strands of hair from the cut.

She was still in her costume, a dark green satin gown. It hugged her under her breasts, and he knew that beneath the dress, her stays were tightly laced around her ribs. She should be released at once from those constraints, and although he was still afraid of hurting her, he hesitated only momentarily. He turned her on her side, unfastened every hook in a long line down her back, and then rolled her to her back again to pull the dress off her arms. She fell limp as a rag doll when he turned her. After removing her shoes, he pulled the dress off at her feet.

She did not moan in pain, and that was good. But pain was at least a sign of life. She lay there before him like a corpse, white and motionless. He unbuttoned her one petticoat at the waist and pulled it down her legs and off her feet. Then he unlaced her stays and removed them. Instantly, she seemed to breathe more deeply and easily. Now she lay before him in nothing but her camisole and pantalets. Gently, he pulled the white linen sheet up over her arms. Then, taking a blanket from his chest of drawers, spread it over her for warmth. He removed the few remaining strands of hair from her face with his fingertips.

Pulling a slipper chair to the side of the bed, he sat and rested his head against the mattress. He was thinking that if he lost Mariette, the world would end for him. When the fire broke out, she'd been playing the scene in which he always felt she was talking to him across the footlights. Her character Odette was crying for her lost love, the man who could never be her husband, and in his heart Philippe knew why Mariette *became* Odette in that scene.

Perhaps he was jealous of the energy and emotion she gave to her acting instead of to him. Perhaps he wanted to be the only recipient of all those outpourings of joy and love and sorrow. Maybe that was why he had fought her acting. But if she survived, he swore to himself, he'd never badger her again about the theater. He'd let her do exactly as she pleased. Anyone as beautiful and gifted as Mariette had to be shared with the world.

He'd been right the very first night he'd met her. She should not be a *placée*. She should be a Creole's wife, the lady on his arm at the opera. He had tried to do it the right way, to marry her with his parents' consent. And they had refused. But with or without their blessing, he'd marry her, if God spared her life. He frowned and choked back a sob.

CHAPTER 39

Philippe sat beside the bed, realizing that the wedding arrangements, which had been made for the coming Saturday at St. Patrick's Church would surely have to be changed. Mariette lay before him, motionless, hardly breathing. *Mon Dieu*, he prayed, *let her recover. Nothing in this world means anything without her.* He reached out for her hand and held it tenderly, rubbing the cool, slender fingers with his thumb.

He must write a note to Desiree. She'd be crazy with worry as to where Mariette was and whether or not she'd been hurt. He sat at his *escritoire*, took a pen and a sheet of vellum from the drawer, and wrote.

Dear Madame Delon,

Mariette is with me at my town house. I've sent for a doctor to care for her. She was knocked unconscious by a falling beam during the theater fire. Please do not come here or write and do not tell Soniat or Delissard of her whereabouts. I promise to visit you tomorrow with news of her condition.

Philippe

Realizing that her maid Adelle, who was also her dresser, would send for Soniat if Mariette were missing, he took another sheet and wrote...

Dear Adelle,

 Mlle. Delon is fine. She was hurt but not seriously, and she will be attended by a physician. Do not send for M. Soniat, or there will be grave trouble. I cannot tell you who or where I am, but I promise you she is well. If you care for your mistress, do nothing. More news will come soon.

Philippe heard the front door slam and then heavy footsteps coming up the stairs. He folded both notes, putting a name on the outside of each and marking Desiree's note with an X. He opened the door of the guestroom and greeted the physician.

"Philippe, I see you're well," the doctor said. "Your man said you'd been injured."

"I told him to say that, Doctor, but it's Mam'selle Mariette Delon who's hurt. Do you know of her?"

"The actress?"

"Yes."

The doctor cleared his throat. "I'd better take a look at her," he said. He came into the guestroom and looked at the figure on the bed, then at Philippe. He began to examine Mariette, saying nothing about her state of undress. He listened intently to her lungs and then carefully examined her head.

"I'll dress the wound on her forehead, but first I must get her back to breathing properly."

Philippe nodded, his hand clenched around the bedpost. "Will she be all right, Doctor?" he asked.

The doctor did not answer but set to work. Turning the covers

aside, he straddled the young slender body. The bed ropes creaked
loudly as he pressed against her ribs and then lifted his weight,
pressed again, and then lifted again, all in an even, rhythmic motion.
After many minutes of silent work, he turned her onto her stomach.
Then once again, he straddled her and repeated the process.

At last she coughed, a deep, choking cough, and then she
moaned. Philippe smiled, his eyes shining, waiting for a verdict,
but the doctor said nothing. Carefully, Dr. Meynard turned her over
on her back and studied the gash on her head.

"You washed out her wound?" he asked. Philippe nodded. "You
did well. I'm glad you took those stays off, too. I don't know how
women can breathe with those ridiculous things." He looked at the
pitcher and bowl. "Empty the bowl and get me some fresh water."
Philippe took the pitcher and bowl. He found Jean Baptiste sitting
in the hallway, doubled over, sleeping lightly, but within calling
distance. Philippe shook the man's shoulder.

"Jean," he said. "I want you to deliver these notes for me." He took
them from his pocket. "The one with the X on it is the most
important," he said. "Deliver it first. It goes to Mam'selle's mother.
She is Madame Delon. A black woman. She lives in a shotgun house
on Rampart Street. This is the address." He handed Jean Baptiste the
card on which Mariette had written her address the day they'd had
coffee at Vincent's.

"I'll find it, Michie," the servant said.

"Then go to a house in Faubourg Marigny on the New Levee
Road. Do you know that neighborhood?"

"Yassuh."

"This is a new mansion in the second block from Esplanade, the
only house in the block. Ask if it's the residence of M'sieur Soniat.
Can you remember that?"

"Yassuh. M'sieur Soniat."

"And give it only to Adelle."

"Adelle." Jean Baptiste nodded and left on a run. He would find the houses. He was bright, and Philippe trusted him. Now he went down to the kitchen. He rinsed out the bowl and pumped fresh water into the pitcher. Back in the room, he watched Dr. Meynard wash the gash again and remove the splinters. He applied an ointment to the long red gash and covered it with a square of gauze and a bandage which he tied around her head.

Now he turned to Philippe. "She'll be all right. She inhaled a good bit of smoke, but her lungs are all right now. The blow to her head no doubt caused a concussion, but there's no fracture that I can detect. The best medicine is rest. As for the wound, it's superficial. It will heal. I'll leave this ointment with you. You can apply it twice a day and change her bandage. In a couple of days, take the bandage off. I'm afraid she's going to wake up with a terrible headache. I'll leave you some valerian powders. If you need me, you know where I am." He placed a few small packets on the night table.

"I don't know how to thank you," Philippe said, leading the doctor from the room. "And as for her being here, well, I was at the theater when the fire started. I saw the beam strike her, so I ran onstage and carried her out."

"You didn't know her before?"

Philippe scratched his head. How much should he say? "Yes, Doctor, I knew her. In fact, I'm going to marry her. My father has refused his consent and doesn't know I have her here. You're the only one who knows, you and my servant."

"And you're hoping I'll keep it that way." A tired half-smile pulled the doctor's lips to one side.

Philippe returned the smile. "Yes. Will you?"

"Of course. My work is always confidential."

"Thank you, Dr. Meynard. Thank you very much." He opened his *porte-monnaie* and paid the doctor's fee.

Dr. Meynard took the bill, smiling impishly, and left the room. Philippe escorted him to his rig. He waited until the doctor had left the yard. Then he rushed back inside and took the steps two at a time to the room where Mariette lay.

How still she was! How shallowly she breathed! Like a statue carved in ivory, she lay beneath the linen sheet, one slender arm on top the blanket. Her long hair lay in tangles against the pillow, the skin of her cheekbones diaphanous in the candlelight.

He snuffed out the candles he had lit in the sconces above the bed and those in the candelabra on the mantel. Now only the night candle burned. Pulling up the slipper chair, he rested his head against the mattress. The ropes beneath the mattress creaked. He found Mariette's left hand and held it lightly in his own. Then, closing his eyes, he began to pray again, but sleep descended upon him and stole the prayers from his lips.

CHAPTER 40

In the middle of the night, Mariette woke up screaming. "Fire! Fire! They can't get out! Get them out!" Philippe was at her side, holding her, trying to awaken her.

"Mariette, it's all right," he said. "It's over. You're safe, you're with me. Sleep, *mon amour*. Try to sleep."

She let herself go limp in his arms, but by the light of the night candle, he could see the frown of pain on her forehead. "Oh, Philippe! My head! It hurts so bad!"

"I have a headache powder for you, *cherie*. I'll pour you some water." He poured the water, brought the powder to her lips, and helped her with the glass. He could see by her stiff posture how intense her pain was. At last, she fell into a light sleep, and he sat in the chair once again and kept his vigil.

In the morning, Mariette was awakened by the chant of a vendor in the *Rue Royale*, regaling his vegetables from the French Market. "Ah got okra, Lay-dee! Fresh sweet white corn, two bits a dozen ear." She opened her eyes and tried to sit up. She gave a little cry of pain, then slowly lowered her head back to the pillow. It throbbed agonizingly. She looked up and saw an unfamiliar ceiling in an unfamiliar room. Turning her head ever so slightly, she saw Philippe resting against the side of the bed, his body slung like a hammock from a slipper chair to the mattress. The vendor hadn't awakened him. *He must be dead to the world.*

Was she in Philippe's rooms? How had she gotten here? The last thing she remembered was the fire at the theater and the beam coming down. How had she survived that? Who had told Philippe she was hurt? Who knew enough about them to bring her here?

Gently, she touched his head, closing her eyes against the fresh onslaught of pain. Tears rolled from the corners of her eyes, but she did not sob or move for fear of making her headache worse.

Philippe felt her fingers on his hair. Quickly, he lifted his head and saw her tears, her body convulsing with restrained sobs. In one quick motion, he was off the chair and kneeling at her bedside.

"Mariette, *mon ange*," he said softly, not daring to touch her, "tell me what hurts you."

"My head," she whispered hoarsely. She stopped her sobs by sheer force of will, knowing they would only make the throbbing worse.

"Oh, my love," he said, in an agony of compassion for her. "The doctor said you had a concussion, but not a fracture. He says you'll be fine, but you're to rest. You could take another headache powder now."

She nodded without speaking and with as little movement as possible.

Instantly, he was on his feet and over to the night stand. The pitcher was empty.

"I'm going downstairs for cool water, Mariette," he said. "I'll be right back."

She heard him return but she kept her eyes closed and her head completely still. Water gurgled into a glass and a paper packet cracked as it was unfolded. Now Philippe was beside her, holding her gently by the nape of the neck and helping her take the powder.

After an hour had gone by, she was still in agony. At last, she appeared to fall asleep, and he was grateful she was having even momentary relief. At ten o'clock, Jean Baptiste opened the door and brought in a tray for Philippe, but Philippe waved him back and followed him out into the corridor, for fear of disturbing Mariette. Frightened that her injury might be worse than the doctor had expected, Philippe said, "Go get Doctor Meynard right away, Jean. Tell him Mam'selle is suffering badly. Ask him if he has any stronger pain killer he can bring."

Jean Baptiste ran down the stairs and left on horseback through the *porte-cochere*. In a half hour, the doctor was back with laudanum for the pain. Mariette had been sleeping lightly, but she awakened when he entered the room.

"Mam'selle Delon," he said, "I'm Dr. Meynard. I examined you last night and treated your wound."

Mariette opened her eyes to see the man, then winced with pain. She raised her hand to examine the bandage. "My head hurts," she whispered.

"I know," he said, kindly. "I'd like to change your dressing while I'm here and examine your head again."

She nodded only slightly.

The doctor changed the bandage, but when he leaned over the bed and put both hands to the back of her neck, lifting it from the pillow, she groaned, and her eyebrows pulled together in a frown of agony. Philippe winced.

"There's no fracture, Mam'selle," he said. "It will take you a few days to get over this blow, but you'll be all right. I'll give you some laudanum now, and you'll sleep most of the day. By tomorrow, with bedrest and Philippe's good care, you'll feel much better. When you wake up this evening, please eat something. It will help your headache.

"You were a very lucky young woman," he added. "If that beam had hit you directly, you would not be here to talk about it. You can also thank Philippe for rescuing you."

Frowning, she looked up at Philippe. "I don't understand."

"I was there, Mariette."

"Where?"

"In the theater, in the third row."

"Why?"

"To see you playing Odette." A smile trembled on her lips, but she closed her eyes again. "I called your name," Philippe said. "I think you heard me, but you couldn't see me in all the confusion."

She smiled. "I...heard...you." She sobbed, and tears fell from beneath her closed eyelids.

"Don't cry, *mon coeur*. It will make your head worse." He took her hand and pressed his lips to it. Philippe told Mariette how she'd been hurt and how he had rescued her.

"And when he reached you," the doctor added, giving them both a start, "he picked you up and carried you through the stage door to his rig and brought you here to his townhouse. That's where you are now." He smiled, enjoying his part in telling the story. Philippe grinned. The old doctor was indeed a romantic. "Did you know where you were?" the old man asked, dying to know.

"No," she said. "I've never been here before."

The men exchanged glances, and Philippe smiled, vindicated. At least the doctor knew Mariette was not a loose woman, and Philippe's feelings for her were not casual. Perhaps now, he could rest easy, knowing the doctor would not tell his father. Philippe wanted Mariette to be able to stand on her own two feet when they were married. They would be lucky if that would be Saturday, as Philippe had planned. But until they were married, he could not let his father know she was in his house.

The doctor gave her the laudanum and signaled Philippe to come out of the room. "She'll sleep now," he said. "You ought to leave her alone to rest quietly. Go bathe and shave. She'll want to see you looking dandy when she wakes up." He was grinning like a Cheshire cat.

Philippe chuckled. *Dandy?* Dr. Meynard was full of surprises. The old reprobate had probably hoped he *was* sleeping with Mariette. Who knew what kind of a ladies' man *he* had been when he was young?

"She's a beautiful woman, Philippe," he said, when they were walking downstairs. "I wish you much happiness with her." And the doctor climbed into his rig and rode away, humming one of Mariette's show tunes.

CHAPTER 41

Philippe sighed. She would be all right. It was all he had to know. He would do as the doctor said. He would have a wash and a shave and a big breakfast. Suddenly he was famished. As he washed at a basin in the kitchen, he tried to think if there was anyone he hadn't notified, anyone who'd be anxious about Mariette and might inquire as to her whereabouts.

Caldwell. Assuming, of course, that Caldwell himself had not been hurt. When he was dressed, he'd take his mare and go to Caldwell's house. Then suddenly he realized he hadn't reported in to work. He hadn't even sent a message. Any time now, his father would be sending someone to check on him. Worse yet, he might be coming himself.

The front door knocker clacked loudly.

"Damn!" Philippe said, afraid it would be his father and afraid it might awaken Mariette. Rushing through the downstairs corridor with nothing but a length of toweling around his hips, he saw Jean Baptiste open the door very slightly, speak with someone, close the door, and come toward him. "Yo' papa sent a messenger. He wonts to know is you comin' to work t'day?"

"Tell him no. Tell him I'm going directly to meet a boat on the riverfront. I'll report to the office later, after I've... taken the client to lunch."

"Yassuh."

That should buy me some time. Philippe listened, as Jean Baptiste repeated the message word for word. The messenger left, and Jean came to the kitchen.

"He said he tell yo' papa. He look lak he b'lieved it."

"Good. I'll take that breakfast now," Philippe said, skimming the straight razor over his chin. In a short time, he'd eaten, dressed, and left the house. He stopped first at Desiree's to give her the details and assure her that Mariette would be all right. "You must say nothing to M'sieur Delissard," he warned, with such a serious mien that Desiree nodded. "If you do, he'll send for Soniat, and the man will come in brandishing a sword."

"Oh, *Mon Dieu!*" Desiree said, crossing herself. "I won't say a word."

Philippe knew she was frightened enough to keep that promise. "Madame Delon," he said, "I want to marry your daughter. I've wanted that ever since I met her. I knew how impossible it seemed, but as you know, I still took her to meet my parents."

"I know that. I was so afraid she'd be shamed."

"They refused us their blessing, but we're going to be married secretly on Saturday."

Desiree's eyes opened wide. "I hope she recovers quickly. It would mean everything if she were married before Soniat came back."

"I understand that."

Desiree, seeing the heightened state of his emotions, placed a gentle hand on his arm. "You should know that she never would have agreed to *plaçage* with Soniat, except that..."

"Yes, I know. Her father struck you."

"Yes. And he struck her, too, more than once, it shames me to say. But in the end, she was protecting me. That's what made her give in to him."

He nodded, frowning. "We'll marry as soon as she's well, Madame. But for now, she's a sick girl, and I'm taking good care of her. Just promise me to tell no one where she is."

"I promise."

Philippe was about to take his leave when Desiree reached up and planted a kiss on his cheek. He smiled down at the pretty mulattress, then took her in his arms and hugged her.

His second stop was Caldwell's home on Esplanade Avenue, six blocks from the river. It was a narrow, two-storied house with a leaded glass door downstairs and a wrought-iron balcony upstairs. He tied his horse's reins to a small iron lawn jockey and approached the building. At the door, he dropped the knocker.

In a minute, a pretty little woman, some ten years older than Caldwell, opened the door. His wife? Philippe had never seen her before. When he'd come here to find out where Mariette was some weeks ago, Caldwell had been alone.

"Yes?" the woman asked. Her dark hair, tied in a knot at the nape, was disheveled, her clothes untidy.

"Madame Caldwell?" he asked politely.

"Mrs. Caldwell," she said, smiling.

"My name is Philippe Grillet," he said in French. "I'd like to see M'sieur Caldwell."

"Excuse me, I speak no French," she said.

"Oh! Well, I speak English... a little. I am learning. Is Mister Caldwell at home?" he asked in English.

"Yes. Come in." She led him into the first parlor. "Sit down," she said. She was not shy about looking Philippe over thoroughly. She tilted her head to one side coquettishly, gazing into his eyes, examining his clothes. "I'll call him," she said.

Everyone knew that when Caldwell married her she was a beautiful, wealthy widow. He'd dragged her with him from one Southern playhouse to another, until at last he'd settled in New Orleans and become a property owner, an entrepreneur, the holder of a franchise for gas illumination, all due largely to her fortune. Philippe wondered how she liked her life now, with her husband so seldom home. Did she know about his womanizing?

Caldwell entered in his dressing gown and house slippers, his hair in disarray, as if he'd just gotten out of bed.

"Mister Caldwell," Philippe said, "I'm glad to see you were not hurt in the fire."

"I was lucky, Mr. Grillet," Caldwell said, falling into an over-stuffed chair and waving Philippe toward a settee. "Sit down, please. Would you like some coffee?"

"No, thank you."

"I was at the stage door when I heard the cry of fire. I would have gone back inside to help the others, but people were jamming the exit, and there was no way to get back in." Whether or not that was true, Philippe would never know. Caldwell was a coward, but the story sounded plausible. "You've come to try to find Mariette again," Caldwell said. "Did you try the New Levee house?"

"No. This time, I've come to tell *you* where she is."

Caldwell's face lit up. "You mean you know? I've been worried to death."

"She's at my townhouse. I was in the theater when she was struck by a falling beam. I carried her to my rig and took her home. My doctor says she'll be fine, but she must rest."

"So!" He was smiling broadly, enormously pleased. "Mister Grillet, I can't tell you how grateful I am to you, for rescuing my actress and for ending my anxiety. Please, you must stay for lunch." He got up with a sudden burst of energy.

"No," Philippe said, irritated that Caldwell had the audacity to think he had done it for him, and galled that the man was only relieved because she was his actress. How petty he was and self-centered! "I have other errands, M'sieur," Philippe said, "and then I must return to Mariette." He pulled on his driving gloves as he spoke. "I came to see how you were. Mariette will want to know. And to tell you she was well. But more than anything else, I came to make sure you would not go inquiring as to her whereabouts. I must insist you tell no one where she is, especially not Louis Soniat. He will challenge me if you do. I can easily kill the bastard, but I don't want that to upset Mariette's recovery. The doctor said she was to have rest. Anything else, and you may no longer have an actress, do you understand?"

"I do. Indeed I do, Mr. Grillet," Caldwell said. "You can rest assured no one will know of her whereabouts from me."

"I'm going to count on that." Philippe's voice was threatening.

"Of course," Caldwell said. Philippe noticed a trace of perspiration on the actor's brow, although the day was cold.

"For Mariette's information," Philippe continued, "were any of the other actors or actresses hurt?"

"Yes." Caldwell's bushy eyebrows came together in a frown. "A fine young man, Patrick Duffy, one of our new actors this season, died this morning at Charity Hospital. He had inhaled a great deal of smoke."

"I'm sorry."

"Three actresses were taken to the hospital, but they're home now and well. They sent me word this morning."

"That's good," Philippe said. "And the patrons?"

Caldwell shook his head. "Fifty people killed by fire or smoke or falling timbers." He shook his head. "The worst theater tragedy I've seen."

Philippe shook his head. "I'm so sorry. What about the theater?"

"Burned to the ground. Nothing left." He stopped suddenly, gazing past Philippe, as if seeing once again the inferno in his mind's eye. "The fire started in a coffin factory to the rear of the building. Do you know the place?"

"I do. Yes."

"It spread to the theater workshop, where paints were kept, and you know how highly flammable they are." Philippe nodded. "Well, in minutes, it was out of control, before anyone even knew about it. I think Mariette was the first to smell smoke, and the audience knew when she stopped saying her lines, there might be fire in the house."

"Well, be thankful to Mariette that more people weren't killed."

"Oh, I am. But what worries me is that all those people will be wondering where she is. And *how* she is."

Philippe scratched his chin with his gloved fingers. "Well," he said at last, "they'll just have to go on wondering, now won't they?"

Caldwell nodded vigorously. "Yes. Oh, definitely yes. They will have to."

Philippe left the house and ran down the steps. He mounted his mare, snapped the reins, and took off at a gallop. He had one more stop to make.

At Grillet and Son, he greeted his father.

"What's the matter, Philippe?" Grillet asked. "You look pale today. Are you ill?"

"I went to meet the ship, but it didn't show up," Philippe lied. "I checked at the steamship office, and they told me it wasn't due in till next Wednesday. I guess I marked my calendar wrong. I have been a bit off lately. Raw throat and a bit of fever last night."

"That so?" His father appeared concerned. "You've been working too hard, *mon fils*," he said, trying for reconciliation once again. "Take a few days off. Take care of yourself. Someone else can do the work."

Just what Philippe wanted to hear. "Thanks, Papa. I think I'll do that." He left the office without another word and was on his way home to Mariette. For tonight, at least, he'd have his beloved girl safe and sound under his roof. *Please God, let her be suffering less.* He wanted to find her feeling better so that he might spoil her and pet her and tell her about their wedding.

For now, at least, all possible dangers had been put at bay. Mariette must eat and rest and get well. A whole new life would be starting for them soon.

CHAPTER 42

"How is she?" Philippe asked Jean Baptiste.

"She still be sleepin', Michie," the black man answered.

Philippe pulled his pocket watch from his waistcoat. "Three o'clock," he said. "I was hoping she'd be awake so she could eat something. The doctor said it would help her headache. What have we got in the house, Jean? You may have to go to the market."

"Ah had some carrots an' taters an' snap beans fum de vendah dis mawnin,' an' a nice peice of soup meat in de pantry. Ah made some soup fo' de lady. Dere's enough fo' us, too. Made a big pot in de cookhouse. An' ah fix some egg custard. Dat be good fo' sick peoples."

"Wonderful, Jean. You're a jewel. Now that I'm here, take a run down to the bakery and get a French bread and something light for Mam'selle, maybe soup crackers or melba toast. Get all three." He gave Jean Baptiste a bill. "By the time you get back," Philippe said, "she should be awake and she'll be hungry. You could fix her tray then."

Jean Baptiste left by the side door, and Philippe ran up the steps to the guest bedroom, to his darling girl, his beloved. He couldn't wait to feast his eyes on her, to hold her hand. He let himself into the room where the shutters had been closed against the brightness of mid-afternoon. Mariette lay on the bed in the darkness, still sleeping, the covers thrown aside. He felt like an intruder gazing wickedly at a goddess.

She lay on her side, her features profiled against the pillow, her hair a mass of shining ebony tangles, the bandage on her forehead pushed askew. One hand was beneath the pillow, the other on the sheet. She was still in her camisole and pantalets, one shapely calf flung toward the side of the mattress, the small white foot hanging down. He wanted to lift the foot back onto the bed, but he dared not risk waking her, possibly to more pain.

He stood motionless, watching her, loving her. She turned onto her back, spread-eagling herself, stretching, trying to come out of a drugged, unnatural slumber. Ashamed of having invaded her privacy, he covered her with the sheet and blanket. He didn't want her waking up to the sight of him ogling her, which was exactly what he was doing.

She slept on. As silently as possible, he took off his coat, his cravat and collar, and sat in the slipper chair to wait. He watched her thick, dark lashes for a sign of her awakening, but they were motionless, like two black silken arcs against her ivory cheeks. Her jet black brows were partly hidden by the bandage; yet even in sleep, her expression was engaging. There was no color in her cheeks, but a luminosity he had seen only in paintings.

Her throat was fair and slender. Her luscious breasts, partly visible above the covers, rose and fell with her even breathing. Hurting with passion for her and not daring to touch her, he rested his head on the mattress. Only the slightest creak came from the mattress ropes, but it resounded in the quiet room, an accompaniment to Philippe's smothered groan.

"Philippe," she said softly.

His head was up. His hand reached for hers beneath the covers. It was warm and soft and pliant in his own. "My love," he said. "How do you feel?"

"Did all those people die in the fire?"

"No, *mon ange*, don't think about that now. You have to get well. How is your headache?"

"Better."

"I'm so glad. But take care. Don't make any sudden moves."

"I won't, but if you're going to be my nursemaid, I'll have to ask you for a few things."

She was better. Sweet Jesus! She was so much better. "Like what, dear heart?"

"I need a *pot de chambre*, a bathtub of hot water, and some food. In that order."

"Oh, Mariette. Beloved. You don't know how happy I am to be your nursemaid." He kissed her hand, hesitated, then took her small face between his hands and brushed her lips with his. "I get no pay," he said with a half-smile, "but I do expect special privileges."

She smiled for the first time since the fire. How glorious to see that dimple once again. He walked around her bed, opened the door to the commode, and took out the *pot de chambre*, lifting its china cover.

"Do you need help getting up? Or *on?*" he asked. "Don't be embarrassed, my love."

She was blushing furiously. "I can get up," she said. "Just go get the other things, and please leave the room. Quickly."

She was smiling when he left. He wanted to sing on his way downstairs to the kitchen. Jean Baptiste had brought the soup kettle into the house and hung it on one of the pothooks in the huge kitchen hearth. The aroma was wonderful. He'd placed a tray on the work table and set it with utensils, a white linen napkin in a silver ring, a soup plate, and a teacup.

Philippe smiled. Jean Baptiste, like the doctor, wanted to play a part in her recovery. Philippe pumped three buckets full of water and hung them to heat on other pothooks over the fire, moving the soup kettle to a trivet in the corner of the hearth. When the water was hot, he'd have Jean Baptiste bring up the hip tub, and while Mariette was bathing, Jean could finish preparing her tray.

Philippe went up to his own room to look for the bar of lavendar soap he had bought for his mother. He took a thick length of toweling from his dresser, a hairbrush from his high-boy, a cotton nightshirt and a soft new bathrobe from his armoire. They would be enormous on her, but she could wear them while Jean Baptiste laundered her underthings.

It would be awkward taking the *pot de chambre* from the guest-room. Also, if she were not strong enough to get in or out of the tub, she would be embarrassed if he had to help her. They had never seen each other naked. Just the thought of it was enough to set him on fire—but he would not make a mistress of Mariette. She was going to be his wife. Until then, he'd keep his hands off her, if that was possible.

CHAPTER 43

The knocker sounded. "Damn!" Philippe said. Frowning, he rushed through the corridor and opened the door to see his sister Jeanine standing on his doorstep, carpetbag in hand, like a waif who needed shelter.

"What on earth...?" Philippe began, a smile turning up the corners of his mouth, but she interrupted.

"Papa sent word you were sick, so I came to be your nurse. Now what in the world are you doing out of bed?" With those words, she walked past him into the house, dropped her carpetbag on the floor, and skimmed her hat in the general direction of the hat rack.

Philippe laughed out loud. He put his arms around his sister and hugged her tight. Jeanine was so outrageous, she always amused him, especially when she shocked their mother. And here she was, his only ally where Mariette was concerned, to do the things he could not do for her.

"What's the big brother act for? You must want something," she said brashly. "I smell soup, and I'm starving."

"Jeanine, come into the parlor and listen to me. Can you keep quiet for a minute?"

"Sure," she said, following Philippe and plopping herself on the settee in her tomboy fashion.

"Do you know Mariette Delon?" he asked.

"The actress? Yes, I know of her. Why?"

"Well, she's here."

"Here?" She pointed toward the floor. "Under this roof? You mean you know Mariette Delon?"

"Yes. So do you. She's the beautiful young lady I brought to *Belle Fleur* for our parents to meet."

"That Anne-Marie Something?" Jeanine smiled.

"deBoisblanc. Yes, she's the one. We made up that name."

"But why?" Jeanine giggled. "I don't understand."

"I didn't want Maman and Papa to think 'theater' and immediately rule her out as an unworthy wife for a great catch like me," he said, facetiously, teasing his sister.

"I thought she was simply gorgeous," Jeanine said, "but Papa said you can't marry her. What're you going to do now?"

"Marry her anyway. I'll be dismissed from the family and the business, but I'm still going to marry her."

Jeanine gasped. Philippe smiled at her reaction to his news. For once, he had astonished her.

"How...? When...?"

"Keep still and I'll tell you." He related the story of the fire, of his rescuing Mariette and bringing her to his apartment, and of the pain she'd suffered since last night. For once in her life, Jeanine was speechless. Recovering at the end of his story, she had a dozen questions.

"Has she seen a doctor? Who knows about her being here?"

Philippe answered her questions. He told her he'd let her in on the details of the wedding as soon as he'd discussed them with Mariette, but she would have to promise to keep his secret.

She made an X over her heart with her index finger and pantomimed locking her lips and throwing away the key.

Philippe chuckled. "Now, first of all, I'm not sick. I just told Papa that so I'd have a few days off to work things out. Thank God he sent *you* here, instead of Maman."

Deirdre beamed. "Can I go upstairs and see her? Is she in your room?"

"No, you devil! She's in the guest room, where she belongs, as this establishment's most illustrious guest...ever!"

He had said the words theatrically, and Jeanine giggled. She was the same age as Mariette and yet so different. She was not nearly as mature and ladylike as Mariette, but a lot more brash and outspoken. She was totally herself, in her manners and style of dress. She was a rebel. She did what she wanted to do, parental rules notwithstanding. She had liked boys for as long as Philippe could remember, and he was sure she not only knew about sex, but might have tested the waters already.

"I could use you as her nurse for a day or two. Would you be willing?"

"Of course!" she answered. "I can't believe this. I'm going to be a nursemaid to Mariette Delon, that gorgeous actress. Wait'll I tell..."

"You can't tell anyone." He did the lock sign on his own lips. "Remember?"

"Oh, sure. I won't. Just a slip of the lip, big brother."

Philippe got up and walked out into the corridor, his sister at his heels. "We'll talk more about it later. Now go on up and help her with the commode. Here," he said, leading her to the hat rack, where he'd put the things for her bath when Jeanine knocked at the door. "Take all this up to her, and tell her a tub and hot water are on the way."

"Oh, Philippe! Lavendar soap! I love it." She rummaged through the pile. "What's this? Your nightshirt?" she fairly shrieked.

"Why don't you open the window and shout it out, Jeanine? I think someone on Chartres Street may not have heard."

"Sorry!" she whispered.

"I had no choice. I have nothing else for her to wear."

"Well I do. She can wear the nightgown and robe I brought for myself. What's she wearing now?"

"Her underwear. You know, the cotton thing with the straps, and the long drawers?"

Deirdre smiled wickedly. "You saw her in them?"

"Yes. What else was I to do? You hadn't come yet." He smiled.

"Oh, Philippe," she said, hugging him with the towel and bathrobe between them, "I love you. I'm so glad I came." When he shushed her, she whispered, "I'm so glad I came."

"So am I, Sweets. Now get on up there, and here, take your carpetbag," he said, putting it on top the pile of things in her arms. "And remember, she's still quite ill. Remind her of who you are, and keep your voice down." He gave her a smack on the rump to speed her on her way.

Jean Baptiste returned with hot French bread, soup crackers, and melba toast. The warm bread filled the house with a delectable aroma. Philippe told him Jeanine had come and he watched as a smile lit up Jean Baptiste's face.

"Oh, Miz Jeanine be perfect. She can do de ladies' things, an' no need to worry 'bout her. She kin keep a secret, and she love devilment, so dis oughta suit her fine." He chuckled.

The hip tub was soon deposited in the bedroom, followed by bucket after bucket of steaming water. Jeanine had put the soap in the tub, and the bedroom smelled of lavendar and came alive with Jeanine's chatter.

First, she put the covered chamber pot outside the door, to be disposed of later. Then, she arranged the towel and face cloth and hairbrush on the footlocker at the end of the bed. Her running commentary delighted Mariette.

"Here, let me pin your hair on top your head," she told Mariette. "Then get undressed and slip into the tub and soak a bit. That ought to pick up your spirits. Nothing makes you feel better than a good hot bath. And when you're ready, I'll scrub your back."

Mariette soaked and Jeanine chatted. She reported the news about Philippe getting a few days off by playing sick and explained that that was the reason for her being here. She said nothing about the casualties from the fire, which she'd read in the morning paper, thinking Philippe might not want Mariette to know about them.

"Did the theater burn down?" Mariette asked, as if reading Jeanine's mind.

Jeanine hesitated for a moment, then answered bluntly, "To the ground."

"Was anyone killed?"

"I don't know," Jeanine lied. "Philippe will have to get a newspaper. He'll tell you later." And then to distract her, she said, "I loved your play, *Lock and Key*." She clasped her hands before her breast. "When you cried for your lover, I cried buckets, even after I got home."

Mariette smiled. But her smile was soon replaced by a frown. "I thought you didn't know me when I came out to *Belle Fleur*," she said.

"Well, I felt as if I'd seen you before. You know the feeling you get. I went to the play with my friend and her mother while I was spending a few days in town. And from the stage, you looked older...different than you did at *Belle Fleur.*"

"It's the makeup," Mariette said.

"I guess. And Philippe called you Anne-Marie Something, so I didn't really put it all together."

Mariette nodded. Immersed in the steaming bath, she rested against the back of the tub. As soon as she closed her eyes, she was back in the burning theater, where hundreds of helpless people were climbing over seats and pushing past one another to get to safety. It haunted her. It probably always would. Surely many must have died.

"Does your head still hurt?" Jeanine asked.

"A little. This bath feels wonderful. I'd stay in longer, but I'm famished."

"Then let me help you wash. Jean Baptiste has soup on the hearth and hot French bread."

"Mmmmm."

Jeanine lathered the cloth with fragrant lavendar soap and covered Mariette's body with the velvety white foam. Minutes later, she was pouring rinse water over her, patting her dry with the thick toweling, then pulling her own cotton nightgown over Mariette's head. Weak from the steaming bath, Mariette let Jeanine help her back into bed.

Jean Baptiste knocked at the door to announce he'd left her tray outside.

"Eat first," Jeanine said, getting up. "Then I'm going to brush your hair." She piled pillows against the headboard, and Mariette leaned against them. Jeanine carried the tray in. They both looked at it, then at each other, and smiled. A steaming bowl of dark, rich soup with vegetables and beef floating in the broth was surrounded by buttered slices of crusty French bread, cup custard, and a cup of hot tea.

"That looks wonderful," Mariette said. "Aren't you going to have some?"

"You bet I am," said Jeanine. "I'll go down and have Jean fix me a tray, and I'll bring it up and keep you company. Can you manage without me for a few minutes?"

"Oh, yes."

When Philippe heard what was going on upstairs, he told his sister, "If you think you're going to have all the fun, you're wrong, Sweets. I'm coming up, too."

Jeanine smiled warmly at her brother. In minutes they were upstairs in the guest bedroom, Philippe sitting on the side of the bed, facing Mariette. He was wielding the soup spoon, feeding her, then stopping to break off chunks of hot buttered bread, which she devoured. He pulled her napkin from her lap, tucked it into the neckline of her gown, and used the end to catch the butter at the corners of her mouth, restraining the urge to lick it off himself.

"You've lost your bandage somewhere," he said, looking at the thin red scar on her forehead.

"In the tub, I guess," Mariette said.

"Well, it's healing well." Her tangled hair had formed little corkscrew curls all around her face. And her cheeks, glowing from her bath, were like December roses. His desire for her was so intense, his breathing was ragged. The spoon trembled in his hand. She opened her mouth and took the soup, and he heard himself groan. Every act he shared with Mariette was becoming a sensual experience.

Their eyes met and she understood. She touched his hand and took the spoon from him. "I'll feed myself," she said softly. And she did, as quickly and ravenously as Jeanine, who was gobbling hers noisily, sitting in the slipper chair in the far corner of the room.

Mariette ate every morsel and then lay back, sighing with satisfaction. She closed her eyes and lay very still, looking weak from the effort of bathing and sitting up to eat.

"I want you to rest now, *mon amour*," Philippe said, removing her tray.

"But I was going to brush her hair," Jeanine complained.

"Later, little sister," he said kindly. Jeanine nodded. And Mariette made no protest when they both left the room.

CHAPTER 44

An hour later, Philippe crept back into the guestroom and sat in the slipper chair. In his shirt and trousers, unemcumbered by coat and cravat, and wearing his comfortable house slippers, he dozed in the quiet room. He'd had little sleep the night before. Early shadows of the short winter day were beginning to invade the bedroom.

Mariette's eyelids fluttered, then opened. "Every time I open my eyes, you're here," she said, smiling.

Startled, he awakened. He took her hand and rubbed her knuckles gently. "Is that bad?"

"No. That's good," she said. "Will Jeanine be coming up?"

"No."

"She's been so good to me, lending me her nightgown and bathrobe. She wanted to brush my hair. It really needs it."

"I told her I'd do it. I asked her to stay away." Philippe smiled. "She understands." Mariette returned the smile. "May I take it down now?" he asked.

She nodded. She sat up in bed and turned her back to him. Philippe lit the night candle beside the bed and began searching for hairpins in the tangled mop. They were deep inside the dark mass and not easy to find, but the chore was a delightful one. He put the pins, one by one, on the nightstand and reached for the hairbrush on the footlocker.

He brushed the knots from the ends first, and she lolled her head and sighed, enjoying the attention. Then he began taking one thick strand at a time and working through it. It was like fine ebony silk, but in massive quantities, and he relished the feel of it in his hands. When he'd finished, he twisted the rope of hair and let it fall over her left shoulder.

"Your neck is so lovely," he said huskily. He looked at her nape, soft and white and powdery from her bath, and pressed his lips to it. Unable to restrain himself, he slipped his hands under her arms to find her breasts and cradle their fullness in his palms. He heard her quick intake of breath, matching his own uneven breathing. She turned around to face him, flushed and trembling. She lifted one hand to touch his face.

"Philippe, make love to me," she begged.

Heat flashed through Philippe's arteries. He tried to recall all the vows he had made to keep his hands off her body, but somehow he couldn't bring them into focus. He wanted her as he'd never wanted a woman in his life.

She slipped her arms around his neck and drew him to her. He kissed her mouth, gently at first for fear of hurting her, then taking her lips hungrily, with an almost-devouring kiss. He bit at her full lower lip, groaning with desire for her. Then, letting go his self-imposed restraints, he delved with his tongue for the sweet inner recesses of her mouth. She went limp in his arms. A moment later, she pulled off her nightgown and turned back to embrace him.

"Beloved," he said huskily, "we shouldn't. You need rest."

"Philippe," she whispered, "I need *you.*"

"I'm going to marry you, *mon ange.* I said we would wait for that. You're not a *placée* to me."

"Don't talk, Philippe. Don"t analyze. Make love to me."

There were no more words. He got out of bed and locked the door. He gazed at her in the flickering light of the candle, her cheeks like roses, her eyes glassy with desire. He pulled off his slippers and rushed to be rid of his clothes. At last, he blew out the candle and slipped into bed.

She moved over to make a place for him, and he slipped into her bed, warm from her body and scented with her bath powder. He lay full length beside her, pulling the featherbed over them both. He took her in his arms, and when they came together, her breasts pressed against his chest, her thighs warm against his, the contact was heart-stopping. He held her to him gently, and although he was already painfully aroused, he did not rush. He wanted to give her pleasure when he made love to her. He knew he could not long hold back the passion that was building inside him. But to his surprise, she too was so driven by urgent yearnings, so filled with need to be possessed in loving tenderness, that when he lay above her and slowly entered her, she lifted herself to accept him completely.

Sweet primal sounds of need came softly from her throat surrounding him like a chorus of sirens, carrying him beyond his need to breathe. Together they found their rhythm of love, a driving, maddening force that broke at last, when a shuddering release overtook her. She caught a breath, an almost soundless cry, like a rose petal falling, and he, who had yearned for her so long, was close behind with his own burst of fire. Then, sweetness, beyond all sweetness, and peace.

For a few moments, he lay atop her, consumed with the delight of her warm body beneath him. Then, taking her with him, he rolled to his side. He reached out his free hand to gather her long hair, now fanned out across the pillow. He twisted it in a rope and pulled it down over her shoulder. He rubbed her forearm gently. Now that he had possessed her, he could not stop touching her, kissing her, reveling in her.

They lay on their pillows, eyes seeking eyes, and in the meager light, he studied the fullness of her lips, the dimple at the corner of her mouth. When she laid her hand on his chest, exploring it, his body responded instantly. Her fingertips skimmed the center of his chest, and he groaned in renewed desire, from a pit that seemed endlessly full.

"Oh, Mariette," he whispered hoarsely, "you don't know what you do to me." He kissed her deeply. They lay together, sated, gloriously alive, silent except for murmured endearments and sweet gratuitous kisses. Neither wanted to move, for fear of disturbing the golden moments of waning pleasure. Limbs entwined, they rested.

To Philippe, it was a completion. Whatever had been lacking in him before--the yearnings, the needs--all were now filled, and filled to overflowing. He knew that whatever happened to them tomorrow or the next day, neither he nor Mariette would ever willingly depart from this fulfillment. It would be their reward for all the obstacles they might face and all the roadblocks along the way.

Mariette rested in his arms, luxuriating in the moment, wishing it to last forever. She had astonished herself by experiencing such total sensual fulfillment. After all she'd been through with Soniat, she had never expected to know such fierce carnal pleasure. She supposed that was love. With her face resting in the curve of Philippe's shoulder, she smiled a small proud smile into the darkness.

CHAPTER 45

In the morning, Philippe walked into the dining room, fresh from his bath and shave, in a dark blue frock coat, tan riding pants, and leather boots. Jeanine was already at the table eating her breakfast, and he wasn't eager to face her. She'd undoubtedly spent the night in his bedroom, since he'd remained with Mariette behind closed doors in the guestroom. Jeanine would take one look at him and start zinging her barbs. If there was one thing he didn't need this morning, it was teasing from his kid sister.

Philippe helped himself to eggs and sausages from the salvers on the sideboard. He sat down at the table and poured his coffee, trying not to meet his sister's gaze. But looking up once, he saw her eyeing him wickedly from beneath lowered lids.

"I take it the patient has improved," she said.

"She has."

"Some treatment that must have been!" she teased.

Philippe's nostrils thinned. His eyebrows came together in a frown. Why should he have to report on his love life to his sister? "Look, Jeanine, I don't need a chaperone. I appreciate your help but..."

"I'm one person too many this morning, right?"

"No, Sweets. Forgive me. Just don't tease me. I'm a bit on edge about anyone finding out Mariette is here."

"Sure, Philippe. I understand."

"I have to go get a morning paper. I have to know what the reporters are saying about Mariette."

Jeanine said, "I heard Papa say yesterday morning there was a story in the paper about an actress that was missing, kidnapped or something during the fire. I didn't pay much attention. Do you think they meant Mariette?"

"Possibly. I've got to find out," he said. He looked at Jeanine. "I promised I'd tell you my plans."

He took a sip of his coffee. "Is today Friday?" he asked.

"Yes."

"Well, tomorrow, if Mariette is well enough, she and I are going to be married." Jeanine sucked in a silent gasp. "I've made arrangements with a priest at St. Patrick's Church for 9:00 o'clock Saturday morning. I have both our birth certificates in my coat pocket."

"Oh, Philippe, that's wonderful!" Jeanine said.

Philippe smiled at his sister's pleasure. "Now I need you to stay for today to look after her. I have a few urgent errands to make. By the way, how would you like to stand up in your brother's wedding?"

"Oh, Philippe! I'd love it!"

"Good! Then I'll make my errands and get back here."

"Don't rush."

"Thanks. Now go up and see to my lady's needs. She'll be wanting her breakfast, too, I think."

"I'm going," she said, leaving the table. She was getting that devilish gleam in her eye again. "I'm sure she must be famished."

Philippe followed her to the stairway, taking careful aim before throwing a fringed pillow at her backside. She started running, and then he heard her giggling until the sound was swallowed up behind the guestroom door.

CHAPTER 46

After breakfast, Philippe left the house on his mare. He stopped at the newsstand in the French Market, picked up a copy of *L'Abeille*, dropped some change in a wooden box, and began reading as he walked back to his horse. The story of the fire took half the front page, and this was the second news day on the subject. His eye went to the banner headline.

MARIETTE DELON, STAR INGENUE, STILL MISSING

Philippe felt as if he'd been punched in the stomach. Now Soniat would know, and he'd come running. Philippe would have to get her out of his apartment and into a safe hiding place without delay. He read on.

Not a word has been heard of the whereabouts of the actress Mariette Delon since fire razed the Camp Street Theater Tuesday night, nor has anyone come forward to identify the man who ran up on the stage and carried away the unconscious actress.

When the fire broke out, this courageous young woman told the audience that the theater was on fire and they were to run for their lives.

Lies! Philippe thought. She did nothing of the sort!

Immediately after this warning, she ran toward the back of the stage, where she was hit by a falling beam and knocked unconscious. What happened to her after that is a mystery. A reliable source, however, saw a young man pick her up and carry her off, no doubt a kidnapper in search of ransom. Has she died since then? Is her abductor afraid to admit his guilt, thinking he'll be hanged for murder?

James Caldwell's new star, acting in her first major role, has disappeared. Caldwell himself knows nothing of her whereabouts, nor could he offer any insight into the mystery.

Anger almost suffocated Philippe. The mystery was that the lying muckraker who'd written the story was still walking around alive. If he'd been free to disclose himself, Philippe would have walked into the newspaper office and broken his writing fingers.

An older gentleman who had accompanied the actress to the theater every evening cannot be found for questioning. One of the actresses told this reporter about their relationship, but had no idea who the man was or how he could be reached.

Philippe slapped the newspaper against his palm. How dare they! How dare they ruin her reputation, writing about her relationship with an older man?

The reporter wrote on about the young actor from Ireland, Patrick Duffy, who had died in the fire. Then came a more complete list of casualties, including some whose bodies had been dug out in the last twenty-four hours. But the reporter had written Mariette's story first, with headlines, knowing her current popularity would sell newspapers.

Philippe mounted his mare and sat in the saddle staring into space, wondering if Soniat had the New Orleans newspapers delivered to his plantation in Jefferson City. If so, he was probably already on his way back to search for Mariette. He decided to take the newspaper back to his townhouse so Mariette could find out what was going on.

He felt a prescience of imminent danger, of Delissard finding his townhouse, of Soniat breathing down his neck. He must find a place to hide Mariette where the lecher couldn't find her, at least until tomorrow morning, when they would be married. After that, Soniat could never hurt her again.

Back home, he ran up the stairs and knocked at the guestroom door.

"Come in," Mariette answered.

He found her sitting up in bed, propped against her pillows. Jeanine was sitting on the slipper chair, reading to her.

"Would you mind waiting downstairs for me, Sweets?" Philippe asked his sister.

Jeanine nodded and left the room.

Philippe looked back at Mariette. Her hair was braided in a thick, shining rope that hung over her shoulder. Her radiant smile told him she was still basking in the glow of last night's love-making. It almost made him forget the urgency of his mission. She held out her hand. He took it as he stood beside her bed.

"You're gorgeous this morning," he said.

"You're gorgeous yourself," she said. "Sit down here, by me," she said, patting the place on the side of her mattress.

Philippe sat and took her in his arms. Once again, he was so fully aroused, he could have easily slipped into bed beside her, but he had vowed to himself that he would not make love to her again until they were married. He backed away and glanced at the wound on her forehead. "That gash," he said, gently moving her hair to the side with his fingertips. "It's healing nicely. Does it hurt?"

"Nothing hurts." She almost purred.

"Tell me how you feel."

"Reborn," she said, smiling brightly. "I feel…"she stopped and stared at the ceiling, choosing her words carefully. "I feel as if I've been rescued from a life that was revolting to me and transported to paradise." She pressed her cheek into the palm of his hand. "Here with you, I can be a whole, happy, radiant being. It breaks my heart that it took a tragedy like the fire to make it happen, but I cannot help it if I am consumed with love for you."

Philippe took her in his arms. "My darling girl," he said breathlessly. "My beloved Mariette." He backed away and devoured her with his eyes. "You fill me with such joy, I am drunk with it." He, too, hesitated, trying to find the words that would be equal to his passion. He pressed his cheek to hers and closed his eyes. "I will love you till the day I die," he said.

CHAPTER 47

"I'm so worried, Philippe," Mariette said. "There are things I have to know."

"Like what, *mon ange?*"

"About the theater." A frown line marked her brow. "Jeanine said it burned to the ground."

"It did."

"Many people must have died. I have nightmares about the screams and all those people fighting to get out."

Philippe held her hands and locked eyes with her. "It was horrible, my love," he said. "I won't tell you otherwise. I was sitting in the third row behind the orchestra. Someone screamed 'Fire!' and everyone panicked. People were climbing over each other. They were crying and choking on smoke. I couldn't move. I was in shock, I guess. Then I heard a crumbling noise, and I looked up to where you were standing on stage and saw that a heavy beam was about to break away and fall. That brought me out of it. Otherwise, I might have stayed frozen to the spot."

"Oh, Philippe, it must have been terrible."

"It was a disaster. Fifty-one people killed. Here," he said, handing her the newspaper he'd carried home. "You can read about it."

"Mary, Blessed Mother of God!" Mariette whispered. "Were any of the cast killed?"

"A young actor named Patrick Duffy. Did you know him?"

"Only to say hello. He came over from Ireland as a digger for the canal. Then he tried his hand at acting. Said he'd done a bit of theater back in Dublin. Can you imagine, Philippe? He made it through the yellow fever epidemic two summers in a row in that canal, when so many diggers perished, only to die in a theater fire." She shook her head in disbelief.

"Horrible," Philippe said. "Two men from the orchestra died, too, from breathing in smoke. The rest of the casualties were all people in the audience." He shook his head. "Most of them were trampled to death or killed when the walls collapsed. They're still digging out the bodies."

A look of horror came over Mariette's features. Philippe took her in his arms again and stroked her back lovingly. After a time, she lifted her head. "All those people," she said, shaking her head. "They came to see a play, and for that they lost their lives."

She pressed her head to his shoulder. But suddenly, as if a new realization had come to her, she backed away again. "What do they think happened to me? Does the newspaper say?"

He unfolded the paper. "You can read about it. All the lies they tell about you, about how you were injured and an unknown man took advantage of your helplessness and kidnapped you."

"Oh, *Mon Dieu*! What a lie!"

"Well, that's the press. Already, they had the most dramatic story in years— certainly the most tragic— but it wasn't enough, so they made up a kidnapping."

"And is that what everyone believes?"

"I dare not ask anyone, for fear they'll think I carried you away... which, of course, is basically true."

Mariette smiled half-heartedly, but suddenly her smile became a frown, as all the possible consequences of that article began to occur to her, as they had to Philippe. She placed both hands on his lapels.

"Philippe, does my mother know where I am?"

"Yes," he said, taking her hands in his. "I sent her a note Tuesday night and went to see her yesterday morning. I told her what the doctor said and I promised I'd take good care of you."

With a sigh, she leaned back against the pillows, relieved. Then her eyes widened again. "What about Caldwell?"

Philippe nodded. "He knows, too. I went to his house. And by the way, he's fine. He just *happened* to be at the stage door when the fire broke out. He'll always manage to save his skin. I told him he'd better not tell Soniat where you are or he might be very sorry. Can you believe that egotistical bastard thanked me for saving you for *him*?"

"Forget about Caldwell," Mariette said, dismissing it as inconsequential. "Do you really think I'm in danger from Soniat?"

"Not as long as I'm alive. By the way, I told your mother not to tell your father where you were, or there would be dire consequences."

Mariette rested against her pillow and lost herself in thought. "There might be dire consequences if she *doesn't* tell him. Dire to her, anyway. Did you consider that?"

Philippe nodded, clearly aware that Desiree was a pivotal player in this drama.

Mariette frowned, as all the possible consequences of the article began to occur to her, as they had to Philippe. "If my father has read this paper," she said, "he's probably on his way back to New Orleans.

He may already be here," she said. "Should I go back to the house on New Levee Road?"

"Absolutely not! We're together now, and we're going to stay together."

Mariette smiled. Those were the sweetest words she'd ever heard, but she knew that she and Philippe were far from safe. She trusted Philippe to protect her from Soniat *and* her father. But no one had to tell her that danger lay ahead.

"I sent a note to your maid Adelle," Philippe said. "I knew you wouldn't want her to worry."

"Thank you for that."

"I told her you were well, but I didn't tell her where you were and I didn't sign my name. I was afraid she'd come to take care of you."

"Yes. She would have done that."

"Or she might have told Soniat who signed the note, and he'd know where to look for you," he said.

"How would he know? I didn't tell him your name."

"No, but you told your father, remember? Soon after the Quadroon Ball? He knows the name Grillet. He does business with *my* father, and he could get my address through him."

Mariette's breath caught. She remembered her conversation with her father. "Oh, Philippe, how could I have been so foolish?"

He held her close and stroked her hair. "Don't blame yourself. You could never have anticipated this." He moved back again to look into her dark troubled eyes. "I think you're safe here now. But not for long."

"What can we do?" she asked.

"I'll find a place to hide you, just for tonight and tomorrow morning. After that, we'll be married. I haven't told you about my new arrangements with Father Maher."

Mariette brightened. "What new arrangements?"

He smiled. "We're to be married at St. Patrick's Church tomorrow morning at 9:00 a.m."

"Oh, Philippe!" she said, drawing him close. "Can it really be true?"

"*Oui, ma belle*," he said, caressing her smooth nape with his fingers. "After we're married, you'll be safe. You'll be my wife, and neither your father nor Soniat can manipulate you then." She pressed her head to his shoulder, savoring the moment. "We'll move into the building I've rented in the American Sector, and I'll start my own business."

She allowed herself the luxury of a smile. He smiled back, happy to have given her some pleasure. He got up and stood beside the bed, still holding her hand. "Meanwhile, you must rest and recuperate."

Suddenly, she frowned, as if a new problem had just presented itself. "I'll have to get married in my Act Three costume. It's all I have with me."

"I'll get something from your mother. I have to go there anyway. But our main concern now is to get you out of here. Take a nap, *mon amour*. When you wake up, I'll have it all worked out."

Mariette nodded. Weakness washed over her. She slipped down under the covers and closed her eyes.

Philippe let himself out of the room and ran down the stairs to talk to Jeanine in the parlor. He sat beside her on the settee. "I have an idea where to hide Mariette," he said, "but I think it's best if even you don't know about it."

Jeanine frowned. "Why are you hiding her?" she asked.

"I'm sorry, Sweets, I can't tell you that. She's in harm's way. That's all I can say. Maybe some day, I'll be able to tell you the whole story, but not now."

Jeanine looked disappointed. Then in one of her quicksilver changes, she patted her brother's arm lovingly. "All right, big brother," she said. "You know I could simply die of curiosity, but I'll go along with you on this one."

"Thanks, Jeanine," he said soberly. "You're a great co-conspirator."

"Sure, because I don't know anything."

Worried as he was, he laughed. "Even if Mariette gets better today, you still can't go home yet."

"Why not?"

"Because Papa will think I'm well, and he'll expect me in the office tomorrow. And tomorrow, God willing, will be my wedding day."

"Oh, Philippe! That sounds so glorious! But why can't I just stay here?"

It's exactly what Philippe would have liked, but he knew that things might be dangerous in his townhouse before morning. If Jeanine stayed, he'd have two women to hide and protect instead of one. As well, he didn't want Jeanine to find out that Mariette had been a *placée*. Soniat was probably on his way back to New Orleans to look for Mariette, and might very well come to his townhouse. His sister would then be in on Mariette's secret. He hoped none of his family would ever know that unfortunate part of her past.

"You can't, Sweets, and it's too hard to explain. I'll tell you what. Go visit Elise. Stay the night. I'll have Jean Baptiste drive you there and come for you in the morning. If for some reason, he doesn't show up, have Elise's driver take you back home."

Jeanine nodded, but her disconcerted frown remained. "I love you, Philippe," she said.

"Love you too, little sister." He followed her through the corridor to the hat rack, where she began shoving all her things into her carpetbag.

"Can I still stand up for you?" she asked, looking disappointed.

"Maybe yes. Maybe no. Till tomorrow, we'll be living from one minute to the next. I'll go get Jean." He smiled "Jeanine..."

"Yes?"

"Thanks for everything, Sweets."

She reached up and kissed his cheek. "My pleasure."

CHAPTER 48

When Jean Baptiste returned from driving Jeanine home, Philippe was ready for his last errand. He rode away from the townhouse, heading for Desiree's house on Rampart Street. After arriving, he tied his mare's reins to a branch of an oak in a vacant lot thick with trees, just across the street from the little shotgun. He got down, sat well hidden in the brush, leaning against the oak, and prepared to wait. He felt certain that either Mariette's father or Louis Soniat would be coming here today to ask Desiree if she knew where Mariette was.

Almost an hour later, when he was dozing after a sleepless night, he heard a carriage pull up to the house. The carriage driver hopped down and opened the door. Raoul Delissard, Mariette's father, walked briskly up the path to the gallery. Philippe had never seen him with Mariette, but he remembered him as a client of Grillet and Son. Delissard knocked at the door, and Desiree let him in. Philippe took his watch from his waistcoat pocket. Twelve noon.

Philippe rubbed his eyes with his thumb and forefinger. What would she tell him? If only he could be sure of her silence. She had promised, but there was a limit to the brutality any woman could take.

At twelve-fifteen, Delissard retraced his steps to the carriage and his driver pulled away. Desiree was nowhere in sight. Philippe waited a few minutes, then ran across the street. He knocked, but no one answered. Finding the door open, he entered to find Desiree lying on the floor in the parlor.

"Madame!" Philippe cried out, rushing to her side. Her hair was loosened from the knot at her nape, and there was blood at the side of her mouth. "What happened? Did he strike you?"

She opened her eyes and tried to get up. She groaned as if in pain.

"Here, let me help you," Philippe said. He lifted her from the floor and helped her to a chair. He put a pillow behind her back. Then, hunkering beside her, he saw a swelling on the right side of her face near her eye. She had obviously been struck.

"Did you tell him where she is?" he asked. "Tell me quickly, so I can go home if he's on his way there."

"No," she said weakly. "I told him nothing. He said he read in the paper that Mariette was missing. Kidnapped. He asked if I'd heard from her. I told him no." She choked on a sob. "He hit me hard."

Philippe took a folded handkerchief from his pocket and pressed it to her lips. "I'm sorry," he said. "Is there anything I can do?"

"Go home and take care of Mariette."

"Did he say where he was going?"

"He said he'd have to go tell Soniat. I suppose he's on his way to Jefferson City. After he hit me, I saw him coming toward me again, so I said I'd received a note, trying to placate him. He asked if it was a ransom note. I said no, it just said she was safe, and I was not to worry." She shrugged her shoulders. "I thought that might appease him."

"Did it?"

She shook her head. "No. He doesn't care about Mariette's safety. He only wants her back in Soniat's house." She took his handkerchief and dabbed again at the corner of her mouth, and then handed it back to him. "He asked to see the note. I told him I'd burned it. He was furious. He hit me with his fist. Then he left."

"You were very brave, Madame," Philippe said.

She stared past Philippe. "It's the land. That's all he's ever wanted. He's talked about it for years. Now it's his, but only so long as Mariette keeps her contract." She turned her dark eyes on Philippe. "Keep her away from Soniat, please."

"You can count on that," he said venomously.

"Raoul never cared about me...or Mariette."

Philippe knew exactly where Desiree's sentiments lay. To her disbelief, Delissard had turned vicious toward her, and she was heartsick with disappointment. She knew now how little he cared for her, and her revulsion for him knew no bounds. She might be doing it for all the wrong reasons, but she'd never tell Raoul Delissard where Mariette was. It was her only revenge.

"I'll go now, Madame," Philippe said. "I've got to prepare myself for what's coming. I'll take good care of Mariette. I promise you that. And you must be strong and never tell them where she is."

"Never! You can count on that."

Philippe smiled kindly and patted her hand. "Will you please give me a few of Mariette's things, some underclothes, a nightgown, and perhaps two dresses. Daytime dresses."

"Of course. I'll put them in a carpetbag." She went quickly to the back of the house. When she returned, she handed him the things he'd requested. Then he left on a run, mounted his mare, and galloped homeward.

On his arrival, Jean Baptiste told him that Mariette had eaten her lunch and was resting. Philippe paced the downstairs corridor, running his fingers through his hair, trying to concentrate on the dangers crowding in around him. How long was the trip to Jefferson City and back again? Four hours each way? It depended on whether he came on horseback or by packet. Would he drop everything and head for the city? Or would he wait until morning?

Philippe knew that Mariette's father would give Soniat his name. If Soniat tracked him down and found them in the townhouse together, what would he do? Philippe was not worried for himself, for he could surely defend himself against Soniat. It was Mariette he was concerned about. If Soniat found her here, he'd get even with her for the damage to his pride. Philippe knew he had to hide her now and keep her hidden till the danger was past.

When he entered Mariette's room and sat on the slipper chair, she awakened, although he hadn't made a sound. He took her hand. "I stopped at your mother's house," he said.

"Was that wise, Philippe? Suppose Soniat had been there?"

"I didn't go in right away. I watched and waited from the woods across the street. I was well hidden." He told her he'd seen her father coming and going, and then repeated his conversation with her mother. Mariette winced and bit at her bottom lip.

"I've got to get you out of here," Philippe said. "Your father's on his way to Jefferson City to tell Soniat you're missing, if he doesn't already know it. Soniat will come back to New Orleans. Very soon. Your father will give him my name."

Philippe paused, as if hesitant to tell her what came next. "I have an idea," he said. "I hope you won't object to it." Mariette waited, nodding him on. "If you were to hide in Jean Baptiste's room," Philippe said, "I'd stay there with you till bed time. Then when you retire, you could take his bed. It's clean, I assure you. Jean Baptiste is a fastidious person."

"I wasn't concerned about that."

"You could lie facing the wall with a tignon wrapped around your head. If he entered the room, he'd never doubt you were my maid servant asleep for the night."

Mariette was silent for a moment. "And where will Jean Baptiste be?"

"Outside in the carriage house, keeping watch to protect us both." Philippe paused. "He will be armed, of course. And he's easily roused."

"Well, yes, if you think that's best." She looked up into Philippe's eyes and slipped her hand into his. "When do you think he'll come?"

"Late tonight or early tomorrow morning. Just to be safe, we should stay downstairs this evening to be close to Jean Baptiste's room. That way, you can slip inside quickly if necessary." He stared away, thinking. "I'll cut you a large square of fabric from an old tablecloth. Can you fashion a tignon?"

"Oh, yes." She pinched her lips together in fear. "Philippe," she said, "please hold me. I'm frightened."

Philippe sat on the side of the bed and took her in his arms. He held her close till her trembling died down. He didn't speak but kissed her brow and drew her hair gently from her forehead with his fingertips.

The evening was long. Philippe tried to keep up a running conversation, telling her about the arrangements for their wedding tomorrow, and how delighted Jeanine was that he had asked her to stand up for them. He opened the package her mother had sent and Mariette put on one of the day dresses. Then they hid the packaging, turned down the bed, and tidied the room. Philippe kept talking to keep her mind occupied, but she jumped at every sound of the house settling. At six o'clock, Jean Baptiste served them a light supper, did the dishes, and moved his coat and shoes out of the room. When the sun had set, Philippe suggested they all take their places for the night.

Standing at the door of the small bedroom, Philippe took Mariette in his arms. "Take heart, *mon amour*," he said. "You have two men here to protect you."

"I'm not worried for myself. It's you I'm worried about. And Jean Baptiste, of course."

"Don't worry, *mon ange*. I'll sleep in the guestroom where you were, and have my pistol loaded in the nightstand."

"But he might kill you both as you sleep."

"There'll be little sleep for me tonight, Mariette." Philippe lit a night candle and opened the door to his servant's neat little bedroom. He placed the candle on the nightstand. "Listen to me, Mariette," he said. "He may not come at all tonight. Perhaps not for another day or so. He may be tied up in business or out of town. Or your father may not tell him right away."

Mariette shook her head. "He'll tell him."

"If he's not here by morning, you and I will go to St. Patrick's Church on Camp Street and be married," Philippe said.

"Tomorrow!" She turned her gaze to meet his. In the light of the night candle, her eyes were wide and shining. "But Philippe," she added, remembering the point she wanted to make, "what did you do about your birth certificate? You told the priest you were Quadroon."

"And so my birth certificate shows." He allowed himself the luxury of a smile. "I changed the 'W' to a 'Q', and I did a good job of it, too." He gazed into her wide, astonished eyes, reflecting the night candle.

"But I can't let you do that, Philippe," she said.

"It's done."

"Too much is at stake."

"And none of it worth anything, if I can't have you."

"Oh, my darling Philippe!" She rested her head against his chest and circled his body with her arms. "I would've thought, if anything, you'd change mine."

"I can't. It shows "Father Unknown," and I can't change all that."

"Philippe, are you sure you want to do this? To make this sacrifice?"

"What sacrifice?" He kissed her softly. "Now wrap the cloth around your head and get settled down on Jean's cot. We'll all get through the night somehow."

CHAPTER 49

Philippe shook himself out of a light unwanted slumber. Thin slices of pearl gray light lay across his bed from between the slats in the shutters; yet, everything in the room was visible. He strained to listen. The house was silent. Outside, on the street down below, a heavy wagon groaned on the wet cobbles. His senses were attuned to every sound. A churchgoer's footsteps creaked on the gunwale *banquette*. His ear even caught the soft babble of voices in the French Market two blocks away.

After moving Mariette to Jean Baptiste's bedroom, Philippe had taken the guest bedroom. Fully clothed, he had spent the night in the slipper chair, fully awake until the silence of early morning finally lulled him, and he drowsed. Just outside his bedroom door, the floorboards creaked, awakening him, and as he watched, mesmerized, the glass doorknob began to turn. With lightning speed, he reached for the pistol in the night table drawer. But he had not yet grasped it when the door flew open and Louis Soniat burst in, his knee slamming the drawer shut before Philippe could extricate his hand.

"Where is she?" Soniat shouted, his face dark with anger. The men had never laid eyes on each other, but neither had any doubt who the other was. In a split second, Soniat pulled a kitchen knife from behind his back and raised both arms, his two hands grasping the knife handle.

Philippe saw the gleaming blade, honed to paper thinness, hovering over them both. He lunged for Soniat's waist, and the force of his shoulders pushed the breath from Soniat's lungs. Soniat fell backward, his arms coming down with the weapon but missing his target.

The men rolled over on the floor, locked together in a death grip. Philippe grabbed Soniat's wrist and held it so fiercely he trembled. The knife dropped from his fist and rattled on the hardwood floor. Philippe struggled with Soniat, forcing him to his back, and at last, he straddled him, pinning him to the floor. Philippe grabbed the knife from where it had fallen and held it to Soniat's throat, its sharp point just above the skin, ready to plunge.

"I could rip out your jugular, you bastard," Philippe said, "and I'd do it with pleasure, but I'd hang for it, and I have plans I won't let you spoil."

"You've had Mariette," Soniat said. Philippe knew he was trying to rile him. "After that, what other plans could you have?"

Philippe's teeth bared and the knife trembled in his grasp.

"Philippe," Mariette said, from the doorway. "Don't do it. Drop the knife."

Philippe looked up at her, surprised. Soniat looked too. Philippe knew that until this moment Soniat had not been certain she was here. "You should not have shown yourself," Philippe told Mariette brusquely.

"It doesn't matter now," she said. "Don't kill him. They'll hang you. Give me the knife."

Philippe sat back, still straddling Soniat, holding him to the floor. He threw the knife onto the bed and took hold once again of Soniat's wrists. Mariette came barefoot into the room in a daydress. She climbed onto the bed and put the knife under the pillow.

"Did Delissard give you my name?" Philippe asked. When Soniat hesitated, Philippe said, "Tell me, or I'll strangle you with my bare hands." He caught the man's throat in a vise of steel.

Soniat nodded, his eyes distended. Philippe released his hold, and Soniat let his head roll back, his eyes fall shut. He was breathing heavily. "He.thought she was kidnapped, but... after he saw Desiree ..."

"After he *beat* Desiree," Philippe corrected.

Soniat smirked."He decided it was all a lie," Soniat continued. "He thought...Mariette was in hiding...I can't talk this way." He coughed. "You're choking me. Let me up."

"No, *cochon*," Philippe said. "You'll tell it where you lie, or I'll strangle you and hang if I must."

Eyes closed, hardly able to speak, Soniat went on. "He said that Mariette had told him...months ago...that she was in love..with a Philippe Grillet. So..." His voice was hoarse, his speech almost inaudible. "I knew...where your father's office was, and he gave me your address."

"Did you tell my father you were looking for Mariette?"

"No," he groaned, then frowned quizzically. "Maybe I should have. He might have... come with me...and brought...every constable on the force."

"Well, that's your misfortune, isn't it?" Philippe asked, still straddling Soniat. "But now the choices are mine. I could have you arrested for breaking into my house. That would be easy. But I am a man of honor, and I'm willing to challenge you. No, better yet, I'll

292 Mary Lou Widmer

let you challenge me, since you appear to be the cuckold here."

Mariette sat motionless on the bed, her face a mask of misery. Her *tignon* had been discarded and her long hair fell around her shoulders. Her teeth were tucked into her lower lip and she was trembling visibly. She felt the sharp sting of guilt for having brought two men to each other's throats, fearing that only one would live to tell of it, and it might not be Philippe.

She looked at Soniat, holding her breath, waiting for his answer. Was it her imagination, or was there mockery in his eyes? Was he amused at the effrontery of Philippe's challenge? Perhaps he was thinking Philippe had played right into his hands, instead of killing him when he'd had the chance. Soniat was an expert swordsman. Her father had spoken often of the number of men he'd sent to the St. Louis Cemetery. No doubt he considered the duel an easy task, one he could dispose of before breakfast.

Philippe removed his hand from the man's throat and Soniat breathed easily again. "Tomorrow," he said. "At dawn in Pere Antoine's Garden behind the Cathedral."

"No, Philippe!" Mariette begged. "Let him go. Forget the duel. We have each other."

"Maybe just having you isn't enough, *ma belle Mariette*," Soniat said, getting to his feet. "I know it wasn't much when I had you." He turned to look at Philippe. "At least I broke her in for you." He smiled sardonically. "You can thank me for that."

Philippe, now standing, grabbed the man by his linens and dragged him to the wall, then pounded his head against it.

"Philippe, stop!" Mariette shrieked. She was afraid Philippe might kill him. His eyes were glazed with a crazed kind of anger. But Soniat soon recovered. He opened his eyes and raised his hands to defend himself.

Philippe dragged him out into the corridor. He dropped him like a dead weight on the upstairs landing. Without another word, Soniat picked himself up and limped down the stairs. Breathing heavily, he made it to the door and let himself out.

Soon after, Jean Baptiste came in through the back door, his head showing a bloody gash.

"Jean!" Philippe cried out from the landing, "Are you all right? Did he hit you?"

"Yassuh. Wit de horsewhip. But it ain't too bad. Ah'm sorry ah didn't stop him fo'you."

"And I'm sorry you had to take that blow," Philippe said. "Go take care of yourself, and I'll come down and make some coffee. He's gone. It's over now."

CHAPTER 50

Mariette knelt in the last pew of the Cathedral beside her mother, her rosary beads moving slowly past her fingers. In dark dresses and bonnets, with veils draped over their faces, the two women prayed in the light of a dozen votive candles flickering in a nearby rack.

Mariette had spent the night at her mother's house, rising when it was still dark to dress for five o'clock Mass. Mariette had much to pray for. Forgiveness, first of all, for having made love to Philippe. But how was she to obtain forgiveness without contrition? And she was not the least bit sorry for having known the greatest joy of her life.

Strange how the Church kept them from marrying by upholding the State laws against miscegenation. And the same Church forbade them to make love without its blessing, for that was fornication. Was there no way their love could be blessed?

If they'd come together in *plaçage*, the Church, while not condoning their union, would have winked at it, respecting the virtuous *placée* unless she was untrue to her protector.

What it boiled down to was, if she made love to Soniat, whom she despised, and to whom she *was not* married, the Church would have covertly approved the union, but since she'd lain with Philippe, whom she adored, she was a sinner who could not be granted absolution.

But this morning, it was not absolution she was praying for. It was Philippe's life. Not that she wished Soniat to die instead. In a way, he was not to blame for the situation they were in. He had offered her an accommodation, and she had accepted, albeit against her will. Then she'd given herself to another man. It was *she* who had wronged *him*, and for that, someone would pay, perhaps with his life. She prayed that both he and Philippe would consider their honor satisfied if one merely pinked the other with his rapier.

The altar boy rang the bells. The priest came onto the altar with the covered chalice. Mass began. "*Dominus vobiscum*," he prayed.

"*Et cum spiritu tuo*," the altar boys replied.

Was it possible that in little more than an hour, Philippe could be dead, condemned at twenty-nine to lie in a tomb with nothing more to mark his passing than an inscription reading, "Died on the field of honor"?

Weak with fear, she sat back in the pew, the words of the *Kyrie* washing over her. She could not concentrate on the Mass. She was recalling all that she and Philippe had talked about yesterday after Soniat left.

Philippe, it seemed, had taken fencing lessons for years. He had fought one duel and emerged the victor. Though he had taken a cut on his thigh, his opponent had been killed. The memory of that terrible event seemed not to disturb him at all.

"He had challenged me," Philippe argued, "about a political difference. After he'd drawn first blood, he was asked if he was satisfied. The bastard said no, so he dug his own grave."

Mariette had winced at this cold-blooded statement. "Doesn't it bother you that you killed a man?"

"Why should it? It wasn't murder."

"*Quelle difference?* He's dead."

"A world of difference. In a duel, one follows rules of fair play. Your opponent must be one you respect. No one would fight a duel with a man he would not have to dinner."

"How civilized!" Mariette had remarked. "So, besides becoming a master of the foil, you must learn how to take an insult politely and how to die honorably."

"That is exactly so," Philippe had answered.

"It's madness, Philippe!" Mariette had argued. "I could understand it better if you'd killed him in the heat of passion."

"But I'd have hung for that."

"I see," Mariette said.

"Of course, dueling, too, is against the law, but no official would try to enforce it or he, too, might be challenged."

Mariette shook her head. "Where did this barbaric custom come from that lets men die in their prime, while their killers go unpunished?"

Sitting in church, she considered the looseness of the laws that governed men of aristocratic blood in this wild port city. Civil law forbade duels, yet the authorities upheld the institution and let hundreds of young men die. They died honorably, of course, in a way that would comfort their families. It was idiocy!

Philippe had tried to assure her that he was well prepared. He'd served as second in many a duel. He knew weapons and he could hold his own with Soniat. She was not to worry.

Not to worry! Her world was ending, and she was not to worry! The Mass was over. She had been far away in her thoughts.

After Mass, she and her mother walked through the flagged alley alongside the cathedral to the garden in the rear. Mariette thought it sad that so green and peaceful a garden should be the site of so much bloodshed. She led Desiree to a stone bench behind a niche holding a statue of St. Anthony, the patron saint of the long-ago pastor for whom the garden had been named. She pressed her fingertip to her lips and her mother understood. They would remain silent and unseen.

Philippe had spent the night at *Belle Fleur*. He'd told her exactly what he planned to say to his father: that Soniat had insulted him and he, Philippe, had offered him a challenge; that the insult had to do with Anne-Marie, who was, in reality, Mariette Delon, the actress, whom Soniat also loved; that he'd rescued Mariette from the theater fire and taken her to his townhouse for care; and that Soniat, assuming the worst, had broken in and attacked him.

And so he had told his father his story, which was mostly truth, on the eve of what might be his last day on earth. He'd told him everything except that Mariette had been a *placée* to Soniat, and therefore a Quadroon. He'd even told him he still planned to marry her after the duel, if he survived. He *had* to tell his father the reason for the duel, she realized, since he wanted his father at his side, as his second, in full knowledge of his love for her and the circumstances that had brought them to this impasse.

No doubt Francois Grillet thought all the arrangements for the duel necessary and honorable, just as Philippe did. Creole men were all fools. But no doubt, his father despised her for bringing his son to this end. When it was over, if Philippe lived, he would still try to stop him from marrying her. But if God spared his life, she would not hold Philippe to his promise of marriage.

CHAPTER 51

Dawn was beginning to break, and the first early light brought the moss-draped oaks into view. The grass was wet with dew, and an early breeze riffled the leaves.

Carriage wheels creaked on the *Rue Royale* at the far end of the garden. A carriage stopped. Muffled sounds of male voices broke the early stillness. Then the clank of an iron weight to anchor the horses' reins. Now boots on the wooden *banquette*. Mariette's heart slammed against her ribs. She peeped around the side of the little niche.

In a space between ligustrum hedges, she could see them approaching: Philippe, in a dark frock coat, light trousers, black boots. He was dressed for a special occasion. *Mere de Dieu, don't let it be his funeral.* His father, Francois Grillet, who would be his second, was close behind, followed by two other men, cousins perhaps, for they resembled Philippe. And Doctor Meynard. She sucked in a gasp to see the doctor there. Then she remembered Philippe saying that each man could bring his own surgeon to be on hand if needed. Bringing up the rear was Jean Baptiste. Poor Jean, how devastated he would be if...no, she must not think of it.

Ten minutes passed and another carriage came rolling down Orleans Street, to the point where it ended at the *Rue Royale*. The driver stopped, hopped down to open the carriage doors, and two men got out and walked across the street to enter the garden.

From her vantage point behind the bush, she could see Soniat. He and his second were dressed to the nines. Soniat wore a top hat, a gold chain draped across his waistcoat, white linens at his throat. Soniat's second approached. Philippe was the challenged duelist; he and Soniat, in their infinite male wisdom, had agreed on that. This, it seemed, gave Philippe the right to name the weapons and the distance. And so he had chosen rapiers and a distance now being measured off in the prescribed manner.

Death by the rules. Murder in the aristocratic style. Mariette closed her eyes and shook her head. She wanted to run out to the center of the garden and scream at them all, *Are you crazy? Don't you see what you're doing? You're making a ceremony out of death. It's insane! Stop it now, before one of you is in his grave and the other walks away, guiltless and honorable! Sweet Mother of God!*

But her lips were stilled. An outcry like that, the only note of sanity in the whole mad scene, would bring Philippe's scorn upon her for having overstepped herself in a man's world. It would make him appear a coward. It would be gauche. Death was not gauche, but her outcry would be gauche.

Soniat's second raised his hand to indicate the direction. Now the case of weapons was carried to Soniat, who, as the challenger, got first choice of blades. He selected a rapier, its hilt of chased Toledo steel. He took it in one hand, hefted it for weight and balance. He sliced the air with it a few times and nodded, satisfied. Philippe took the remaining weapon. Their seconds were telling them where to stand when, suddenly, the sun rose, sending fingers of light down through the moss-draped oaks.

Philippe and Soniat took off their coats, handed them to their seconds, rolled up their sleeves. They took their prescribed places, their swords at their sides in their right hands, their left hands balled into fists behind their backs. Their blades were raised in salute, catching the morning sunlight. Mariette reached out for her mother's hand. Philippe's father gave the signal and the duel began.

The blades came together, tapping, chiming in the morning stillness, as the two men tested each other. They circled, feinting and parrying, trying each other's skills, learning the strength of each other's wrists. Back and forth they shifted, each watching for an opening.

Mariette threw back her veil. She had to see well.

The tempo quickened. Soniat lunged and Philippe parried, giving ground. Now, in a sudden display of skill, Soniat pushed Philippe back. Philippe countered, defending himself well, deflecting Soniat's strategies with his own. Murmurs from the bystanders rose and fell.

Shoes scuffled on the hardpan soil. Labored breathing rasped in the early morning air. Soniat attacked again and again, displaying the skills Mariette had heard so much about. Sweat broke out on Philippe's face and neck. His shirt clung to his shoulders and arms. His curly hair hung wet over his forehead.

Soniat fought harder, lunging and striking Philippe's sword again and again. He whirled the tip of his blade in a *riposte*. He leaned forward, and when he drew back, there was a red stain on Philippe's shirt, just above the waist. Mariette gasped. She squeezed her mother's hand. Then the two seconds were in the arena of battle, stopping the duel. Mariette held her breath. Philippe was still standing. If it could only end now!

"Sir, according to the Code," Francois Grillet said to Soniat, "I must ask you if your honor has been satisfied."

Mon Dieu, Mariette prayed, let him say yes.

Soniat looked at Philippe with loathing. *"Non!"* he said so loudly that his voice echoed in the treetops.

Mariette sobbed silently. Philippe's father sent him a sorrowful glance. How desperately he must have hoped his son would be reprieved! But as a man of honor, he stepped back to his place and announced that the match would resume.

Again the swords clanged. Again Soniat attacked. Again Philippe retreated. Mariette wondered how Philippe could fight with his wound, but his swordplay seemed to be more evenly matched than before. His competence as a swordsman was only now coming into play, like an athlete whose skills have not been tested for a while.

Soniat, sensing Philippe's ability, pounded him with a shower of attacks, pressing the advantage of Philippe's wound. All honor had gone out of the contest. Now it was a matter of revenge. Soniat was out for murder.

Philippe's strength was waning. Sweat poured from his head. The red stain on his shirtfront blossomed. The duelists' blades crossed, but when the men drew apart, it was Soniat who was ready for the first lunge. Philippe fell to the ground, and a new wound, just above his heart, spurted blood. His arm was extended along the wet grass, his hand still clutching his sword, but his head had fallen back, and his eyes were closed.

"Mon Dieu!" Mariette said, falling weakly against her mother. "Philippe is dead!"

CHAPTER 52

Mariette's eyelids fluttered. Desiree's strong arms enveloped her and drew her to sit on the stone bench behind the statue. She picked up her wrist and massaged it. Minutes later, Mariette opened her eyes. Resting her head against her mother's shoulder, she wept in heart-wrenching sobs. "He's gone, Maman. My Philippe."

Desiree held her, rocking her body with her own, rubbing her back gently. Desiree, too, was weeping, sharing her daughter's sorrow.

Suddenly, Mariette raised her head. Her dark eyes were immense in a face as white as paper. "Maybe he isn't dead," she whispered. Fighting her weakness, she got up and looked back through the ligustrum hedge. Soniat had already walked to his carriage and left the scene.

She focused on the figure lying on the ground, his left arm extended, his left knee raised as he had fallen. The two wounds, one extending beneath his ribs and across his lower left arm, the other above his heart, were bleeding profusely, red stains spreading over his white shirt. Dr. Meynard knelt at his side, facing in Mariette's direction. He felt for a pulse at the carotid artery and nodded at Francois Grillet, who was standing at Philippe's feet. "Still living," he said, "but he's losing a lot of blood. We must get him to a hospital at once."

Mariette's breath caught. "I must go to him," she told her mother.

"No, Mariette, don't go," Desiree begged, holding her daughter's hand. "His father must surely hold you to blame. *Mon Dieu*! Who knows what he'll say to you?"

"I must go," she said, breaking away. Leaving the back of the niche, she ran across the dewy grass to the place where Philippe lay, her hooded cape flying on the wind like the wings of a bird. Francois Grillet and the doctor looked up as she approached, her face wet with tears. Without a word to Francois Grillet, she looked down at Philippe. His skin had a grayish cast. His face was beaded with perspiration, now cooling in the chill breezes of early morning.

The scene was a sketch in quiet desolation, Philippe stretched out on the ground bleeding, the doctor kneeling over him, his father standing at his feet, holding the case in which the rapiers had been replaced. Mariette knelt beside him, facing the doctor. A sob escaped her throat. She extended her hand toward him, but she did not know where to touch him. His shirt was wet with blood, and she did not wish to disturb his wounds. With her face over his, she wept silently, her body heaving with the intensity of her grief.

"Will he live?" she asked the doctor.

"I can't say, Mam'selle," Dr. Meynard answered. "He's losing a lot of blood. We'll have to take him to the hospital now. I can offer you no hope."

Mariette sobbed aloud, tears streaming down her face.

"Mademoiselle Delon," Francois Grillet said. Mariette looked up at Grillet, her face a mask of pain. He was formidable in his grief, his own tears falling freely. "Please leave us now," he said. "You can blame yourself if he dies. I pray that I never lay eyes on you again."

Mariette looked back at Philippe, her lips pressed together. She lifted Philippe's hand and kissed the cold fingers. She was so weak it was all she could do to rise to her feet. But she stiffened her back and looked directly into Grillet's eyes. "I loved him very much," she said. "If we'd been allowed to marry, it would never have come to this."

Ignoring her words, Grillet handed the rapier case to the doctor, stooped down where Mariette had knelt, and lifted his son's body. As Mariette watched, her cheeks wet with tears, her hands pressed to her lips, Grillet carried Philippe to their carriage, his arm falling away lifelessly, his head hanging back. The movement of his body brought on a fresh flow of blood, and Mariette could see a trail of crimson drops falling into his palm and from his fingertips.

She ran back across the garden and into her mother's arms. Grillet could not hurt her with his words. Her heart was already broken. Philippe would die, there was of little doubt of that. Like a very old woman, she walked slowly, laboriously back to the rig and let Desiree handle the reins. Celine had a hot breakfast waiting when they returned but Mariette took only coffee. Even as she drank it, she was in another world, mesmerized by heavy sorrow. Her mother ate in silence. The quiet of the room was broken only by Mariette's sobs.

"Come, *ma fille*," Desiree said afterwards, "I'll help you change to a nightgown and you can lie down for a while."

Mariette followed where her mother led. She had neither the will nor the strength to resist. She lay in her bed and closed her eyes, not caring if she ever got up again. If Philippe died, there would be nothing to get up for, ever again.

When she awakened, she gazed blankly at the tester above her head. Her mother came in and sat in a chair at the bedside. She pulled a folded paper from her apron pocket. "A messenger came with a note this morning," she said.

Mariette turned her head toward her mother.

"It's from Soniat." Desiree said.

Mariette faced away.

"Shall I read it to you?"

"I don't care."

Desiree unfolded the paper.

"*To Mariette Delon*," she read.

"*This is to dissolve our relationship as patron and placée. I hereby reclaim possession of all property at Number 350 New Levee Road, including house, furniture, slaves, carriage, clothing, and jewelry. You have broken your contract as placée by the act of fornication with Philippe Grillet. I am no longer interested in an alliance of plaçage.*

In addition, I hereby reclaim the land granted to Raoul Delissard in Jefferson City, which action was predicated on our liaison de plaçage. I regret what has come to pass, but the fault is not mine.'"

Louis A. Soniat

Desiree held the note out for Mariette to take it, but when she did not, she folded it and put it back in her pocket. She waited. "Talk to me, Mariette. What are you thinking?"

Mariette did not turn to face her mother. "What difference does that paper make?" she asked. "I would have died before going back to him, so I'm glad he feels the same. That chapter in my life is ended."

"And the house?"

Mariette turned now and looked incredulously into her mother's eyes. "Do you think I ever cared about that house? I *hated* that house. And I'm *glad* my father lost the land. He deserves worse punishment than that, but since it meant so much to him, it will probably be enough." She paused, narrowing her eyes. "He's a vicious man, Maman."

Desiree said nothing. She looked down at her lap.

"Well, don't you know he is? He beat us both brutally. He forced me into a cruel relationship. I'll never forgive him."

"I know. You're right."

"I'll take care of you, Maman."

"It isn't that."

"Don't tell me you still love him." Desiree did not answer. "How can you?"

"No. I don't love him. I feel a great deal of anger and shame about what he did to me. To both of us. But you don't cancel out a lifetime of love so easily."

"*He* did." Mariette huffed sardonically. "I can't believe how cruel he was to you."

"But he was good to me for a very long time, when I had no one else."

"Why wouldn't he be good to you?" Mariette asked acidly. "He was getting what he wanted from you."

Desiree shook her head in shame. "I had hoped I meant more to him than that."

"You should have known what you meant to him years ago, when he married without even telling you. And *still*, he expected you to be at the front door, waiting for his visits."

"That's *plaçage*, Mariette." She caught a sob in her throat. "I knew the rules from the beginning."

Mariette touched her mother's hand in pity. "Don't cry for him, Maman. He was never worthy of you."

Desiree sighed heavily. "Well, he's out of our lives now."

"Thank God for that!"

CHAPTER 53

For the next two days, Mariette stayed in her room. She had no appetite, no strength, no desire to go on living. Desiree and Celine made custards and soups that were her favorites. She took one look at the tempting food and turned her head.

At last, on a bright sunny day, when the temperature rose to seventy-five, she got tired of being in bed. She got up, washed and dressed herself in a fresh print dress. Her knees were wobbly as she walked to the kitchen to have breakfast with her mother. Life goes on, she decided, and it's no easier lying in bed.

She asked Celine to brush her hair. Then, taking her needlepoint, she went out to the gallery and sat in a rocker. Desiree soon joined her.

"Did he die?" Mariette asked, her voice breaking on the words.

"I don't know," Desiree said. Silence fell for the space of a few heartbeats. Robins nesting in the oak tree in the front yard broke the stillness. Mariette knew her mother had something on her mind. At last, Desiree spoke. "There are wrongs on both sides, you know, Mariette," she said.

"What do you mean?"

"You blame your father for everything, including the duel. But look to yourself, *ma fille*. You slept with Philippe when you were contracted to Soniat. You should never have done that. Never!"

"I don't know how you know that, but it's true. And why shouldn't I? I loved Philippe. You knew that. I never wanted the contract with Soniat. And there's something else you didn't know. When Soniat took my virginity, he took it harshly, like an animal, thinking only of his own pleasure. He used me roughly, like a whore, never caring if he caused me pain."

Desiree grimaced. "I didn't know," she said softly.

"Can you blame me," Mariette asked, "for loving a good, caring man who treated me gently?"

Tears came to Desiree's eyes. "Oh, *ma fille*, I didn't know."

"If only we'd married that last day before Soniat came. We had plans to be married the morning before the duel."

"What plans?"

"We were to go to St. Patrick's Church on Camp Street at nine o'clock Saturday morning. A Father Maher was to marry us. Philippe had made all the arrangements. When I couldn't find my birth certificate, we went to the St. Louis Cathedral and had a copy made of my baptismal certificate. And since it would have been impossible for Philippe to change the words "Father Unknown" on my certificate, he changed his *own* baptismal papers to show Quadroon." Desiree frowned and shook her head in disbelief. And Mariette added, "He changed the W to a Q."

Desiree's jaw dropped. "Did you see it?"

"No." A small frown appeared between her eyebrows. "But I know he did it."

Desiree shrugged. "I've never heard of that, Mariette. In all my years of *plaçage*. And another thing. Knowing Soniat was coming, why didn't he bring the priest to you that last night?"

"He didn't know for sure that Soniat was coming that morning, Maman. And the priest had told him his schedule was crowded and the earliest he could marry us was Saturday." She looked at her mother and frowned. "What are you trying to say?"

"That if you'd been married, Soniat could have done nothing. If Philippe had just had a marriage certificate, you would have been safe."

"Well, I know that. And I *was* safe. It was Philippe whose life was in danger. But he was so confident he could win over Soniat."

"Yes. He was confident. That's youth." Desiree rocked slowly, in silence, watching Mariette's eyes and studying her every expression. "And if he had won the duel, what would he have done then? That's what I keep wondering."

"Why, he would have married me, of course."

"Perhaps."

Desiree and Mariette sought each other's dark eyes. After a moment, Desiree got up and left the gallery. Mariette stared out beyond the gallery. Her mother had never believed Philippe would marry her, and she hadn't been satisfied till she'd tried to plant seeds of doubt in her daughter's mind.

The following day, Mariette answered a knock at the door and smiled for the first time since the duel. Jean Baptiste was standing on her gallery.

"Jean!" she greeted the servant effusively. "Please come in. How is Philippe?"

Jean Baptiste entered sheepishly, holding his hat in his hands. "Ah come to tell you 'bout dat 'cause ah knows you be worried. Michie Philippe, he be real sick, Mam'selle."

"But he's alive. Oh, thank God! I didn't even know that." She smiled, brushing a tear of joy from her cheek. "And he's going to get well, isn't he, Jean?"

Jean Baptiste turned his hat around in his hand. "Ah hope so, Mam'selle."

Mariette frowned. "You mean, there's still a chance he might die, Jean?" She stood, facing the black man, begging him to say no.

"Ah don' t think so, Mam'selle. He be young an' strong. He got over bad things befo."

"Oh, *Mon Dieu*," Mariette said, sinking to the settee. She gathered her thoughts and then asked, "Does he ever say my name, Jean?"

"No'm, not dat ah heard."

"Are you ever alone with him?"

"Yes'm."

"And he doesn't ask for me then?"

"No'm."

"But he told you to come here today."

"No'm. I jes' come 'cause time be passin', an' ah knows you be worryin' yo'sef."

"Oh. I see. Please sit down, Jean. Tell me what happened after the duel."

Jean continued to stand, all the while turning his top hat around. "At fust, they took him to de horspital to try to stop de bleedin'," Jean Baptiste explained. "Den, dey brung him to his Papa's house on de bayou, an' dey been nursin' him dere. De doctor come evah day to change his dressin' an' look at his wounds. They be deep, Mam'selle. Plenty stitches. De big one, de one down in his arm, got to festerin' an' dey keepin' a close watch on it."

Mariette sucked in a sob. "Do you think I could come and see him, Jean?" she asked. Out of the corner of her eye, she could see her mother shaking her head.

"Oh, no, Mam'selle," he said. "I think Massa Francois, he turn you way fum de door. Ah hates to say it." He looked down, shifting his weight from one foot to the other.

There was nothing left to say. Mariette nodded sadly. She led Jean Baptiste to the door and thanked him for his visit.

CHAPTER 54

Spring came in early March with soft, balmy breezes, bushes ablaze with azaleas, and warm drizzles. From Mariette's bedroom window, she studied the flagged patio, the blaze of fuschia hibiscus bushes, and the banana tree, now greening and fountaining. And still no word from Philippe.

A robin lighted on her windowsill, chirping happily. Mariette was deaf to its song. Each day her heart grew heavier. Two months had passed since the duel, and she'd heard nothing from Philippe. No letter. Not even a message carried by Jean Baptiste.

She felt certain that Philippe had not died. She'd sent Celine or gone herself to the newsstand in the market every day since the duel to buy a paper just to check the death notices. If a man from a prominent family died, not only was he listed, but his obituary was a half column long, telling of his genealogy and his survivors. When noted personalities died, fliers were tacked to lampposts to notify the public of the times and locations of wakes and burials. No fliers announcing the funeral arrangements for Philippe Grillet had ever been posted.

Mariette reasoned that in two months time, if he hadn't died, he should have recovered. He had to be up now and walking around, perhaps even back at work. She had an almost uncontrollable urge to go up to the commission house and walk right in, just to know if he was there, and whether or not he still cared for her.

It was possible, and she knew it well, that in the last two months, in the bosom of his family, nursed and spoiled and cosseted, he could have had second thoughts about marrying her. He'd had plenty of time to realize the folly of his earlier plans, if he'd truly had any plans. Why on earth should a man like Philippe marry a woman whose grandmother had been a slave in San Domingue? Why give up his inheritance and his livelihood? Be shunned by his friends and business associates? Philippe was the most eligible bachelor in New Orleans. For him, life could be comfortable, luxurious, uncomplicated. Perhaps Desiree had been right all along in doubting his intentions. Mariette had never actually seen his altered birth certificate.

A new problem had entered the picture, making the outlook for her future as bleak as it could possibly be. For several weeks, she'd felt a queasiness early in the morning. This past week, she'd lost her breakfast twice. Her mother knew it, of course, had known it since her first complaint of nausea. They exchanged worried glances. Desiree could read her thoughts. *What will I do now?* Of course, it was Philippe's baby, thank God for that. She remembered well that she had had her courses on that Christmas day when Louis Soniat had been called back to his plantation in Jefferson City to settle the matter of the runaway slaves. And she had never had to submit to his brutish lovemaking since then.

Desolate, she sat each morning on her gallery, holding her needlepoint but never pushing the needle through the screen. It was only a prop. She watched as neighbors did their spring cleaning.

They shook out rugs, hung curtains on the line, or sat on their porches in their rocking chairs, wielding palmetto fans and sharing gossip. Mariette only nodded in their direction. She had nothing to say to them. Her heart was raw with pain.

One afternoon, when she was sitting outdoors, she was delighted to see the tall figure of James Caldwell walking from the livery stable in the direction of her house. He carried a bouquet of flowers in one hand and a paper cornucopia in the other. She got up from her rocker and ran down the steps to meet him at the gate. "Mr. Caldwell!" she cried out. "I'm so happy to see you! You look wonderful! Come in! Desiree will want to see you, too."

"These are for you," he said, handing her the flowers.

She smiled, cradling the roses in the crook of her arm. "Thank you," she said. "They're beautiful. Come inside so we can visit."

"I knew you'd been injured in the fire." He hesitated. "I would've come sooner, but I didn't know where you were. The papers said..."

"I know," she said. "The kidnapping. It was so ridiculous. Not a word of it was true. I was injured, but I'm fine now, and that's all that matters."

In the parlor, the greetings began again when Desiree saw Caldwell. "These are for you, Madame," Caldwell said, handing her the cone-shaped paper package.

Surprised, she opened it. "*Dragees*!" she exclaimed. "*Merci*!"
Soon they were all seated on the settees, sipping anisette and enjoying Desiree's sponge cake. "Delicious cake, Desiree," he said. "You must give me the recipe for my cook. I've never tasted better."

Mariette translated for her mother, and Desiree nodded at Caldwell. But Mariette was curious. Caldwell hadn't come to Rampart Street to get the recipe for sponge cake. He finished his cake and put his plate on the table beside him.

"Now!" he said, smiling. "Remember I told you, after your first appearance in *Lock and Key,* that my new theater would be opening the first week in May?"

"Oh, yes sir, I do."

"Well, my dear Mariette, the building is almost complete and in another month, at most, it will be unveiled."

"Oh, Mr. Caldwell!" Mariette exclaimed. "How wonderful!" She translated for her mother.

He smiled proudly, squaring his broad shoulders and clamping his hands on his knees. He was so vital, so full of energy, it seemed out of character for him to remain seated for a full ten minutes. "The formal opening date will be right on time. May first."

"Only two months away!" Mariette added.

"It will open with a wonderful play, *School for Scandal,* starring Edwin Forrest. He will be playing opposite Jane Placide. There are two other fine roles. I will be playing one, and I've come to offer you the other. The role of ingenue, if you are well enough to work."

"Oh, Mr. Caldwell, this is the best news I've had in a very long time. I've been able to work for weeks. Of course, I'll come. When do rehearsals begin?"

"At once. I must reorganize my troupe right away. Would Monday be too soon for you? At one p.m.?"

"I'll be there," she said. "It will be wonderful to be working again." Caldwell picked up his hat.

"But where will we rehearse, with the Camp burned down?" Mariette asked.

"At the new theater, my dear. The St. Charles. The stage and dressing rooms are finished, and I want everyone to get the feel of their new surroundings. It's so enormous, we'll have to find new ways to project our voices." He was smiling proudly. He started to get up.

"Don't go yet, please," Mariette begged. "Tell me more about it."

"Well, I wouldn't want to take away the thrill of your first glimpse, so I'll just say it's magnificent. But on April first, the protection fence will come down, and my beauty will be revealed."

Mariette gasped with delight.

"I've planned a bit of a 'do' for the second week of April," Caldwell continued, "mostly to get some free press coverage. The mayor will cut the ribbon and a band will play some of the show tunes we've done in the past. I'm having a grandstand built across the street, where my actors will sit. Then, when the speeches are over, the actors can be tour guides for the patrons. One view of the interior will whet their appetites for the first play."

CHAPTER 55

On Monday, March 15, at one p.m. the actors and actresses of Caldwell's repertory company met outside the fence of the new St. Charles, greeting one another like long-lost friends. Soon Caldwell arrived and led them down the side of the building to a back service alley, from which they could enter the new theater. They passed through a double door to find themselves at the back of the enormous stage.

Like the showman he was, Caldwell threw the switch that lit two hundred fifty gaslights in the central chandelier. The actors looked up to the ceiling and ah-h-ed in unison. The fixture was thirty-six feet in diameter, or so the papers said, an object of wonder in its own right.

From the stage, they could see that the auditorium was laid out in a horse-shoe design, edged with theater boxes. Draperies of blue, red, and gold hung across the boxes, which were separated by Doric columns. In the vast theater, four levels of seats had been provided to accommodate more than four thousand people. It was awe-inspiring.

The actors walked around, shaking their heads in amazement, examining the parquet, the pit, and the orchestra. They asked Caldwell if they might go up to the second tier to see the stage as the audience would see it. Caldwell waved them on. He had no control over them that first afternoon. There was too much to see and he was proud that they were so thrilled with his Temple of the Muses, as the newspapers were calling it. It wasn't until the second day that he managed to get them to walk through the blocking for Act One.

The last weeks of March flew by. Costume measurements were taken and the ladies in the sewing room worked feverishly to get the wardrobe ready in time. Bleachers went up across the street from the theater, and on April 1, the fence that had surrounded the new St. Charles Theater was torn down.

Residents of the American Sector crowded into the street to exclaim over the magnificent new building. The facade was embellished with figures of the Muses in high relief. People gazed, studying the facade, for there was nothing else like it in all New Orleans, and possibly in the South.

Sitting in the bleachers on April 15, Mariette felt certain she was not showing yet. She'd made herself a new pink dress for the occasion, larger in the waist than her other dresses. She thanked the Lord every night in her prayers for having learned from Madame Delacroix how to cut a pattern and sew a dress. At this point in her pregnancy, she could keep her secret and still look fashionable.

She estimated she was three months pregnant, and as yet, she had only a thickening of the waist and a swelling of the breasts as evidence of her condition. It had been many weeks since the actors had seen one another, and it was not likely that anyone would associate an added ripeness of her bosom with pregnancy.

The play was to begin May 1 and run for two weeks. She could make it that far without showing, she felt certain. Now that she'd passed her third month, her nausea had left and she was feeling strong again and healthy, except for the debilitating anguish of missing Philippe and the growing realization that he had no intention of returning to her.

She wanted to act in the play. She needed the exposure just now. It would enhance her career just in time, before she had to go into hiding. Then perhaps, after her baby was born, she could go on with her acting. She'd need an income from some source to support her child. How she would keep the child a secret, Mariette did not yet know.

With her parasol open against the noonday sun, she watched as the mayor cut the ribbon and the band played. Then at last, Caldwell invited one and all to follow his actors into the theater for a look.

Opening night came quickly. In her costume, a dress of sapphire blue brocade with a deep decolletage, Mariette looked through the peephole at the men in their black evening attire taking their seats in the parquet. On the second tier, the center boxes were filling with extravagantly dressed ladies, all jeweled to the hilt. She suddenly had a severe case of stage fright. The orchestra was tuning up. Its familiar discordant sounds made her feel at once more nervous and more comfortable.

"Five minutes," a voice called out, and quickly, Mariette ran to her dressing room for one last look at her makeup. After closing the door, she embraced her mother, trembling.

"Remember, Mariette," Desiree said, powdering her daughter's smooth white shoulders. "After your first line, you'll forget the audience."

"I know," Mariette said.

Out in the wings, she saw the curtains part and she gasped at the sight of thousands of people in the handsome horseshoe, facing the stage, smiling, waiting to be entertained in style. The ring of gas footlights illuminated the actors' faces, and when she heard her cue, she found herself gliding onstage, ready with her first line in the role of Marceline.

The curtain calls were endless. All four stars received thunderous applause. Mariette had her own ovation, both with Caldwell and alone. The audience went wild.

In the newspapers the following morning, every critic called it the hit of the season. The theater, big as it was, was sold out for the two-week run.

CHAPTER 56

In the second week of the run of *School for Scandals*, William Niblo, the noted theatrical impresario from New York City, was spotted sitting in the stage box of the St. Charles Theater. At the first intermission, word spread like wild fire that he was there. When someone like Niblo came to see a play, he was looking for talent. To all actors, working on the New York stage was the epitome of success. It elevated them to a whole new plateau in the theater world. Would Niblo be making any offers tonight? Every member of the cast was holding his breath, hoping to hear a knock at his dressing room door.

After the third act and the endless curtain calls, it was Mariette who got the nod. Desiree, working with the costumes, hid behind the changing screen to hear what was said. Mariette opened the door to see Caldwell with a stranger, a balding, middle-aged gentleman holding a silk top hat and a silver-headed cane.

"Mariette," Caldwell said, "May I have the pleasure of introducing you to Mr. William Niblo of New York. Mr. Niblo, this is our ingenue, Miss Mariette Delon." Caldwell backed away. "Now, against my better judgment, I'll leave you two alone."

"I'm honored to meet you, Mr. Niblo," Mariette said, extending her hand and smiling incredulously. "Surprised, too." She was thinking of all the other actors who'd give anything to be in her shoes at this moment. "Please come in."

Niblo bowed over her hand and entered. "The honor is mine, Miss Delon."

"Won't you sit down, Sir?" She waved him toward the settee.

Niblo sat on the settee, placing his hat beside him. Mariette took a chair facing him. "Miss Delon," he began, "I think you are a gifted and promising young actress with a great future in the theater."

Mariette smiled. "Thank you, Mr. Niblo. Coming from you, Sir, that is indeed a compliment."

"It happens," he said, leaning forward, both hands on top of his cane, "that I am in need of an ingenue in my troupe at Niblo's Gardens. Truth to tell, I am always in need of beautiful young ingenues." He paused. Mariette nodded him on. She enjoyed his clipped Northern accent, so different from the slow Southern drawl of New Orleanians, and so different, of course, from her own French accent. He continued. "If you would be free to relocate to New York to act with my troupe, I can promise you important roles and fine wages." He paused. "You're a single lady, I understand."

It was an important question. Married actresses were trouble. Husbands were rarely willing to pull up stakes and follow their wives to New York. And if the actresses left them behind, sooner or later they returned to them.

"Yes, I'm single," Mariette said. "And your offer is most attractive." Mariette's mind was racing ahead. If she could go to New York now before anyone in New Orleans knew she was *enciente*, if she could have her baby there, and if she could then act on the stage for Niblo afterwards, she'd have the means to support her baby and her mother, without shame. As to the missing father, they could always make up a story about him in New York, a city where no one knew them.

"The problem is," Mariette said, "I have family matters that keep me from coming to New York at this time." *It's a Godsend. If only he takes me on my terms.* "But if you don't think me too forward, Sir, I'd like to ask you something."

"Anything, Miss Delon," Niblo said, grinning broadly.

He wants me. I can tell. I've got to try. "If you think you'd still be interested, say next October or November, I'd be free then, and I'd be delighted to join your company."

"Well, I won't deny I wish you could come right away," he said effusively. "But if you can be there in the fall, I'll be enchanted to have you. I have several theaters in New York City. Plays change every two weeks. And as I said, we're always in need of beautiful, talented young actresses."

He rose from the settee and took a business card from his coat pocket. He handed it to her. "Find me any day at this address. If I'm not there, someone will know where I am."

Mariette took the card. It was the address of Niblo's Garden, his principal theater. "Thank you, Mr. Niblo. I'm very grateful."

"No, my dear. It is I who am grateful."

On this dramatic note, he bowed over her hand and left the room. A second later, Desiree came out from behind the screen.

"Mariette, it's the answer to a prayer!" she said. She hugged her daughter. "Do you realize that?"

"Of course. We'll go now, you and I, to New York City, but we won't tell Mr. Niblo we're there till after the baby's born. Then, I'll have you to take care of the baby while I'm at the theater. Will that be all right, Desiree? It seems I'm planning your life along with mine."

"It will be wonderful, *cherie*. I *want* to be part of your life. Always."

Mariette sat on the settee. Desiree sat beside her. Mariette's eyes scanned the walls of her dressing room, the wheels of her mind in motion. "I have money saved up for our passage, and we could sell the house. That should pay our expenses for a good long time. Do you think Celine would come with us?"

"No, I don't think so. She always said that if she had to leave us, she'd go to her sister in Minden, Louisiana. Celine is getting old. She suffers with rheumatism."

"We'll make her a free woman before she goes."

"Yes. We should do that," Desiree smiled, unable to keep the joy from her voice. At last, Mariette had found a way out of her dilemma. "Oh, Mariette, we'll have to make plans. We must check the schedule for packets sailing from here to New York."

"We can't leave till the play ends, of course."

"I know, but that's just a matter of days, *BéBé*. We must start packing our things. And turn the house over to a property agent."

"I wonder if Celine would stay in the house until it's sold," Mariette said.

"Oh, I'm sure she would," said Desiree. "She'll have to make plans herself."

"Then it's settled. We'll go to New York." Enthused by the turn of events her life had taken, she got up, clasped her hands before her, and paced. "We'll rent an apartment. I'll stay close to home so Mister Niblo will have no chance of seeing me."

"Will you tell Caldwell where you're going?"

"No. But after bringing Niblo to meet me, he'll know."

"And how will we explain the missing husband to the landlord in New York?" Desiree asked, carried away with the plans.

"We can say he's out to sea for a year," Mariette said.

"Or dead, better yet," Desiree suggested. "Then if we stay on, we don't need another explanation.

"Desiree, you're really good at this." Mariette smiled.

"I've acted in many plays, *n'est-ce pas?*"

Mariette drew in a deep breath and sighed. For once, she felt she had some kind of a respectable life to look forward to. She had plans to make, too. That would distract her from thoughts of Philippe. Since he obviously no longer wanted her, she would try to make a life of her own without him. But it hurt her to the heart that he would never see his baby.

In her bed that night, she stared up at the tester, her hands behind her head, her mind full of the future and the past. She'd be leaving New Orleans soon. Would she be leaving any chance she'd ever have of marrying Philippe? She shook her head at her own stubbornness. As her mother always said, she never gave up. How foolish to persist with dreams that he could ever care, that he had ever really cared! It was over. Done with.

She thought of her adult life as a play. Act One: her short, detested time as Louis Soniat's *placée*. Act Two: the few glorious days as Philippe's lover. Act Three: Curtain going up! What would she be? A mother? Certainly. An actress? Hopefully. A wife? Probably never. She turned her face into her pillow and tried to sleep.

CHAPTER 57

Mariette was thrilled to see the skyline of New York City. After weeks aboard ship, weeks of continuing grief for Philippe, advice from her mother on every possible subject, and plan-making of the most elaborate kind, she felt a sense of relief when she saw the tall buildings of the city sketched in the distance against the blue Manhattan sky. It was a clear June morning, and she watched the rowboats bringing the *Delta Queen* safely into the dock and the longshoremen on the quay catching the ropes to tie her securely in place.

The noise of the port was deafening. She heard the bellow of orders from the captains of other ships to crew members fitting out their vessels with new ropes and hoisting their mended sails. She heard the screech of pulleys rigged to the mast of the ship alongside them as it took its load and the chant of the crew as they all pulled together. She heard the shouts of vendors on the quay and the cry of seagulls wheeling overhead, waiting to take their share of whatever detritus was washed ashore.

Mariette smelled the rancid odor of filth and sewage coming in on the tide and splashing up against the quayside wall. Leaning against the ship's rail in the early morning, she looked down into the cloudy water to see garbage of every kind and marveled once again that she did not experience nausea.

Their ship was only one in the midst of a forest of masts, so thick, so busy, tied to a quay so much bigger than the port of New Orleans, that she could never have imagined it. To either side of them were fleets of ships, their flags waving, their sails snapping in the wind. And in the distance, beyond the waterfront, heaps of buildings, spires and steeples, the outline of a busy city. It was dizzying.

Leaning against the ship's rail in the early morning, she realized how much farther away from the rail her body was now than when the journey began. Her belly was distended and she was undeniably showing. She was four and a half months pregnant, and thicker than she'd ever been in her life. What else could she expect when all she'd done for weeks was sleep, eat, sit, and rest?

Her depression lingered, but thoughts of the baby occupied her mind more and more as the days went by, especially in her idle state. She had made many plans. When they arrived in New York, she would buy flannel fabric to make baby gowns and caps and receiving blankets. She'd buy lace to trim the tiny garments. She'd buy skeins of woolen yarn and have her mother teach her how to crochet booties and bonnets.

She tried to imagine what the baby would look like. If it was a boy, it should have Philippe's coloring, his olive complexion and sea-green eyes with long black lashes. A girl might have dark curly hair and dark eyes like hers and her mother's. Thoughts of holding her baby lightened her heart. They were balm for her emotional wounds.

Desiree joined her at the ship's rail, and they watched the activity all around them. Ferry boats plied back and forth from Manhattan Island to nearby shores, carrying boatloads of people, wagons, horses, boxes. Everything seemed busy, moving, a scene of relentless activity. The sky was a clear robin's egg blue, with only a few white threads of clouds. The sun lit up the rivers around the island, giving them a coppery sheen. As they neared the docking area, she could hear the ringing of bells, the clinking of capstans.

How grand it would be to touch earth again! To her amazement, she had not had a day of *mal-de-mer*, in spite of her condition. Many others had been green with it, and had had their servants bring trunk trays to their staterooms. Nonetheless, she'd be glad to get off the ship and away from her cramped quarters.

To her surprise, the staterooms on the *Delta Queen*, like those on all passenger steamboats, were assigned to men at one end, women at the other. Being separated from men was a relief to Mariette. Her heart was so bruised she had no desire for anyone's company. With her mother, she didn't have to talk. Her mother understood.

She and her mother had shared a double-decker bunk stateroom. Mariette had offered to take the upper bunk, but Desiree wouldn't hear of it. What if Mariette fell going up or down the ladder? She could injure the baby. No. Desiree held firm. She was still young enough to get into an upper bunk.

Throughout the trip, Mariette slept poorly, waking often when memories of Philippe were too vivid. She saw his flashing white teeth and his handsome tanned face underscored by white neck linens, and her heart ached to kiss his soft, warm mouth and hold his hard body close to hers. How would she ever get over this all-consuming love? She tried to keep her restlessness from disturbing her mother. She knew her mother pretended to sleep through it all, but on one or two occasions, she'd come down to Mariette's bed and hugged her and tried to comfort her.

Her mother had never believed Philippe intended to marry her in the first place, so the disappearance of a lover, an *amoureux*, came as no devastating shock to her. Mariette knew how hard her mother tried to distract her from thoughts of Philippe by making plans for the baby, and it always lifted her spirits.

Rooming with her mother had been providential. They fastened the buttons at the backs of each other's dresses and coiffed each other's hair. These were things Celine had always done for them, and they were not used to dressing themselves. Her mother's company and comfort were playing a large part in the healing that was slowly, ever so slowly, taking place inside her.

At dinner each night, men and women were allowed to mix, and this embarrassed Mariette. She was sorry she had no larger dresses to wear. Her own clothes were so tight they left no doubt in anyone's mind about her pregnancy. She wore her mother's knitted shawl to cover as much of her body as possible. Men would see her face and smile, eager to find a shipboard flirtation to while away the time. Then they'd take one look at her belly and steer clear of her.

"I think it might be a good idea if we pass ourselves off as lady and maid in New York," Desiree told her as they stood at the ship's railing.

"Why, Maman? It doesn't matter in New York."

"Maybe not legally, *ma chere*, but it matters everywhere, to some degree. Our relationship may hold you back in your career. Oh, they'd take you, all right, just to prove they're not as bigoted as Southerners, but you'd always have that shadow over you. We could share an apartment as lady and maid, and in the fall, go to Niblo's that way, just as we did with Caldwell."

"If you think so," Mariette said. She knew she would not be relegating her mother to a degrading position by agreeing to this arrangement. It made for an easier, more comfortable acceptance for them both, wherever they went.

CHAPTER 58

On board the *Delta Queen*, Desiree had managed to make friends with a young man called Edmond St. Paul, a New Yorker, who spoke French. He'd learned the language, he said, because his import-export firm did so much business with New Orleans. In fact, he was, at that very time, returning from a business trip to New Orleans.

Desiree and Edmond chatted in French together each night at dinner, while Mariette sat in smiling silence. Desiree managed to find out from him where the good neighborhoods were in New York, and where they could find an apartment—a flat, Edmond called it in English. She asked him about himself—men always loved to talk about themselves—and they passed the time at the table companionably, Edmond stealing glimpses of Mariette, who turned her face away.

Desiree nurtured the friendship, working to get the information she needed. Edmond St. Paul told her everything about himself, including the fact that he was a bachelor, and Desiree smiled and nodded and told him nothing.

Now suddenly, as the ship pulled into port, he was beside them. Mariette touched her mother's hand and frowned. The one thing Mariette didn't want was anyone keeping track of their whereabouts and knowing about her baby. She and her mother had discussed it in the privacy of their stateroom.

Desiree shook her head almost imperceptibly, and Mariette, reading her signal, knew she meant to take care of it. They had docked at the southern tip of the island at South Ferry. Edmond St. Paul held each of them by an elbow as they descended the gangway and then waited to collect their trunks.

"I'll hire a horse and cart for you ladies," he said. "You just wait right here, and I'll take you wherever you're going." Edmond left on a run toward a cluster of mules and wagons for hire down the street.

Mariette looked at her mother and pursed her mouth. "We can't let him know where we're living, Maman," she said. "He'll keep track of us. He'll know everything."

"Don't worry. When he comes back with the wagon, we'll take it, we'll thank him, and we'll bid him good-bye."

"But we don't know where we're going. We don't know where to find an apartment."

"I do. He told me. Don't worry. I'll handle everything."

In minutes, Edmond returned, sitting beside the driver of a run-down wagon pulled by a gray mule. He helped Mariette step up onto the hub of the wheel to take the seat beside the driver. Edmond helped Desiree into the bed of the wagon. A few minutes later, he found their steamer trunks and, with the help of the driver, managed to lift them into the wagon. Now, he climbed in, obviously planning to sit between Desiree and the trunks. Mariette turned her worried eyes to her mother.

"Edmond," Desiree said, in her most engaging manner, placing her hand over his. "I've enjoyed your company so much on this voyage. I don't know how I'd have made it through all these weeks without you. But this is where we part. Mariette, as you can see, is *enciente*. Her husband is due in from the sea any day now." *We're back to Plan One*, Mariette mused. "He's a very jealous man," Desiree continued. "If he saw you with her, he might do you serious harm. I hate to say that about my own employer, but it's true. So be a dear, and let us get on with our lives. You've made our time on board ship most pleasant." She took his hand in both her own and shook it vehemently. "So we'll tell you goodbye here and now."

"*Au revoir, M'sieur*," Mariette said. "*Merci beaucoup*."

Edmond looked totally crestfallen. He'd clearly expected to go with them, help them find lodgings, and become fast friends. They'd made sure he'd learned nothing aboard ship about Mariette's pregnancy, but he had obviously hoped that the absence of a husband might mean he was deceased, and perhaps he, Edmond, might have a chance with her. Now he was being put out of the wagon and out of their lives. Clearly displeased, he climbed back down and, standing in the bright sunlight on the busy quayside road, with a frown on his face and his hands on his hips, he watched them roll away.

CHAPTER 59

"You'll have to talk to the driver," Desiree said. "Surely he speaks only English." Mariette took one look at the brawny, red-headed Irishman and judged the same. "Tell him to drive a block or two, and when we're well away from Edmond, give him this list of places to go."

Mariette translated for the driver, and handed him the paper. He nodded, flicked his reins and the mule moved. Wagon wheels creaked along the wet cobbled street of the waterfront. Mariette looked to her right at the bustling docks, where bowsprits of one or two of the larger ships extended almost into their path. Wagons queued up, waiting to be loaded with hogsheads of sugar, and boxes and packages of all sizes. To her left, ship chandleries and warehouses lined the sidewalk, an untidy assemblage of ships' stores scattered about outside their doors. She saw quayside coffee shops, as well as the workshops of sailmakers, tanners, rope makers, and shipwrights.

After a city block, the driver took an angled road called South Street, which ran along the East River, and Mariette realized that *this*, indeed, was the heart of the port. She could hardly take it all in. As far as the eye could see, for the next mile or more, was an entire world centered on shipping and commerce. There were coopers and linen weavers, sugar refiners, clockmakers, coach makers, metal workers, even barbers and hair-dressers.

At a busy corner, the driver announced in a booming voice, startling both Mariette and Desiree, "That buildin' there is called the Tontine Coffee House. That's where the merchants do their tradin'," he said with authority, in the manner of a tour guide. "Some does it inside the buildin,' some roight out here on the streets. You can see 'em there." He thrust his chin forward in their direction. Mariette smiled in surprise at his garrulous manner and raised her eyebrows to her mother. But then she gave her attention to the merchants standing in the street outside the Tontine Coffee House in their ascots and frock coats, their faces serious, their arms waving. They were obviously selling something, whatever the ships had brought into port. And she stashed away the information, knowing that if Philippe ever came to New York looking for her, his ship would probably dock right here at South Street, and he'd go into this building, where merchants carried on business. She would remember the Tontine Coffee House.

In the midst of the deafening noise of carters going in every direction, sailors calling out orders and carrying heavy burdens down creaking gangways, she studied the buildings they were passing, all three and four stories high, made of brick and mortar with gabled roofs and chimneys, and along the waterfront, on every inch of ground and wharf were barrels of rice, flour, and salt, and crates of tea saturating the air with aromatic fragrance.

Overcoming her astonishment, Mariette handed the driver the list of three city blocks Desiree had given her. They were in different neighborhoods, Edmond had said, but they were all fine places where they might find good housing. The man drove another city block to a place where there was less noise and they could hear one another.

"Beggin' your pardon, Ma'am," he said to Mariette, "but would ye be knowin' Mahattan a-tall?"

"No, sir. We're new in town."

"Please call me Danny," he said. Mariette nodded. "Now I don't mean to overstep," he said, "but are ye planning t'live in New York permanent?"

"Well, yes, we are." Mariette frowned. "Why do you ask? Are those bad neighborhoods?"

"Oh, no, Miss," he said, "quite the contrary. The neighborhoods are new, built up in the past few years, an' if there's any to let, 'tis sure I am they'd be dear." Mariette tilted her head, not understanding the term. "They'd be costly," he clarified. "But I'll take ye there, if that's what y'want."

"Oh!" She translated for her mother. They both looked crestfallen. "Well, surely they can't *all* be new."

"Yes, Miss, they can. Y'see, 'twas only…oh…say twenty years ago, all the people in Manhattan was huddled down near the waterfront below Canal Street. But then the guv'nor come up with a plan to lay out all o' Manhatten with streets runnin' north t'south and east t'west, makin' up more than 2000 brand new city blocks." This he said as proudly as if all the blocks belonged to him.

"Oh, my! So many!" Mariette said, thinking of the few blocks in all the French Quarter in New Orleans and just double that number in the new neighborhood lately occupied by the Americans above Canal Street.

Danny went on. "Now today, people are buyin' up them lots t'the

344 Mary Lou Widmer

north of the island and puttin' up houses almost as you watch," he said. "But the *first* people to buy in the new part of town were the swells, like Astor an' his friends. And it's mansions they built…an' hotels. An' those are the neighborhoods on yer list, an' they're fancy," he said. "I'll show you." He snapped the reins and the mule moved faster.

They rode several blocks away from the waterfront, then turned, driving north along a wide cobbled avenue. "This here is Broadway," he said.

Mariette perked up. "Oh? So close to the waterfront?" she asked.

"Oh, yes, ma'am. Broadway runs the whole length of the island."

"I didn't know. Will we be seeing any theaters as we go along?"

"Oh, no ma'am. They're farther north," he said. "There's a lot more on Broadway than just the-ay-ters."

Mariette nodded. She was glad. No need to risk seeing Mr. Niblo at this point. She settled back against the old leather upholstery to enjoy the scenery. This was obviously the oldest part of Manhattan, if the aged homes and buildings were any indication.

"This was the Old Dutch town," Danny said, as if reading her mind, "settled 200 years ago."

Two hundred years ago, Mariette thought, *New Orleans was still a swamp in the crescent of the Mississippi River.* "Please," she said, eager to learn of her new whereabouts, "point things out as we go along."

Danny smiled. He reddened a bit, but looked as pleased as if she'd given him a prize. After a few more blocks, he took a turn into a street he called Broad Street, which led directly up to an imposing two-story building, where the street ended. The building was old but elegant, with a balcony and columns on both floors. "That there is Federal Hall," he said. "That's where our first president, Mister George Washington hisself, took the oath of office in 1789."

Mariette gasped and brought her hands together as if in prayer. "I can't believe it! Look, Desiree," she said, and briskly she translated. Desiree smiled. "Oh, Danny, what a wonderful tour guide you are!" she said. Mariette knew that this was a sight she would remember during the long months of her confinement.

Encouraged by her praise, he went on. "Now the street that runs in front of Federal Hall is called Wall Street. That's where tradin' is done these days in stocks an' bonds. D'ye know of it, Miss?"

Mariette shook her head. "Very little."

They turned into Wall Street and rode several blocks, and soon she was seeing finer, newer, more expensive residences, three stories high with arched entryways and multi-paned windows. Mariette felt her breath catch at the lineup of extravagant mansions, standing shoulder to shoulder down the block.

The houses were of brick, with party walls, like some in New Orleans, but in New Orleans, most single houses were small, built in the shotgun style for lack of land, and one-storied because of the swampy soil and the high water table. They were of cypress, painted pastel colors, and each had a little porch with an ornate cornice. She had always thought them pretty, but they were like doll houses compared to these mansions.

"Oh, my!" she said. "These are the most beautiful homes I've ever seen." Mentally, she excluded Soniat's mansion, and of course *Belle Fleur*, which was a plantation, and another thing altogether.

After leaving the area of Wall Street, they were soon back on Broadway, where Danny pointed out the City Hall, a white building a whole block wide, with its balcony and cupola, and right across the street from it, the fabulous Astor House Hotel. "This is the biggest hotel on the island," Danny said, "built by John Jacob Astor." Mariette was once again stunned by the size and majesty of the building.

They passed through a shopping district that was busy and exciting. She secretly hoped they'd find quarters not too far away for her to shop in these stores before she became too big to go out. The shops were all two and three-stories high, with canvas awnings stretching out across the brick sidewalks to provide shade for shoppers. The traffic thickened, and Danny's wagon was soon threading its way between a public horse-drawn omnibus and a line-up of carriages, hackney cabs, and wagons. Pedestrians gathered on the sidewalk, and at the far end of the block rose the majestic steeple of a church.

At last they pulled up before a three-storied building that looked like a mansion to Mariette. "Is this one of the houses on the list?" she asked, frowning.

"Yes, ma'am," Danny said. He added nothing, waiting for her reaction.

"And in such a mansion, do they rent rooms?"

"Yes, ma'am. I happen t'know this one does."

"Oh, no," she said, shaking her head. "I could never afford it. You're right about that." She and Desiree shared a frown of confusion, both wondering why Edmond had thought they were so well off. Perhaps *he* lived in such a domicile and thought everyone did.

Danny drove them to the two other neighborhoods on the list and stopped before houses he knew to be rental property. The story was the same. "I'd have to be wealthy indeed to afford such living quarters," Mariette said. Looking at her knowledgeable tour guide, she asked, "Danny, do you know of a nice, clean neighborhood where I could live with my maid, where the rent wouldn't be too high?" she asked humbly. "I have limited funds and I'm going to have to stretch them out for a while."

Danny smiled a fatherly smile. "Sure an' I do, Miss," he said. "Don't you be worryin' yer head." Then, without further delay, he turned the wagon around and went back down Broadway toward the waterfront. When he came to a wide intersection, he said, "This here is called Bowling Green. Now I'm goin' t'show ye a block I think ye'll like, with five row houses, all rental property. They're in an old neighborhood, but real nice. You'll see."

He turned into Bowling Green, and, within a few blocks, they were pulling into a cul-de-sac where there were five red brick houses, each approached by ten steps. On the second level, bay windows dominated the façade. The buildings were three stories high, with dormers and chimneys on the rooftops. The sidewalks were clean, the buildings attractive. Just across the street was a little park, an oasis in the the heart of a busy neighborhood, with wooden benches set in the shade of maple trees. Mariette loved the setting. She prayed there would be a vacancy.

"Now around this little park, they's alweez a few horses an' carriages you can rent fer a ride down Broadway to the shops or the the-ay-ters," he said. "And these here flats won't take yer last penny, Miss."

"Oh, Desiree," Mariette said, smiling. "Isn't it fine?"

Desiree smiled back and nodded like a dutiful maid.

Mariette addressed the driver. "Now, Danny," she said, "do you know any of the owners of these properties? Which one would you think I should approach? We have to have a place to sleep this very night."

The red-headed Irishman took off his cap and scratched his head. Then he smiled and took over the situation once again. "I do, now that you ask, Miss," he said. "There is a Missus O'Flaherty, a friend o' mine, who recently lost her boarders and is lookin' to replace them. She's in the middle house there," he said, pointing to the central building.

Mariette sucked in an audible breath. "My, I hope she hasn't found anyone yet," she said. "I would be most delighted to live in this neighborhood."

"Then I'll wait till you've had a chance to talk to her, an' tell her Danny sent you," he said. "If you reach an agreement, I'll get yer trunks outer the wagon."

After the long journey and the disappointments of the morning, finding such a delightful place to live was more than Mariette could have asked for. There was indeed a Mrs. O'Flaherty, and she did indeed have a "flat" to let. She was a short plump Irish lady with iron-gray hair pulled to the back of her head in a knot. She opened the door to a knock, and Mariette looked past a vestibule into a long wide corridor, giving off to an apartment on each side. She said she still had a vacancy and ushered them into the apartment on the left of the corridor. It was a furnished flat with a living-dining room and two bedrooms. Mrs. O'Flaherty explained that no cooking was allowed in the rooms, but she always had coffee on her stove for her tenants. And they could cook in the dependency—a building to the rear—where they could also do their laundry and use "the necessaries." And, of course, commodes would be provided for the apartment.

Mariette smiled at her mother. Desiree nodded. The rent was agreed upon, the first month paid, and the landlady placed a large copper key in Mariette's hand. Now she returned to the driver, who carried their trunks up the steps for his fare and a few extra coins.

Alone in the flat at last, Mariette and Desiree hugged each other and laughed with glee.

"It's perfect, *ma fille*," Desiree said.

"Oh, yes. We can take the baby to that little park across the street. We'll have to get a pram." They walked over and knelt on the window seat to look at the little shaded area through the glass. Smiling, Mariette looked at her mother. "The best part is that Edmond will never find us in this neighborhood," she said.

"You're right. Oh, we can make a good life here, Mariette," Desiree said.

"Yes, my dear Desiree," she said, "I think we can."

CHAPTER 60

"*Mon ami*," Armand called out, as Philippe entered the office of Grillet and Son, "you're looking well today. How are you feeling?"

A disapproving frown creased Philippe's forehead, and he signaled Armand with a nod of the head to join him in his private office. When they were seated in the half-glass-enclosed room, Philippe behind his desk, he said, "Armand, I have asked you before and I must insist. Do not ask about my health. I am well. I have recovered and I don't want to be thought of as an invalid." Philippe looked through his glass enclosure at the many merchants in his father's commission house, engaged in buying and selling goods from recently arrived ships. He lowered his voice. "In fact, when I feel certain that I can earn my own living ...in my present condition... I'll be leaving here."

"But you can earn your own living now, *mon ami*. You've proved that many times over. How many cargoes must you sell before you get your confidence back?"

Philippe looked amused. "My father makes it easy for me, Armand, you know that. He sends all his best clients my way and makes it look as if they asked for me. I'm not a fool. Before the duel, he used to enjoy competing with me for contracts... but no more."

Armand did not reply. He knew the truth of Philippe's words. With comfortable familiarity, he took a cheroot from the box on Philippe's desk and clipped off the end with his pocket knife. He struck a match on the side of the box and lit the cigar.

"He wants to build up my confidence, don't you see?" Philippe asked. "He's a good man, my father, but as long as I'm with him, I'll never know if I can manage on my own."

"And is it so vital to you, *mon ami,* to know you can manage on your own?"

"Well, it's *everything*!" Philippe said. "My whole future depends on it."

"Why so, *mon vieux?* Why can't you enjoy the benefits of an established business? You're more fortunate than most. If you go off on your own, what will be different, except that you'll put yourself at risk?"

Philippe leaned forward and met his friend's dark gaze. "If I do well on my own, in time, I'm going to ask Mariette to marry me." He paused. "I've never changed my mind about that."

Armand shook his head and smiled a patient smile. After all his friend had been through, he still would not accept the fact that such a thing was impossible. "I know there's no other girl in your life, Philippe," he said, "but I can't believe you're still thinking of marriage."

Philippe shook his head. He sighed. "I've been wanting to talk with you. I need to confide in someone who understands." Philippe shifted in his chair. He did not know how to begin, for he knew his plans would seem absurd, even to a sympathetic friend. "You see, Armand, there are things that must happen before I go to her. Did I ever tell you that I was looking to rent an office in the American Sector, close to the New Basin Canal?"

"No. Never. I'm amazed to hear it."

"Well, I've bought a property there, and I was lucky to get it." Philippe smiled proudly, as if sharing a treasured secret.

"Lucky indeed," said Armand, "with all the Americans buying into that area. When that canal opened, every merchant in the South wanted to be in New Orleans doing business with the Gulf Coast cities."

Philippe grinned. "It happens I have a friend in real estate," he said. "He's been holding this building for me, for a small down payment, until my townhouse was sold."

"Oh, *mon Dieu,* your town house! You had to give it up!"

Philippe nodded. "My father put it up for sale after the duel, when I was at *Belle Fleur.*" A frown darkened Philippe's face. "I truly loved that house. I left my most cherished memories there. But it was for the best, I suppose," he said, waving his hand. "It sold in a month. It's valuable property in a good location. He got a good price for it and put it in my account. With that, I was able to pay off my new building, with some left over, and that's what I'll live on till my own business is established."

Armand smiled slowly and with admiration. "I am astonished. Truly," he said. "Does your father know of your new property?"

"Not yet. I'm still living at *Belle Fleur.* But I plan to tell him today. I have nothing at the new place yet. I was hoping you'd come with me one morning to look for a few pieces of office furniture."

"Gladly," Armand said. "And the furniture from your old townhouse?"

"...is in storage, but after I've broken the news to Papa, I plan to have it delivered to my new place. I'll live upstairs and work in the office on the ground floor."

"And you'll ask Mariette to marry you?"

"After I'm sure I can make it on my own. And… if she'll have me the way I am now."

Armand shook his head with an almost imperceptible movement. "Philippe, Philippe!" he said. "As my grandmother used to say, 'When something is in your head, it isn't in your feet.'"

Philippe smiled. "That's true."

"Oh, *mon ami,* if she loves you, it will make no difference at all," Armand said.

"I pray you're right."

"So why not go now? Don't wait months and months. Present yourself, declare your love, let her see you and understand what life has in store for you both. Then find out if she still loves you."

Philippe nodded. "The problem is," he said, "I'm not sure where she is."

"She's not in New Orleans?" he asked, surprised. "Have you been to the house on Rampart Street?"

"Many times. At first, I just rode past, looking around. I saw that the house was up for sale, but no one was about. "

"And?"

Philippe tapped his desk with a pencil. "I went back several times. Once I saw their black woman shaking out a rug and I rushed to talk to her, but she ran inside and bolted the door. I knocked but she told me through the closed door that her mistress was no longer in New Orleans, that she didn't know where she was." He sighed. "Oh, she knew, all right, but I think she was sworn not to tell."

Armand frowned, gathering his thoughts. "So then..."

"I went to see Caldwell."

"Oh, yes, of course. He would know."

"He denied knowing anything at first. Said she'd left town, but that was all he knew. But then I threatened him, not physically, of course." Philippe grinned. "I hinted that I had much inside information about his *affairs de coeur* that his wife might be interested in." He laughed. "Then he told me everything. His wife holds the purse strings, you know. It's *her* money he's invested in that monster of a theater."

"Well, what did he say?" Armand demanded.

"Well, it seems an important impresario from New York, a man named Niblo, visited Mariette in her dressing room one night after a performance, and although Caldwell was not privy to the conversation, he felt sure the man offered her a contract to act in his theater in New York."

Armand smiled. "So then you *do* know where she is!" he said.

"Well, New York, yes, but it's an enormous city." He sat forward and met Armand's eyes. "First of all, I don't know if I can trust Caldwell. And secondly, this Niblo may not have hired Mariette at all, if and when she arrived there. It's the hub of the theater world, and Mariette would be a small fish in a big pond."

"But if you're determined to find her, then that's where you must go, *n'est-ce pas?*"

"Yes." Philippe nodded. "But it won't be easy. Not for me, anyway. It takes six weeks to get there by boat, and when I arrive, with my limitations, I'll have to find a place to live and a commission house to work in."

"Will Jean Baptiste go with you?"

"Oh, yes. I couldn't go without him. He helps me dress and lifts things for me... whatever I can't do for myself. I've told him my plans, and he's looking forward to it."

Armand nodded.

"I'd ask you to come work with me at my new office, my friend, but I won't be there permanently. I'm sure you understand."

"But of course," Armand said.

"It's just a trial run," Philippe said. "As soon as I know I can succeed on my own, I'll sell the building and leave town."

Armand stood up and paced a few steps within the office walls. "You'll be doing all this on Caldwell's word alone, you know, and you may be on the wrong track altogether."

Philippe nodded. "That's true. But I don't think so, Armand. I feel in my heart that she's there, maybe waiting for me. Isn't that possible?" He found his friend's dark eyes.

"Of course, it's possible, Philippe," Armand said. "Anything is possible."

"Wish me luck. No matter what my father says, I'll be moving to the American Sector in a few days." He rubbed his forehead briskly, as if trying to rub away his worries. "I have so many plans to make, but first I must tell Papa." He heaved a sigh and Armand waited. "Strangely enough, I don't think he'll object, not to that, anyway. He's always encouraged me to be independent. I think he might admire my ambition."

Armand assumed an expression that told Philippe he was about to express an opinion. "I think you're just putting things off, Philippe," he said. "You can make it on your own. You could go to New York today."

"No, Armand, I must try my own wings first."

Armand smirked. "Hard head," he said, knocking on his own head.

"So true." Philippe smiled. "Just as your grandmother said."

CHAPTER 61

It was a good life, Mariette conceded, except for the heat. It was
August, and Mariette was almost seven months along in her
pregnancy. She was big as a house, awkward, and always uncomfort-
ably hot. A rivulet of perspiration constantly ran between her
breasts and down the center of her back. She'd expected it to be cool
in New York, even in the summer, just as it was hot almost all year
round in New Orleans, but she'd been in for a surprise.

For a small woman, she'd gained a great deal of weight. Her baby
kicked incessantly, sometimes knocking her knitting right out of
her hands. Her stomach was like a shelf, and it was hard to avoid
using it as one. But she always got a kick in return for her trouble.

Yet, it was a good life, if she could only forget Philippe. Mrs.
O'Flaherty told them that she, like so many other Irish women in
New York, was an expert midwife. She offered to deliver Mariette's
baby when it came time. Both Mariette and Desiree were
inexpressibly grateful.

They had told Mrs. O'Flaherty that they were mother and

daughter, and why they had pretended to be lady and maid. They asked her to keep their secret. And since she would be delivering Mariette, only the three of them would have to know about the baby. They confided in her about Philippe as well, and found her not only understanding but sympathetic and grateful for their confidence. She promised not to tell another living soul.

Mariette had decided, the first month in New York, to teach her mother English, which she thought would be an absolute necessity if she were to live and shop and converse with the people here. Each day, they spent an hour or more in Bowling Green Park, sewing or knitting baby clothes, and as they worked, they reviewed common English words for everyday objects. Then Mariette started teaching her verbs, which were the most difficult part of the language. Tenses in particular made Desiree scratch her head.

"Don't worry too much about whether you get the tenses right," Mariette said in French. "They'll know what you mean, and it will be no novelty to them. Lots of foreigners live here."

The lessons went better than Mariette could have dreamed, and afterwards, for the rest of the day, Mariette tried to speak only English to her mother, to help her learn. Only when they became irritated with each other, due mostly to the heat, did they revert to their easy French.

"When I think of the Germans and Irish and Africans who live on this island, I sometimes wonder how they understand each other at all," Mariette said, holding up for inspection the baby gown she was working on. "The Irish speak English, of course, if you can call it that." She chuckled, thinking of Danny with his heavy brogue, and wondered fleetingly if they'd ever see him again.

Desiree frowned, concentrating on what Mariette had said. "The Africans...are they all slaves, *ma fille*, or do you know?"

Mariette put down her sewing and looked at her mother. "I'll tell you what I know. One day, Mrs. O introduced me to the tenant on the third floor, that Irishman named Mohnihan? Do you know who I mean? He wears a top hat and cane and goes to work at seven in the morning."

"Yes. I've seen the man."

"Well, he tells me things from time to time. He says it wasn't so long ago that all the slaves on the island got their freedom."

"Really, Mariette?"

Marette nodded gravely. "Well, of course, many Negroes were already free, some from the very beginning when they came over with the Dutch settlers. That's what he said."

Desiree nodded, concentrating. "So black people have been here all along."

Mariette nodded. "He says there are as many colored people in Manhattan now as white."

"And how are they treated, I wonder. Did he say?" This was, of course, a subject vital to Desiree.

Mariette sighed. "In some ways better than in the South, Maman. In others, just the same, Mr. Mohnihan says."

"What do you mean?"

"Well, there's no law against free Negroes eating in the same public place as white people, which, of course, could never happen in New Orleans. But then, the rich white people have their own clubs and eating places, where no black people would dare to go. Mr. Mohnihan says the blacks mostly mingle with sailors, both black and white, in the low-class taverns around the waterfront."

Desiree was glad she had decided to live in New York in the guise of Mariette's maid. That would make her life easier all around.

Desiree had found a market within walking distance of their residence, where she was able to buy fresh fruit and vegetables; a bakery where bread was baked daily; and a butcher shop, where she could purchase soup meat, chickens, and various cuts of beef, which were plentiful in New York.

She'd used Mrs. O'Flaherty's hearth in the dependency to the rear of the boarding house to do her cooking, and she'd seen the good Irish landlady eyeing her and shaking her head, as if trying to reach a decision.

One day, the landlady said, "I know 'tis hard fer you t'cook for yerself an yer darrter in that buildin' outback, comin' down from the second floor an' all. An' it'll be worse when the hard winter sets in. I was thinkin' maybe ye'd be willin' t'pay a wee bit more per week and take yer meals with me, like boarders, y'might say."

Desiree was so overjoyed with the suggestion she wanted to hug the landlady on the spot. "That's a grand idear," Desiree said, having learned some of her English with an Irish brogue. She couldn't wait to tell Mariette. And boarders they became, and even faster friends, as Desiree helped Mrs. O with the cooking and cleaning up.

One morning, as they were sitting on the benches in the little park, enjoying the shade and an occasional breeze, Mariette asked, "Do you miss New Orleans, Desiree?" She always called her mother by her given name, and planned to do so indefinitely, to avoid mistakes later, when it would matter.

Her mother put down her knitting and gazed absently at a horse and wagon rolling by and two children playing hopscotch on the brick sidewalk. "Yes, I do," she said. "I thought I wouldn't, but I do." She sighed softly. "Once it was over for Raoul and me, I was glad to get away and start a new life." Desiree was speaking French, and

Mariette didn't object. The subject was sensitive. It called for sensitive words.

"And now?" Mariette prompted.

"Well, now that the house is sold and Celine has left New Orleans, I feel as if my lifeline has been cut, and I'm drifting in a foreign country."

"I get that feeling, too," Mariette said. "I miss the cathedral bells, for one thing." She unwound some thread from a ball of blue yarn and went on crocheting. I miss Caldwell." She laughed. "He's a rascal, but a nice man. He knew I was *enciente*, I think. That's why he was so generous about letting Niblo talk to me."

"That was good of him, Mariette."

"Yes. He's a flirt and a bit of a coward, but he's kind."

"And the theater? You miss that, I'm sure."

"I miss acting, yes, but I didn't get to know the St. Charles Theater the way I knew the old Camp. She knotted her thread and cut the ends with a small pair of scissors. "There are some things I never told you," Mariette said. She stopped knitting, trying to find the words to tell her story. "I met Philippe quite by accident at the gumbo counter in the French Market one day soon after the Quadroon Ball."

"Oh?" Desiree took off her glasses. "Tell me."

Mariette told her mother all about their chance encounter, the walk to the cornstalk fence, the stop at the coffee shop. And the kiss. She was dreamy-eyed as she spoke of it, that long ago afternoon that seemed like a beautiful storybook tale.

"And you were never to go out of the house without a chaperone," Desiree scolded gently.

"I know. But if I'd had a chaperone, all those wonderful things would never have happened."

Desiree looked at her daughter. Mariette's eyes were moist and her lips parted in a small smile after the word *kiss*. "That must have been something special, that kiss," Desiree said.

Mariette sighed wistfully. "Oh, my dear Desiree, you'll never know." She looked past her mother, as if recapturing the moment. "It was the beginning of our romance."

Once Mariette started confiding in her mother, she wanted to tell her everything. She talked about Christmas night, when he'd come to Soniat's house after Desiree had gone home and the servants had left. She said that Philippe had come looking for her and found her there alone.

Desiree listened intently to her daughter's story. She frowned at first, but then smiled when she learned that Philippe had refused to make love to her there. Mariette knew that her mother was beginning to believe that Philippe had truly loved her, and may indeed have made definite plans for their marriage. Mariette spoke of Philippe's fear of fires, of the episode of fire in his childhood, of his rescuing her from the theater fire in spite of his phobia. Desiree watched her expression as she spoke of Philippe. Mariette knew that in a way, Desiree loved him too, for his gentleness, and for saving her life in spite of his fears.

They revealed many things to each other as the months went by, and Mariette grew bigger and the baby kicked harder. They watched as the trees in the park came to full fruition in the summer months, thick with shining leaves and blossoms and alive with birdsong. And during the first cool snap in September, when Mariette saw the leaves turning red and gold and swirling in a shower all around them, she knew that her time was almost upon her.

CHAPTER 62

On a perfect fall night in late October, when they were sitting in their living room, Mariette told her mother she was having hard pains, like her menses pains, low in her belly. Desiree knew it was time. Mariette was going into labor. She'd no sooner come to that conclusion than a gush of water down Mariette's legs confirmed it.

"Desiree! What's happening?" she asked.

"Don't worry, *ma cherie*," Desiree said. "Your water broke, that's all. It happens to everyone."

"*Mon Dieu*! I thought I was bleeding to death."

"No, no, you're going to be just fine. I'll go get Mrs. O'Flaherty. I'll be right back."

"What should I do in the meantime?" Mariette asked.

"Dry yourself off. Put on a clean nightgown. Walk up and down. And pray," she said.

Like most babies, the infant was born inconveniently at two o'clock in the morning. It was a beautiful little girl, with fair skin, dark eyes, and a head full of black hair. Mrs. O'Flaherty laid her on top of Mariette's stomach while she cut the cord. Then she removed the bloodied linens and cleaned up both mother and child.

Mariette was exhausted. She'd never worked harder in all her life than she had giving birth to that baby, but she'd had a perfectly natural birth, or so Mrs. O'Flaherty said. The baby'd been in good position from the start, and there had been no problems. The pains had been excruciating at the end, and the pushing had worn her out, but when Mrs. O'Flaherty at last laid the baby in Mariette's arm, in a receiving blanket, all memory of pain vanished. She passed her trembling hand over the baby's head and gently touched its silky cheek. She looked at her mother who was bending over her, admiring the baby. "She's beautiful, Desiree, *n'est-ce pas?*"

Desiree took her daughter's hand. "She's beautiful, *ma fille.*"

Mariette stayed in bed for five days, but after that, no one could keep her down. Her mother and Mrs. O insisted that the usual recovery time was ten days, but Mariette felt so strong and so happy, she knew it was not too soon to be up doing things.

She nursed the baby, keeping the bassinet alongside her bed, feeding her on demand when she cried. Often they fell asleep together in the double bed, and Desiree gently removed the infant, changed her nappie, and put her down on her stomach in her own little bed.

Mariette named the baby Desiree, to her mother's great delight. To avoid confusion, she nicknamed her Daisy. In New York, they were leaving their French behind, getting more American every day, and in America, nicknames were the rage.

With two women sewing and knitting for her, Daisy had more nightgowns and day dresses, aprons and bibs than any ten babies in New York. Mariette loved nothing more than bathing her baby, dressing her up, curling her hair in ringlets around her finger, and taking her to lie in her carriage in the park across the way, where passing strangers could stop and admire her. She was, to Mariette, the most beautiful baby in the world.

On November 20th, a month after Daisy's birth, Mariette decided it was time to go to Niblo's and find out if he still wanted her in his acting company, or if she'd have to look for another acting troupe. She looked forward to the outing, even if she was a bit worried about the outcome. She'd been cloistered in the house and the little park for months, not even going to the shopping center in Manhattan she'd seen her first day in the city. She felt claustrophobic, eager to break out of her confinement.

Mrs. O'Flaherty, who knew Mariette was an actress, and was apprised of her upcoming visit to Niblo, knocked on the door of their apartment that morning and offered the use of her copper hip tub. "I can get the yardman to bring it up an' get you a coupla buckets o' hot water," she said.

"That would be the greatest favor you could do for me," Mariette said graciously. She and her mother had been washing "by piece" from a pitcher and bowl since they'd arrived, and the walk downstairs for hot water had been anything but easy. "I accept your kind offer and I'll see that you get two tickets on the aisle to the first play I'm in."

"Now won't that be grand!" the landlady said, laughing as she left to make the arrangements for the bath.

For this first visit to Niblo's, Marriete decided to go in style. A lineup of horses and carriages for hire parked every day in the half circle around Bowling Green Park. With money in the bank from the sale of the house on Rampart Street, Mariette felt they were in high clover and she could afford to hire a carriage. Her mother would go as her maid and Mrs. O'Flaherty would keep the baby.

After her bath and shampoo, Mariette dressed in a blue taffeta gown. It felt a bit snug after her pregnancy, but with her stays pulled tight, her mother had managed to fasten the hooks. For the first time since she'd arrived, she wore two petticoats, which Desiree had starched and ironed. With her parasol and reticule, she decided she was as ready as she'd ever be. Mariette and Desiree, lady and maid, left the house and rode off toward Niblo's Garden.

CHAPTER 63

After her long confinement, Broadway once again amazed Mariette, with its mansions, its many shops and interesting landmarks. She had inquired with the drivers of hackneys on the Bowling Green cul-de-sac if any of them knew a red-headed Irish driver named Danny, and to her amazement, one of them said yes, and she'd been able to locate him. With delight, Danny came to pick her up, not in the wagon he'd first taxied her in, but in a fine hackney, which he'd bought since he'd last seen her. Mariette was so pleased to see him, she had to restrain herself from giving him a hug. But her face said it all, and if Danny noticed that her waistline was no longer thick, he had the good manners not to mention it.

Danny drove along the cobbled thoroughfare with obvious experience in a quagmire of traffic. He wove in and out of the tangle of horse-drawn streetcars, hackneys, and carriages, while their drivers shouted obscenities at him and at one another. Mariette reveled in it all, feeling free at last from the flat where she'd thought of nothing but motherhood for so many months.

She hadn't seen the workaday world of Broadway since their arrival, for they lived off the beaten track, in the quiet south end of the island. But as the hackney rolled northward, she took in all the details once again: the signs over the doorways of workshops, where grocers, bakers, seamstresses, leather workers, and blacksmiths plied their trades. Men and women jostled each other entering and leaving cobblers' shops, and women picked up loaves of bread for the evening meal.

Danny said he knew the location of Niblo's Garden, so Mariette enjoyed the scenery, not having to concern herself with finding the address. "Y'know, Miss," Danny explained, unable to withhold his vast fund of knowledge, "just a little time back, Broadway was almost all foine houses, but little by little, it's becomin' a street of shops an' hotels an' the-ay-ters." Mariette nodded. "Now about this Niblo's Garden, where ye're goin?' It useta be just a place where people could sit outdoors an' lissen t'music an' watch fireworks an' such. But I'll tell ya what made it the big theay-ter it is t'day"

"Please do," Mariette said.

"One night, Mr. P. T. Barnum, a great showman, put on an act there at Niblo's Garden, featurin' a woman who claimed t'be one hunderd an' sixty-one years of age an' the former nurse of President George Washington hisself."

"No!" Mariette exclaimed, smiling and bringing her hands together.

"Yes, ma'am. An' with that act, Niblo packed the house, and it's been one act after another ever since. Of course today, he puts on plays."

"Well, what ever happened to Mr. Barnum?" Mariette asked.

"Oh, he has his own museum now, across the street from Niblo's. He packs 'em in with all kinds o' freaks. But they say he's goin' t'bring in a wonderful singer. It's the great Jenny Lind, the Swedish Nightingale."

Mariette became distracted from Danny's chatter at this point, for they were nearing Niblo's Garden. She reached inside her reticule to make sure his business card was still there. When the carriage stopped, she looked up at the building in awe. It was a spectacular edifice, with central triple-arched doors running two stories high and Doric columns all across the front. Painted tiles on the marquis spelled out the words *Niblo's Garden,* and a modest billboard advertised the current play.

Her heart racing, Mariette paid Danny and stepped down to the sidewalk. Then, with Desiree two feet behind her, she entered the huge, magnificent building. She was overwhelmed at the size of the theater, which was comparable to the St. Charles in New Orleans, and she realized for the first time that Caldwell had every reason to be proud. The St. Charles was probably the most extraordinary theater in the South, and it was only now that Mariette was aware of it. But this was New York, where such theaters were common, she supposed, and she was grateful she'd had a chance to act in the St. Charles, for the experience it had given her in such a showcase.

Seeing a rehearsal in progress, she sat in the darkened audience and watched, unnoticed, some few rows behind the director, whom she hoped was William Niblo. Reaching inside her reticule once again, she drew out the card the impresario had given her…a lifetime ago, it seemed. Could it be only five months?

Would Niblo remember her? Perhaps he gave out cards like this all over the country. Maybe actresses by the dozen were constantly descending upon him. It was possible he had no place for them all, or else had forgotten them, despite his flattering offers.

At last a break was called. Mariette drew in a deep breath,

pinched her cheeks to bring color to them, shook out her skirt, and rippled her fingers in a little wave to her mother. Her knees were weak from apprehension, just as they'd been that very first day at the old Camp, but she walked down the aisle and called out, "Mister Niblo, sir." The man turned around.

Coming closer for a better look in the dark aisle, Niblo knit his brow, then smiled a radiant smile. "Why, it's Miss Delon from New Orleans, I do believe," he said.

She breathed a sigh of relief. "How kind of you to remember," she said, smiling. "I've come to live in New York, now that fall is here, and hopefully, act in your theater, if you'll still have me."

"Have you!" He was grinning from ear to ear. "Of course, I'll have you, my dear. I couldn't be more delighted. Come. I'll introduce you to the actors in my company."

Niblo was a small man, except for the girth around his middle, held neatly inside a waistcoat of embroidered silk cloth. He wore a smart white cravat beneath his fleshy neck, and was more nattily attired than James Caldwell on his best day. His head was bald, encircled by a St. Anthony halo of dark hair mixed with gray and decorated with mutton chop whiskers. He had a smooth round face, ruddy cheeks, and eyes as dark as jet and crinkled at the corners from smiling. He was an agreeable man, obviously kind and happy in his work, as his words had indicated.

Now, with his hand at her elbow, he escorted her to the stage and introduced her to the cast of the production that was to open that very night. Everyone smiled and shook her hand, all with cautious reticence, which she'd expected. Actors were insecure people, afraid of being upstaged by newcomers, or worse yet, replaced by them. But Mariette couldn't concern herself with that. She needed a job and she hoped to find it here.

Before the afternoon was over, Niblo had offered her a supporting role in a production which was to go into rehearsal in two weeks. "I'm looking forward to having you in my company at last," he told Mariette. "New York audiences will take you to their hearts. They'll be charmed by your French accent."

"Do I still have an accent?" she asked, with all sincerity.

"Yes, and please don't ever lose it. It's worth its weight in gold to me."

"Thank you, Mr.Niblo," she said.

Niblo's words were indeed prophetic. The role of Hannah in the play *The Little Drummer* proved an outstanding vehicle for Mariette on the New York stage. After her very first performance, the critics of three newspapers gave her rave reviews, praising her sensitivity in the role and delighting in her French accent. How different it was here from New Orleans, she was finding out. In New Orleans, Frenchmen were becoming more American every day. In New York, on the other hand, where "American" was the norm, a French star was a novelty.

For the next few months, Mariette had only one hiatus, and before it was over, she had to begin rehearsals on a new production. Each play, as Niblo had said, ran for two weeks, and was followed immediately by another play. This meant that unless they used alternate actors, cast members performed in one play six nights a week with a matinee on Sunday, while rehearsing in the daytime for the upcoming drama. It was exhausting, but Mariette was young and strong and the money was good.

Their only other income consisted of monthly interest checks received from the Chase Manhattan Bank, where they had deposited the payment from the sale of the Rampart Street house, in amounts sufficient to support their frugal living. Mariette deposited all her wages from acting in a savings account, for she knew, as her mother often told her, that she must earn what she could now, for her years on the stage were limited. When she grew fat and her hair turned gray, she would be lucky to get occasional character roles, or maybe none at all. As a young actress, she must make the most of her time.

Mariette was grateful to have her mother with her to care for Daisy, and confident that nothing could ever happen to her baby while she was away. But she regretted the amount of time she spent at the theater, instead of at home with her baby. By the time she was six months old, Daisy was so beautiful, so animated, so smart, she was doing everything but talking. And of course, she was happy and content to be left with her Grandmaman. Mariette wasn't sure if she was glad about that or just plain jealous. She left the house each morning, after a dozen kisses to Daisy's smooth rosy cheeks. But before she'd even departed, Daisy had lost interest in her mother. She was too busy making sounds for Desiree to take her out of her high chair and bundle her up for their outing.

Mariette had lived all her life in a tropical climate, and found the cold winds and snows of the New York winter cutting and painful. She had to admit, however, that there was a certain beauty in the winter cityscape, for the leafless branches of the tall trees in the park were like black lace against the slate gray sky, and her very first view of snow gave her an indescribable thrill. She had to get outside, where she could feel it and catch the flakes in her palms and on her tongue.

Daisy seemed to thrive in the cold weather. Bundled up in her woolen snowsuit, her jet black hair forming ringlets about her cap, she was ready for Bowling Green Park and her line-up of passing admirers. Desiree agreed with them all that Daisy was an extraordinary baby. Her nose and mouth were part Mariette and part Philippe, but her complexion, like a magnolia petal, was her mother's. When her first two teeth came in, she looked like a bisque doll on a shelf in an emporium.

When Mariette had time at home, she couldn't wait to take her out for her airing, so she could be the one on the receiving end of the compliments. She couldn't keep her hands off the child. Instead of letting her sit in her pram, which she was perfectly content to do, Mariette picked her up and held her on her lap, where she could hug her around her waist and gently pat her mittened hands together.

Mariette was so constantly in the limelight in Niblo's Garden, her name became a household word. Though she could have afforded a fancy apartment and a Phaeton, which would have enhanced her image as a glamorous actress, the idea of moving from Bowling Green Park held no appeal to her.

Her one luxury, other than the young Irish girl Sarah, her dresser, was Danny Dugan, her driver and the first friend she'd met in New York. She hired him on a weekly basis to take her to and from rehearsals and performances. She called no undue attention to herself except for the inevitable publicity interviews, on which Niblo insisted. Yet, there was not a theater-goer in New York who did not know who Mariette Delon bought her clothes from, what Mariette ate for breakfast, even the name of Sarah, her dresser. A "Mariette" bonnet appeared in a Broadway millinery shop window. The "Mariette" petticoat in a nearby lingerie boutique became a "must" for every young girl.

She went through her days like a whirlwind, wearing herself out so she could sleep at night. Yet sleep rarely came. Her mind was filled with thoughts of Philippe, with his curly hair and his broad shoulders and his beautiful blunt fingers that had touched her body and made her blood sing. She loved him. She missed him. She grieved for him. She wanted him to know his baby.

Mrs. O'Flaherty had made life easy for them in many ways. Besides making them "eat-in" boarders, she'd arranged for a copper hip tub to be left permanently in their apartment. She kept Daisy whenever it was necessary, taking joy in the baby's company. In all, she became their closest confidant and their caring, concerned friend.

She was still the only one who knew they were mother and daughter, and she was flattered to have been entrusted with their secret. Mariette and Desiree loved her. She was family. They'd never leave Bowling Green. Mrs. O would have to put them out.

CHAPTER 64

Upon arriving in New York, Philippe found an ad in the newspaper describing a flat that seemed ideal. It was one he could share with Jean Baptiste, and it was on Canal Street, near the waterfront. He figured that no matter who he worked for, the commission house would probably be near the port, and he could easily walk the distance. The flat consisted of a living area with a fireplace, a large bedroom, a small kitchen, and a good-sized wardrobe room, where a cot could be set up for Jean Baptiste. Philippe told Jean that it if he was successful in business, he would provide him with better quarters, but the black man seemed satisfied with the arrangements.

His next order of business was a stop at City Hall. Having no idea where to look for work and finding himself awash in a myriad of ships and merchants trading goods at the South End of Manhattan, he knew he needed direction and advice. What Armand had said had proved prophetic. This move was indeed a risk, and letters from his father would have been pure gold in this Babel of a commercial world. But Philippe would never have asked for them, since Francois had been so opposed to his leaving New Orleans.

Philippe had said nothing, of course, about going after Mariette. That would have been the last straw for Francois Grillet, who long ago had considered that affair a closed book. In the end, he had given in to his son's leaving, and they had parted on amicable terms. His mother had wept a few tears at his departure, but trusted his judgment and took solace in the fact that Jean Baptiste would be with him and would let them know if ever he needed assistance. Jeanine said only that she wished she were going with him, that New York must be the "most divine place on the globe." With that, she gave him a hooded look that told him she knew *exactly* what he was doing.

At City Hall, he got down from a hired hackney cab, with Jean Baptiste at his elbow. He climbed the steps of the white stone building. It was a bright sunshiny day, bitter cold, but not windy. He felt wonderful. His health was fully restored, he had regained his weight and upper body strength. Best of all, he had left a thriving business behind him in New Orleans, a firm whose success his father had grudgingly admired, enough to buy from him both the property and the list of clients at a surprisingly good price.

Satisfied that he had succeeded in the first part of his plan, Philippe was about to embark on the second leg of his journey. Success in New York would enable him to find and marry Mariette, the only girl he had ever loved.

He took a firm hold on his silver-headed cane with his one good hand. The cane attracted no attention, since canes were very much in style. But to Philippe it was indispensable, since it gave him posture and balance, which he needed if he were to make the proper impression, not only on his future employer but on the company managers and ships' captains he'd be dealing with.

Dressed in a new dark-blue greatcoat, which he'd purchased on his arrival in New York, he was comfortable and warm. It was a coat not seen in the shops of New Orleans: a heavy wool garment, knee length, with a single row of buttons and a velvet shawl collar. He had splurged as well on close-fitting trousers of tan wool, a few fine linen shirts, stock collars and silk ascots. It was important to look good for his initial introduction into the business world, in spite of the pinned-up coat sleeve where his lower left arm should be. Walking close behind him, Jean Baptiste carried his master's satchel and umbrella.

Past the massive doors and inside the high-ceilinged corridor of the first floor, Philippe forced himself not to look up or about in the manner of a tourist. He directed his steps to a clerk seated at a table who appeared to be dispensing information.

"Is the Chamber of Commerce in this building?" he asked. He knew his English was still highly accented, but hoped it was at least understandable.

"Yes, sir," the clerk said. "Take the aisle to your left and enter at the second door."

Philippe nodded. He had understood what the clerk said. He knew enough English to get by, and when the visit was over, Jean Baptiste would fill in whatever he had missed.

Jean Baptiste had turned out to be a jewel in helping Philippe learn English on the voyage to New York. What Philippe had never known was that the black man had been born into a family of second-generation slaves on a tobacco plantation in South Carolina, where he'd learned English as the slaves spoke it. It was their own version of English, all bad grammar and a few African words thrown in, but Jean was smart, and he understood the language completely, even if he'd never spoken it correctly. It wasn't until he was sold down river to New Orleans that he'd had to learn French, and his speech had become the patois Philippe knew so well. But reverting to English was easy for Jean, and once Philippe discovered this, he set up a regimen of lessons in the privacy of their stateroom that had brought him to this point, where he could at least converse with Americans.

Philippe found the office of the Chamber of Commerce with no trouble. Jean Baptiste handed him his briefcase, opened the door for him, and sat on a waiting bench outside the office. Almost at once, Philippe was ushered into an impressive room with paneled walls, a work table, and many chairs. A large window looked out on a huge tree, bare of leaves, sketching a graceful design against the magnificent façade of the Astor House Hotel across Broadway.

He was asked to have a seat. Behind the desk sat a wiry little man, with a nameplate on his desk, announcing that he was Edward A. Stern. He had a handlebar moustache and a harsh look beneath bushy eyebrows, and his frowning countenance lived up to his name.

When at last he had the man's attention, Philippe explained that he was looking for work as a commission merchant in New York, that he'd just left his own successful commission house in New Orleans, that he had twelve years experience in the field, and would be obliged if Mr. Stern would give him the names of one or two commission houses in Manhattan where he might inquire.

Edward Stern looked Philippe up and down, his gaze resting for a long time on the empty sleeve. He shuffled through a box of cards and pulled out two. Before he spoke, he clacked the edges of the cards on the desk top, studying Philippe rudely. Then, suddenly he asked, "D'you think you can do the job with a missing arm?"

Philippe had to pinch his lips together not to laugh. The question was so outlandish, it was funny. It was also unnecessary, since he'd just said he'd left a successful commission business in New Orleans. "Yes. I'm sure I can," Philippe said crisply. "I've worked for four months since I lost my arm and had one of the richest commission houses in New Orleans."

"Oh," the man said, and nothing else.

Philippe had papers in his satchel, Balance Sheets and Statements of Profit and Loss, but decided not to show them to Mr. Edward A. Stern, unless of course, the man refused to give him the names on the cards. Finally, after another thorough perusal of Philippe's physique, Edward A. Stern dipped his quill pen in ink and wrote out the names and addresses of two firms on the back of his business card. Philippe bid the man good day and left the office.

The first commission house he visited was called Darensbourg's and the owner, Herman Darensbourg, a red-faced German with a hearty laugh and a rough brown beard, looked him over. After Philippe had shown him the impressive records of his company for the past four months, he hired him on the spot. As to comments on Philippe's appearance, he had only one thing to say. "Son, if you go out like that, you'll be the best dressed man on the waterfront, and no doubt about it."

Philippe smiled. He liked the man. "I had no warm clothes for your hard New York weather," he explained, "so I bought these when I arrived. But I'll be wearing less expensive ones in the spring."

"Better wait till summer, Mr. Grillet," Darensbourg said. "Sometimes our winters last all spring. And don't be apologizin' for lookin' spiffy." Then, almost as an afterthought, "When would you like t'start work, I wonder?"

"Right away," Philippe said, grinning at the prospect.

"You've got a heavy accent there, my boy," Cobb said, good-naturedly. "Think you can talk to the captains of English ships?"

"I'm learning more English every day," Philippe said. "I'm sure I'll do fine." Philippe knew that his ace in the hole was Jean Baptiste, who'd be with him at all times, carrying his satchel and translating when necessary.

"Well, I'll tell you what, Son. Come in tomorrow at 8 a.m. It happens I've got a ship comin' in in the mornin', if it's on schedule and the tide is right. The captain's French, an' he'll be overjoyed to do business with a Frenchman."

Philippe left the commission house walking on a cloud. He asked Jean Baptiste to take a walk with him along the waterfront to see what was going on. In New Orleans, he'd always loved to watch ships unloading their cargoes, and he was astounded at the number of ships in the New York harbor and the magnitude of the business in progress. What a flourishing town for merchants who knew what to sell to whom, and he vowed in that moment to learn what came in and out of this port, where it came from, exactly who wanted it, and how it should get there. Oh, yes, he would succeed here. And what luck that the commission house was only three blocks from South Street, where he'd do most of his trading. His legs were strong, and he knew he'd enjoy walking from the commission house to the waterfront each day.

On that first walk, he bid the time of day to sailmakers and tanners and ship chandlers. It was a good day and a good start. If all went well, he would soon find his beloved girl, and nothing on God's earth would stop him from marrying her.

CHAPTER 65

One evening, three months after she'd been acting at Niblo's Gardens, Mariette arrived at the theater to find that she'd soon be starring in a new play, *The Foundling of the Forest,* opposite an actor called Robert Courtney, recently arrived from London. He was a handsome man with a rich voice and a long string of credits in the English theater. He had been a student and later an instructor at the Royal Academy of Dramatic Arts in London, and he'd left England at the height of his career, the matinee idol of the London West End theater district.

Every member of the cast was wondering why he'd left such a successful career in England to try his luck "across the pond." Mariette was puzzled, too, for here was this theatrical star, the toast of two continents, teamed up with a relative nobody from New Orleans in a play that the critics predicted would be the favorite of the season.

Even during their first rehearsal, it was easy to see that he and Mariette worked well together, that there was chemistry between them that would be sure fire at the box office. Courtney was tall, auburn-haired, mellow-voiced, a consummate actor. And Mariette, the fair-skinned brunette with the French accent, was small and delicate with an undeniable sensuality. They complemented each other, and when the plot called for an embrace or a kiss, they were so convincing in their performances, the audience purred as one. Each was a perfect foil for the other, and the theater-going world hoped there would be a romantic relationship between them.

As Mariette expected, gossip about a romance was not long in coming, although Robert had never so much as touched her hand unless it was required in the course of the play. But *Foundling of the Forest* was a romance, and his words and embraces and the ending kiss were so deliciously sensual, there was no convincing the rest of the cast—to say nothing of the audience and worst of all, the newspaper reporters—that these two beautiful people did not continue their romantic activities in private. Columnists blatantly hinted at liaisons that had never taken place, with questions like "What English actor has been seen squiring a certain young French star about town in the last few weeks?" It was lies, *all lies.* He'd never even spoken to her except on stage, and the words he'd spoken there weren't even his own.

Viewers would not dismiss it. Robert and Mariette were both unattached, they were handsome, and their loving embraces were sizzling. Or so it seemed. Even William Niblo hoped that a real-life romance would ignite between them, for it would pack his theaters forever. As it was, during the run of *The Foundling,* it was all but impossible to get seats, and the play had to go into additional weeks to satisfy the romance lovers of the city.

Mariette found Robert a delight to work with. He was so convincing as a lover that she found herself returning his on-stage embraces with equal ardor, more so because she knew that he did not take them seriously and he would walk away from her at the end of the play as if she were a stranger.

Truth to tell, he was cool and stand-offish in his attitude toward her offstage. It gave her reason to wonder if she was still attractive or if she was getting old and losing her looks. She certainly wasn't interested in romantic entanglements; but on the other hand, it seemed an affront to be totally ignored. Mentally she shrugged, not really caring, but her fellow actors kept talking in whispers behind their hands, thinking it all a great act the two stars were putting on, saving their amorous engagements for private moments.

Mariette simply thought of Robert as the Mystery Man, the name he'd been given in the newspapers, the Man with an Unknown Past. It was his business, and a relief in a way. So long as he didn't confide in her, she did not feel obliged to confide in him, and it was so much better that way. Mariette had learned long ago that a secret was only a secret so long as only one person knew it.

At last one evening, to her great surprise, as she and Robert were leaving by the stage door at the same time, he addressed her. "Miss Mariette," he said. She started, surprised at the unexpected voice. "May I see you home? I have my Phaeton waiting just around the corner."

"Oh!" she said. "Thank you, no. I have a standing engagement with a driver who takes me back and forth to the theater."

"If you show me where he is, I'll be glad to tell him...and pay him...that is, unless you have other plans."

"No. No other plans," Mariette said in a small voice. She was not at all happy about this turn of events. He seemed to be taking matters out of her hands altogether. If she let him take her home, she would definitely not invite him in. Her mother would be asleep and so would Daisy, and he must not see either of them in any case. No one in New York knew of her family, and Robert Courtney was not going to be the first to find out.

But Mariette had been brought up to be polite and she didn't know how to say no. She sighed audibly and then smiled a small smile. "I'll tell him myself," she said. "But I can't stop anywhere along the way. I must go directly home. I'm very tired."

"Of course," he said.

There was little conversation along the way. Mariette twisted the tassle of her reticule, trying to think of something inconsequential to say. She didn't want to ask where he lived or anything about his personal life outside the theater. At last, she thought of a safe subject, one of interest to them both.

"The play is going very well, don't you think?" she asked in a thin voice.

"Oh, yes, well indeed. Niblo says he may have to keep it going for a third two-week run, but he'll have a problem there."

"Oh? I should think he'd be glad it's so popular."

"Well, I'm sure he is, but you see, some of the actors in the play that follows this one are threatening to look for work elsewhere unless their play starts soon."

Mariette considered this conundrum. "Hmm. But that's a good problem to have, wouldn't you say?" she asked, smiling. "It shows how successful his plays are. I wonder why he doesn't just move our play to one of his other theaters."

Robert smiled. It was the first time Mariette had ever seen him smile except when a smile was called for in the play. "Do you remember the Old Testament story of Solomon's advice about splitting the baby in two?" he asked.

"Yes, but..."

"Well, that's what he'd have to do with us, because we're in the cast of the next play as well."

Mariette laughed girlishly. "Oh, yes," she said. "I'd forgotten that."

When they reached Bowling Green, Robert looked around well, taking in the little park with its trees and benches, and the three-story red-brick houses that formed the cul-de-sac. "Charming neighborhood," he said.

Mariette wasn't at all glad he knew where she lived. It was as if he now had a foot in the door. And God only knew what he would ask of her next. But on the other hand, the ice was broken. They worked so closely together, it seemed a good thing for them to be friends. After parking the Phaeton, he walked her up the stairs, not even holding her arm. And after she'd taken her key from her reticule, he unlocked the door and let her pass through, returning her key and nodding his head in a small bow as a friendly goodnight gesture. When she was inside, she breathed a sigh of relief. He had not asked to come in. He had not made the slightest romantic advance, and yet, they knew each other a little better now. And for that, she supposed she was grateful.

CHAPTER 66

It wasn't Philippe's idea to go to the Astor House Hotel dining room for a mid-day meal, but his boss had been urging him to do so for months. "You're a fine-looking young man, always dressed in good taste," Herman Darensbourg said, with his perpetual smile. "You should be mixing with the 'big people' in town. It never hurts to know the upper crust, and it's good for business. Take my word for it."

So, on a day when he had no afternoon appointments, Philippe went to the Astor, not expecting to enjoy himself. In New Orleans, he'd known the kind of "big people" Darensbourg was referring to and he'd never liked them. Oh, there were one or two wealthy men who were down-to-earth and hard-working, like the merchant Maunsel White and his friends, the Byrnes brothers, who were the brains behind the New Basin Canal. But then there were his father's friends, society moguls of great wealth, who were out to impress the world with their importance. They talked of their trips abroad and their Phaetons and their daughters' coming out parties till they made him sick. He smiled, remembering his sister Jeanine, who'd absolutely refused to be introduced to society. This had been taken as an insult by her friends, who'd considered their debuts the highlights of their young lives, and as a disgrace by her mother, who had taken to her bed for a week. What would she tell her friends, she kept asking Jeanine. But to no avail. There would be no coming out party for Jeanine Grillet.

But here he was at the elegant restaurant, in the Garden Room, surrounded by potted palms and seated at a huge glass window overlooking one of the most beautiful gardens he'd ever seen— flower beds of lilies and roses and hardy bushes in topiary designs of birds and swans, all surrounding a long reflecting pool. He decided he was glad he'd come. Manhattan was indeed an island of many sights and sounds, and he had only just dipped his toe into the pool. What surprised him most was that there was so much land around this hotel, and around everything in New York. This was new to him, this surfeit of land, for Philippe had come from a city where every inch of cleared land was occupied.

The waiter came, and he ordered his meal, delighted to find the menu in French. He found himself relishing filet of sole, fresh asparagus, and trifle for dessert, altogether the most delicious meal he'd had since leaving home.

As he ate, he took his time looking around, knowing he'd have to report to Mr. Darensbourg. To his amazement, Mr. John Astor *himself,* as everyone in New York seemed to say, showed up for lunch and ensconced himself in his private dining area, set off by an arbor, but still in full view of his guests. He was there to have lunch, like everyone else, and yet somehow the arbor set him apart, like a monarch. The arbor amused Philippe, who watched the man for a while and was amazed to see him mix all his food together, dessert included, and use his knife to shovel it into his mouth. And if that wasn't bad enough, he wiped his hands on the table cloth. Philippe wanted to laugh, thinking how his mother would react. But the waiters' faces were as rigid as the Sphinx, and not a guest in the room raised an eyebrow, for this was John Jacob Astor, and he could do as he damn well pleased. It was his hotel, and if he ate like a pig, he brooked no criticism. For Philippe's part, he didn't care if the man was the world's greatest real estate genius. He still had the worst table manners Philippe had ever seen. He shook his head in wonder.

Looking around the room, Philippe spotted journalists whose columns he'd read and two important men he'd heard about, Commodore Vanderbilt and one of the Roosevelts. He began to understand that it was a place where the "big people" came to be seen. After his coffee, he asked the waiter to bring his accounting, and while opening his *porte-monnaie*, requested that he give his compliments to the chef, for he had rarely enjoyed a meal so much.

"I'll do that, sir," the waiter said. Then, responding to Philippe's amiability, asked, "Are you new in town, sir? I haven't seen you here before."

"Yes," Philippe said, smiling. "I've been in Manhattan only a few months."

"I thought I might point out to you the gentleman over there, the one in the gray frock coat? He's the stage star, Robert Courtney. Sometimes newcomers go to the theater and they like to see a famous actor in real life."

Philippe's heart raced. He had read the newspaper hints about a romance between Robert Courtney and his Mariette. At first he hadn't believed them, but when the reporters continued to harp on the subject, he'd begun to wonder.

"He's a British star," the waiter added, noticing the small frown of interest playing around Philippe' s forehead. "He's in a play at

Niblo's with a new French star, Mariette something or other, who's all the rage these days."

"Thank you," Philippe said curtly. He put some bills on the waiter's tray without comment. Sensing his customer's change in attitude, the waiter departed swiftly.

Philippe had, of course, already seen Mariette on stage. A few days after his arrival, he'd bought tickets and he and Jean had sat side by side in the last row on the first floor at Niblo's, Jean with a smile on his face a mile wide. Never before had he sat beside a white man in a theater, never anywhere but in the third balcony, reserved for Coloreds, where he could not hear or see a thing. As for Philippe, he'd spent the whole performance smiling too, but smiling with love for the beautiful actress in the play. He was so proud of her and so light-headed, seeing her for the first time in over a year, he wished that he'd had the courage to go backstage and declare himself to her. But he had a plan, and he decided to stick with it. At that time, he hadn't been sure at all that he'd be successful in business in New York. More than that, he admitted in all honesty; he was afraid to show himself for fear of rejection.

Many times since then, he'd seen her on stage, loving her more each time, but still holding back. And then one night, he'd seen her acting with Robert Courtney as her leading man. His face burned with anger when the man took Mariette in his arms and kissed her deeply and long. He'd had a hard time watching that obscenity. He kept telling himself it was only a play, it meant nothing, but all the while he was seething with jealousy. And since then, he'd tried to put it out of his mind. But that was impossible when the newspaper reporters wrote, true or false, about their secret romance. At any rate, he hadn't gone to see her then, or since. And maybe now, it was too late. Maybe she really was in love with Robert Courtney.

If that was true, and Philippe presented himself to her, she might, with her generous heart, feel compelled to be loyal to him, to pretend it didn't matter about his arm, while all the while, she'd be agonizing over Courtney and the compromise she'd been forced to make.

Philippe sat a minute and took a good look at Robert Courtney. He allowed grudgingly that the man was handsome in a rugged way that would appeal to men as well as women. He was meticulously dressed: diamond in his cravat, barber shave, the works. Philippe cringed, thinking how he undoubtedly enjoyed being paired with his beautiful Mariette, onstage and, for all he knew, offstage as well. Yes, it was very possible she was already in love with Courtney. He was her leading man, and things like that happened.

Philippe felt the urge to cross the room and, and with his one good hand, punch the man right in his handsome British face. It brought him up short to realize that if he did, the man could not strike back since Philippe was lame. Suddenly, there descended upon him an all-consuming depression. He knew in that instant he could no longer defend himself physically. There would never be another duel. Not even a fist fight. Not that he was by nature aggressive, but it was still the bleakest blow of all.

He was suddenly overcome by nausea and a severe pain in his abdomen. He was afraid he might lose the dinner he'd just enjoyed. With a heavy heart, he left the dining room, and fortunately found, adjacent to it, a reading room where he sat down in a soft leather chair to rest his nerves and overcome his distress. He laid his head back and closed his eyes. Drawing in a deep breath, he forced himself to relax. But he could not escape the reality that if Mariette loved Courtney, everything he'd accomplished up to this point was a pathetic waste.

Some minutes later, a voice called out, "I say, old chap, are you ill?" The voice was deep and mellifluous and totally British, as it resounded in the silent reading room.

Philippe opened his eyes but remained in a reclining position and did not even turn his head. Across the room, seated at a reading table, Robert Courtney had stopped in the middle of turning a page of the newspaper. Philippe looked around. There was no one else in the room.

"No. I'm fine," Philippe said.

The Englishman would not be put off. Slowly, he folded his paper, got up from the table, and walked over to sit in an easy chair facing Philippe. "Are you sure you're all right?" Courtney asked, "You look a bit flushed. Is there anyone I can summon?"

Philippe wanted to tell the man to mind his own business, to go to Hell and leave him alone in his misery. He wanted to say that if he was ill, it was all Courtney's fault. But the actor was being solicitous. And Philippe realized with a blinding insight that if he didn't befriend Robert Courtney, he'd never find out what he had to know—if Mariette was in love with him. He must force himself to make conversation.

He pulled himself up to a sitting position and answered. "Just a bit of indigestion, I think."

"Well, perhaps I could get you some kind of restorative," Courtney said. "I'm sure the Astor Hotel would have something. Should I ask a waiter?"

Philippe shook his head. "I don't think the Astor dining room would appreciate a request for a stomach restorative." He forced a wan smile. "But thank you, anyway."

"I'm Robert Courtney," the man said, extending his hand in greeting.

Philippe moved forward and shook the actor's hand. He decided in that moment to give a false name and not reveal too much about himself. Courtney might tell Mariette about their meeting and give her his name, and he wasn't ready for that yet.

"Gerard Dupre," Philippe said, calling from memory the name of a fellow student.

"Glad to know you. May I give you a ride to wherever you're going?"

"No. Thank you. I have a servant waiting for me outside in a rig."

"From France, are you?"

"Yes," Philippe said. The man knew his accent, of course, and this was as good a lie as any.

"I'm European, too," said Courtney. "From London. I'm an actor, working at Niblo's Garden. Do you frequent the theater?"

"Yes," Philippe said. "I saw your play. It was excellent."

"Thank you." He did not pursue the subject. "And what is your line of work, old chap?"

The reference rubbed Philippe the wrong way. "I'm a commission merchant." Philippe thought fast. Making up a whole new identity was not easy, though he'd done it once before for Mariette. He'd have to remember his lies. And he wasn't feeling well enough to strain his brain. "I was working out of Marseilles for several years," he said, "but once the Erie Canal opened here, everyone in commerce seemed to be making a fortune from it. So I decided to try my luck in New York."

"Is that so?" Courtney smiled, genuinely interested. "And have you been successful here?"

Against his inclinations, Philippe liked the man. He was not only concerned about a stranger's health but eager to hear about his business. He seemed like a good man. It wasn't his fault if he'd fallen in love with Mariette. Who wouldn't, if he held her in his arms and kissed her every night and twice on Sundays?

"Quite successful," Philippe answered. "There's no place else in America—or Europe, for that matter—where there's so much trade that there aren't enough ships and merchants to handle it."

"That good!" Courtney exclaimed ingenuously. He sat back and crossed his legs, making himself comfortable in the posture of a man on the verge of a long conversation. "Tell me about it, old man, if you're up to it. I'm eager to know everything about this country."

Another point scored, Philippe thought. He found that he'd recovered from his anxiety attack, now that he'd accepted the fact that Robert Courtney meant no harm, and was indeed personable. Strange as it seemed, in other circumstances, he would've been pleased to have such a friend. God knows he needed one. For several months now, he'd had no friend at all in this foreign frozen tundra, except for Jean Baptiste, and he couldn't take Jean everywhere with him. The Astor was a good example of that.

Philippe began talking about a subject he knew and enjoyed thoroughly. "Well, it was the Erie Canal that did it. They say it's the greatest feat of engineering since the Egyptian pyramids."

"Really?" Courtney asked, entranced.

Philippe nodded. "It was an idea a hundred years ahead of its time. It was conceived and carried out by the will of one man, a man of vision, Mister DeWitt Clinton."

Courtney's intelligent eyes locked with Philippe's and he nodded, ingesting this bit of information. "Well, what was the idea?"

"The Erie Canal was built to connect the immense wealth of the interior of the American continent with the port of New York, by way of the Hudson River. It was genius; everyone knew it, but it was thought impossible at this time, even by President Jefferson."

"But he did it?" Courtney asked. "Clinton, I mean."

"Oh, yes. He built a ditch, an artificial river, 350 miles long through swamps and hills in upstate New York. It took nine thousand men to do the job." Philippe found himself warming to the subject with the innate pride of an American.

"Remarkable!"

"So, if a merchant can't make a living here, he can't make it anywhere." At last, he smiled a genuine smile. He was thinking how good a living he was making here, how he and Jean Baptiste had become a well-known sight on the waterfront, wending their way from one ship to the next, the French one-armed merchant and the black man who carried his satchel and umbrella. They were a curious and recognizable pair, easy to spot among the brawny Irish and Germans on the docks.

Courtney smiled. He laced his fingers and sat back to listen. "Give me a typical day of your work," he said.

"Well, my first assignment here was easy for me. Since I spoke French, my employer sent me to meet a ship's captain who also spoke French. He came to New York with a shipload of Parisian clothing, fabrics, fans, things like that. So I wined him and dined him and won the account. The merchandise was then consigned to my employer, to be sold to wholesalers in those industries." He smiled proudly and rested back against his chair. "Then, you see, after I made the connection, word spread in the network of the shipping world and other contracts followed...for me *and* for my employer."

"Good show!" Courtney said, smiling with a flash of white teeth. At this point, Robert Courtney stood, and Philippe did the same. He appreciated the fact that Courtney did not try to help him to his feet. When both were standing, he shook Philippe's hand. "I'd like to give you two tickets to tomorrow night's performance. I'll leave them at the box office in the name of Dupre. Will you come?"

"If I am able." Philippe smiled.

"And would you have lunch with me next week?" Courtney asked. "I've enjoyed our talk." He hesitated before saying, "I hope you won't think me presumptuous, but I believe you and I are in the same situation…that is to say, without friends in a foreign city."

Philippe nodded. "You're right."

"So will you meet me here next Monday at noon? The theaters are closed on Mondays."

Philippe hesitated. The last thing he wanted was a close friendship with his sweetheart's lover, if indeed Courtney was that. But that was what Philippe had to find out. He'd have to encourage the comradeship, at least for a while. "Yes. I will," he said, and hoped he was doing the right thing.

CHAPTER 67

More and more often, Mariette found Robert Courtney waiting at the stage door after performances, in the hope of taking her home. He was always smiling in anticipation of their meeting, always immaculately attired, and always surrounded by adoring female fans, who peppered him with questions about his private life and paid him every kind of compliment, delicate and otherwise.

By their attentions, he was neither pleased nor annoyed. He was accustomed to female adoration and comfortable with it, giving even the humblest fan a kind smile or a nod. But he did not engage in conversation with them. He made it clear by the way his eyes never left the stage door, that he was waiting for Mariette. And when she at last appeared and stood at the top of the stairs, his adoring fans were silenced momentarily, diminished by jealousy. Then, as if on cue, they returned their gaze to Robert with more sighs and more requests for autographs.

Mariette had to admit that he was a treat for the eyes, a true matinee idol, and she couldn't help feeling proud that she was his leading lady. After a week of such obviously planned meetings,

Mariette dismissed Danny, explaining that it would only be tempo-rary, and she knew where to reach him in time when she needed him. She felt bad about it and paid him an extra week's wages to make up for the inconvenience.

She enjoyed her rides home with Robert. Both she and Robert played their roles with such intense realism that they were spent at the end of a performance and needed a brief respite afterwards. For a while, they rode along in companionable silence. Then, when the tension eased, Robert smiled engagingly at Mariette and offered a bit of conversation. They sometimes began talking at the same time, then laughed at themselves, and began again, with small compli-ments for each other's appearance and performances. Their relationship existed solely in the theater world, and in that sphere, they were at ease in each other's company.

Mariette was pleased to discover that conversation came easily, although their topics were limited. They enjoyed critiquing their nightly performances, discussing how they might have been improved. "If only I had spoken in a quieter, more masterful voice in the first scene," Robert once said. And on another occasion, Mariette suggested, "I think our blocking was wrong in Act Two. We should have been standing closer to the audience for the last argument. We should ask Mr. Niblo about it." Like the conscien-tious professionals they were, they provided each other with valuable insights, each bringing up a point the other might have overlooked.

Mariette discovered that she had missed male companionship. In truth, until Robert entered her life, she'd had little companionship of any kind. As for close women friends, she had only her mother and Mrs. O'Flaherty. The actresses she worked with daily were distant and aloof in their relationship with her. They made it clear that they were not her friends, and they considered her an inexperienced upstart from a small port city. In spite of that, she knew that to them, she was a threat. She often caught glances and smirks that spoke of criticism, resentment, and jealousy, and she saw nothing to be gained by trying to convince these women that she meant them no harm, that she was simply earning a living, and she had no ambitions that might work to their detriment.

And so she refrained from engaging in conversation with them altogether and felt no loss when they were cold with her. She was working in an arena she loved, doing the only work she knew. Acting came easily to her, and she needed the income to support her mother and child. It was as simple as that.

She hurt no one and asked no quarter. She accepted the wages Niblo paid her–generous wages, to be sure–and asked for nothing more. She enjoyed the privacy of a simple, if not luxurious, dressing room. It was small but clean and adequate, and she would never have asked for better accommodations. Except for the pain deep in her heart at the absence of her beloved Philippe, she was content. And when that overwhelming depression gripped her, as it so often did, she turned her thoughts to her beautiful, wonderful baby, and it helped restore her peace of mind.

Her nightly ride home with Robert turned out to be a bright new interlude in her otherwise routine life. For some reason she could not fathom, with this elegant Englishman, who had landed in her world as if from another planet, she could be herself. Although she and Robert came from worlds apart, or maybe because of it, she could relax with him and enjoy a pleasant impersonal chat. He was charming, witty, and not at all stuffy, as she had thought he'd be. It was as if neither had a personal life outside the theater. And Mariette meant to keep it that way.

Robert told her about the differences between the theaters in London and those in Manhattan, a subject which she found endlessly fascinating. He regaled her with stories about British royalty, stories that enthralled her. He spoke about the British wars against the French, which he always called "the French wars," the reference he'd obviously learned in school. "The French wars," he said, "always ended in British victories." He said it with a winsome teasing smile, knowing of course that Mariette's background was French.

Mariette, no fool when it came to English and French history, countered with the story of the Battle of New Orleans just twenty-five years earlier, in which the Frenchmen of New Orleans, along with a rag-tag army of Americans, had soundly whipped the British, making America a world power and one to be reckoned with. She told her story in a voice that rang with pride, emphasizing that her home town was now a valued port city, second only to New York, and that New Orleans had contributed much to the strength of the new nation.

It was only after she'd made this proud declaration that she realized she'd revealed New Orleans as the place of her birth, inadvertently giving Robert a piece of the puzzle of her previously hidden past.

"You have a fine grasp of the significance of the battle, Mariette," Robert said with obvious admiration. "But of course, you know that history is always written by the victor," he added, raising an admonishing finger.

"Of course," Mariette admitted. "That was why we had to make sure we won."

Robert laughed good-heartedly. Gently, he took her gloved hand and kissed the back of it, swiftly, carelessly, and then released it, as if it made no difference at all, but suddenly, Mariette felt her cheeks warm. It was their first physical encounter offstage. It was a small gesture, indeed, but it spoke of approval and affection, and it was totally unexpected. It left her breathless and confused.

Robert, seeing her discomfort, rushed in to fill the silence. "You must have studied the battle well," he said.

"I had good tutors," she said humbly, and then no more, deciding she had opened enough windows to her private life for one evening.

CHAPTER 68

Their nightly rides led to late night suppers in out-of-the-way hotels and eateries. For a foreigner, Robert seemed to know all the nicest restaurants in New York, cozy little places with crisp linen tablecloths, shaded candles, and little vases of fresh flowers. Gloved waiters were always in speedy attendance, laying out crystal and silverware before them.

Weeks became months and their relationship deepened. One evening, to her surprise, Robert gave Mariette a glimpse into his personal life. They were seated at their favorite table in a small restaurant. They had ordered their meal and were making small talk. "I don't think I ever told you about a young Frenchman I met a few months ago at the Astor dining room," Robert said. "A nice chap. Very knowledgeable." He took a cracker from a small china dish on the table and spread butter on it. "He's from Marseilles. We've been meeting for the past few weeks for lunch on Mondays. He has no friends in New York, either, so it was fortuitous that we met."

Mariette's heart lurched when he said a Frenchman, but as soon as he said Marseilles, she settled down again, knowing she was grasping at straws.

"Well, I'm glad for you, Robert," she said. "It's good to have a friend when you're new in town." She had a faraway look that Robert recognized as loneliness and he decided to change the subject. He spoke of their new play, *A House of Cards*, which had followed *The Foundling of the Forest.* Based on their previous success acting together, Niblo had given them the starring roles, and once again their performances packed the theater. And after each performance, Mariette found herself looking forward to Robert's company.

The newspapers had, of course, picked up on their secret rides and dinner engagements, hinting at every imaginable kind of clandestine activity, although not a single romantic word had passed between them. Mariette worried about the stories, wondering if she should put an end to their nightly rendevous. She could not bear to think that Philippe might be in New York and might read what the reporters were saying and decide to stay out of her life altogether.

One afternoon, she found her mother in the kitchen, enjoying her cup of strong dark tea and a small cake. It was Desiree's one concession to her sweet tooth, that mid-afternoon *gouter*. Mariette sat at the table across from her and rested her chin in her palms. "I may have to tell Robert I can't see him any more," she said in a small sad voice, "and I hate to do it." She sighed. "Until he met me, he had no other female companionship. And I'll be sending him back to that life of loneliness." She thought of the stranger Robert had befriended, but knew that was not the same as having a woman companion.

"And what about your own life of loneliness?" Desiree asked. She sipped her tea. Mariette shook her head slowly, saying nothing.

"Mariette, get yourself a cup of tea and come talk to me," she said. Mariette got up and poured herself a cup from the china pot on the trivet. She sat once again on the kitchen chair facing her mother and added cream and sugar.

"Is Daisy napping?" she asked.

"Yes, she's good for an hour or more. I just put her down. Now I want you to listen to me." Desiree stirred her tea and gathered her thoughts. "First of all, it's not your fault that Robert Courtney has no female companionship," she began. "He's chosen to be a recluse, for whatever reason. He doesn't even confide in you as to what the reason is."

"Nor do I confide in him," Mariette argued, but gently, knowing the truth of her mother's words. "And by the way, he's not exactly a recluse. Not any longer. He made friends with a young man from France. He meets him for lunch every week, so perhaps he's not as mysterious as people say."

"Well, good for him," Desiree said curtly. "Now you won't have to feel so sorry for him in his loneliness." In truth, Desiree didn't understand her daughter's relationship with the handsome British actor at all. "And as far as female companionship is concerned, just as he began a relationship with you, he can do the same with someone else, *n'est-ce pas?*"

Mariette nodded uncertainly.

"*He* was the one who sought *you* out, not the other way around." She waited, but Mariette said nothing. "You've never committed yourself to him in any way, have you?"

"No. Never."

"You've been clever, Mariette."

Cleverness has nothing to do with it, Mariette thought. She wanted to object to the spin her mother was putting on her friendship with

Robert, but Desiree raised her hand to silence her. She had not yet had her say. "Now consider this, *cherie*. He seems like a good man, and obviously not without means. He's very much attracted to you. I think he may be in love with you." Mariette shook her head, but Desiree pushed on. "Or if not now, he probably will be. But it is his way to take things slowly. And that's good. It gives you a chance to look to your future and make the right decision. In time, I feel sure he'll ask you to marry him, and I don't think it would be such a bad idea."

"But suppose Philippe..."

"Philippe! Philippe!" Desiree sighed aloud with exhaustion. "He's probably dead, Mariette." Mariette's heart gave a giant thud at the sound of the harsh, cruel word. "And if he's alive and he still wants you, he can certainly find you. You're a star on the New York stage, and no one is easier to find. Philippe is no fool. And if he needs help, Caldwell will certainly point him in the right direction." She waited but Mariette had no reply. "So? Doesn't that tell you something?"

Mariette stared blankly at the kitchen wall. It told her something, all right, something she didn't want to face. She sipped her tea and said nothing, but Desiree knew she had given her something to think about.

"It may be good for you to marry Robert Courtney," Desiree said thoughtfully. "I think he would treat you well."

Mariette turned her face away. She didn't want to hear about marriage to Robert. Her mother should know, after all this time, that she would never marry anyone but Philippe, but she had wearied her mother with talk of her long lost love, and she didn't have the strength for an argument.

Desiree took her daughter's chin between her thumb and forefinger and forced her to look into her dark eyes. "You could do worse, Mariette. You won't always be young and beautiful. Your stage career will not last forever. It might be the best thing for you...and for Daisy...to have a good man to support you when you're no longer playing leading roles on Broadway."

Mariette kept her own counsel. It occurred to her that her mother had said nothing about where she, Desiree, would fit into that picture. If Mariette married Robert, Desiree would no doubt be pushed into the background in her daughter's life, possibly into another flat in another part of town. If she married Robert, she might stop acting altogether and stay home to take care of her own baby. Perhaps she might have more babies. That might be Robert's wish. And where would that leave Desiree, her loyal mother, the loving grandmother of her baby? It occurred to her that Desiree had never blamed her for uprooting her from her home town and making her a live-in nurse for her baby. Mariette sighed heavily, as if the weight of the world was on her shoulders. She had no idea what the future held in store for either of them. The biggest decisions in her life always seemed to be made by other people...her father, Philippe, and possibly, in the near future, Robert.

Slowly, she stirred her tea and took another sip. Desiree left the kitchen, and Mariette remained where she was, surprised that her mother had given her situation so much thought. She drank her tea, washed her cup in the kitchen sink, and walked slowly to her bedroom. She would try to take a short nap before Daisy woke up and called out to her again.

CHAPTER 69

Wide-eyed, with no hope of sleeping, Mariette lay in bed, wondering what would happen if Robert proposed. He knew nothing at all about her. How would she explain having a mulattress mother and a baby but no husband? Maybe Robert wouldn't want her when he knew all about her. Well, that would be the end of it, *n'est-ce pas?* She could certainly never keep her family a secret.

She tried to tell herself, though she knew it was not entirely true, that the only reason she had not yet asked Robert to come to dinner and meet her mother was that their relationship had not progressed to that level. Meeting a lady's parents was a step on the road to the altar, or so she'd always believed, until she'd been forced into the despicable world of *plaçage*. That was something else she'd have to tell Robert if she agreed to marry him. The memory of that shameful period in her life, and the fact that she felt duty bound to reveal it to anyone she planned to marry, lay like a heavy stone in her chest, and from time to time, she thought she'd be physically sick from it. It was only Robert's company that had chased away those bad memories and lightened her mood. But the road ahead was still frightening.

Walking the floors that night, Mariette wondered if the facts about her hidden family would turn Robert away from her. She imagined he knew nothing whatsoever about *plaçage*. How could he know? It was a way of life that flourished in New Orleans because of the many black women of many shades of color that populated the city. There was also the fact that many light colored women had the delicate features of their white fathers. So many beauties, Mariette mused, whose only destiny was to provide forbidden sex to white men. How would Robert react if he knew that she, Mariette, had been part of all that?

Maybe Englishmen were more liberal than Americans when it came to having illicit sex and producing children out of wedlock. She knew one Englishman who lost no sleep over his own clandescent affairs and had accepted her arrangement with Soniat with delight. James Caldwell. She had been forced to allow him to think the worst of her. And yet, to Caldwell, free love was not a vice, but a most satisfying way of life.

She knew from personal experience that French fathers in New Orleans guarded their virginal daughters with their lives, never allowing them to be in the company of gentlemen admirers without chaperones until the marriage vows had been said. Yet the same strict fathers might take virgin quadroons in *plaçage*. How could they live with such irreconcilable points of view? What hypocrites they were! So genteel in their own parlors and so base in the bedrooms of their *placées!* Naturally, her father and Louis Soniat leapt to mind, and she had to swallow hard to keep the bile from rising in her throat. But Mariette reminded herself that all that had happened in New Orleans, and she was not in New Orleans any more and might never live there again.

She was a Broadway star now and she loved everything about her new life, except... well, she wouldn't even say his name, or the tears would fall again. Her mother was right on that subject. She was tiresome even to herself. She determined in that moment that, at least for the time being, she'd just continue to enjoy Robert's company. If they wanted privacy, they'd simply have to find more remote meeting places, or start arriving and departing separately. This they must do, until he stated his intentions more clearly.

CHAPTER 70

After supper with Robert one night, Mariette pressed her serviette to her lips and placed it across her lap. She looked across the table into Robert's hazel eyes. "Robert," she said, "have you been reading the items about us in the newspapers?"

He nodded.

"Then you know what they're writing about our rendevous and our late night suppers."

A frown line formed between his heavy brows. "So?" he asked. "They must always have someone's secrets to reveal, true or false. It doesn't bother me. I'm the Mystery Man, remember?" He smiled.

"But it bothers *me*, Robert," Mariette said. "I don't want my reputation bandied about for the sake of a news story. I don't know what to do but I cannot allow it." Her tone sounded haughty, even to her own ears, and in that moment, she did not know herself. Was she becoming the actress Mariette Delon? She hoped not. But Robert seemed to find no fault in her. On the contrary, he was quick to shoulder the blame for having put her in a bad light.

"Oh, my dear," he said softly. He placed his coffee cup in the saucer and took her hand in his. "How unfeeling I've been, thinking only of myself." He laced his fingers through hers. "I have no one in this country who can be hurt by vicious stories. But it may be different with you. I don't know. You've never told me, and even now, I'm not asking you to say anything you don't wish to reveal."

Gently, Mariette released her fingers from his. She looked down at the table, silent, wondering if this would be the time to put an end to their secret meetings. At last, she folded her hands on the table top and faced him squarely. "You know how much I've enjoyed your friendship and the time we've spent together..."

"Mariette, wait," he said. "Please don't say you can't go on seeing me. Don't deprive me of your company. It means everything to me." He signaled the waiter to come clear their table. When every dish was taken away, Robert took Mariette's hands in both his own. "My dearest girl, we've done nothing wrong," he said. "I've respected your reluctance to discuss your private life."

Mariette closed her eyes and shook her head slowly. "Robert, you are entirely without fault. You have not even asked if I've ever been married."

He pressed a kiss to the back of each of her hands. "But I'm going to ask you now. Have you ever been married, my dear girl?"

"No, Robert. I am not married now, nor have I ever been married. But my dear friend, there are other things to know."

"Then tell me. Please tell me."

She sighed wearily. Where to begin? How much should she say? He'd been so good to her, and they'd worked so closely together. Yet, she knew that in telling him about herself, she'd be opening up a Pandora's Box and letting out all the heartaches and shames of her past life. Once out, they could never be hidden again. But she could not dismiss this good man without some explanation, and if she was to say anything at all, it would have to be the truth. So she vowed in that moment to tell him about herself, but only what she felt she could disclose.

"I fell in love with a young man in New Orleans two years ago," she said, " a man who wanted to marry me, but there were obstacles to our marriage, obstacles which I cannot explain to you." She met his gaze timidly, knowing she was treading in dangerous territory. Then, seeing the disappointment in his eyes, she added, "Well, not yet, anyway." He nodded, waiting patiently.

She gazed past his shoulder, not willing to meet his eyes, as she remembered the times of greatest turmoil in her life–the fire, the duel, and the long months after the duel when Philippe seemed to have disappeared from her life, and then, most frightening of all, when she discovered she was pregnant. She decided not to tell him these bitter memories, not only because they would be painful to expose, but because he had no right to share them. They were hers and Philippe's. At least she knew that much.

"I was acting in James Caldwell's new St. Charles Theater in New Orleans two years ago," she said, "and Mr. Niblo came to see the performance. He visited me backstage and offered me a contract to work in New York. And I accepted, because I wanted to put distance between myself and the man I loved, since he could never marry me. Now, Robert, this is what you must understand. If that man is still alive, and if he has followed me to New York, he will read in the newspaper that I am acting at Niblo's and that I have formed a serious romantic liaison. If that happens, he may never come to me." Tears welled in her eyes.

Robert took her hands again and held them a bit more firmly. She watched his face grow dark and she saw the frown line deepen between his heavy brows. "So, you're still in love with him."

Mariette withdrew her hands from Robert's. She placed them in her lap, laced her fingers, and found his eyes in the candlelight. "Yes, I am," she said. Robert waited, knowing she would say more. "As long as my relationship with you was unknown, I was happy to be with you. I've enjoyed our friendship more than I can say."

Now it was Robert's turn to be heard. "Mariette, I want you to listen to me. I'm going to tell you things I have told only Niblo. I felt he had a right to know, as my employer, since he might question my permanence with his company. And of course, he has an investment in me."

Mariette nodded. The waiter came and asked if they wanted to see the dessert cart, and Robert waved him away. He looked into Mariette's eyes. "I was married for five years to a beautiful woman, an actress, whom I loved dearly. When she became pregnant, we were both overjoyed. But to our great misfortune, she was unable to deliver the child. It was a breech birth...and...and...she died." He paused and cleared his throat. "The baby died, too," he said, almost inaudibly. He closed his eyes for a moment and then began again. "It's been three years since then, and even now, I'm hardly able to say the words."

Mariette placed her hand on the cuff of his frock coat. "Oh, Robert," she said. "I'm so sorry."

He nodded. "I couldn't bring myself to talk to anyone about it. And since it seemed frivolous to talk about anything else, I didn't talk at all. And so I became the Mystery Man." He smiled a one-sided smile and tossed his head to one side as if the gossip meant nothing to him. "But I've always felt that if a person was happy in a marriage, then he should marry again, because it is a life that suits him." He looked into Mariette's eyes with a look of anguish. "I won't ask you why the man can't marry you, or even why he may not still be alive. I will love you no matter what you tell me. The only thing I had to know was if you were free, and now that I know that, I would like you to consider this a proposal of marriage...that is, if and when you are ready."

Mariette had anticipated it. Her mother had anticipated it. And yet, now that the words hung between them, she was as uncertain about her answer as she had ever been.

"I know you don't love me, darling girl," he said. "You have been honest with me, and I admire your sincerity. But if he is in New York, if he's come here for you, he can easily find you."

It was what her mother had said, and it was undoubtedly true, but she found it hard to believe that Philippe would know where she was and would choose to stay away.

Robert rubbed the back of her hand fondly. It was a gesture he used on stage that endeared him to his fans. With actors, Mariette mused, one never knew where their stage mannerisms ended and their real-life gestures began. She supposed that an actor brought to his role what he knew from real life, what he *did* in real life, for that was what he was and he could not be otherwise. "I must add, though," Robert said, "that I find it hard to believe that any man would not want you."

She smiled weakly at the compliment and reached inside her reticule for her handkerchief. She pressed it to her eyes before the tears began falling.

But Robert was not yet finished. "We get along well together, Mariette. We have our work in common. We love the theater. I think if we were to marry, it might be an ideal life for us both, but I won't press you to answer me. Not yet."

Mariette knew in that moment that she would never marry Robert, even if he were willing to accept her heritage and her single motherhood. They were from different worlds, and she did not love the man, though hundreds of women would give anything to be in her shoes.

He waited. She found his hazel eyes in the dusky, candle-lit corner of the restaurant. "Robert," she said, "dear Robert...I am so sorry for all the heartache you've had in your life, and I admire you for being able to go on with your career in spite of it." She sighed heavily. She patted his hand. "I may marry someday. I don't know." She looked directly into his eyes. "But not now."

"I can wait," he said. "I will give you all the time in the world to decide."

She smiled with gratitude. She regretted hurting a man like Robert, but she couldn't give up on Philippe. She felt herself retreating into a private world where Robert had no place. Robert had changed the subject to relieve her anxiety. He was talking about some mundane event of the morning, but Mariette was far away–at an early morning Mass and a dueling field in Pere Antoine's Garden. In her mind's eye, she was looking down at her beloved Philippe stretched out on the dewy morning grass, unconscious and bleeding his life away. She was suddenly aware that Robert had stopped talking and was waiting for her to react...to something.

"I'm sorry, Robert. I was distracted. What did you say?" she asked,

"I was telling you about my unusual outing this morning."

"Oh?" She frowned, not the least interested.

"Yes, I went with my new friend to the waterfront to see him do his work. It was most enlightening."

"And what kind of work is that, Robert," she asked, annoyed at having her thoughts shunted to some unimportant detail in Robert's day.

"He's a commission merchant," Robert said.

Mariette felt her knees turn to water.

"They buy large cargoes of merchandise and sell them."

"Yes, I know what they do." She frowned, wondering how to fashion the question. "Is he from New Orleans?"

"No, my dear. Marseilles. Remember, I told you?"

"Oh, yes. Marseilles."

He picked up his story. "I was surprised to discover how brilliantly he operates. He's quite a salesman, although his English is highly accented, like..."

"Like mine?" Mariette asked, touching her throat with her fingers.

"Well, yes. And what surprised me," he said smiling, "is that he's quite a well-known sight on the waterfront, he and his black servant."

Jean Baptiste! It was Philippe! She had no doubt of it. She wanted to grab Robert's coat and shake the information out of him. "A black servant?" she asked.

"Yes, my friend is lame, you see, and the man carries his satchel and umbrella, and lifts things for him."

Mariette felt all the breath leaving her body. She knew in that moment that Philippe had come, that he had befriended Robert, and that he was just biding his time to come to her. She felt suddenly limp with a debilitating weakness. But there were questions she must find the strength to ask.

"In what way is he lame?" she asked.

"He lost his left arm below the elbow."

Mariette gasped.

"But he manages quite well. He never talks about it. And he's such an intelligent and likeable fellow, one soon forgets his incapacity."

"What is his name, Robert?" she managed to ask.

"Gerard Dupre. I've told you that." He frowned. "Why? Do you know the name?"

She shook her head. Philippe had no doubt given Robert a false name. "Did he ever tell you how he was wounded? Did he mention a duel?"

"A duel?" Robert gave her an astonished glance. "No. Never." He hesitated, frowning.

She closed her eyes and shook her head. She could say no more. Her premonitions were far too unrealistic to sound sane. And the story of the duel was the story of her life in plaçage and the disaster it had brought them to. She could not speak of it.

Silence fell between them like a pall. Each was rushing from one conclusion to another. For Mariette, all conclusions were beyond possibility, beyond hope. And yet she *had* to hope. She felt the room suddenly spinning around. A cold sweat broke out on her brow.

She took hold of Robert's coat sleeve and pushed on. "Robert, I know this sounds impossible, but I think your companion may be...oh, I know how foolish it seems, but ..." She could say no more. She was blacking out. She slumped against the chair in the restaurant and her eyes fell shut. Robert signaled the waiter and dropped a pile of bills on the table. He asked the man to help him carry Mariette to his Phaeton. And he drove her home.

CHAPTER 71

"Mariette! *Mon Dieu!*" Desiree said. "Why did you sleep in your clothes last night?"

Mariette awoke with a start to see the first gray light of dawn giving shape to her four poster bed and her night stand. Her mother stood over her with her back to the slatted shutters, a dark figure in the dusky room.

"Maman," she said, confused at being awakened so suddenly and surprised to find herself still fully dressed, her bedspread not even turned down. "Oh, yes, I remember. I was very weak last night in the restaurant, and Robert had to take me home in a hurry."

"But you should have called me, *ma fille.* I could have helped you off with your clothes and taken care of you."

"No. No, I couldn't call you. Robert took me to the door. I managed to walk up the stairs on my own. Then he wanted to wait while I called someone, but I think I almost closed the door in his face, poor man."

"But why, Mariette? I was here. Why didn't you call me?"

Mariette sat up and put her legs over the side of her bed. "Maman, try to understand. As sick as I was, I knew that if you and Robert came face to face, I'd have to explain who you were, and I just couldn't do that. Forgive me. I was too weak to make big decisions last night, so I let myself in the house and made it to my bed. And I guess I just fell asleep."

Desiree nodded. She understood. She might not like being hidden away and denied the title of Mother, but this was not new to her. It was the story of her life. And Mariette's. Without further word, she felt Mariette's forehead, but quickly convinced that there was no fever, she began to unbutton the back of Mariette's dress, as the girl sat limp and motionless. This done, she pulled the dress off, first by its long sleeves, then by its hem. Watching her daughter out of the corner of her eye, she walked quickly to the cedar robe and took out a soft cotton nightgown. Mariette neither moved nor spoke. Returning to the bed, Desiree loosened the strings at the back of Mariette's corset. At last, relieved of this constraint, Mariette drew in a deep breath.

"I don't know how you slept with all this on," Desiree said, shaking her head. She proceeded to remove Mariette's two underskirts and her drawers, and put the gown on her over her head. She turned down her daughter's counterpane and blanket and punched up her pillow. "There now. Go back to sleep. It's only 6:00 o'clock. Daisy isn't even awake yet. When she wakes up, I'll give her some breakfast, and then we'll go outside and let you rest this morning."

"Desiree," Mariette said weakly, "he's here. Here in New York. I know it."

"Who, Mariette?" Halfway to the door, she stopped and turned to face the girl.

"Philippe, of course," Mariette said, with an edge to her voice. *Who else would she be talking about?*

Desiree faced her daughter and shook her head. "And how do you know this?"

"Robert met him. Believe it or not, they've become friends." Seeing her mother's tight lips, she told the story quickly: how Robert met a Frenchman at the Astor Hotel in the dining room, and how they'd been meeting for lunch once a week. "He gave him a false name, of course, and said he was from Marseilles, but I know it is Philippe. I know he's come for me. I feel it inside."

But Desiree's eyes narrowed. "Mariette, that could be anybody, *ma fille*. You don't even know that Philippe was injured, or if he *is* lame. And if he is, it's even less likely that he would have made it to New York on his own and found himself a useful occupation."

"But Desiree, it *was* his occupation. It was what he did for a living in New Orleans."

"And based on that alone, you leap to the conclusion that it's Philippe." She shook her head. "He doesn't go by the name Philippe Grillet." Her voice was rising with irritation. "He doesn't say he's from New Orleans. And he's never mentioned a duel." She pursed her lips." Yet you're positive it's Philippe."

"He has a French accent, Maman, and he's a commission merchant."

"Mariette, do you know how many commission merchants there are in New York City? This is the biggest port in the country, *ma fille*. The city must be bursting with them."

"I know. But still..."

"And if he *is* here, which is highly unlikely, isn't it very coincidental that he would be friends with Robert, of all people?"

"But that's just it, Maman. He must have read about him in the newspapers, acting on the stage with me, and he sought him out, probably to find out if Robert and I were in love. Maybe he didn't want to ruin my life. Maybe he thought that if Robert and I were planning to marry, he would disappear from the scene altogether. Isn't that possible?"

"It's possible, yes, but highly unlikely! And if he is here, why wouldn't he come to you instead? Why wouldn't he propose to you and find out for himself how you feel? I know Philippe well enough to know that he's direct."

Mariette nodded. Yes, Philippe was direct. But if he was seriously disabled, he might be afraid she'd reject him. But she did not answer. She'd had enough discussion with her mother and she was glad to sink back beneath her covers and lay her head on the pillow.

Desiree walked to the door and turned to face Mariette. "I'm going to fix you some toast and tea. Then I want you to sleep all morning. Will you let me send Mr. Niblo a message that you aren't well and you'll be missing rehearsal this morning?"

"Yes. Send it. I know the play by heart. Mr. Niblo knows that."

Desiree raised her eyebrows. She was surprised by Mariette's compliance. She never missed rehearsals. She had to be truly exhausted.

⚜

By eleven o'clock, Mariette was up and dressed and relieved not to have to go to Niblo's Garden until 8:00 o'clock that evening. She had worked steadily for so many days and weeks that a day off was almost like a vacation. She was also too overwhelmed by last night's revelations to sleep longer. But the bright spot in her day was that she'd be able to spend time in Bowling Green Park with Daisy and Desiree.

She washed and dressed herself in a morning dress with long sleeves. Then, after encountering the first crisp autumn breeze at her front door, she turned back to the hatrack in the foyer, grabbed a shawl, and swung it around her shoulders. Walking down the steps, she felt the wind blowing her long hair across her back. She had not coiffed it, but brushed it with a center part, and caught it at the nape with a ribbon.

She found Desiree seated on the park bench with Daisy on her lap, telling her a story. What a picture they made together, Mariette thought, in the dappled shade of the maple tree, now in its glorious autumn dress of red and gold, shedding its leaves almost as she watched. The pram stood alongside them, but Daisy was seldom willing to stay in it any more. She was a toddler now, and if she could find a place to set her feet down, she would walk all day with someone leaning over her, holding her little hands as she took her first uncertain steps. This job usually fell to Desiree, who complained that it broke her back, but Mariette was home today, and she took over happily.

When Daisy saw her mother coming, she reached out her arms and Mariette scooped her up and swung her around joyously. What a treat it was to spend the day with her baby. She sat on the bench alongside her mother and put Daisy in her lap. But not for long. Daisy scooted off her mother's knees, landing with the soles of her shoes on the bricked walkway, and if Mariette had not grabbed her hands, she would have been off on her own, falling down every other step and then getting up to try again. Mariette took her hands in both her own and let her toddle and fall until she was worn out. Then she picked her up and sat her on her lap, singing a lullaby she knew Daisy would sit still for.

"It's a beautiful day, *n'est-ce pas?*" Desiree asked.

Mariette looked around her. The clear morning sky was like a hard dome of cerulean blue, broken by rooftops and steeples. It was cool and sunny, with the first hint of winter in the air. The two huge trees in the circle of the park were alive with birds, and neighbors were sweeping their steps and watering potted geraniums.

"It's glorious," Mariette agreed.

Mariette put Daisy in her pram, and the baby picked up her stuffed bear, plugged her thumb in her mouth and her eyelids started to close. The exercise and the balmy weather had worked their magic, and Daisy would fall into a light slumber, at least for a little while. Now Mariette moved over to sit beside her mother on the park bench.

Desiree was knitting a garment for herself, a soft black woolen shawl with a fringe. It was a project that would take time to finish, and Desiree was in no hurry. Knitting was her passion.

"Robert proposed to me last night," Mariette told her mother.

Desiree stopped knitting and gave her her attention. "And what did you say?"

Mariette shrugged. "I told him I was still in love with a young man from New Orleans, and I hoped he would come find me and marry me. But I also said that if this does not happen, I may want to marry someday. But not now."

"And he is willing to wait for you?"

"He said he was."

Desiree went back to her knitting. "Well, you're a lucky girl, but I wouldn't keep him waiting too long. He's a good catch, Mariette."

Mariette nodded. "I haven't told him about Daisy yet."

Desiree found her daughter's eyes. "Or about me," she said, her eyes hooded.

"No. I would have told him everything last night, I think, but the conversation took a strange turn." She hesitated, knowing her mother would take each item of coincidence and show how it proved nothing. And Mariette could not deal with that this morning. And yet she had to talk about it or she'd go crazy. "He began to tell me how he'd gone with his friend to the waterfront to see first hand how a commission merchant deals with his clients."

Desiree put her knitting in her basket and took off her glasses. Mariette had her attention.

"Now, listen to me, please," Mariette said. "It's true his friend gave him the name Dupre and said he was from Marseilles originally, but I think Philippe would do that, if he didn't want his presence known yet in the city."

"And why would that be, Mariette?" *A bit of impatience beginning?*

"Because he wanted to befriend Robert Courtney, the actor, and find out if what they say in the newspapers is true, that Robert is in love with me and that I return his love."

"And what will he do then? Go back to New Orleans?"

"I don't know. He might. He's just honorable enough not to want to ruin my life...again."

"The man is from Marseilles and his name is Dupre. And just because he's a commission merchant, you're sure it's Philippe."

"And he has a black servant..."

"Anyone can have a black servant, Mariette."

They sat in silence for a few moments. Desiree reached out and placed her hand on her daughter's arm. *"Ma fille"* she said softly, "you have been so miserable for so long. All this is wishful thinking, my child. Philippe is gone. He's a closed book in your life. Why don't you let this good man marry you and take care of you? Forget about Philippe." Seeing that Mariette was about to object, she rushed on. "If you want to find out if it's really Philippe, ask Robert if you can meet his friend. Come face to face with him, Mariette. The man cannot be Philippe. It's impossible. Once you know that, you can marry Robert and have a good life."

Mariette met her mother's eyes. "Maybe you're right," she said. "I'll think about it."

Desiree went back to her knitting. A neighbor came by and looked at the sleeping child and spoke softly, so as not to wake her, complimenting Mariette on her baby's beauty. Ladies shopping at the greengrocer's and the butcher shop waved as they passed by, happy to see Mariette at home for a change. She knew that in the neighborhood, she was a celebrity, and she tried not to be aloof. She spoke with everyone, inquiring about their health and commenting on the weather. They always asked her about Robert Courtney, as though he were her personal property, and they asked about upcoming plays.

After an hour in the fresh air, Mariette felt herself becoming sleepy, but it was too late now, for Daisy was waking up and getting ready for more exercise. Mariette smiled at her baby and noticed suddenly that she was holding something in her hand, something she was waving.

"What's that piece of paper she's holding?" Mariette asked her mother.

Desiree frowned. "I don't know."

Mariette took the paper from the child's little fist and returned to her bench.

"It's a note," she said. She opened the paper and saw that the message was printed in ink on thick white paper. She unfolded the square of paper and read. "THAT'S A PRETTY BABY YOU HAVE THERE. TAKE CARE!" Mariette's hand began to shake. "Maman, it's a threat!" Mariette felt the gooseflesh rise on her arms and she started to tremble. "Who could have....? What do you think it means?"

Desiree got up and picked up the baby from her pram, as if to protect her with her body. She looked all around, up and down the street and in every doorway along the sidewalk. Mariette walked to the carriage and passed her hand beneath the coverlet and the padding. There was nothing else there.

"Who could have put it there?" Desiree asked. "I've watched her every minute. Maybe when I left the carriage outside and took her in to change her nappie…" She looked at her daughter. "Let's go inside, Mariette." she said. "Come quickly!"

CHAPTER 72

Once inside the flat, Mariette double-locked the door, took the baby from her mother and carried her to the rocking chair in her bedroom, where she proceeded to hold her close to her body and rock her almost frantically. Desiree followed and sat on the bed facing her. The baby, sensing her mother's panic, began to whine.

"Oh, my poor baby," Mariette said, easing her grip on the child. "I'm holding you so tight, I'm frightening you." Then turning to her mother, wide-eyed, she said. "We must never take her out to the park again, Maman." In her fear, she had fallen back into her comfortable way of addressing her mother. "We must keep her in the flat."

"Yes. Yes," Desiree agreed.

"And I won't go to the theater for rehearsals until we know who is threatening us." She looked past Desiree, trying to gather her thoughts. "I suppose I'll have to go at night for performances, but not unless Mrs. O'Flaherty is here with you."

"Yes," said Desiree, "and maybe Mr. Mohnihan from upstairs."

"We'll ask him."

"And we must always...*always*...keep the doors double-locked."

Mariette nodded. A growing panic spread throughout her body. "Why is someone threatening me, Maman?" she cried out. "What do they want from me? How can anyone be so evil as to think of harming my baby?" Her voice broke on the words, and she sobbed broken-heartedly.

"I don't know, *ma fille*. I don't know."

"I have no enemies. I can think of no one, certainly not at the theater, who would hate me that much. None of them even know about Daisy." She was trembling and sobbing, and Daisy was crying with her.

"Here, give her to me," Desiree said. She took Daisy in her arms and rocked her standing up, shushing her sobs and trying to pacify her.

"Someone would have to really despise me to think of making such a threat, and the only two people I know who could hate me that much are part of my past, long forgotten...at least by me."

"You're thinking of Louis Soniat, of course," Desiree said.

"Yes. And my father."

"But Mariette, if your father is here and he's seen you with Daisy, he knows it's his grandchild. Could anyone wish to harm his own grandchild?"

"My father could. Oh, yes. He's evil, Maman."

Desiree didn't answer. Mariette knew she was recalling the many beatings he had given her. Yes, he was evil. "But why would he be here in New York?" Desiree asked. "And why would he have tracked you down so far, just to make this threat?"

By now, Daisy had fallen asleep, and Desiree carried her to her bed in the back bedroom. She put her down and covered her with a blanket. Desiree signaled Mariette to follow her to the kitchen.

Mariette sat at the table and pulled her mother's arm to make her sit down facing her. "It's the land, Maman," she said, gripping her mother's wrist tightly. "He never did get his precious land from Soniat, and he's never given up."

"Oh, but Mariette, that's impossible. After all this time, the only way he could get it...oh, no, he couldn't possibly think that you would..."

"Yes." She nodded. "He could think it. He would try to put me back with Soniat, as though nothing had ever happened."

"He has to know you wouldn't go. He has to know you have a career on the stage."

"What is that to him, Maman? He's the most selfish, evil man I ever knew. How did he get me to submit to his will in New Orleans? By beating you until I gave in. Well, now that he's seen Daisy, he has something even more convincing to hold over my head. "

"Oh, I can hardly believe that."

"Believe it." Mariette's jaw was hard, and for the first time in her life, she knew what it was to truly despise a person.

"But he would have to convince Soniat to take you back, even though you have a baby now."

"Well, he probably told Louis the baby was his. How would anyone know? I was with Louis very shortly before I made love to Philippe. Daisy looks exactly like me, so she could be anyone's baby. I am the only one who knows for sure that she's Philippe's child."

"And you're positive of that, Mariette?"

"Oh, yes. I'm positive. Remember, Maman, it was Christmas day when Soniat was called back to his plantation to see about the runaway slaves. At that very time, I was having my period. And I was never again with Soniat after that. But I *was* with Philippe. But how can I ever prove that?"

"You should not have to prove it, Mariette," Desiree said sympathetically.

"But he may threaten to tell Mr. Niblo everything, and my career would be over."

"Threats work both ways, Mariette. You could threaten to show up on his doorstep and tell his family about his placée of twenty-three years and his quadroon daughter."

"You know, Maman, I don't think he'd care if I did that. He knows his wife would never leave him. It would be too much of a scandal. And there's too much money involved. Besides all that, it's so commonplace for Creoles to have placées in New Orleans."

Desiree shrugged. "You're right. He might just risk it."

"And you know the land means more to him than his family," Mariette said. "He's not afraid of the little power we hold over him. It's nothing compared to what *we* have to fear."

Desiree looked into her daughter's eyes and took her hand. "Maybe you should tell Robert everything and if he still wants to marry you, accept his proposal, Mariette. Once you're married, you're safe. Do it for Daisy's sake."

"No. No, Maman. I will not let my father push me into marriage to escape his evil threats. I'm going to find Philippe, if he's here, and tell him everything. He's the only one who can help me now."

CHAPTER 73

On a Wednesday morning, after being closeted with her mother and baby for a week, with all the shutters closed and the door double-locked, Mariette heard a demanding knock at the front door. Her heart leapt to her throat. Desiree was immediately at her side. She walked to the door and pressed her ear to it.

"Who's there?" she asked.

An unfamiliar voice answered. "I have a letter here for a Miss Mariette Delon."

"Who are you?" Mariette asked.

"Don't matter. You don't know me."

Mariette looked at her mother. Desiree frowned and shrugged. Mariette was afraid to open the door. Her father could be standing behind the messenger and might force his way into the house.

"Who is it from?" Mariette asked.

"The gen'mun didn't give me no name," the man said, "but he says he's yer father."

Mariette drew in a frightened gasp. She had expected it. "Is he with you?"

"No, Ma'am. He said you'd know where he's at when you read the letter."

Desiree walked over to the living room and peeped through a slat in the shutters of the bay window, trying to see the messenger. She scurried back to Mariette. "I see only one man. He's a stranger, but he's small. I think it's all right to take the letter."

Cautiously, Mariette slid the bolt lock but left the chain secured. Then turning the knob, she opened the heavy door an inch. The man standing in her line of vision could never do her harm. He was small and thin, with threadbare clothes and disheveled red hair, someone her father had no doubt picked up off the street, someone he might even now be watching from behind a tree or a building in the cul-de-sac.

"Here. Give me the letter," she said, grabbing it, slamming the door, and throwing the bolt again. She carried the folded paper to a gas lamp in the parlor and turned up the wick. After lighting the lamp, she tore open the letter and began to read.

My dear Mariette,

  Louis Soniat is willing to forgive your infidelity and take you back again.

"Willing to forgive! *He's* willing to forgive *me?*"

"Read, Mariette."

Now that he knows you have given birth to his baby, he is willing to reconcile with you. He has never sold the house in Faubourg Marigny, and he wants you and the baby to come back there as his family.

"But of course he wants the baby," Mariette shouted. "Who wouldn't want the baby? But it isn't his, Maman, and he will never lay his hands on that child." She was trembling with rage and fear. "Only I know for certain that the baby is Philippe's. But Soniat may very well lay claim as a parent, and with his great wealth, he could hire clever lawyers who could make a good case for his paternity."

"Finish the letter, Mariette."

Her hands were shaking so badly now, she had to press the paper to the table to read on.

Louis will come for you and see that you and the baby are returned to New Orleans in the finest accommodations aboard a luxury steamboat, with a nurse in attendance. He will allow you to go on acting in New Orleans, if that is your choice, or stay at home with your baby.

"My choice! How generous!" Mariette said acidly. "The same old promises! The same old luxuries thrown at me! If I didn't want them the first time around, why would I want them now?" Her voice was filled with rage. "And what has my father to gain from this magnanimous intervention?" She looked at her mother with a sinister grin. "The land, of course."

"You're right," Desiree said. "He still wants it. And now he thinks you've put it in his lap, by having Soniat's baby. He'll fight for that, Mariette."

"But he won't win, Maman. He'd have to kill me first."

"Read the rest."

Mariette looked back at the letter.

I will call on you Monday at noon, when you return from rehearsal. I will expect your answer then. You can hope for no better future than you will have with Louis Soniat. He will treat you like a queen.

"Treat you like a queen! I've heard those words before and lived to find out what kind of treatment that was. Of course, I'll never go back," she said, her lips trembling, "but I'm in serious trouble here, Maman." Her eyes filled with tears.

She walked over to the settee, and Desiree followed. The episode had taken all her strength. She was exhausted by fear and hatred. She sat heavily, and Desiree sat beside her.

Mariette looked back at the letter. "He says 'when you return from rehearsal.' Do you realize what that means? He's been watching me, for God knows how long—where I went, what I did."

"Oh, *mon Dieu!* That scares me to death." Desiree clasped her hands before her as if in prayer. "He says he'll come Monday. That gives us four days."

Mariette looked at the letter. "He signed it, Your father, Raoul Delissard. He only admits to being my father when he wants something from me." Desiree nodded. "And something else, Maman, he makes no mention of you at all. He's seen us together, obviously. He knows you're here. What does he think I'll do with you? Leave you here in New York?"

"That's the least of his worries, Mariette. He was finished with me when I wouldn't tell him where you were after the fire. No, even before that, when I first refused to sign the contract."

Mariette put her arms around her mother and sobbed against her shoulder. "I'll never abandon you, Maman, you know that. And I'll never go back to Soniat. They can take me to court, and I'll tell them how I know it isn't his baby. They may not believe me, but I'll never let that man put his hands on me or on Daisy."

"How can I help you, Mariette?" Desiree asked, her own eyes moist with tears.

"There's no way, Maman. I can't even help myself. But Philippe can help me." She paused. "He can verify dates. I'll see Robert tonight and tell him he must bring his friend to the theater tomorrow night. I know it's Philippe. I know it in my heart."

"I'll pray for that," Desiree said. Then suddenly, Desiree's face brightened. "Mariette," she said, smiling wanly, "if it *is* Philippe, do you realize he doesn't even know about Daisy yet?"

"I know." She smiled through her tears. "I've been planning to surprise him. I wanted to take him home and present her to him as a beautiful gift." Her eyes were shining with a mixture of joy and apprehension. "I didn't want to go to him after all this time with life-and- death problems to solve." Then, recovering, she said, "But I can still surprise him, can't I?" she asked. "Let him have the joy of seeing her before I tell him the threat I'm under?" she asked. "Once he's seen her, he'll never let them take her away."

Mariette tossed and turned in bed that night. She got up and brushed her hair. She said her rosary. She went to the kitchen and warmed some milk. Then, back in her bedroom, she walked the floors, almost crazy with fear that she'd be dragged through the courts and in the end, have to go back to Soniat if she wished to keep Daisy. No. She would never let that happen.

The miracle was that she had lived in New York as long as she had without anyone learning about her mother and baby. Her neighbors knew Desiree as her maid. They knew she was an actress, and they knew she had a baby, but somehow, this information had never found its way to the newspapers. It was remarkable! With fame and fortune came a loss of privacy. Every actress could expect that. But she had kept her family hidden for almost a year, and till now, she'd been lucky. But an avalanche of revelation was coming. Not only revelation, but threats and possibly dire consequences.

Her chief concern was no longer that Philippe might think she was in love with Robert. That had suddenly become secondary in her list of anxieties. Now, she must remove the threat her father held over her–the threat that she must do his will and bring her child to the man she most despised.

Although she felt in her heart that Robert's friend was Philippe, it was still possible that he wasn't. A shiver snaked down her spine. If that were so, she'd have no one to help her. What would she do? She might be forced to marry Robert, a man she did not love, just for her own protection. *Dear God*, she prayed, *let it be Philippe. And let him come tomorrow night. Please, Sweet Savior, my life depends on it.*

She checked the time on her mantle clock. Two a.m. She lit the night candle on the small mahogany table beside her bed and walked barefoot to the door of her mother's bedroom. Desiree was snoring softly, and Daisy, lying on her stomach with her legs pulled up under her, slept like a cherub with all her covers off. Mariette smiled. She was almost a year old, walking and saying a few words. She was the greatest joy in Mariette's life.

She knew she shouldn't pick her up. She might not want to go back to bed afterwards, but her yearning to hold the soft, warm body was overpowering. Mariette placed the night candle on the bedside table, turned the baby over, and took her in her arms. Daisy curled up on her mother's shoulder and put her thumb in her mouth. Mariette picked up the small blanket and covered her sleeping baby. Then with Daisy in her left arm and the candle holder in her right, she walked to her own bedroom. If Desiree woke and found her missing, she would not be alarmed. This was not the first time Mariette had paid her baby a nocturnal visit.

In her bedroom, she placed the candle holder on her table and sat in her cane-back rocking chair with Daisy cradled in her arms. Mariette rocked her gently, softly crooning a little nonsense tune she had sung long ago in a play at the old Camp Theater. She pressed soft kisses to her baby's neck and knew she had never felt such an all-consuming love for another human being.

Suddenly, Daisy lifted her head and opened her eyes to see in the dim light of the candle who was kissing her. Her thumb left her mouth with a smack and she smiled at Mariette, her dimple very much in evidence. "Ma-ma!" she said. Mariette smiled. They were Americans now, and Mariette had taught Daisy to call her Mama, as American children did.

Mariette kissed her full on the lips. "Yes, it's Mama, my precious love." She hugged her close and began rocking her again. Daisy made singing sounds, telling Mariette to go on with the song. It was one of her favorite tunes, and she loved her mother's voice. So Mariette rocked and sang until Daisy was once more asleep. Then she walked softly and put her back in her grandmother's bed.

CHAPTER 74

After the threat note and the frightening letter that followed, Mariette knew she could no longer timidly hint to Robert that his friend might be Philippe. It was no longer a matter of sparing his feelings. Her life, her future, and the future of her child were on the line, and only Philippe could save her. She had to know the truth.

At the theater that night, she sent a message to Robert's dressing room, asking if he could come see her right away. Since Mariette had told him never to come there for fear of gossip, he was surprised by the invitation. Without hesitation, he rushed to her room, already dressed in his Act One costume. Mariette was still in her street clothes though curtain time was near. Her dresser Sarah was behind the changing screen holding Mariette's costume, preparing to get her ready.

"Sarah, would you mind stepping outside for a minute?" Mariette asked.

Sarah put the dress back on the rack and skittered from the room.

Robert looked at Mariette. He could see by her pale face that she was troubled.

"What is it? Are you ill?" he asked.

"No. Not ill. Sit down," she said in a hasty, clipped manner. Robert sat. "Robert, I am in danger," she said. "Of course, you know nothing of my personal life, but there are people in my past who would do me great harm, and one of them is here in New York, threatening me and those close to me."

"Oh, my dear," he said, standing and taking her hands. "Who are these people? How can I help you?"

She took a deep breath. "Robert, it's a very long story, and one I'd prefer you'd never know, but trust me when I say my future life is at stake, and there's only one thing you can do to help me."

"I'll do anything, you know that."

"I hope you will. I'm depending on it." Mariette closed her eyes, then opened them again to face Robert directly. "I want you to bring your friend, the commission merchant, to the theater tomorrow night. I have a strong feeling he's the man I was in love with in New Orleans."

"Is he the one who's threatening you?" he asked, angrily.

"No. Quite the contrary. He is the only one who can help me resolve the threat. He's the only one who can bear witness to facts that will save me." She paused and lowered her eyes. "I'm sorry. That's all I can tell you."

"I see." Silence fell for a few seconds. Then Robert spoke. "You're asking me to bring a man to you who may take you away from me forever."

"Yes. That's what I'm asking you to do."

"And if he's the man you love, will you marry him?" His eyes were hooded, his mouth tight.

"If he asks me, yes."

Robert smirked, knowing there was little chance that he would not.

"I need you to do this for me," she said emphatically. "It's no longer a matter of love alone, take my word for it, Robert. I've received notes that threaten my future life, and only marriage can protect me."

"Then marry *me*, my love. *I* will protect you."

"No, Robert, dear Robert. I can never marry you. I don't love you." She reached up and cupped his cheek with her palm "You're a good man, Robert, and I know you'd love me and care for me, but I will not marry you just to protect myself against those who would harm me. It wouldn't be fair to you."

"I wouldn't care why you married me, Mariette. You'd come to love me in time. I'm sure of it."

Mariette shook her head and moved away. She sat on the settee, and Robert sat beside her.

"Robert, listen to me." She drew in a deep breath. "Something has happened. Something frightening. It is imperative that I find out the identity of your friend. I know he told you his name is Dupre, but don't you see? If he is the man I love, he would have given you a false name. He wouldn't want me to know he's in New York. He's waiting to see if I'm in love with you." When he didn't answer, she found anger building inside her. "If you don't bring him to me tomorrow night," she said, heat rising in her cheeks, "I'll go to every commission house in Manhattan until I find him."

Robert remained seated, his head lowered to his hands. He knew he would do her bidding, and in doing so, lose her forever. Without raising his head, he nodded.

Standing, she touched the top of Robert's head gratefully. "You'll never know what this means to me," she said. "And I hate to add to your heartache, but I think it would be best if we don't go on having dinner after the show or even meeting here in my dressing room. At least, that will stop the gossip mongers from writing about our romance." She sat down beside him and kissed his cheek. Then she took his arm and walked him to the door. "Hurry now," she said. "It's late, and I must get into my costume. Tell Sarah to come back in."

Robert left, but when they were on stage together, the question of Robert's love for her was unmistakable. It was there, alive, pulsing between them. And she realized in this performance especially that his physical desire for her had taken over his stage persona. Only on stage could he put his arms around her, kiss her tenderly, and hold her close, pressing his body to hers. She was fully aware that this was not an act for him, but an expression of ardent love, and the audience seemed to sense it as well.

There was a kiss at the end of Act Three that was deep and sensuous, and tonight, Robert lengthened the kiss. When his mouth covered hers, the heat that was passing between them made the audience fall silent as a tomb, holding its collective breath. Not a sigh or a cough could be heard. Mariette felt the passion of the kiss invade her body and send coils of fire down to her toes. She was at his mercy during the kiss, for the only way to end it would have been to push him away, and she knew that William Niblo, kind man that he was, would have fired her on the spot.

This was "the kiss" that was talked about all over town. It was "the kiss" that was selling standing-room-only tickets and bringing patrons in to see the same performance over and over again.

Although the kiss had always been passionate, this night in particular it was scorching. It was Robert's goodbye kiss. And when it ended, and the heavy curtains began to close, the patrons, caught up in the passion of the moment, moaned softly as one and then broke into applause that lasted a full five minutes.

After the performance, Mariette sent a messenger with another note to Robert, asking him to come back to her dressing room. She had Sarah help her change, as well.

When she heard a knock at her door, she signaled Sarah to answer it and then wait in the corridor. Robert entered and closed the door. "You have my promise, Mariette," he said. He sounded heartbroken. "What else can you want from me?"

"Robert. I think you know why I've called you here."

"No. I don't know why." He seemed affronted.

"When we were on stage together tonight, I..." she hesitated, closed her eyes, and tried to find the right words... "I found that your lovemaking was unnecessarily prolonged and...heated." She blushed at the word.

A small smile played at the corners of his mouth. "Heated?" he asked. "Isn't that what Niblo wants of us? Isn't that what the patrons pay for?"

Mariette faced him squarely. "You're making the kiss in Act Three into a sensual display that shames me more and more each night. You're making a whore of me on stage."

Her words seemed only to further arouse his passion. "Mariette," he said, his face flushed with desire. He took her face between his hands and slanted his mouth over hers with a deep and passionate kiss that left her weak and angry and confused. At last she found the strength to break away.

"I want you, Mariette," he said, holding her in his arms.

"And you *had* me out there on stage tonight, didn't you, Robert?" she asked, her eyes narrowing. "You had me in your power...in the kiss...whether I wanted it or not."

"And did you want it, Mariette?"

She closed her eyes. Then, opening them, she looked past his shoulder. She could not meet his gaze. "Yes," she said. "I wanted it. I'm not made of stone. I have passion."

He came closer, placing his hands at her waistline, but she pressed her palms to his chest to keep him from taking her in his arms.

"I cannot have a love affair with you, Philippe," she said. She gasped, realizing what she had called him, praying he was too caught up in his own desires to catch the name. But that was too much to hope for.

"Philippe!" Robert whispered hoarsely. "So that is his name...my friend the merchant."

Mariette broke away from Robert and sat on the settee in her dressing room. She rested her head against the cushioned back and closed her eyes. She nodded. "Yes," she said.

"I think you're throwing away our happiness...yours and mine."

'No, Robert, no." She shook her head, and tears flew from her eyes. "If your companion is Philippe, I will have all the happiness there is for me in this world."

Silently, he nodded, convinced by the force of her statement. "Then our time on stage is my only chance to hold you and kiss you as I'd like to kiss you when we're alone." He slipped his arm around her waist where they sat and kissed her cheek and her throat. "My darling girl, I love you so. It makes me crazy to hold you in my arms and know that after the curtains close, you're out of bounds to me. Can't you see what torment you're putting me through?"

"And what do you think it does to me, Robert? I'm not in love with you, but you're such a masterful lover, you arouse my passions, and I can not let that happen."

"Then tell me what to do, Mariette, or I'll go mad for wanting you."

"Bring your friend here tomorrow night. Put him in the first row center, then bring him to my dressing room after Act One. I have to know if it's Philippe. You'll do that, won't you?"

He nodded. "I've already promised."

Mariette got up and looked into her dressing table mirror. She couldn't remember if she'd combed her hair or taken off her stage makeup. She decided she'd leave the theater as she was. She'd go directly home. It didn't matter how she looked.

"I have to go now," she said. "I can't keep Sarah waiting in the corridor, while you and I are alone in my dressing room. That's bound to draw a crowd. We have no private lives." She grabbed her hooded cape and a large carry-all cloth bag, throwing into it her make-up remover, her brush and comb.

"I'll take you," he said. They locked glances, each taking the measure of the other.

She looked away, trying to find the proper words. "Will you promise not to try to hold me or kiss me?"

He nodded. "Yes."

✦

They rode along Broadway in silence for a while. Then Robert spoke. "What do you want me to tell Gerard? About tomorrow night, I mean."

"Tell him that Mariette Delon says she's certain he's the man she was in love with in New Orleans, and she wants to meet him."

"The man called Philippe," Robert added somberly.

"Yes. Philippe Grillet. Ask him if that's his real name, and then you'll know."

Robert nodded. "I hope you know now that I'd do anything for you."

Mariette took Robert's hand and tried to find his eyes in the darkness. "How good you are, Robert!"

"I love you, darling," he said, as if it were all the explanation she needed. "But don't hold out too much hope that he'll be your long lost love."

"Why not?"

"Because he knows how to find you, Mariette. If he came to New York to marry you, he would have come to you on his own."

"Not if he thinks I'm in love with you, Robert. Can't you see that? He's waiting to find out. That's why he befriended you. He may not want to ruin my life...again."

"Again?"

"Yes. He fought a duel for me once. Remember I asked you if he'd ever mentioned it?" Robert nodded. "I saw it all from a secret place and made my presence known afterwards. He was lying on the ground, close to death. His father said I was to blame, and he hoped he'd never see me again."

"Were you to blame, Mariette?"

"In a way, I suppose I was. I can understand how his father thought so." She brought her hand to her throat, closed her eyes, and leaned back against the horsehair upholstery, as scenes of that terrible day flooded her memory. "It was very complicated, Robert. You'd have to live in New Orleans to know the reasons why men fight duels. It's insane. I begged him not to fight, but he considered it a matter of honor." She put her face to her hands and shook her head. Robert put his arm around her shoulder. "Weeks after the duel, his servant visited me and said he was very ill. But after that, months went by, and I didn't know if he was alive or dead."

She sighed heavily, then sat up and straightened her back. She had to finish her explanation and make him understand. "So, don't you see," she asked, "when you told me your friend was lame and he was a commission merchant, which is what Philippe was in New Orleans, and he had a black servant," …she stopped to draw a breath and placed her hand on Robert's arm, "it all added up. Your friend probably is my Philippe."

Robert flinched when she said *my Philippe,* and she knew the words had pierced his heart like an arrow. "If that I so," he said sorrowfully, "it will be my misfortune."

CHAPTER 75

Mariette could never remember a longer day. From the time she awoke in the morning till she left for the theater that evening, she was such a bundle of nerves she couldn't even do the smallest task. When she tried to feed Daisy, the spoon trembled in her hand, and she finally had to turn the task over to Desiree.

In the afternoon, she tried to nap, but it was out of the question. Her body was one taut wire. *What if Philippe didn't come tonight? Would she give up all hope of ever seeing him again? Would she have no one to speak for her to prove that Daisy was not Soniat's baby?* Unless she could put that doubt to rest, she could not make plans that would affect the rest of her life...and Daisy's...and her mother's.

And what of Robert? He'd agreed to step aside and let her see his companion first, to find out whether or not this was "her Philippe." And if he was not, would Robert be standing in the wings, heart in his hands, waiting to take her as wife or lover, whichever she chose. Was that a fair treatment for a man like Robert?

And of course, there was still another hurdle to leap. She'd never yet told him about her mother and her fatherless baby. Would he be willing to take on such a family? It was a rare man indeed who would. And even if he did, she wouldn't marry him. She didn't love him. She was back to that again. At last, she abandoned the idea of a nap and walked the floors of her bedroom.

It all boiled down to one thing. If Philippe didn't come back into her life tonight, nothing else mattered. She might lose Daisy, and before she'd let that happen, she'd take her baby and her mother on the first boat to Europe and disappear there.

She walked to the kitchen to make herself a cup of tea and found her mother there. Desiree was as tense as she, waiting impatiently for night to come, not knowing how to advise her daughter.

"Mariette," she said, "sit down, *cherie*, and let me fix you some tea."

Mariette sat, as weary as an old woman, though she had done nothing the whole day. In minutes, Desiree had boiled the water, spooned in the tea leaves, and found cups and saucers and spoons. "I've been thinking over everything you said, and you're right. I'm sure you'll see Philippe tonight."

Mariette smiled. "Do you really think so, Maman?"

"Yes. I'm sure of it. Try to think about that, and calm yourself. When you see each other, you'll both know what your future holds for you."

"Of course, when I *see* him, Maman. *If* I see him. But till then, I'm a wreck."

"I know, BéBé," Desiree said. "If I could make the clock move faster for you I would."

"Suppose he doesn't come at all," Mariette said.

"Don't try to second guess the future, *ma fille*. Things will happen when they happen. Time will pass and you'll know everything."

CHAPTER 76

At seven p.m., Mariette kissed her baby and her mother and signaled a cab to take her to the theater. By eight she was coiffed, made up, and dressed in her costume. At 8:30, she was standing behind the curtain, lifting the circle of velvet cloth to watch as patrons began to take their seats on all three levels of the house. The orchestra pit was filling up, the dissonant musical notes a soothing ambience to her wildly beating heart. She was glad she knew the play so well, for she would not have all her wits about her tonight.

"Five minutes!" a young man called out from backstage. Still no occupant in the first row seat on the aisle. The players in Act One rushed to their dressing rooms for one last look in the mirror. From habit, Mariette did the same. She almost collided with Robert in the wings, and they both stood stock still.

She raised her eyebrows in question, but her throat was too dry to form words.

Robert nodded. Yes, he was here. His friend was here. Was it Philippe?

At nine o'clock on the dot, the curtains were drawn, and Mariette stepped out onto the stage. The audience applauded. She forced herself not to look down into the audience. Then, in the middle of the first act, when she could wait no longer, she looked across the footlights and saw Philippe. Her knees almost buckled under her, and she felt faint. She stopped in her monologue, not more than a second, and then continued in what she hoped was a normal voice, saying the words by rote, as she stared, stunned at the sight of the man she loved.

He smiled, his dazzling white teeth revealed in glorious contrast to his olive complexion. She couldn't believe how handsome he still was and how much she still loved him. How long had he been in New York? A few months? Six months? How could he have stayed away? Didn't he know how much she loved him? The tears were close behind her eyelids.

Recovering herself, she channeled her energies into her performance. At the end of Act One, she took her curtain calls with Robert and the other actors, smiling a fake smile, and then ran to her dressing room and closed the door behind her.

"Sarah!" she called out. From behind the screen, the young Irish woman came quickly. "I feel faint. Get the smelling salts."

"Yes, ma'am," the girl said. She found the bottle and passed it beneath Mariette's nose. "What is it, Miss Mariette?" she asked. "You're white as a sheet."

Mariette sat on the settee, closed her eyes, and shook her head. She hadn't the strength to answer. Then, as she had expected, a knock came at her door and she gave such a start, she frightened Sarah.

"I'll get it, Miss Mariette," Sarah said.

Mariette sat transfixed, waiting. This was her moment. She'd waited all these months for him, made up a dream world about him, and now she would know if it had been only wishful thinking. She watched Sarah open the door and stand to one side, and she had her first glimpse of her beloved Philippe. He stood, framed by the doorway, in formal dress, black tie, white ruffled shirt, his top hat in his right hand. He was more handsome than ever. But he was different now, a bit awkward, off balance. And of course, she knew why.

Her eyes fell shut.

"Miss Mariette!" Sarah shouted. "Are you sick? D'ya want me t'call a doctor?"

Philippe walked into the room. Wordlessly, he made the girl understand she was to leave them alone. For some reason, Sarah trusted him and left.

When Mariette opened her eyes again, it was to see Philippe sitting beside her, looking at her, fanning her with his hat.

"Mariette," he said, so softly she would not have heard him had she not been looking at his sensuous mouth. He had grown a mustache since she'd last seen him. It complimented his aristocratic features, and when he smiled, slowly, as he was doing now, it stood in sharp contrast to his fine white teeth. Mariette couldn't speak. "Mariette," he repeated. "It's Philippe, my darling. I've come to ask you to marry me."

She rested her head against his shoulder. At last, the words came. Weakly, she said, "Oh, Philippe, I have loved you every day of my life, even when I didn't know if you were still alive."

He took her hand and drew her into his embrace. She was still in shock. A rag doll. Sensation had not yet returned. She didn't know how to fashion the questions. Before she could say a word, he brushed his lips to hers, his mustache soft, wondrous against her mouth. He held her gently but possessively, and kissed her again, deeply, starting a fire kindling down deep in her body, ready to catch and blaze. She circled his neck with her arms.

When their lips parted, she looked up into his eyes, seeking the answers to all her questions. Her hands followed the contour of his shoulders and his arms until they reached the empty sleeve of his frock coat, where the fabric had been folded up and pinned. He had lost his arm. Her beautiful man had lost his arm. She'd known it, of course.

"Philippe," she said, touching the empty sleeve. "Was it the duel?"

"Yes. The rapier made a wound beneath my ribs. It ran wide and made a deep cut in my arm. It was neglected while the doctors worked on the deeper wound near my heart. And by the time they gave my arm their attention, gangrene had set in and the arm had to come off." He'd said it matter-of-factly, but she knew it had been the most tragic loss of his life.

"Oh, my love!" she exclaimed, pressing her hand to her lips. Her voice trembled. "Was it terribly painful?"

"I was in and out of delirium. I don't remember."

She knew he remembered, but he'd never tell her.

"Five minutes!" the stage hand called out in the corridor.

"I must get ready for the next act," she said. Her words sounded hard and uncaring to her own ears, as if she had no concern for his loss and his misery. What she wanted to say was *My darling, I love you, I need you, it doesn't matter, take me wherever you want to go*, but there wasn't time. And there were so many things she must know from him before saying anything.

"Do what you have to do," he said. That voice, deep, mellow, the music of her heart. "I'll be here when you come back."

She found it hard to get up from the settee. Her knees were weak. She couldn't breathe. With difficulty, he helped her up, his right hand reaching over to grip her arm.

She walked to the door and called Sarah to come back into the room. With deft touches, the girl powdered Mariette's face, throat and shoulders, applied fresh color to her cheeks, and placed a rouge paper between her lips. Mechanically, Mariette pressed her lips together. The girl touched a hairbrush to the sides of her coiffure, fastened her braided crown with hairpins, and straightened the folds of her skirt. Fortunately, there was no costume change for the second act.

Mariette looked at Philippe like a lost child trying to find the words to tell him what was in her heart. Leaning over him, she touched her cheek to his, and then ran out into the corridor.

Act Two had never seemed so long. When it ended, she did not even take a curtain call but rushed to her dressing room and threw the door open wide, but no one was there. "He's gone! *Mon Dieu!* He's gone!"

She collapsed on the settee and let her eyes fall shut. She'd lost him by not saying the right words, by not reassuring him that it didn't matter about his arm. Sarah came rushing in and knelt before Mariette. "He's gone," Mariette said again.

"Oh, no, Miss, he's comin' back," Sarah said quickly. "He said to tell you he didn't want to upset you durin' your second intermission, but he'd be back after the performance."

Mariette's eyes flew open. "Are you sure? He said he was coming back?"

"Oh, yes, ma'am. He was most definite about that."

Mariette sat forward and took a deep breath. She smiled weakly. "Thank God!" she whispered.

"We have a costume change, Miss Mariette," Sarah said. "I have everything ready."

Mariette moved swiftly. One dress was unhooked and dropped to the floor, and she stepped into another. Fortunately, nothing had to pass over her head so neither her hairdo nor her makeup was disturbed. She sat at the dressing table and looked at her pallid reflection. The maid fussed around her, securing hairpins in her braided crown.

"That's good enough, Sarah!" she said. "I've got to go out and see if he's in his seat. I would've looked during the second act, except that I thought he was here in my dressing room." She ran backstage, found the peephole in the curtain, and lifted the circle of cloth.

The lights were on in the auditorium, and he was there, in his front row seat. She closed her eyes and breathed a sigh of relief. *Thank God! He could easily have left me, thinking I didn't want him any more, the way I acted, with my fainting and my empty words, as if the loss of his arm was too much for me to deal with.*

She worried herself through the last act, paying little attention to the fact that Robert was not holding her and kissing her as passionately as he had the night before. No doubt he felt uncomfortable, knowing Philippe was in the audience, and sensing Mariette's anxiety. Perhaps he'd decided to stand aside and let things happen.

After her curtain calls, she rushed back to her dressing room. She sat on the settee waiting. Sarah busied herself, straightening the dresser, waiting as anxiously as her mistress. At last, the knock came. Mariette gasped aloud, and before Sarah could move, Mariette was on her feet. *Please God,* she prayed, then opened the door. It was Philippe.

"Oh, sweetheart, come in," she said, her hands trembling. "Sit down, my darling. Please...sit here beside me."

Sarah walked past them and out of the dressing room, closing the door behind her. Philippe sat beside Mariette and she looked up into his eyes, those marvelous green eyes. "I wouldn't have blamed you if you'd never come back," she said, her eyes misting over. "But you have to understand, dear heart, I had so many questions to ask you, and no time to ask them. I was afraid you misunderstood the way I rushed out of here." She stopped to catch her breath, and he smiled, waiting for her to finish. "I wondered why you had come to New York in the first place. And if you had come looking for me, why you didn't find me. I have grieved so for you."

He smiled. He moved his left shoulder forward to allow the empty sleeve to fall to his side. At last he began. "After the duel, when I recovered from my long illness, I left my father's firm and went into business for myself."

"But why…"

"Wait," he said, placing a finger on her lips. "I had to be sure I could run a commission house on my own, even though I was incapacitated."

"Yes. Well…"

"Well, after four months, I was satisfied that I would have no problem."

"And when did you come to New York?"

"Almost a year ago," he said. "Last January."

Daisy was three months old. A wave of sorrow filled Mariette when she thought of the time he had missed with his baby—the first teeth, the first words. He could never get those back again. "Why did you wait so long, Philippe?" she asked. "Why didn't you come to me when you first arrived? Surely Caldwell told you where I was."

"He told me, but I was never sure you'd want me…this way." He turned his head in the direction of his empty sleeve.

"Because of your arm, my darling?" she asked incredulously. "How could you doubt my love? You still have your brilliant mind and your handsome face, and everything else that matters. Did you know what I thought all this time?" she asked.

He shook his head. He took her hand and fondled it.

"I thought you didn't want me at all, knowing the disaster I had brought into your life, the split I'd caused in your family. I thought that maybe you'd decided that our bloodlines were too different after all."

"Never for a moment," Philippe said, finding her dark brown eyes. "But when I got here, I began to think you had fallen in love with Robert. The newspapers said..."

"They were wrong, Philippe. I worried myself sick that you'd read those stories and believe them. Robert was a friend to me. Nothing more."

"He told me he loved you, Mariette," Philippe said. "How could he not? Holding you in his arms every night. The first time I saw you on stage together, I hated him for that."

"But it was only acting, Philippe," she said, knowing she was stretching the truth a bit, at least as far as Robert was concerned. "And there will be no more kisses between Robert and me. I will give Mister Niblo my notice and leave the theater."

Philippe smiled for the first time in their long and difficult conversation. "Are you sure you want to do that, *mon ange?*" he asked.

"Oh, yes," she said, savoring his endearing word.

"Then listen to me well," Philippe said. "I love you, Mariette. My life is meaningless without you."

"Oh, darling," she said, so relieved that she was robbed of words.

"I want to marry you and make a home for you here in New York, where it doesn't matter who or what we are."

"But you were well enough to come to me many months ago, long before Robert was the issue. I was in New Orleans until last

May. I acted in Caldwell's first play at the new St. Charles. Surely you knew that."

"Yes, I knew, Mariette. There is nothing I didn't know about you."

Oh, yes, my love, there's one thing you didn't know. "Well, why then..."

He placed his forefinger on her lips once again. She kissed it and took his hand in hers. He said, "I couldn't get up the courage to knock at your door and have you see me after they'd taken my arm."

A painful lump came to her throat. She heard a loud sob and realized it was hers. "Did you think I would love you any less?" she asked, her face wet with tears.

"I should have known," he said, gathering her in his arms to hold her close. Then backing away again, he tried to explain. "Before the duel, I thought all our obstacles were created by society and the law. I worried about birth certificates, and matters of family." He shook his head. "But after I lost my arm, I knew there were more bitter realities for us to face, if we still wanted to be together."

"If! How can you say if? Do you know how I've grieved for you, cried for you? Do you think the loss of your arm would make any difference to me, except that I'd share in your loss?"

She rested her head against his shoulder, sobbing softly. He turned and encircled her shoulder with his right arm. Then, slowly, he lowered his mouth to hers. The kiss was like their first kiss in the arcade of the vacant store in the *Rue Royale*. It was warm and tender and filled with promise. Her lips opened to his, and he deepened the kiss, drawing heated urgings from deep in her body. She put her arms around him and drew him close, her fingers fondling the dark hair that curled over his collar. She cupped his face with her palm, wanting him as she'd never wanted him before.

"Come home with me, Philippe. We'll talk along the way." She got up from the settee and went in search of Sarah. Again she found the girl outside her room.

"I'll be going home in my costume, Sarah. I won't need you any more tonight. Is your husband here to take you home?"

"Yes, ma'am. He's waitin' to turn off the lights. Can I do anything more for you?"

"No, thank you, Sarah." She paused in the corridor, looking back into her dressing room. Philippe had gotten up from the settee, but was out of earshot. "And Mr. Robert?" Mariette asked Sarah. "Has he left the theater?"

"Yes, ma'am. A good quarter hour ago."

Mariette nodded. Robert knew what was going on. He knew Philippe had gone into her dressing room and had not come out. No doubt he'd told Philippe he knew his real name, and Philippe had explained his duplicity. Now Robert knew everything. Dear Robert! At least her conscience was clear. She'd never said she loved him, and she'd never agreed to marry him.

She took her cape from her wardrobe closet and wrapped it around her shoulders. She handed Philippe his top hat and cane, and he took them slowly, thoughtfully. She could tell he had something more to say. "You'll have to do many things for me, Mariette," he said. His voice was hoarse, raspy.

Mariette placed her hand on his chest. "And I will relish them all," she said. "You saved my life once, remember that, Philippe? And you had to face up to your worst nightmare to do it." She took his face between her hands and kissed his lips. "You nursed me...and fed me... and sat beside me day and night." Her voice broke on the words. "It will be a privilege to take care of you, Philippe, and not because I owe you," she sniffled…"but because I love you."

A frown of anguish brought his dark brows together. "I can't take your beautiful face in my hands any more," he said. "I can't take you in my arms."

"Then I'll take you in mine." She wrapped her arms around his body underneath his greatcoat. "Same thing," she said, sobbing softly. She felt his heartbeat, heard his sobs, joined her own to his. Then looking up, she smiled. "Kiss me," she said, "and let's go home."

CHAPTER 77

The carriage wheels creaked down Broadway toward Bowling Green Park. Gas lamps cast gleaming bars of light across the cobbles. Mariette always enjoyed the ride home, but never more than tonight. Tonight, she was coming home with the love of her life and the father of her baby, holding inside her the secret that would fill him with more joy than he had ever known. She was euphoric.

She sighed deeply, oblivious to the tall brick Federal houses they were passing by. All was quiet and peaceful, except for an occasional theater emptying out. Tonight, a church spire pierced the full moon, a hat pin against the creamy disc.

She'd taken her place in the carriage on Philippe's right, so he could put his right arm around her. When they made love, she'd have to remember to lie on his left, so when they faced each other, he could touch her face with his right hand. She'd learn. She could hardly wait to learn.

There was so much she wanted to know. How to begin? "So you're working for a commission merchant here now?" she asked.

"Oh, yes, I have been, for several months. Darensbourg's Commission House."

"And you waited all these months to come for me, just because you thought I might not want you?" Her voice rose sharply and he could not mistake her disbelief.

"Yes, that, and also, I had to be sure I could earn a living here, lame, and on my own."

"And are you sure now, Philippe?"

"Yes, I'm sure. First I had to make it on my own in New Orleans. But once I saw my business was a success, I decided to take a chance working in New York. And I've done quite well. Apparently, an arm doesn't matter much in the commission business. It's experience."

"I see. So you're financially...comfortable." And on a sadder note, she added, "And you've broken all ties with your family."

"Yes. That was inevitable. But what I don't understand is why *you* ever left New Orleans."

Mariette smiled in the darkness. Her heart began to race. She couldn't wait for him to see Daisy. "I had a good offer," she said. "I've established a name on the New York stage."

"But you were beginning to do that in New Orleans. It was just a matter of time."

She smiled. "You sound as though you don't mind my acting any more."

"I don't. I'm proud of you. You're beautiful and talented. And if you want to continue your career, it's all right with me, as long as they don't keep casting you opposite Robert Courtney."

"Please. Don't worry about Robert."

"I won't," he said. "I was just happy you made the offer to leave the stage to please me. But no, my darling girl, do whatever you like. Other men can only dream of making love to Mariette Delon. I've got the real thing." Philippe gathered her to him with his strong right arm. She rested her head on his shoulder and sighed a deep sigh of contentment.

"As you can hear," he said, "I've been learning a lot more English." He explained how Jean Baptiste had given him his first lessons on the voyage to New York. "Of course, the English lessons were a bonus. I really brought him along to cook for me and help me dress."

"Well, I'll be happy to relieve him of those duties," she said. She tried to laugh but found she was crying instead and rested her head in the curve of his shoulder. When she was able to control her tears, she found a handkerchief in his vest pocket and blew her nose.

The carriage slowed, made a U-turn, and stopped at the curb before the central two-story house in Bowling Green Park. Philippe looked around at the buildings and the park across the way. "Nice little park there," he said.

"Come in, my love," she said. "Maman will be so happy to see you."

Neither by word nor expression did she reveal her million-dollar secret.

CHAPTER 78

Philippe got down from the cab and paid the driver. Then, coming around the hackney, he helped Mariette to the carriage block. He did it so adroitly that it wasn't until afterwards that she realized how graceful he was, in spite of his loss. Philippe had the build and the strength of an athlete, and she was beginning to see that his lameness would hardly limit him at all.

Mariette slipped her arm through his to walk up the steps of the house. At the front door, she reached inside her bag for her key. He took it from her and unlocked the door. Smiling up at Philippe, her heart beating like a drum against her ribs, she entered first and he followed.

Mariette knew that her mother and Daisy were sleeping. She led Philippe in quietly, and ushered him through the foyer and into their flat.

"It's a lovely apartment," he said in English, with his strong French accent.

"A flat," she corrected, raising a forefinger.

"Right. I knew that." He looked around. Mariette had decorated the place comfortably, if not luxuriously. Her favorite part of the parlor was the graceful bay window that overlooked the street and the little park, and the windowseat with its many pillows. While she was lighting the sconces that flanked the fireplace mirror, Philippe walked over to the window, pulled back the lace curtain and looked out. Turning back to Mariette, he said, "Nice view."

Mariette nodded. She tried to see the parlor with Philippe's eyes, as if for the first time. The focal point was the fireplace with its marble mantel, laid with a lace lambrequin, edged with passe-menterie. A settee faced the mantel, two wingback chairs flanked it, and an inexpensive carpet of Persian design marked off the area. The gaslight sconces above the mantel to each side of a gilt-framed mirror now illuminated the room with a soft, yellow light. A marble-top table stood before the settee. Beyond the parlor was a small dining area with a claw-foot oval walnut table and four cane-back chairs.

Mariette took off her cape and hung it on the back of a chair.

"Come sit down," she said, leading him into the parlor. She rubbed her hands together. "Oh, my, it's cold in here. I'll start a fire."

He didn't offer to do it. She felt a sharp jab at her heart, knowing that in so short a time, he'd learned to accept his limitations. It was best, of course. She must do the same. She knelt before the fireplace, made a little tent of kindling. Then, after placing two logs across the andirons, she reached for the tinderbox and started the fire. In minutes, blue flames were licking up the sides of the logs. "It will be warm in no time at all."

She got up and sat beside him. "How about hot cocoa? I'll fix some, and then I'll call Maman."

"It's late, *mon ange*. Aren't you too tired for all that?"

"On the most important night of my life?" Her voice was shaky, thin as a reed. "You know, when we first moved in," she said, patting his lapels, trying to gain control of her emotions, "Mrs. O'Flaherty said we were not to cook in the flat, but now we're like family. We have our main meal with her at noon, and she had a ring of gas jets installed for us some time back, so we can fix tea or coffee or oatmeal for...a light *dejeuner.*

Almost slipped that time. He must not know about Daisy till he sees her.

"May I come with you?" he asked.

"Of course."

She took his arm and led him to a small room behind the dining room, where she and her mother had arranged a pantry. Within a cupboard, shelves held boxes of tea, cocoa, sugar, flour and baby biscuits. She grabbed the tin of cocoa, lit the burner and put the teapot on. With quick efficient moves, she arranged a serving tray with teacups, spoons, napkins, a sugar bowl. She spooned a bit of cocoa into each cup.

"It will be ready soon." She reached up and kissed his cheek. "Why don't you wait in the parlor. I'll go tell Maman. She'll want to come see you."

"No, please don't disturb her."

"What? She'd kill me if I didn't." She led him back to the parlor. "You just wait for me in here. It's getting warm now."

He did as she'd ordered, unwillingly, she knew. Mariette took off her shoes and ran in her stocking feet to the room where her mother and Daisy slept. "Desiree!" she whispered, trying not to wake the baby. She struck a match and lit the night candle. The room came into view.

Desiree was instantly awake and sitting up. "Mariette, was it Philippe?"

"Yes, Maman. It was my Philippe. And he's here!"

"Thank God! Oh, *ma fille!*" Desiree's eyes filled. "And when you saw each other, all your questions were answered, *n'est-ce pas?*"

"Oh, yes. You were right. We both knew."

In the dim light, Desiree saw her daughter's coffee black eyes, more radiant than the candle, glowing as they hadn't glowed in a year. Her unshed tears and her smile told the story.

"I've known it all along, Maman…that it would be Philippe," she said, tears spilling over her lashes. "He's come for me. He wants to marry me."

In an instant, Desiree was out of bed, hugging her daughter. "Oh, Mariette, *ma fille*, I'm so happy for you."

"*Vite! Vite!* Put your robe on. Come and see him."

Daisy sat up in the bed, awakened by the commotion. She looked at the two women hugging. "Ma-ma!" she said. They both laughed softly. Mariette took her in her arms, kissed her cheek, and put her back down on a baby pad.

"Maman, please change her nappie. Then just put on your robe. The tea pot's whistling. I'll go take it off the burner."

"I'll be quick. Don't worry." Desiree laughed softly. "This I have to see."

In the pantry, Mariette moved the tea pot to a pot rest, turned off the gas jets, and rushed back to her mother's room. Daisy lay on her back, her arms reaching up for her mother. Desiree slipped the second pin through her clean diaper. She pulled up the baby's long white stockings and pinned them to the diaper. Then she pulled down Daisy's little flannel nightgown. She wrapped a small blanket around the child. Daisy was smiling.

"She thinks we're going out," Desiree said, chuckling.

"Her hair!" Mariette said. "Wait. Let me."

Mariette and Desiree giggled like two schoolgirls. They fumbled for the baby's hairbrush and pulled it through her jet black curls. Daisy giggled, too, bubbles forming at the corners of her mouth. Mariette picked her up.

Desiree put on her house robe, tied it at the waist, and pulled her long braid over her right shoulder. Now the procession began. From Desiree's room to the parlor, Mariette carried the child straddling her hip, holding her head against her shoulder. Daisy was yawning, awakened too soon from a heavy slumber, but in good disposition nonetheless.

Philippe knelt before the fire, his back to them, placing another log across the andirons. The women approached so softly he was unaware of their presence until they were almost upon him. He saw their feet first and gave a start. Then, dropping the log, he got up to his feet, bracing himself with his right hand on the marble-topped table.

Standing up to his full height, he saw Mariette with Desiree behind her, the two women smiling, their eyes shining. Mariette was holding a baby with eyes of *cafe noir* ringed with a fine line of blue around the pupils. The baby was looking at him curiously. She had a head of curly black hair, and her lips were like a cupid's bow.

He looked up at Mariette, whose face mirrored the baby's. Mariette's eyes were brimming with tears of joy. A sob shook her body.

"Mariette!" he said softly in astonishment. "She's your baby!"

"And yours." Mariette's sobs were louder now. The baby turned around to look at her mother. "Ma-ma!" she said, reaching up to touch her face.

"Philippe!" Desiree said, coming toward him and seeing the empty sleeve for the first time. "*Mon Dieu!*" she said, her hands flying to her face. Her gaze traveled from the sleeve to Mariette and then back to Philippe's eyes. "Was it the duel?"

"Yes. But I'm fine now. Back at work many months." He smiled at Desiree. "I didn't get my kiss yet."

Desiree smiled through her tears and reached up to kiss his cheek. "So what do you think of your daughter?"

He pressed his lips together, closed his eyes, and sobbed. "I think she's...a miracle. An angel. I didn't know. I would've come. I..." He gathered Mariette and Daisy to his body, sobbing as if his heart would break. To the baby, he said, "Come, *mon ange*, let me sit down and hold you." He looked at Mariette. "What's her name?"

"Daisy. Short for Desiree."

He looked at the proud grandmother. She beamed. He smiled. He sat on the settee, his right arm braced by the curve of the furniture. Mariette sat beside him and placed the baby in his lap. Gently, he held her to him, his lips pressing a kiss to the top of her warm silky curls.

Obligingly, Daisy turned to look at the man. Grabbing his coat lapels, she stood up on his lap in her stocking feet, and his arm went around her to support her. Mariette watched, every nerve in her body taut, consciously keeping her hands in her lap, not reaching out to protect her baby.

"You're doing very well," Mariette said, as sobs shook her body.

"She's doing it herself," he said. "She's holding on. Isn't she wonderful?"

"Yes." Mariette laughed softly.

"How old is she?" he asked.

"Almost a year."

Knowing she was the center of attention, Daisy put her arms around Philippe's neck and hugged him. It was too much for

Philippe. He held her close and kissed her neck and her face as the tears ran down his cheeks. *"Mon enfant,"* he whispered hoarsely. *"Je t'aime."* He kissed her again and again in soft possessive little kisses.

Daisy looked at her mother, who was smiling, nodding. Soon she pulled away and sat back down on her father's lap, her arms extended to her mother.

Mariette took her from Philippe. "She went to you very well for the first time, Philippe," she said, her face wet with tears. Everyone in the room was crying now, with the exception of Daisy. The child was busy examining her mother's Third Act costume, which she had never seen before. It was all glitter and brocade and gilded lace, with strands of pearls at the neck and on her ears. Daisy reached out for the necklace, but Mariette took her little hands in hers and handed the baby to her mother.

Silence fell for a moment, broken only by soft sobs and joyous sighs.

"Try to put her back to bed, Maman, if you can."

"She'll stay if I do. And I'll leave you two alone to have your cocoa." She looked at Philippe. "I'm so glad you're here," she said. "I love you, Philippe." She stooped down and kissed his cheek.

Philippe's throat tightened. "I have no words tonight," he said by way of apology.

"I understand," Desiree said. "We really surprised you, didn't we?"

Seeing her grandmother kiss the man, Daisy leaned over out of Desiree's grasp, pursing her lips to him. Philippe gave her a sweet, loud smack on the lips and she giggled.

He watched Desiree walk away with the child and disappear into the darkness of the hallway. He remained seated on the settee, too overcome with joy and astonishment to speak. Mariette sat beside him, her left hand resting on the empty sleeve and the shoulder of his left arm. She rubbed it gently, letting him know it didn't matter. It didn't matter at all.

Philippe spoke first. "She calls you Mama," he said, with love in his voice.

"Yes. And she calls my mother Maman."

"What will she call me?" he asked.

"Papa, I suppose," she said. "We're still French, although we're getting more American every day."

She sighed deeply, wearily, happily. It was time to talk. She had so much to tell Philippe. But she decided to get comfortable first. She drew a few central pins from her elaborately coiffed hairdo, and the braided ropes were released from her chignon, snaking out to curl over her shoulders. Hairpins pinged against the arm of the settee and fell to the carpet. Mariette combed through her hair with her fingers. Philippe reached over and touched her hair.

How long had she dreamed of being with him again! And he was here with her, and they could have their fill of each other. But then suddenly she became somber. "Our troubles are not over yet, Philippe."

"Yes, they are," he said. "We're together. Don't tell me this isn't paradise." He smiled and pulled her to him. "We'll be married here in New York and start a whole new life."

"I know, my love, but there are things I haven't told you because I didn't want to spoil your homecoming." She drew in a deep breath. "Something terrible has come up that threatens our future. There is a serious danger right on our doorstep. This was why I had to see you tonight, my love. I'll tell you all about it."

CHAPTER 79

Mariette got up from the settee and walked to the mantelpiece. From beneath the lace scarf, she drew out two neatly folded papers. Holding them between her thumb and forefinger, she brought them to the sofa and began her explanation.

"About a week ago, when my mother and I were out in the little park across the street, Daisy was sitting in her pram, waving this piece of paper. I took it from her, and you can see what it said." She handed him the note and he read. THAT'S A PRETTY BABY YOU HAVE THERE. TAKE CARE!

Philippe frowned. "TAKE CARE? What does it mean?"

"Well, I didn't know, but I was frightened half to death."

"Well, you must have been."

"It sounded like a threat that someone might take her away. But who? I wondered. Who could hate me enough to hint at such a horrible thing?"

"And of course you thought of Soniat."

"Yes. And my father." She paused. "My greedy father, who never got his land from Soniat. And I was right. My father's here in New York, Philippe, and only to bring more misery into my life."

Philippe took her hand. "How do you know that?"

"Wait. I'll tell you everything," Mariette said. "Maman and I took Daisy and ran into the house and double-bolted the door. I knew someone could have been watching us even then. So for a whole week, we all stayed indoors with the door locked and the window shutters closed. I sent word to Mr. Niblo that I couldn't make rehearsals for a few days. But I had to go to the theater at night, and I was so afraid to leave Daisy. I had Mrs. O'Flaherty come and stay with my mother and Mr. Mohnihan, a nice old gentleman from the third floor. He brought his pistol down just in case."

"But why didn't you call the police? They would have…"

"No, Philippe," she interrupted. "I could not call the police. No one in the theater world knows about Daisy *or* my mother. I've always passed for white. You can imagine what the newspapers could do with that story: *Mariette Delon found in hideaway with mulatto mother and fatherless child.*"

Philippe nodded. "Yes, but no matter. The baby's life was in danger."

"Not really. Listen to me, Philippe. No one wants to kill our baby. I know that. If that were the case, they could hang me in Washingtom Square, and I wouldn't care."

"Well, what *do* they want?"

Mariette took out the second piece of paper. "Yesterday," she said, "a messenger came to the door and handed me this letter." By this time, Mariette was trembling, and Philippe drew her to him.

"My love," he said, "Please try to calm yourself. I'm here with you now, and I'll never let them take that baby. Give me the letter."

Her hand shaking, Mariette handed it to Philippe. His eyebrows came together in a frown, and he read aloud.

My dear Mariette,

Louis Soniat is willing to forgive your infidelity and take you back again."

Philippe looked at Mariette and laughed aloud. "Willing to forgive! The son of a bitch!"

Now that he knows you have given birth to his baby, he is willing to reconcile with you."

"Good God in Heaven! *His* baby!"

He has never sold the house in Faubourg Marigny, and he wants you and his baby to come back and live there as his family. He will come for you and see that you and the baby are returned to New Orleans in the finest accommodations aboard a luxury steamboat, with a nurse in attendance. He will allow you to go on acting on the stage in New Orleans, if that is your choice, or stay at home with the baby.

Philippe looked at Mariette, his face a mask of hatred.

I will call on you Monday at noon when you return from rehearsal. I will expect your answer then. You can hope for no better future than you'll have with Louis Soniat. He will treat you like a queen.

Your father,
Raoul Delissard

Philippe looked into Mariette's troubled eyes. His own eyes reflected disbelief and fury, as well as a comic reaction. "The man's a lunatic! How could he think you'd ever go back to Louis Soniat? Your father has told you that before, that Soniat would treat you like a queen! Could he really expect you to fall for that again?"

"I said those very words to my mother, but don't you see a threat hidden there? In the first note, the words TAKE CARE! Then in the second letter, he seems to hint that if I say no, he means to force my hand."

"What can he do? Take you to court? You were never married to Soniat."

"No, but he can claim the baby is his."

"But you can prove that it's not. I'm sure you've given it much thought already."

"I've worn myself out going back over dates, and I can prove it, if they'll take my word."

"Tell me the dates."

"It was Christmas Day, if you recall. Soniat had left the house in Faubourg Marigny to go to his plantation to punish some runaway slaves. My mother had had Christmas dinner with us. She can testify that I was having my monthly period at the time he left, and I told her then that he had not been to my bed since my period began. And, Philippe, as God is my judge, I have never slept with that man since then."

"But you have with me."

"Yes." She smiled weakly. She paused for a moment. "It was the most glorious night of my life."

"And mine." He took her in his arms and held her tenderly. "But can you give dates?"

"Of course. It was two nights after the Old Camp Theater fire, which was in all the papers. The fire was on January 20, 1841. We can research it, of course, and get a paper of that date in the library, but you made love to me two nights later. That would make it the 22nd of January. And Daisy was born, most obligingly, exactly nine months later, minus two days."

"When is her birthday?"

"October 20," Mariette said. "My landlady can confirm that. She was the midwife."

"And I know someone who can confirm the date of conception," Philippe said, smiling, "other than you and me."

Mariette smiled shyly. "Who in the world would *that* be?"

"My sister Jeanine. She was there. She knew we were in the guestroom together that night. That's why she had to sleep in *my* room."

"Of course I remember. But would she testify?"

"Mariette, *mon ange,* she would consider it the highlight of her life."

Mariette giggled. "She was so good to me, Philippe. I think she was intrigued by the whole affair."

Philippe laughed too, thinking of his outrageous sister. "She was delighted to be in on our secret love affair. I think what appealed to her most was how shocked our mother would be, if she knew."

The reference to his mother suddenly saddened Mariette. "Oh, Philippe, if she testified, your whole family would be in on our secret life; not only that we have a baby, but that my mother is a mulattress and I'm a quadroon."

Philippe touched Mariette's cheek with his fingers. "I don't care, Mariette. I've already broken away from my father. I'm on my own now. It doesn't matter what they know. Trust in me, my love," he said. "I'll never let them take our baby away."

Mariette was not satisfied. "Others will know, too, Philippe."

"Yes, including your father's white family. I don't think he'd want them to know."

"I'm not so sure. I was telling my mother just today that *plaçage* is so common in New Orleans, I doubt if his wife would be too shocked. She wouldn't divorce him and part with all that lovely money." She gazed into space, thinking. "You must remember he is mean and avaricious. And that Soniat has great wealth to bring to the courts, and he counts many important attorneys among his friends."

"My sweet Mariette," he said smiling. "There is one major factor you have overlooked." Mariette gave him her full attention. "Soniat will not want the baby without you, even if your father's attorneys could prove she's his. And once we're married, there's no way he can legally get you back."

Mariette's lips turned up at the corners in the beginning of a smile.

"Think about it," Philippe went on. "Whether or not we can prove it's *my* baby," he said, touching his chest with his fingers, "he has no legal claim on you. You had a contract, which would never stand up in court, except in New Orleans, and even *there*, it would only serve to deprive you of the house and all the material goods he gave you."

As if in a dream, Mariette said, "And I gave all that up long ago…willingly. No…*eagerly.*" She smiled, for the first time since she began her story. Then brightening even more, "And there's one other thing you don't know," she said. "Soniat sent me a letter a few days after the duel, declaring our contract null and void."

"And have you kept the letter?" Philippe asked.

"Among my most important papers," she said proudly. "I discarded it at first. Then I retrieved it…just in case I needed it later on."

"Then you have nothing to fear. No court in the land can force you to go back. And most importantly, we will be married, and after that, neither your father nor Louis Soniat will have any control over you."

Mariette smiled a full smile. "How soon can we be married,

Philippe?" she asked, knowing she was working against time. "My father is coming here Monday."

"What about tomorrow, *mon ange*? We'll go to the Justice of the Peace and come home with a marriage certificate. How does that sound?"

"Heavenly." Mariette was so overcome with relief that she allowed herself the luxury of a smile. She reached once again for the handkerchief in Philippe's coat pocket and dried her eyes. Then, putting it back, she sighed. She turned to face him, so that she could lie with her head in the crook of his strong right arm and receive his kiss. He lowered his mouth to hers and kissed her deeply and with longing, and they both knew a hunger that must soon be satisfied.

"Philippe! My beautiful man," she said, raising her right hand to his face. "I can't believe you're here with me at last, after all the doubts and worries and yearnings. Now you know the real reason I had to leave town. I was pregnant and unmarried. I was desperate to save my good name and have a way to support my mother and my baby. Then suddenly, like an answer to a prayer, I had this offer from Niblo to act in New York. Of course I had to take it."

"And that was the one eventuality that never occurred to me. What a fool I was!"

"No. You could never have known."

"But what did you do about Mr. Niblo? He knew you were pregnant."

"No. He never knew. Even to this day, he doesn't know I have a baby." She sat up beside him to explain. "You see it was May when he offered me the contract, and I wasn't showing yet. I told him I couldn't come to New York till the fall, and he said he would take me then."

"So where were you when the baby was born?"

"Here in New York. Maman and I came right away, in May, but Niblo didn't know we were here. We stayed close to home and far from the theater. Then a month after Daisy was born, I went to Niblo's Garden, and the dear little gentleman welcomed me into his troupe, bless his heart!"

"Mariette! What a designing woman you are!"

"I had to be. My whole future, and Daisy's, depended on it."

"And I was no help to you at all."

"You were sick, my darling. It's only now that I know how sick you really were. And all the hoops you had to jump through to finally get to me."

He leaned over and pressed a few gentle kisses to her forehead, and she sighed with glorious contentment. "A month or so after I got to New York," he said, "I read in the paper that Mariette Delon and Robert Courtney were starring in a play called *Foundling of the Forest*. I bought a ticket and sat in the last row and watched the performance."

Shocked by this revelation, she got off the settee and, with her glittering costume poofed all around her, knelt before him on the floor, so she could look into his eyes. "Philippe Grillet! You were in the theater, and you didn't come back stage to see me! I can't believe it."

"I couldn't," he said. "I had good reasons. I had just gotten a job and I wasn't sure I could manage on my own and be able to support you. And then later, there was the other, more important reason I've already told you—the stories about the love match between you and Robert."

"I *knew* that would happen. I *told* that to Robert. I knew that if you read those stories, you'd stay away from me. Robert and I were never lovers, Philippe. You have to believe that."

"I know that now, but I didn't then. And it was the strangest thing, the way we met. I was having lunch at the Astor dining room, and a waiter pointed him out to me. Well, you can't believe how my blood boiled just at the sight of him. I was so jealous of his closeness to you. I had seen you on stage with him, as I told you, and I was smothering in my hatred for him."

Mariette could not help smiling at his expression of vicious envy. To think she had ever doubted his love!

"Why are you smirking?" he asked, trying to hide his own smile.

"I'm so happy you love me so much. Oh, I wish I'd been able to end your anxieties and tell you those love scenes meant nothing. We were just acting, darling." Mariette grinned.

"Too convincingly, I'm afraid. And then, there were those stories in the papers..."

"The damned papers!" Mariette said.

"Mariette! I've never heard you swear before," he said, grinning.

She adopted a serious mein. "I've learned a few swear words to help me get through the bad times."

Philippe shook his head and smiled. "Tell me something. If Robert didn't know about the baby, where did you hide her when he came here?"

"He never came inside, Philippe. I never let him through the front door."

"He didn't *ask* to come in?"

"No. Oh, he would've come if I'd invited him, but I never did. I told you we were not lovers."

"I believe that, but you did a remarkable job of hiding your baby and your mother."

"Until my father came to town," she said. "He found us with no trouble at all."

So they had come full circle in revealing all their fears, and now she was content that they'd be married and Philippe would protect her...and Daisy. A peaceful silence settled between them. The Ormulo clock ticked on the mantle. A log broke, fell from the andirons and hissed in the ashes. Philippe held her hand and looked into her coffee black eyes.

"We can be legally married here, my love," he said, "which means we can be married in the Church, since the Church follows state laws."

She smiled. "Oh, Philippe, how wonderful!" She rested her head against his shoulder.

"Two years ago," he said, "I tried to fool myself that I could alter the records and that would allow us to have a church wedding. But that would have been a sham, and I think we both knew it."

"You're right."

"So, I was thinking," he said, "that tomorrow, we might have a legal ceremony first, to get that marriage certificate and have it in our hands, for your protection...and Daisy's. But then," he turned her by her shoulders to look deep into her eyes, "we could go to St. Patrick's Cathedral and set a date for a church wedding. How does that sound to you?"

She nodded. "I think it will be the happiest day of my life." Her eyes were brimming with tears. "In New Orleans, society made no place for us. But here in New York, we can be a couple, a respected couple."

"We can be a *family*," he added, "and Daisy can be baptized."

"Oh, yes," she said, a small sob escaping her throat. She reached up and kissed his mouth, and tears fell down her face. "You love her," she said, discovering the wonder of it. She wept then in soft, heart-felt sobs. Then, she laid her head against his chest and rested in wondrous, glorious peace.

"Mariette, *mon ange*," Philippe said, choosing his words, "when that baby stood on my lap and held onto my lapels, I felt such an overhwelming love for her, that even now, if I'd listen to myself, I would run to her bed and pick her up and kiss her all over her beautiful little face and her soft sweet neck."

"Oh, my dear Philippe," Mariette said, embracing him so closely he could barely breathe. "Isn't it amazing?"

"Yes." He backed away to look into her eyes. He was deeply pensive. "I want to raise her to be a whole and happy young woman, free to choose her own path in life. I want to give her everything. I will deny her nothing. I will love her and cherish her."

"You will spoil her," Mariette said, between laughter and tears.

"Yes. I will. I most certainly will."

Mariette laughed softly, tearfully. "You will ruin her."

"No. I will make her happy to be alive, every day of her life."

Mariette sniffed and sobbed. She patted Philippe's chest. She could not speak. Then, after a few silent moments, she got up from the settee. She walked to the mantle shelf, picked up a taper, and carried a flame from the wall sconce to a candle on the marble-topped table. She snuffed the sconces and secured the fire screen. The room was now in darkness except for the light of a single candle. Now she stood before Philippe.

"Give me your hand," she said. Taking his right hand in her left, she helped him up from the settee. Then, picking up the candle, she linked her arm with Philippe's and led him to her room. No one would be having cocoa until morning.

THE END

EPILOGUE

September 15, 1842

My dear Soniat,

It is with great disappointment that I write to tell you that our plan for reinstating a certain party in your residence as placée has failed. The lady in question has rejected your offer, denied that you are the father of her baby, and, to put finis to the whole affair, has married a Creole from New Orleans, whom we both know only too well. She is now under his protection in the state of New York, where they plan to reside. I regret that I was unable to convince her, before she took this drastic step, of your good intentions for her and for the baby. I did my best for you, Louis, since she is dear to me, and I considered your offer both noble and generous.

Her husband had a second copy of their marriage certificate made and presented me with it when I called at their residence on Bowling Green Park this past Monday. He told me to frame it, lest I forget that she is no longer my bargaining chip. Insolent dog! When all I ever wanted was her happiness and security with a man I could trust.

If you have any plans to bring the matter of your paternity to court, I am certain you would have a good case, and I would be eager to serve you in any capacity.

I am still most interested in the parcel of land you offered me for my services to you, which have sent me to the cold unfriendly North and exposed me to rude people and coarse circumstances, so foreign to my normal lifestyle. Can we not come to terms about that land? We are still friends, you and I, and the land means so much to me.

I remain your servant,

Louis Delissard

<hr>

October 20, 1842

Delissard,

I am in receipt of your letter of September 15, and I now see the futility of any further pursuit of the lady in question. As for her child, I have no use for it, unless it comes with the mother. I am not a family man, nor do I hope to become one. Dismiss from your plans any court battles on my behalf.

As for the land that means so much to you, you will never have it while there is breath in my body. You have failed in your pathetic attempts to assist me, and I refuse to grant you ownership of that property either as a gift or a purchase, no matter what price you offer.

You say we are friends, but we are not friends. To put a fine point on it, we are enemies. The matter of plaçage is ended. The matter of paternity is of no interest to me. And the matter of granting you my land, now or at any time in the future, is fichu.

Louis A. Soniat

AUTHOR'S NOTE

The word "Creole" —

According to the late John Chase, (*Frenchmen, Desire, Good Children*), the word **Creole** derives from the Spanish *criollo,* "a child born in the colonies"; therefore, native born New Orleanians of French and Spanish descent were designated Creoles. The meaning changed when their own children and grandchildren were born, all of whom were called Creoles. Many believe that a Creole is a black person. This is not so; however, there *are* black Creoles, descendants of the original free black French and Spanish settlers.

Early New Orleans theater —

Tradition has it that New Orleans theater began in the fall of 1791 when a group of actors and musicians from Cap Francais in San Domingue (Haiti) arrived in New Orleans, following the slave uprising and mass migration from that island. This troupe of itinerant French actors, which included mulattos and quadroons, was directed by Louis Tabary, who established permanent theater in New Orleans. The troupe first performed in tents, then in empty shops, and finally in a two-story building on St. Peter Street.

The first three theaters in New Orleans were: 1) the St. Peter Street Theater (1792) on St. Peter between Royal and Bourbon; 2) the St. Philip Street Theater (before 1809), later converted to a dance hall; and 3) the Orleans Theater (1809), which burned in 1813 and was replaced by a larger, more sumptuous theater. The second Orleans Theater, whose impresario was Charles Boudousquie, was one of the city's showplaces.

James H. Caldwell, a British actor and entrepreneur, brought an acting troupe to New Orleans in 1820 to perform in the English language. He inaugurated the annual theater season. For a while, his English language company performed at the Orleans Theater on alternate nights with a French language company. Caldwell helped develop Faubourg Saint Mary, the neighborhood on the upriver side of Canal Street in the 1830s and 1840s. He built hotels, theaters, and gas works, owning the rights to the latter. Settled by Americans, the area was called by several names during this period: Faubourg Saint Mary, the American Sector, and the Second Municipality.

James H. Caldwell's first theater was the Camp Street Theater on Camp between Gravier and Poydras Streets, which opened January 1, 1824 and was destroyed by fire September 23, 1842. The second was the St. Charles Theater whose cornerstone was laid in May, 1833. The theater opened in November, 1835, and burned down on March 13, 1842. Theater fires were common in the early 19th Century due to flammable materials kept in the buildings. Fire prevention laws were few and fire fighting was sadly ineffective.

The author has taken a liberty with the date of the fire of the Camp Street Theater, but in no other way were the theaters fictionalized. The description of the interior of the magnificent St. Charles Theater was accurate and not exaggerated.

Plays produced in New Orleans in this period and named in the story included *Lock and Key, The Boarding House, The Day after the Wedding,* and *School for Scandals.* Actors who played in these theaters were James Caldwell, Jane Placide, Edwin Forrest, and Lydia Kelly. All others mentioned are fictitious.

All information about New York theaters at that time is authentic.

CPSIA information can be obtained at www.ICGtesting.com
Printed in the USA
LVOW10s1328130913

352351LV00002B/66/P